THE NINE CLOUD DREAM

KIM MAN-JUNG (1637–1692) is generally accepted as the author of *The Nine Cloud Dream* (*Kuunmong*), often considered the greatest classic Korean novel. He is said to have composed it in exile as a comfort to his mother. A member of the *yangban* (ruling class) literati, Kim Man-jung rose to become the head of the Confucian Academy. His other works include *The Record of Lady Sa's Journey South* (*Sassi Namjeonggi*).

HEINZ INSU FENKL is a writer, editor, translator, and folklorist. He is the author of two novels, *Memories of My Ghost Brother*, a PEN/Hemingway finalist, and *Skull Water*. He is an associate professor of English at the State University of New York, New Paltz. His nonfiction includes *Korean Folktales*, which he wrote following a Fulbright fellowship. He serves on the editorial board of *Sijo: An International Journal of Poetry and Song* and is a consulting editor for *Words Without Borders*. He is a recipient of the Global Korea Award and the Buddhist Yushim Prize for his contributions to Korean literature. His fiction and translations have been published in *The New Yorker*.

KIM MAN-JUNG

The Nine Cloud Dream

Translated with an Introduction and Notes by
HEINZ INSU FENKL

PENGUIN BOOKS

Dedicated to Musan Cho Oh-hyun
& all my teachers

_____

PENGUIN BOOKS

An imprint of Penguin Random House LLC
penguinrandomhouse.com

A portion of this book first appeared in different form as "The Ghost Story" in
Azalea: Journal of Korean Literature & Culture, Volume 7, 2014.

Illustrations from *The Cloud Dream of the Nine* translated by James Scarth
Gale (London: Daniel O'Connor, 1922). Artwork on page 16 comprises
portions of these illustrations, assembled by Heinz Insu Fenkl.

The Nine Cloud Dream is published with the support of the
Literature Translation Institute of Korea (LTI Korea).

LIBRARY OF CONGRESS CATALOGING-IN-PUBLICATION DATA

Names: Kim, Man-jung, 1637-1692, author. | Fenkl, Heinz Insu,
1960-translator, writer of introduction, writer of added commentary.
Title: The nine cloud dream / Kim Man-jung ; translated with an introduction
and notes by Heinz Insu Fenkl.
Other titles: Kuunmong. English
Description: New York, New York : Penguin Books, [2019] |
Includes bibliographical references.
Identifiers: LCCN 2018036733 (print) | LCCN 2018050575 (ebook) |
ISBN 9781524705022 (E-book) | ISBN 9780143131274 |
ISBN 9780143131274(paperback) | ISBN 9781524705022(ebook)
Subjects: LCSH: Korean fiction--To 1900--Translations into English.
Classification: LCC PL989.415.M3 (ebook) | LCC PL989.415.M3 K813 2019 (print) |
DDC 895.73/2--dc23
LC record available at https://lccn.loc.gov/2018036733

Set in Sabon LT Std

Contents

Introduction

The world . . . is like a passing cloud, like an imaginary
wheel made by a whirling torch, like a castle of spirits, like
the moon reflected in the sea, like a vision, a mirage, a
dream.

The Lankavatara Sutra

*New readers are advised that this introduction makes
certain details of the plot explicit.*

The Nine Cloud Dream, or *Kuunmong* (九雲夢구운몽, c.
1689),[1] is the most elegant of Korea's earliest literary novels
and one of the most beloved masterpieces of Korean literature.
It is a fantastical romance, full of intrigue and deception, the
idealized story-within-a-story of the poor son of an abandoned
single mother becoming the veritable golden boy of Confucian
culture. Over the course of the narrative, the main character
becomes a great poet, musician, diplomat, general, and brother-
in-law to an emperor; his romantic partners (wives and concubines) are said to be the eight most beautiful women in the
world. But that idealized romance is framed within the story
of a promising young monk who learns a profound lesson
about worldly desire as he follows the Buddhist path. And so
Kuunmong—with all its excellent imitations and reworkings
of Chinese Tang poetry, metaphysical conundrums, thinly
veiled autobiography, and court satire—also serves as a moral-
ity tale dramatizing the themes central to the worldview of a
Buddhist artist-intellectual in seventeenth-century Korea. All
this is found in a single work.

SEOPO KIM MAN-JUNG AND HIS TIMES

Both Korean and Western scholars are in general agreement that Kim Man-jung 김만중, 金萬重 (1637–1692), also known by his penname Seopo (서포, 西浦, meaning "Western Shore," "West Bank," or "Western Port"), is the author of *Kuunmong*. This is based primarily on Kim Tae-jun's seminal 1933 work *History of Korean Fiction* (趙鮮小說史 *Choson soseolsa*) and the reminiscence of Kim's grandnephew Yi Jae (1680–1746) in *A Record of Three Government Agencies* (三官记 *Samgwan-gi*).[2] Kim himself never claimed authorship, but the Korean literati of his time not only wrote fictional works like *Kuunmong* anonymously, but also customarily disavowed authorship of such "low" works both out of modesty and from fear of sullying their reputations.

Kim was well-known and well regarded in his time. He was a *yangban* (a member of the ruling class) related to eminent scholars; he was also an intellectual and political figure of some note in the court of King Sukjong, the nineteenth king of the Joseon dynasty. Like Shao-yu, the protagonist of *Kuunmong*, he became a government minister after getting the highest score on the national civil service examination. The general consensus in the Korean scholarly community is that Kim, a dutiful son whose father died before his birth,[3] wrote *Kuunmong* during his exile in order to comfort his mother, a highly educated and accomplished woman who had raised him and his brother by herself. The story of Kim composing the whole of *Kuunmong* in a single night is typical of literary folklore (Lao Tzu, for example, is said to have composed all of the *Tao Te Ching* in one night); but in Kim's case, the story may, in fact, be an associative conflation with the story of his mother, who borrowed the Chinese classics she was too poor to buy for her sons' education and hand-copied them overnight before she had to return them the next day.

Kim lived during the latter part of the Joseon dynasty, which lasted from 1392 to 1897. Joseon's political and social structures were modeled after Confucian China of the Tang dynasty (618–907). The carefully defined Neo-Confucian ideals governing the "Five Relationships"—ruler to subject, father to son, husband to wife, elder to younger, and friend to friend (all of which privilege men, and which are significantly dramatized and problematized in *Kuunmong*)—were seen as the key to social and political harmony. Meanwhile, Buddhism, which had been a defining characteristic of Korea during the earlier golden age of the Unified Silla (668–935), had begun to wane during the Goryeo dynasty (918–1392) and was actively suppressed in favor of the social control offered by Neo-Confucianism. During this period, Korean women had gravitated toward Buddhism and made up much of its infrastructure, a fact implicitly invoked by *Kuunmong*'s strong representation of women. Taoism, which had long existed in harmony with Korea's indigenous shamanic religious tradition, was recognized by this time primarily in its more philosophical and intellectual form—centering on texts like the *I Ching*, the *Tao Te Ching*, and the writings of Zhuangzi—while its tantric and alchemical practices were largely relegated to the folk culture of superstition and magic.[4]

Kuunmong is generally dated by scholars at 1689, but its literary provenance has been much debated, particularly in recent years. At one time it was believed that *Kuunmong* was the first major work of Korean literature composed in the native hangul alphabet. However, the current consensus, after the discovery of an eighteenth-century Chinese edition, is that it was composed in Chinese, which was the language of literature and government in seventeenth-century Korea in much the same way Latin was used in Europe for many centuries. It is important to remember that before Korea had its own alphabet, all writing was done in Chinese characters or a combination of Chinese with indigenously developed phonetic scripts that were rather unwieldy. In the mid-fifteenth century during the reign of King Sejong the Great—a golden age for art, science, and culture—hangul was developed in order to encourage literacy among the general population. It was so well designed that the common saying is that "a smart man can learn it before the end of the day and even an idiot can learn it in ten days." Ironically, though it quickly took root in the

popular culture, hangul's very efficiency was its initial down-
fall in literary and official circles. The Korean literati felt it de-
meaning to write in such an easy script, and it is said that, at
the time, Chinese characters were called *jinseo* (true letters)
while hangul was known as *amgeul* (women's script) or *ahaet-
geul* (children's script). It wasn't until the early twentieth century, during the Japanese colonial era, that literary writing in
hangul was revived on a large scale as an issue of national
pride and identity. *Kuunmong*, it is now generally agreed, was
originally composed in Chinese and later reprinted in hangul
to make it more accessible.[5]

THE NOVEL

In its Korean literary and historical context, *Kuunmong* is one
of the seminal works of Korean prose fiction, along with Kim
Si-seup's mid-fifteenth-century work *New Stories from Mount
Geumo* (*Geumo Shinhwa*, 금오신화; 金鰲新話) and Heo Gyun's
The Story of Hong Gildong (*Hong Gildong jeon*, 홍길동전;
洪吉童傳), which dates to the late sixteenth or early seventeenth century.[6] If *Hong Gildong jeon* is like the Korean Robin
Hood, *Kuunmong*, in its status and impact throughout the
years, more closely parallels Dante's *Divine Comedy*. The
Buddhist and Taoist themes in *Kuunmong* played out in Korean literary and intellectual culture in much the same way
Dante's confrontation of political and religious themes reso-
nated throughout Europe. Both works involve the journey of
the central character into another reality, in which he learns
valuable moral, ethical, and religious lessons. Both works are
also deeply personal and laden with satirical agendas partially
stemming from each writer's political exile.

The basic plot of *Kuunmong* is an edifying fantasy: for vio-
lating his vows and doubting his vocation, a promising young
Buddhist monk named Hsing-chen ("Original Nature") is made
to experience an incarnation as Shao-yu ("Small Visitor" or
"Brief Resider"), the most ideal of men, his life full of fabulous
intellectual, diplomatic, martial, and sensual accomplishments.

It is an ironic punishment that plays out like an incarnation-within-an-incarnation, and as the narrative develops, we are slowly and subtly introduced to a world of layered illusions. Shao-yu's view of things is constantly obstructed or occluded by intervening elements, sometimes as subtle as a willow branch; there are minor dream sequences within a greater dream; and there are numerous disguises, deceptions, and misperceptions that play with the idea of compromised and multilayered reality. When Hsing-chen's old master, Liu-kuan ("Six Perceptions"), finally enters the illusory world of Shao-yu—now growing old himself—he causes Shao-yu to remember a dream of himself as Hsing-chen the monk. Liu-kuan accompanies him out of his dream and back to "reality," and in the end the monk wakes up as Hsing-chen back on his meditation mat, to learn that reality and dream are interpenetrating phenomena and are ultimately indistinguishable. He has experienced an entire lifetime in a moment.

Kuunmong addresses this theme of reality and dream in such a way that it poignantly critiques the moral and ethical misconduct of the controversial king Sukjong, who took the throne at age thirteen and ruled from 1674 to 1720. King Sukjong's reign was characterized by intense factional disputes and sudden turns of the political tide due to his amorous, fickle, and shrewdly manipulative nature. His name, Sukjong, 肅宗, which he took as ruler, was the name of the Tang emperor who reigned from 756 to 762, and the Chinese characters can be read as "purge factions." The life of Shao-yu parallels and inverts that of Kim in ways too numerous to be merely coincidental, and Shao-yu's relationship with the emperor seems to be a nostalgic and wishful reminiscence of Kim's once-advisory role to the much younger Sukjong. Kim Man-jung was a member of the Western faction, which was dominant early in Sukjong's rule but lost favor during a controversy regarding the proper period of mourning to follow the death of the king's first wife, Queen Insun. When the Southern faction gained control in 1674, Kim was exiled, and it wasn't until five years later, just before a Southern faction member was executed for treason, that Kim was able to return

to court. In 1687 Kim was exiled again, this time to Seok-
cheon for protesting the king's treatment of a scholar official,
but was allowed to return a year later. Then, in 1689, Kim was
involved in protesting Sukjong's dismissal of his second wife,
Queen Inhyeon. Sukjong was so in love with his consort Lady
Jang (said to be the most beautiful woman in the whole of the
Joseon dynasty) that he made her his queen and her one-year-
old son the crown prince. For siding with Queen Inhyeon, who
was the daughter of a Western faction member, Kim was exiled yet again, this time to the remote island of Namhae, where
he is likely to have written both *Kuunmong* and his other
major work, *The Record of Lady Xie's Journey South*, shortly
before his death.[7]

The plot of *Kuunmong*, when it is considered in light of the
scandalous reign of King Sukjong, reads as an idealized remedy for all of the negative machinations in the Joseon court,
particularly regarding the consequences of romantic relationships and the relationships among high court women, official
wives, and concubines. Sukjong's relationship with his queen
mother was hostile, and his wives and concubines were constantly involved in intrigues that are still fodder for historical
soap operas today. Sukjong's senior concubine, Jang, was the
living historical embodiment of the Korean stereotype of the
seductive and conniving beauty.[8] By comparison, the queen,
the princess, the wives, and the concubines in Kim's novel all
dearly love and go out of their way for each other, practically
outdoing one another in their humility and deference to the
others' wishes. The treachery and deceptions that caused ex-
iles and executions in Sukjong's court are replaced, in *Kuunmong*, by romantic stratagems and practical jokes without
dire consequence.

KUUNMONG AND ITS INFLUENCES

Kuunmong, on its surface, is a historical fantasy novel set in
ninth-century Tang China—a kind of fantasy golden age evoked

by Korean literature of the Joseon era, much as writers in English today look back on the literature of Elizabethan times—and in addition to being originally written in Chinese, it emulates and alludes to Chinese Tang dynasty works so gracefully that Chinese scholars themselves have praised its merits.

As a result, *Kuunmong* needs to be considered in light of Chinese as well as Korean literature. In a Chinese context, *Kuunmong* fits into the genre of *quanqi* ("strange tales") that young Confucian scholars would sometimes write as part of their civil examinations to entertain their elder examiners (and perhaps thus earn a higher score). It also refers back to famous dream stories of the Tang period, most prominently "The Record Within a Pillow" (枕中記, c. 719) by Shen Jiji (also known as Li Mi) and "The Governor of Nanke" (南柯太守伝, c. 794) by Li Gongzuo.[9] In both of these stories the protagonist temporarily enters a dream world before eventually returning to reality, the dream episode involving marriage to a beautiful woman of royal family, attainment of a high-ranking position, military exploits, and ultimate dissatisfaction with material success. Kim Man-jung would certainly have known these works, though they are more tragic and lack *Kuunmong*'s structural and linguistic elegance—suggesting he might have set out to remedy those qualities of the older works.

Kuunmong brims with allusions to Chinese literary texts in a way characteristic of Joseon-era Korean literary works, which idealized and emulated Chinese literary culture. Both the narrator and the characters make constant allusions to Chinese literature and history. The way in which allusions abound even in casual descriptions of landscape suggests the underlying consciousness of an outsider mimicking a tradition—perhaps even overcompensating to show off his knowledge. That, in itself, is not unusual, but what is truly astonishing is the degree to which the allusions are interwoven into the narrative and serve to convey the novel's underlying Buddhist themes in an especially subtle and powerful way. Korean literary culture, for the upper classes in the Joseon era, was characterized by a syncretic interweaving of Buddhist, Taoist, and Confucian themes, but Kim's use of allusions is uniquely resonant with ideas central to Buddhism: the illusory nature of the world (*maya* 麼也), the idea of the interpenetration of phenomena (*tongdal* 通達), and "essence-function" (*che-yong* 體用).[10] These are ideas one finds especially significant and enduring in Korean Buddhism after Weonhyo and Jinul,[11] two great monks of the earlier Silla dynasty, Korea's golden age of Buddhism. During Kim Manjung's time, Confucianism was the state ideology and Buddhism was actively suppressed, and so to write a novel in which an elaborate Confucian pipe dream gives way to dissatisfaction that is remedied by Buddhism would also have been an overt act of resistance and criticism, especially from a writer in exile for rebuking the king.

In its amalgamation of Confucian, Taoist, and Buddhist themes in its plot, *Kuunmong* ends by clearly privileging Buddhism as its underlying moral rhetoric. It does so by offering an analogy by which readers, after seeing Hsing-chen's realization, might model themselves on the young monk and thereby break the "fourth wall" of the text and extend its central Buddhist themes into real life. Just as Hsing-chen wakes up from being Shao-yu, having moved from reality to dream and back again with the realization that the two are indistinguishable, the reader may wake out of being immersed in the fantasy of the novel to realize that its themes are not any different from real life. For a typical Western reader, the analogy may stop here, but *Kuunmong* is an important and especially sophisticated example of Buddhist metafiction. A Buddhist understands that one's consciousness of "reality" is actually only an illusion created by the mind and that the world one "lives" in is a once-removed construct of consciousness. In that context, the trajectory of *Kuunmong*'s plot is especially resonant, because it plays out a life of pleasure and accomplishment into one of depression (the unsatisfactoriness of *dukkha*, the primary Buddhist truth of suffering) and resolves Hsing-chen's depression by having him wake up to follow the Buddhist path to enlightenment. The resonance with which Kim played out the Buddhist rhetoric in *Kuunmong* seems to have made the work widely influential. A hundred years after the publication of *Kuunmong*, China's greatest novel, *The Dream of the Red Chamber* (*Hong Lou Meng* 紅樓夢), would feature similar plot details and parallel themes.

Most critical studies of *Kuunmong* have tended to examine its Buddhist, Confucian, and Taoist themes as separate entities. Reality and illusion in *Kuunmong* have been discussed in detail by academics, though Francisca Cho Bantly's *Embracing Illusion: Truth and Fiction in* The Dream of the Nine Clouds is the only book-length critical work in English on *Kuunmong*. Academics have also taken a Taoist lens to *Kuunmong*, one of the most innovative being Marion Eggert, who makes a compelling case for considering the eight women in *Kuunmong* as a symbolic expression of the underlying cosmology of the *I Ching* (an allusion that would have been far more apparent to readers of Kim's time). From that perspective, Hsing-chen's eight fairies are not a sign of sensual excess, but a necessary number for symbolic completion paralleling the Buddhist resolution at the end. The Taoist *I Ching* has eight trigrams, Buddhism has its eightfold path to enlightenment, and even Confucians call one's fate "the eight characters." But *Kuunmong* reveals its true syncretic brilliance in the way in which its Confucian, Taoist, and Buddhist features converge, and one of the ways to find access to this syncretism is via the symbology of numbers, which both introduces and concludes the novel.

The numbers that bracket the narrative must be examined through a lens of three traditions to be fully appreciated. The number nine is presented even before the story, in the title, and is easy to gloss as the eight fairies and Hsing-chen. But the narrative itself begins with the number *five*, referring to the "Five Peaks" of China on the surface, but implicitly evoking the Buddhist *skandha*s, the "five heaps" that account for how one lives in a world of illusion (i.e.,"cloud dreams") created by the senses. Into this setting of the five heaps amplified into mountains comes the monk named Liu-kuan, meaning "*six* perceptions" (a reference to the fact that there are six senses in

Buddhism, the sixth being consciousness). Finally, Hsing-chen (the *one*) and the *eight* fairies are introduced after this to constitute the *nine* clouds.

Kim's use of the number eight has a range of meanings that are especially relevant because they weave together the three traditions in a way that any culturally literate person of the times would immediately have understood. For example, the eight trigrams of the *I Ching*, mentioned above, are often arranged around the *taijitu* (the yin/yang symbol, which also represents the feminine and masculine principles) in a diagram of cosmic order understood during both the Tang dynasty and Joseon Korea.

With a variant yin/yang in the center and with the trigrams rearranged, this Taoist symbol would eventually be adopted as the *eogi*, the royal standard of Joseon in the nineteenth century (and one of the early designs for the flag of the Republic of Korea).

Even scholars who had not memorized the *I Ching* would have known the eight trigrams, as they were also associated with the cardinal and ordinal directions, with their arrangements in a square three-by-three grid. The empty position in the middle was the ninth position, which corresponded to the center of a squared circle and was also associated with the position of a village well surrounded by houses or fields. This grid was a cosmological and political structure, and would have been well-known to any Joseon intellectual.

☷	☶	☵
☴		☲
☳	☲	☰

In the novel, this structure corresponds to Hsing-chen in the middle with the eight fairies around him or Shao-yu in the center with his eight wives and concubines surrounding him. In Joseon and Tang culture, this diagram was a general model for social organization: houses around a village well, districts around the capital, advisers around the king, buildings around the courtyard, wives and concubines around a lord—a structural model for public as well as private relationships,[12] precisely those whose mismanagement led Kim to criticize King Sukjong.

In Buddhism, the circle made by eight trigrams corresponds to the empty circle at the eighth place in the "Oxherding Cycle" (a well-known series of ten pictures with commentaries that chart the journey of a follower of the Zen path).

This eighth picture is transcendence, the primordial emptiness, the condition from which all things emerge (parallel to Hsing-chen, whose name means "Original Nature," characterized by primordial emptiness, from whose mind the dream narrative emerges), but in the Zen tradition it is required that one return from this state, back into the world, to help others achieve enlightenment.

Finally, the circle and the number eight together represent the wheel of dharma, the symbol of Buddhism, which refers to the Buddha's teaching of the eightfold path (the Four Noble Truths of Buddhism being the more distinct spokes).

The circle itself also represents samsara, the continuous cycle of birth and rebirth sustained by the accumulation of karma. The swirl in the center is parallel to the primordial emptiness from which all reality emerges. The first of the Four Noble Truths of Buddhism is the concept of *dukkha*, generally glossed as "suffering" but more accurately rendered "unsatisfactoriness," which is Shao-yu's condition just before he wakes up.[13] Highlighting these Buddhist themes, many editions of *Kuunmong* use a four- and/or eight-part structure in their printing.

The presence of the number five in *Kuunmong*, after the initial overt reference to the five great mountains and the Five Peaks at the beginning of the novel, will be less apparent to a Western reader because it is implied throughout the rest of the story (except in allusions to the Chinese Five Classics). But to an educated reader of Kim's era, the number five was a matter-of-fact part of one's worldview, with immediate additional associative connections related to cosmology and social structure: the Five Relationships of Confucianism, the five elements of Taoism, the five colors, the five tones, the five cardinal directions (with the center being the fifth). *Kuunmong* implicitly critiques King Sukjong's violation of Confucianism's Five Relationships (ruler to subject, father to son, husband to wife, elder to younger, and friend to friend), which were seen as vital to maintaining social stability, by integrating that structure into the Buddhist theme of dream and illusion.

For a Buddhist, there are five emotions and five spiritual faculties, and a process of five steps that condition one's perception of reality. Here, it is important to remember that, in Buddhism, dream and reality are not a binary pairing of opposites. What Western culture considers reality is, in Buddhist philosophy, simply another layer of illusion because it is a "conditioned" reality, meaning that even our mundane perceptions of the world are a result of the operation of a five-part system, the five *skandha*s (or "heaps") mentioned above: form, sensation, perception, mental formations, and consciousness. We, in our normal state, are never in touch with *real* reality, or the thing itself, but constantly experience a world "conditioned" by those *skandha*s, whose sequential interactions produce our very consciousness. Form is the world and the corporeal body, which experiences sensations, which are then filtered and assembled into perceptions, which give rise to associative mental formations, which finally produce our ego consciousness. (In this way, the Buddhist understanding of consciousness is very close to the current findings in neuroscience.)[14] *Kuunmong* implies that the Five Relationships and the Five Peaks are parallel to the *skandha*s, and thus the very social fabric of Confucianism and reality are illusions, *maya* within *maya*.

Six, of course, follows five, but here it does so in both a numerological and a thematic sense, as *Kuunmong* ends with a prominent reference to the number six. The old Buddhist master Liu-kuan, whose name means "six perceptions," recites a passage from *The Diamond Sutra* that lists precisely those six illusion-like things that serve as an analogy for the "conditioned" world as perceived, via the five *skandha*s, by the unenlightened: one, dreams; two, illusions; three, bubbles; four, shadows; five, dewdrops; and six, a flash of lightning. This summary is the last dramatic moment in the novel, and when the fairies are mentioned again they are "eight new nuns." Finally, the number nine refers to the former fairies and Hsing-chen when they have become bodhisattvas. That nine concludes the novel.

Ultimately, *Kuunmong* is a Buddhist metafiction, a reader-involved demonstration of the Buddhist concept of *tongdal*, the interpenetration of phenomena. When Hsing-chen wakes up on the prayer mat, he first realizes that he has experienced an illusory lifetime in an instant in the form of a dream, but then he further realizes that he cannot distinguish whether his former or current state is the actual dream. Prior to his waking, his "real" life as Hsing-chen had penetrated the dream of himself as Shao-yu on at least two occasions. And even within the "dream," his Shao-yu self had other dreams that challenged the "reality" of that state. Likewise, the novel itself anticipates the reader "awakening" from the illusion of the fantastical story, having been immersed in a waking dream while reading, having lost track of one's reality as one does while engaged in a vivid story. In the same way that the five *skandha*s create our "normal" consciousness (which is technically an illusion), they likewise create our consciousness of the novel as we read the text and assemble images from memory. The words of the novel trigger recollections from our "real" lives, but also from our memory of "illusions" such as other novels, poems, songs, and plays. The act of reading *Kuunmong* is meant to be analogous to Hsing-chen's life as Shao-yu was within the novel. These layers of illusion and reality interpenetrate and, from a Buddhist perspective, become indistinguishable in the conditioned phenomenon of what we call "reality."

Kuunmong's sophistication in its Buddhist themes suggests Kim's goal was far more than simply to write a romantic fantasy to entertain and comfort his lonely and worried mother while he was in exile. He clearly knew that the work would have a wide readership in court, including King Sukjong, for whom it may have been Kim's last poignant advice as minister. It was a message to members of the royal court and to King Sukjong himself regarding the ultimate consequence of politics, intrigue, and romance—not simply a critique, but a remedy for the scandalous conduct of the Joseon court and its fickle monarch. It is no wonder that *Kuunmong* is one of the most beloved novels in Korean history, while Sukjong's reign is one of the favorite subjects for historical soap operas.

❦

Kuunmong continues to play a remarkably visible role in Korean culture to this day. Choi In-hun, a major Korean literary figure, wrote a novel called *Kuunmong* in 1962, applying many of the original's themes in a modern context. More recently, 2014 saw the release of an *otome* game, a gender-reversed animated game/visual romance novel, called *The Cloud Dream of the Nine: Love Story of a Girl*. Uhm Jung Hwa, one of the most enduring K-pop singer-actresses, released an album in 2016 sharing James Scarth Gale's 1922 translation of the title, *The Cloud Dream of the Nine*, featuring a music video of the main track, "Dreamer," that might very well emulate the novel's singing and dancing competition. Allusions to *Kuunmong* are ubiquitous in Korean culture—from subtle nods in the use of coded names and numbers in the works of the avant-garde writer Yi Sang to transparent and humorous parallels in superhero films like *Woochi: The Demon Slayer* (2009). Most recently, the blockbuster 2017 film *Along with the Gods: The Two Worlds*, directed by Kim Yong-hwa, combines themes from *Kuunmong* and Dante's *Inferno* in the story of a fireman who dies and must examine his karma as he is tried in the Underworld. Even outside its Korean context, *Kuunmong* reveals the deep history of the themes one sees in today's international blockbuster mind-benders produced in the West: *The Matrix*, *Inception*, and even *Blade Runner* and its sequel.[15]

My own exploration of the themes in *Kuunmong* began many years ago with my study of classical Korean literature, Tang poetry, Vipassana meditation, and dream theory, and it was this combination of interests that motivated me to set out to do this translation. *Kuunmong* is a novel whose themes subtly—perhaps subliminally—permeate the reader. What began for me as a two-year translation project slowly transformed into a deep engagement with Tang dynasty literature, Buddhist philosophy, Taoist alchemy, Korean folk religion, and Korean religious syncretism. My engagement with *Kuunmong*—or, more precisely, my attempt to understand the original text and convey its complexities in English—has not only provided me with vivid and nostalgic memories of a fantastical romance, it has fundamentally changed my very theory of the interaction of reading and writing. I hope *Kuunmong* will do the same for you.

HEINZ INSU FENKL

Suggestions for Further Reading

Bantly, Francisca Cho. *Embracing Illusion: Truth and Fiction in* The Dream of the Nine Clouds. Albany: State University of New York Press, 1996.

Birch, Cyril, ed. *Anthology of Chinese Literature: From Early Times to the Fourteenth Century.* New York: Grove Press, 1965.

Bouchez, Daniel. "On Kuunmong's Title." *Kuunmong-ui jemog-e daehayoe*<구운몽>의제목에대하여. 東方學志 (*Dongbang hakji*), No. 136, December 2006, pp. 387–409.

Cho, Francisca. "A Literary Analysis of *Kuunmong*." Introduction to the James Scarth Gale translation of *The Cloud Dream of the Nine* by Kim Man-choong. Fukuoka, Japan: Kurodahan Press, 2004.

The Cloud Dream of the Nine. James Scarth Gale, trans. London: Daniel O'Connor, 1922.

Eggert, Marion. "*Kuunmong* and the Sino-Buddhist Sphere." Paper presented at the 2nd International Meeting for the International Convention of Asia Scholars [ICAS], Berlin, 9–12 August 2001.

Eggert, Marion. "*Yijing* Cosmology in *Kuunmong*." Paper issued in Proceedings of the 1st World Congress of Korean Studies, Sŏngnam, Korea, 2002; *Embracing the Other: The Interaction of Korean and Foreign Cultures*, Vol. 1, 2002, pp. 213–18.

Evon, Gregory N. "Chinese Contexts, Korean Realities: The Politics of Literary Genre in Late-Chosŏn (1725–1863) Korea." *East Asian History*, No. 32/33, December 2006/June 2007, pp. 57–82.

Fessler, Susanna. Introduction to the James Scarth Gale translation of *The Cloud Dream of the Nine* by Kim Man-choong. Fukuoka, Japan: Kurodahan Press, 2004.

Kim, Byong-Cook. *Kim Man Jung's* The Cloud Dream of the Nine: *A Modern Korean Translation with a Critical Essay.* Seoul: Seoul National University Press, 2007.

Kim, Kichung. *An Introduction to Classical Korean Literature from Hyangga to P'ansori.* New York: M.E. Sharpe, 1996.

Lee, Peter H., ed. *An Anthology of Traditional Korean Literature.* Honolulu: University of Hawai'i Press, 2017.

McNaughton, William, ed. *Chinese Literature: An Anthology from the Earliest Times to the Present Day.* Rutland, VT: Charles E. Tuttle, 1974.

Moore, Steven. *The Novel: An Alternate History 1600–1800.* New York: Bloomsbury Academic, 2013, pp. 495–500.

Mun, Sang-duk. "*The Cloud Dream of the Nine,* a Buddhist Novel." *Korea Journal* 11:3, March 1971, pp. 24–32.

Pu Songling. *Strange Tales from a Chinese Studio.* John Minford, trans. New York: Penguin Classics, 2006.

Rutt, Richard, and Kim Chong-un, trans. *Virtuous Women: Three Classic Korean Novels.* Seoul: Royal Asiatic Society, 1974.

The Story of Hong Gildong. Minsoo Kang, trans. New York: Penguin Classics, 2016.

Wu Ch'eng-en. *Monkey: Folk Novel of China.* Arthur Waley, trans. New York: Grove Press, 1970.

Yu, Myoung In. "The Role of Keijō Imperial University in the Formation of Korean Literature Studies: The Case of *Kuunmong* Studies." *International Journal of Korean Studies / Kukche koryŏhak* 12, 2008, pp. 165–98.

Yu, Myoung In. "*Kuunmong* and Sinosphere: Focusing on Its Title." Sixth Biennial Korean Studies Association of Australasia Conference, University of Sydney, 9 July 2009.

Yun, Chang Sik. "The Structure of the *Kuun mong* [A dream of nine clouds]." *Korean Studies* 5, 1981, pp. 27–41.

A Note on the Translation

There are only three previous translations of *Kuunmong* in English—an unusually small number, given the novel's literary stature in Korea. It was previously translated by James Scarth Gale in 1922 as *The Cloud Dream of the Nine* and again by Richard Rutt in 1974 as *A Nine Cloud Dream.*[1] It was also translated as *The Nine Cloud Dream* by the English Student Association of the Department of English Language and Literature at Ewha Women's University under the supervision of Kathleen Crane.[2]

Gale (1863–1937), a Presbyterian missionary, and Rutt (1925–2011), an Anglican bishop who later became Roman Catholic, are part of the long lineage of Christian clergy who lived and worked in Korea, and they are distinguished by their deep engagement with Korean culture and language, particularly in their study of the classical Chinese in which the old Korean scholarly and literary texts are written.[3] Their translations, examined in sequence, are a fascinating glimpse into the changes in the English language over the course of a half century and an implicit look at the different cultural attitudes taken by Gale and Rutt to their subject. The two translations also reveal an increasing understanding of and openness to Asian traditions from the perspective of highly educated Christians over that half century. Rutt's builds on Gale's, and each has its particular strengths and weaknesses, but in general terms the latter translation shows a cultural sea change in Western attitudes toward Asian culture. The Ewha translation, which was done by Korean students, makes liberal use of both earlier ones while also providing a much more literal rendition of the language.

My own translation has the good fortune of learning from

all three previous translations. It is based on multiple source texts including the 1803 edition at the Harvard-Yenching Library, the 1890 hangul text at the Kyujanggak Institute for Korean Studies, and the Seoul National University text published in 1972. The 1972 text is a slightly shorter version of what is called the "Nojon" text by *Kuunmong* scholars (so named because it begins with the passage describing the "old monk"). I began with the understanding that I would be translating for a readership whose exposure to the subtexts of *Kuunmong* would be in English. Since it was written in seventeenth-century Korea, while the story is set in Tang China, I also tried to emulate the archaic tone of a historical novel without being too archaic with my language. I had to keep in mind that Kim Man-jung was writing what amounted to a fantasy novel that not only alluded to but imitated earlier Chinese works. He also wrote the novel in Chinese with an eye and ear toward the additional layers of wordplay created by reading the Chinese characters in a Korean context. It is difficult even to set up an appropriate analogy, but imagine if a Russian novelist of the nineteenth century had written a heroic fantasy novel set in the France of the Middle Ages and furthermore wrote it in the French of that time, alluding, throughout the work, to even earlier French literature. How does one do a translation that re-creates such a parallel effect? It was a question that presented numerous challenges.

After surveying both Chinese and Korean classics in English translation, I decided that where Gale and the Ewha group used the Korean readings of character and place names, I would use the more logically appropriate Chinese renditions, as did Rutt. The use of the Korean readings of Tang-period Chinese names would be as odd as anglicizing European names—Joseph for Giuseppe, for example—in a novel set in Renaissance Italy. Where possible, I read antiquated English translations of Chinese classics to explore ways of conveying that style. I also kept the anachronistic Wade-Giles romanizations of the Chinese specifically to make this translation feel slightly archaic in English to emulate how *Kuunmong* must have felt to its original readership. In the Introduction, Notes, and Appendices, on the other hand, I have used the standard Pinyin romanizations, except where other romanizations have become established as the familiar form.

Acknowledgments

First, I would like to thank the Literary Translation Institute of Korea for its generous support in sponsoring my initial translation work for this project, and the State University of New York at New Paltz for the sabbatical that permitted part of the research and writing time. I have many people to thank, even from before the inception of this project, which, I realized a few years ago, was the intersection and culmination of all the major threads of my literary engagements going back to the time when I was a child being told bedtime stories from the *Odyssey* and the *Völsunga Saga* by my father, Heinz Johannes Fenkl. My Korean maternal uncles, Hyongbu and Big Uncle, were consummate storytellers, and I unwittingly began my career as a translator when I tried to write down stories they had told me in Korean in my seventh-grade English notebook in Germany. Big Uncle also demonstrated to me, firsthand, how one could integrate the reading of the Tao into one's perception of commonplace reality and memory of dreams. From my mother, Lee Hwa-sun, I learned the importance of remembering dreams and interpreting their omens.

While I was an undergraduate at Vassar, Professor Walter Fairservis introduced me to the Chinese classics and encouraged me to explore Korean folklore more analytically, while Professor William Gifford encouraged a more story-oriented approach. Professor Susan Brisman, in her Romantic Poetry seminar, taught me the value of close reading paired with original research. During my graduate studies at the University of California, Davis, Professors Marian Ury and Benjamin Wallacker introduced me to the rigors of translating Asian folktales and classical Chinese; Daniel Rancour-Laferriere's seminars in psychoanalysis and semiotics helped make symbolism transparent; and Aram Yengoyan, by mentoring a year-long research project that involved dream theory and the study of the Dream-time and lucid dreaming, lent tremendous insight into the real themes that underpin Kim's novel.

James Scarth Gale and Richard Rutt were inspiring role models and their earlier translations were invaluable resources. In translation theory and practice, I am grateful to the late Song Yo-in; and in pragmatic and historical issues, my thanks to Peter H. Lee for his insights and guidance. Sam Raim, my editor, provided insightful feedback that made this a far better book than its original form. Walter Lew, in our work together during his Kaya days, gave me confidence to tackle this project. I deeply appreciate the support of David McCann and Lee Young-Jun, especially while I finished the first annotated excerpt for the journal *Azalea*; Kwon Youngmin inspired me with his deep analysis of the encoded language of the Korean poet Yi Sang, introduced me to Zen *sijo*, and also gave me his inscribed copy of Kim Byong-Cook's Korean translation[1] of *Kuunmong* as an invaluable resource. Master Cho Oh-hyun, whose Zen *sijo* poetry I translated, helped me to understand the principles of interpenetration and nonobstruction in language, two of the fundamental Buddhist principles expressed in the novel. Master Cho passed away the same day I submitted my final draft of this manuscript, and to him I must emulate Hsing-chen's bow to Master Liu-kuan. And finally, my love and gratitude to Anne and Bella, my first readers, without whose continuous support and patience this project would not have been possible.

The Nine Cloud Dream

PART I

石橋奇緣

I

THE REINCARNATION OF HSING-CHEN

There are five great mountains beneath Heaven.[1] To the east is T'ai-shan, Grand Mountain; to west is Hua-shan, Mountain of Flowers; to the south lies Heng-shan, the Mountain of Scales; to the north another Heng-shan, Eternal Mountain; and in the center stands Sung-shan, the Exalted Mountain. These are known as the Five Peaks, and the highest of them is Heng-shan, south of Tung-t'ing Lake, encircled by the river Hsiang on three sides. Upon Heng-shan itself there are seventy-two peaks that rise up and pierce the sky, some jagged and precipitous—blocking the paths of clouds—their fantastic shapes evoking wonder and awe, their auspicious shadows full of good fortune.

Among the seventy-two peaks, the five tallest are called Spirit of the South, Crimson Canopy, Heaven's Pillar, Stone Treasure-House, and Lotus Peak. They are regal, crowned by the heavens, and veiled in clouds, their bases obscured in mist. They are imbued with divine power, and in the haze of the day they are occluded from human view.

In ancient times, when Yü restrained the Great Flood[2] that inundated the Earth, he erected a commemorative stone tablet on one of these peaks, recording his deed, and though many eons have passed, the inscription is still sharp and clear and one can still read the characters for "cloud" and "heaven" upon the stone.

In the days of Ch'in Shih-huang-ti,[3] Lady Wei, having become a Taoist immortal,[4] settled in these mountains with an attending company of fairies as decreed by Heaven. She was known as Lady Wei of the Southern Peak, and many are the strange and wonderful things she caused to happen there.

In the days of the T'ang dynasty[5] a great monk arrived from India. He was so taken by the beauty of the mountains that he built a monastery on Lotus Peak, and there he taught *The Diamond Sutra*,[6] instructed disciples, and banished evil spirits. In time people said that a living Buddha had descended to Earth. His name was Liu-kuan, and he explicated the sutras so clearly that they called him "Master of the Six Temptations," the Great Master Liu-kuan.[7]

Among his five or six hundred disciples, there were some thirty who were advanced and well versed in these teachings, and the youngest of these was Hsing-chen.[8] His features were fair and handsome, and a light shone from his face like flowing water. He had already mastered the scriptures,[9] though he was barely twenty. He surpassed all the others in wisdom and mental agility, and all knew that the master loved him best and intended, in time, to make him his successor.

When Master Liu-kuan expounded upon the dharma to his disciples, the Dragon King[10] himself—in the guise of a white-clad old man—would come from Tung-t'ing Lake to listen attentively. One day the master called his disciples together and said to them, "I am old now, and my health is failing. It has been more than ten years since I have been beyond the gates of these mountains. I must go and pay my respects to the Dragon King. Who among you will go in my stead to his Underwater Palace?"

Hsing-chen volunteered at once, and the master was greatly pleased. He had the young monk outfitted in new robes, presented him with a ringed staff, and sent him off toward Tung-t'ing Lake.

Just as Hsing-chen departed, the monk who guarded the monastery's main gate came to Master Liu-kuan to announce that Lady Wei of the Southern Peak had sent eight of her fairies[11] to see him and they were now waiting outside.

"Let them in," said Liu-kuan.

And they skipped in through the gate, one by one, circled him three times, and bowed, scattering fairy flowers at his feet. Kneeling respectfully, they recited a message from Lady Wei:

Venerable Master, you live on the west side of the mountain and I on the east. The distance is not far, and we are near enough to be neighbors. Yet I am so busy that I have not had occasion to visit your monastery to hear your teaching of the sutras. So now I am sending my servants to pay my respects and to offer you heavenly flowers, fairy fruit, silk brocade, and other humble gifts. I hope you will accept them as a token of my respect.

With that, each of the eight fairies presented flowers and other gifts to the master, and he received them and passed them on to his disciples, who, in turn, placed them as offerings before the Buddha in the shrine room.

Liu-kuan bowed ceremoniously, with hands folded. "An old man like me hardly deserves such lavish gifts as these you have presented to me," he said, and he gave generously to the fairies in return before they took their leave and set lightly off.

They made their way out through the mountain pass, hand in hand, chatting as they went. "In the past, we were free to go anywhere among these mountains," they said. "But now that the Great Master Liu-kuan has established his temple, some of the peaks are forbidden to us, and for nearly ten years we have missed seeing the places of beauty that were once ours to view. We are lucky that our lady's order brings us to this valley at a beautiful time of year.

"It is still early, so let us take this chance to climb up to the top of Lotus Peak. Let us loosen our garments, wash our scarves in the waterfall, and compose some poems. And when we return our sisters will envy us!"

They set off, walking hand in hand along the high precipices, gazing down at the cascading streams and the rushing waters. It was springtime, and myriad flowers filled the valleys below like a pink mist. The air was fresh and alive with an untold variety of birdsong.

The eight fairies sat to rest on a stone bridge, looking down at their reflections where the streams met in a wide pool as clear as crystal. Their dark brows and radiant faces were mirrored in the water like a classical painting done in a master's hand, and they were so captivated they did not notice the sun descending into the western mountains.

CRÐ

Hsing-chen crossed Tung-t'ing Lake and now entered the Underwater Palace. The Dragon King, hearing that Master Liu-kuan had sent one of his disciples, personally came to the gate with an entourage to greet him. When they had gone inside the palace, the Dragon King took his throne and Hsing-chen bowed and delivered his master's message.

The Dragon King thanked Hsing-chen, and then held a great feast for him, full of fantastic delicacies he had never before tasted. But when the Dragon King offered him a cup of wine, Hsing-chen declined, saying, "Your Majesty, wine intoxicates the mind, and it is against my monastic vows to drink."

"Of course, I know that wine is among the five things that the Buddha forbade," the Dragon King replied. "But this wine is altogether different from the wine that mortals drink. It neither arouses passions nor dulls the senses. It instills calm and contentment. Surely you will not refuse it?"

Hsing-chen could not decline, and he had drunk three cups by the time he said his good-byes and left the Underwater Palace, riding on the wind to Lotus Peak. When he lighted there, he was already intoxicated and overcome by dizziness.

"Master Liu-kuan will be furious if he sees me this way," he said to himself. "He will scold me."

Crouching by the bank of a stream, he took off his robes and placed them on the clean sand. He dipped his hands in the clear water and was washing his hot face, when suddenly he noticed a strange and mysterious perfume wafting toward him. It was neither incense nor flowers, and it clouded his mind. "There must be flowers blooming upstream to put such wonderful fragrance in the air," he thought. "I must go find them."

He dressed carefully and followed the course of the stream upward; and there, quite suddenly, he found himself face-to-face with the eight fairies who were sitting on the stone bridge.

Hsing-chen dropped his staff and bowed deeply as he addressed them. "Ladies! I am a disciple of Master Liu-kuan and I live on Lotus Peak. I am on my way back from an errand for him. This bridge is not wide, and by sitting upon it, you are blocking my way. Would you kindly move aside and let me pass?"

The fairies returned his bow. "We are attendants to Lady Wei, and we are on our way back from delivering her greetings to your master. We have paused here to rest awhile. Is it not written in *The Book of Rites*,[12] concerning the law of the road, that the man goes to the left and the woman to the right? Since this bridge is very narrow, and we are already sitting here, is it not proper for you to avoid it altogether and cross at some other place?"

"But the water is deep," Hsing-chen replied. "There is no other way to cross. Where do you suggest I go?"

"It is said that the great Bodhidharma[13] crossed the ocean on a single leaf," said the fairies. "If you are, in fact, a disciple of Master Liu-kuan and you have studied the dharma with him, then surely you must have acquired some supernatural powers. It should not be hard for you to cross this tiny rivulet, so why do you stand there arguing with women over the right of way?"

Hsing-chen laughed. "I see from your attitude that you require some sort of payment for the right to cross, but I have no money. I am only a poor monk. Yet I do have eight jewels, which I will happily give to you if you will permit me to pass." With this he snapped off a branch from a peach tree and tossed it before the fairies. The fragrant peach blossoms that landed transformed into eight clear, sparkling, fragrant jewels.

The eight fairies laughed with delight. Each of them rose from her place and lifted a jewel, gave Hsing-chen a coy glance, mounted the wind, and flew away into the sky.

Hsing-chen stood at the bridge and watched for a long time looking in every direction, but he could not see where they had gone. Soon the multihued clouds had dissipated and even their fragrance was gone.

In a terrible state of dejection, Hsing-chen returned to the temple and delivered his message from the Dragon King. When Master Liu-kuan reprimanded him for his late return, Hsing-chen said, "The Dragon King detained me, Master, and it was not possible to refuse his generosity. That is why I have been delayed."

The master did not reply to this. He simply said, "Go away and rest."

Hsing-chen went back to his dim meditation cell and sat down alone. He could still hear the melodious voices of the eight fairies echoing in his ears, and his eyes still seemed to see their beautiful forms and faces as if they stood before him in the room. He found it impossible to control his racing thoughts—he could not meditate.

He thought to himself: "If a youth diligently studies the Confucian classics and serves his country as a minister of state or a general when he is grown into a man, he may dress in silks with an official seal upon his jade belt. He may look upon beautiful colors with the eyes and listen to beautiful voices with his ears. He may enjoy beautiful girls and leave an honorable legacy for his descendants. But a Buddhist monk has only a small bowl of rice and a cup of water. We read the sutras and meditate with our 108 *mala*[14] beads hanging upon our necks. It is a lofty and profound endeavor, but it is terribly lonely. Though I may become enlightened, though I may master all the doctrines of the Mahayana[15] path and sit in my master's seat to succeed him, once my spirit parts from my body in the flames of the funeral pyre, who will remember that a person named Hsing-chen ever lived upon this Earth?"

He tried to sleep, but sleep refused to come and the hour grew late. Whenever he closed his eyes, the eight fairies appeared before him, and when he opened them they vanished into nothingness. It suddenly occurred to him that the great purpose of Buddhism was to tame the mind and the heart. "I have been a monk for ten years," he said. "For ten years I have avoided the smallest fault, but these seductive thoughts will cause irreparable harm to my progress."

He burned incense, knelt, stilled his thoughts, and was counting his *mala* beads, visualizing the thousand Buddhas,[16] when suddenly one of the temple boys came to his window and inquired, "Brother, are you asleep? The master is calling you."

Hsing-chen was alarmed. "It is unusual for him to call me in the middle of the night. It must be something serious," he thought.

He followed the boy to the main shrine hall, where all the monks of the temple had assembled. Master Liu-kuan himself was sitting in solemn silence in the light of many candles. His appearance inspired both fear and curiosity, and when he spoke it was with great care, with grave intonation.

"Hsing-chen! Do you know how you have sinned?"

Hsing-chen was kneeling before the dais. He bowed low, until his head touched the floor, and said, "Master, I have been your disciple for more than ten years now. I have never disobeyed you. I have tried to be pure. I am not hiding anything, and I do not know what offense I have committed."

Liu-kuan became angry. "You drank wine at the palace of the Dragon King! On your return, by the stone bridge, you flirted with eight fairy girls, joking with them, throwing them a branch of flowers, which you transformed into jewels. And since your return, you have turned away from the teachings of the Buddha and dwelt on worldly and sensual things. You have rejected your way of life here, and now you cannot stay!"

Hsing-chen wept, bent his head to the floor, and pleaded. "Master!" he said. "I know I have sinned. But I drank the wine only because the Dragon King himself offered it to me and I could not refuse. I bantered with the fairies at the bridge because I had to ask them to step out of the way. In my cell I faced temptation, but I came to my senses and controlled myself. If I have done wrong, you may whip me on the calves, but if you are so cruel as to send me away, how will I ever correct myself?

"I came to you to become a monk when I was only twelve, and so you are like a father to me.[17] I serve you like a son. The relationship between master and disciple is deep and sacred. Where am I to go if I must leave Lotus Peak?"

"I am sending you away because that is what you wish," said Liu-kuan. "Why would I make you go if you wanted to stay? You ask, 'Where am I to go?' You should go wherever your desire takes you."

Then Master Liu-kuan shouted, "Come, constables!" and suddenly they materialized from thin air—the yellow-hatted emissaries of Hell.[18] They bowed and awaited his orders. "Take this man into your custody," said Liu-kuan. "Remove him to the Underworld and hand him over to King Yama."[19]

When Hsing-chen heard this he felt as if his spirit had left him. His eyes overflowing with tears, he fell upon the floor, crying, "Father! Father, please! Listen to what I have to say! In ancient times the Great Master Ananda broke all the laws of the Buddha when he visited the house of a prostitute and had intercourse with her. But the noble Shakyamuni[20] did not condemn him! He embraced Ananda and showed him the dharma ever more clearly. I may have transgressed, but surely I am less guilty than Ananda! How can you send me to Hell?"

"When Ananda fell into sin, his mind was repentant," Master Liu-kuan replied. "You, on the other hand, have lost your heart and mind upon a single glimpse of those seductive creatures. Your thoughts have turned toward a life of pleasure. Your mouth waters for worldly honor and wealth. You fare badly in a comparison with Ananda. You cannot escape the grief and suffering that await you, Hsing-chen!"

Hsing-chen could not imagine leaving, and he continued to cry for mercy until the master finally relented and comforted him. "Hsing-chen, while your mind is impure, you will never attain enlightenment, even up here in the mountains," he said. "But do not forget the dharma. Hold true to it, and though you may mingle with dirt and impurities along the way, your return is assured. If it is ever your desire to return, Hsing-chen, then I shall go myself to bring you back, so do not doubt or question me. Now, go!"

There was nothing more to be said. Hsing-chen bowed low before the master, said good-bye to his fellow monks, and went with the emissaries of the Underworld.

They transported him beyond the Lookout Pavilion to the

outer walls of Hell, and when the guards at the gate asked the cause of their coming, they said, "We have arrested this guilty man and bring him here at the orders of the Great Master Liu-kuan!" The guards opened the gates of Hell and let them through into the inner court, where they once again announced their arrival.

And it was Yama himself, King of the Underworld, who commanded that they bring him in. "Honored sir," he said to Hsing-chen, "though you abide in the hills under Lotus Peak, your name already rests on the incense table before the great King Ksitigarbha.[21] I have thought to myself that in the future, when you ascend the Lotus Throne, all sentient creatures of the Earth will be greatly blessed. So how is it that you have been arrested and dragged here before me in disgrace?"

Hsing-chen was confused and humiliated, and he did not reply for a long time. Finally, he said, "I met Lady Wei's fairy maidens on the stone bridge of the Southern Peak. I failed to restrain my carnal thoughts about them. I have sinned against my master, and now, Your Majesty, I await your command."

King Yama sent a messenger to King Ksitigarbha with the following note:

> The Great Master Liu-kuan of Lotus Peak has sent me one of his disciples, escorted by the Yellow Hats. We are to come to a judgment, here in the Underworld, as to his guilt. Since his case is not like that of ordinary offenders I am asking Your High Majesty's counsel.

King Ksitigarbha replied:

> Each man has his own path to perfection, and each is reborn in order to carry out the things necessary to work out his karma. No man can escape the cycle of samsara, and therefore there is no point in our discussing this case.[22]

King Yama was just about to come to a decision when two demon soldiers announced that the Yellow Hats, by Master Liu-kuan's command, had brought eight more criminals, who were now waiting outside the gate. Hsing-chen was greatly alarmed.

King Yama commanded that they be brought in—and behold!—the eight fairy maidens of the Southern Peak came haltingly through the gate and knelt down in the court. "Listen, fairy maidens of Southern Peak!" said Yama. "You fairy folk live in the most beautiful of known worlds. You enjoy uncountable pleasures and delights. How is it that you come to this place?"

Greatly shamed, they replied in a babble of voices: "Our mistress, Lady Wei, ordered us to pay a visit to the Great Master Liu-kuan to ask after his health and well-being. On our way back to the Southern Peak, we met his disciple Hsing-chen. Because we spoke with his disciple, Master Liu-kuan said that we had defiled the sacred laws of the mountains, and he wrote you to ask that we be banished to the Underworld. All our hopes are with Your Majesty, and we pray that you have mercy on us and allow us to go back to the world of the living."

King Yama then called nine emissaries, and they appeared before him. In a deep voice, he commanded, "Take these nine and return them at once to the world of the living."

He had hardly finished his pronouncement when a great whirlwind arose and carried the eight fairies and the youth off into the void, where they were swirled apart and flung into the eight directions. Hsing-chen was borne along by the wind, hurled and tossed about in endless space until, at last, he seemed to land on solid ground.

When the storm calmed, Hsing-chen gathered his wits and found himself among a range of mountains bordered by a beautiful, clear river. Below him was a bamboo grove, and beyond that, through the shady branches of the trees, he could see a dozen houses with thatched roofs. Several people were gathered there, talking together within his earshot. "How marvelous!" they said. "Hermit Yang's wife is past her fiftieth year, and yet she is going to have a child! We have been waiting for so long, but have yet to hear the infant's cry. These are anxious moments."

Hsing-chen said to himself: "I will be reborn into the world of humans. I can see that I am only a spirit now, for I have no body. I left it on Lotus Peak. It has been cremated already, and I am so young I have no disciples to recover my relics and keep them safe."

As these ruminations about the past filled him with grief, one of Yama's emissaries appeared and motioned him over. "This is the Hsiu-chou township of Huai-nan Province in the empire of T'ang,"[23] he said. "And here is the home of the hermit Yang, who is your father. This is his wife, Liu, your mother. It is your karma to be reincarnated in this household, so go quickly. Do not miss this auspicious moment!"

Hsing-chen went into the house, and there sat the hermit wearing his reed hat and a coat of rough hempen cloth. He was preparing some sort of medicine on a brazier in front of him, and the fragrance filled the house. From the room in back came the indistinct moaning of someone in pain.

"Go in quickly. Now!" the emissary urged again. When Hsing-chen hesitated, the messenger gave him a hard push from behind into the room.

Hsing-chen fell to the ground and instantly lost consciousness. It seemed that he had been propelled into some great natural cataclysm. "Help!" he cried. "Save me!" But the sounds caught in his throat, inarticulate, until they became the cries of an infant.

The midwives quickly announced to the hermit that his wife had borne him a beautiful son, and Yang took her the medicinal drink he had prepared. They looked at each other, their faces full of joy.

Hsing-chen was suckled when he was hungry, and he ceased his crying when he was satisfied. As a newborn he still recalled the events of his previous life on Lotus Peak, but as he grew older and knew the love of his parents, the memories of his former existence faded away, and soon they were entirely forgotten.

When the hermit saw how handsome and talented he was, he stroked the child's little brow and said, "Indeed, you are a gift from Heaven come to dwell among us."

And so he named him Shao-yu, meaning "Small Visitor,"

and gave him the special name Ch'ien-li, meaning "A Thousand *Li.*"[24]

❧

Time passes like flowing water, and in what seemed the space of moments, the boy grew to be ten years old. His face had the quality of jade and his eyes shone bright as the morning star. He was strong, and his mind pure and bright, showing that he was most certainly a superior man.[25]

The hermit said to his wife, "I do not originally come from this world, but because I am with you I have dwelt among the dust of this Earth in this mortal form. The immortals who live on Mount P'eng-lai[26] have called upon me many times to return to them. But because of your hard work and your suffering, I have refused them.

"Now Heaven has blessed us with a son who shows great talent, who is superior to others in his attainments. You may rely on him now, and in your old age you will surely enjoy wealth and honor through his achievements. Therefore, I need no longer delay my departure."

One day, the devas came to escort him, some riding on white deer and some on blue herons, and they flew off together toward the distant mountains. Though a letter would come from time to time out of the clear blue sky, no traces of the hermit Yang were ever seen on this Earth again.

夢

2

THE YOUNG SCHOLAR

After the hermit Yang departed, mother and son were left alone to look after each other in this world. In time Shao-yu showed such extraordinary talent that the local magistrate called him "the marvelous boy" and recommended him to the court. But Shao-yu, out of devotion to his mother, declined the favor.

When he was approaching fourteen, his clear and handsome features were said to resemble those of P'an Yüeh.[1] His poetry was like Li Po's, his calligraphy like that of the great Wang Hsi-Chih, and in strategy his cleverness matched that of Sun Pin and Wu Ch'i. He was well versed in astronomy and geomancy, in the six tactics and three practicalities.[2] In the military arts—spear throwing and swordsmanship—his skill was truly wondrous, and no one could stand before him. Because he had been a man of refined temperament in his former life, his mind was clear and his heart was full of compassion, and he solved the mysteries of life as deftly as one might split bamboo. He was altogether different from ordinary men.

One day, Shao-yu said to his mother, "When my father ascended to Heaven he entrusted the reputation and honor of this household to me. But we are still terribly poor and you are forced to labor even in your old age. If we live like dogs or turtles, dragging our tails and making no effort to better our condition, the family line will become extinct. I shall never make you proud, and I will have failed my father's trust. But I have heard that in a few days there will be government examinations open to any candidate in the empire. I would like to leave you for a little while to sit for that examination."

Shao-yu's mother, knowing her son's strong will, did not wish to keep him from this noble purpose. But she was afraid of him taking the long journey at such a young age, and she worried how long he might be away. "You are still young and inexperienced," she said. "This is your first real journey, so you must be sure to take care of yourself so that you may return safely. I shall wait anxiously each day by the gate to see you again."

Shao-yu bade his mother good-bye and set out on his way on a small donkey with a servant boy to accompany him. In a few days he reached Hua-chou in the state of Hua-yin, not far from the capital at Ch'ang-an.[3] The vistas of mountain and stream he passed were especially beautiful, and since it was still a while before the beginning of the examinations, he took his time, covering only a few *li* a day, lingering at historical spots and enjoying the scenery. Thus he averted the boredom and loneliness of the traveler.

❧

Shao-yu saw a small house in the dappled shade of a beautiful willow grove. A blue line of smoke rose into the sky like a roll of silk unwinding, and in a removed part of the enclosure he saw a beautiful pavilion with a neatly kept approach. He slowed his donkey and went near. The branches swayed like just-washed hair under the strokes of a beautiful girl's brush. Through the shade of the encircling branches and leaves he could barely make out the wonderful fairy world beyond.

Shao-yu pushed aside the foliage; his hand lingered, not wanting to let go. He sighed. "In our world of Ch'u[4] I have seen many pretty willow groves," he said, "but none so lovely as this."

He quickly composed a poem:

> The green silky willow, its slender wands
> veiling the bright pavilion—
> Why have you planted it?
> Was it your exquisite taste?

The long willow drapes, their deep green hue
'round the radiant pillar—
Take care and do not break them,
for they are fragile and they move my heart.

As he sang the poem in a rich, clear voice, the clouds paused and the valley echoed.

In the upper story of the pavilion a beautiful maiden was having her afternoon nap. She awoke with a start and sat up, pushing aside the armrest on which she leaned. She opened the embroidered shade and looked out this way and that through the painted railing. From where had she heard the singing? Suddenly her eyes met Shao-yu's.

Her hair was disheveled, like a soft, warm cloud at her temples, and her long jade hairpin had been pushed askew till it protruded slantwise through her hair. Her eyelids were still weighted with lingering sleep, and her expression was of someone who had just emerged from the world of dreams. Her rouge and powder had been removed by the careless hand of sleep, unveiling her natural beauty, a beauty impossible to picture, such as no painting has ever portrayed.

The two stared at each other, startled, but neither said a word. Shao-yu had sent his boy ahead to get him a room at the inn, and now the boy suddenly returned to announce that it had been arranged. The maiden looked straight at Shao-yu for a moment, and then quickly gathered herself and shut the blind, disappearing from view, leaving only a hint of sweet fragrance that carried to Shao-yu on the breeze.

At first Shao-yu regretted that the boy had disturbed him with his news. Now that the blinds had closed he felt as if a thousand *li* of the Yang-tze had cut him off from all his desire. He went on his way, looking back from time to time to check, but the silken window was shut and did not open again. He arrived at the inn with a sense of loss and homesickness, his mind aswirl with confusion.

Her family name was Ch'in and her given name Ts'ai-feng. She was the daughter of a government official. She had lost her mother early in life and had no brothers or sisters. Now she had reached the age when girls put up their hair,[5] but she was still unmarried.

Her father had gone to the capital on official business, and so she was alone when she unexpectedly met Shao-yu's gaze. She found herself intensely attracted to his handsome features and manly bearing, and hearing the verses he sang, she admired his literary skill.

She thought to herself: "A woman's lot in life is to follow her husband. Her pride and her shame—all of her life experiences— are bound to her lord and master. That is why Princess Cho Wen-chün followed Szu-ma Hsiang-ju when she was a widow.[6] I am yet an unmarried girl. I dread the idea of being my own go-between and proposing marriage, but it is said in ancient times, that 'the subjects choose their king,' so I shall inquire about this gentleman and learn his name and place of residence. I must do so at once. I cannot wait until my father returns—who knows where he may have gone or where I might go searching for him in the four directions?"

She unclasped a roll of silk, wrote a couple of verses, and then gave it to her nurse. "Take this letter to the inn at the guesthall and give it to the gentleman who rode past here on the little donkey and sang the willow song. Tell him that my purpose is to find the one who is destined for me, and on whom I may depend. His complexion is fair and his brows are dark and distinct as in a picture. Even if he is in a crowd, you will have no trouble spotting him because he is like a phoenix among chickens. Go see him now and personally give him this letter."

"I shall be careful to do just as you have commanded," said the nurse, "but what shall I say if your father should inquire later?"

"I shall see to that myself," said Ts'ai-feng. "Do not worry."

The nurse left, but in a few moments she returned and asked, "What shall I do if the gentleman is already married or engaged?"

Ts'ai-feng thought for a moment and replied, "If that is un-fortunately the case, I would not object to becoming his secondary wife.[7] He is young, but who can tell whether or not he is married?" The old nurse went to the guesthall and asked for the gentleman who had sung the willow song, and just at that moment Shao-yu stepped out of the entrance into the court and saw her. He replied at once, "Your humble servant, madam, is responsible for the willow song. Why do you ask?"

When the nurse saw his handsome face, she knew without a doubt that he was the man in question. Softly, she said, "We cannot speak here."

Shao-yu was curious. He led her into the guesthall, and when they were seated he quietly asked why she had come.

"Please, Your Excellency," she said, "will you tell me where you sang the willow song?"

"I am from a remote part of the country and have come near the capital for the first time. The beauty of it delights my soul. Today at noon, as I was passing along the main road, I saw to the north a small, exquisitely beautiful pavilion in a grove of green willows. I could not restrain my joy, and so I wrote a verse or two, which I sang. But why do you ask me of this?"

"Sir, did meet you anyone at that time?" asked the nurse. "Perhaps you came face-to-face with a stranger?"

"I came face-to-face with a beautiful fairy," said Shao-yu. "She gazed down upon me from the pavilion by the road. I can still see her lovely features, and the world is full of her fragrance."

"To tell you the truth, that pavilion is the home of my master, Inspector Ch'in," said the nurse. "And the fairy you speak of is his daughter. From the time she was a child, she has been intelligent and pure of heart, and she has a gift for reading character. Though she saw you only once, she has decided to promise herself to you, but her father is away in the capital at Lo-yang and someone must go and return with him before anything can be done.

"It seems you will be leaving soon, and since life is like a duckweed adrift in the sea, my mistress fears that she will not be able to find you once you are gone. So despite the embarrassment and the risk of dishonor, she has sent me to tell you that this is a matter of karma, and to ask of you your name, your place of residence, and whether you are married."

Shao-yu could not hide his joy. He thanked her and said, "My name is Yang Shao-yu, and my home is in the land of Ch'u. I am still too young to marry. Only my aged mother is alive, and though the consent to marry must come from parents of both sides, I give my word here and now. I swear it by the long green hills of Hua-shan and the endless stretches of the river Wei."

The nurse was delighted by her success. She took a letter from her sleeve and gave it to Shao-yu, who tore it open and found that it was a poem.

> I planted the willow by the pavilion
> so you would tie your mount and rest awhile—
> But you made horsewhips of the willow wands
> to hasten your glorious ride.

When Shao-yu read it aloud, he appreciated its brilliance and freshness, and he praised it. "The great Wang Wei and Li Po[8] were no better than she," he said. Then, on the same sheet of silk paper, he wrote a reply.

The nurse took it and placed it in her bosom. She left through the main gateway of the guesthall, but Shao-yu called out to her again. "The young lady is a native of Ch'in, while I belong to Ch'u. Once we are parted it will be impossible to communicate across the mountains. We will have no proof of the promises we made today, and things will be left uncertain. Do you think she would agree to meet by moonlight? In her letter there is some such suggestion, is there not? Please ask her for me."

The nurse returned to her lady and delivered the message. "Master Yang has sworn by Hua-shan and the river Wei that he will be your husband. He praised your composition most highly, and wrote a reply, which I have brought you." She then handed it to the lady, whose face lit up with joy as she read:

> A hundred willow strands woven into melody,
> heart to heart beneath the moon—

> Let us loose those tangled bindings now,
> and celebrate the joyous spring.

The nurse said, "Master Yang asks you if you would agree to let him come quietly by moonlight and write another verse for the two of you to enjoy together."

"It is not proper for a man and woman to meet before marriage. And yet, since I have promised myself to him, how can I refuse? But if we meet in the night there will be rumors, and when my father hears them he will be very angry. It would be better to wait until morning. We can meet in the hall of the house and say our vows there. Go now and tell him."

So the nurse returned once again to the guesthall and told Shao-yu what her mistress had said. Shao-yu was disappointed, but he answered, "The lady's pure heart and proper words put me to shame." Before the nurse left, he pleaded with her not to let anything go wrong with their plans.

❧

That night at the inn at the guesthall, Shao-yu was unable to sleep. He tossed and turned all night, waiting for the cock to crow, impatient with the long spring night. Finally, the dawn star appeared and the drums beat to announce morning. He called his boy and ordered him to feed the donkey.

Suddenly there was a great noise outside—cavalry riding in from the west, thundering by like a great river. Shao-yu anxiously put on his clothes and went outside. Everywhere, the streets were in chaos—armed soldiers shouting and refugees fleeing, crying out as they were trampled underfoot.

When he asked a bystander what was happening, he was told that the general Ch'ou Shih-liang[9] had raised an army and started a revolt, proclaiming himself emperor. The Emperor was away in Yang-chou on an inspection tour, and so the whole capital was in a state of hopeless confusion. The rebels were everywhere, robbing the homes of the people, and there were reports that many of the gates had been locked so no one could escape the city. People everywhere—rich and poor alike—were being forcibly conscripted into the army.

Shao-yu anxiously ordered his boy to saddle the donkey, and they hastened toward Mount Lan-t'ien, where he planned to hide among the rocks.

At the top of the mountain he saw a small thatched hut in the clouds and heard the echoing cries of a crane. Thinking it must be someone's home, he told the boy to wait and he made his way among the rocks.

He was startled to come upon a Taoist hermit resting against a small reading table. The old man sat up and greeted him, saying, "You must be fleeing from the city. And you must be the son of the hermit Yang from Huai-nan."

Shao-yu was amazed; he bowed low and, bursting into tears, he said, "Yes, I am the son of the hermit Yang. Since my father departed, I have been living alone with my old mother. Though I am unlearned, I wanted to improve our circumstances and was on my way to sit for the civil examination,[10] but I had come only as far as Hua-yin when my way was blocked by the rebellion. In fleeing here to these mountains, I have had the fortune of meeting you. I know that Heaven has helped me in sending me to an immortal. I have not heard news of my father in a long time, and as time passes I yearn ever more for news from him. It sounds as if you know of him. Please, sir, tell me all that you know and give a son what comfort can come to him. Where does my father abide? How is his health?"

The sage laughed and said, "Your father and I were just playing a game of go[11] together on top of Mount Chu-ko. We parted only a short time ago, but I could not tell you where he has gone. His face has not changed and his hair has not gone gray, so do not worry about him."

Shao-yu, still in tears, said, "Please, with your power, help me just once to see my father again."

But the old Taoist only laughed again. "The love between son and father is deep, but the difference between men and immortals[12] is such that though I should like to help you, I cannot. The mountains where the fairies live are far away, and their ten provinces are vast, so it is impossible to know where your father might be. But since you are here, why not stay for a while and go when the way is open once again? It will not be long."

Realizing the old sage had no intention of helping him, Shao-yu soaked his clothes with hopeless tears. The sage comforted him, saying, "Meetings and farewells, farewells and meetings—that is the way of the world. Crying does not help."

Shao-yu wiped away his tears and thanked the old man, and he stayed, entirely forgetting about the boy and the donkey at the bottom of the path.

The old man pointed to a *ch'in*[13] hanging on the wall and asked, "Can you play?"

"I have always enjoyed music, but not having a good teacher, I have never been properly trained."

The old man had the *ch'in* brought to him. He gave it to Shao-yu and told him to give it a try.

Shao-yu put the instrument across his knees and played "The Wind in the Pines."

The old sage laughed with delight. "You have talent," he said. "So I shall give you proper instruction." He took the *ch'in* himself and played four tunes of unearthly clarity and beauty, like nothing heard before by mortal ears. Shao-yu was naturally skilled, and his mind was sharp. He mastered each tune after hearing it only once. This pleased the sage, and he brought out a white jade flute to play a piece on it for Shao-yu to learn. "Even in ancient times it was rare that two masters of music should meet. I present you with this *ch'in* and this flute—you will find them useful someday. Keep them safe and remember what I have taught you."

Shao-yu took the instruments and bowed in thanks. "Master," he said, "you were a friend to my father and I want to serve you as I served him. Please accept me as your disciple."

The old man smiled. "You cannot escape worldly riches

and glory, wealth and fame. How is it that you would while away your time on this mountain with me? Your path and my path are different—you were not meant to be my disciple. But I shall not forget your request. Here is a book of P'eng-tsu's yoga.[14] Study it. His techniques will not gain you immortality, but you will avoid illness and live to a great old age as he did."

Shao-yu rose, then bowed again to receive the book. "Master, you say that I am to enjoy wealth and glory, but I would like to ask you about another matter. I was discussing marriage with the daughter of the Ch'in family in Hua-yin, but I was caught up in the rebellion and had to flee here. I do not know the future. Can you tell me if we will marry?"

The old man laughed loudly. "Marriage is as dark and mysterious as night," he said. "One does not speak lightly about the way of Heaven. But your karma has many beautiful things in it, so do not set your heart only on Ch'in's daughter."

Shao-yu knelt to receive his instructions, then went with the old man into the guest room, where they spent the night.

The old man woke Shao-yu before dawn. "The way is now clear," he said. "The civil examination will be held in the coming spring, and your mother awaits you. Hasten back to her so that she will not worry." He gave Shao-yu some money for traveling.

Bowing his thanks a hundred times, Shao-yu set out with the *ch'in*, the flute, and the book of yoga. As he left, his heart was already full of sadness, but when he turned to look back, the house and the old Taoist had already vanished. All that remained were the sunlit clouds above the mountain.

He had gone into the mountains with the willows still in bloom, and now, with only a day gone by, he was shocked to see that it was already autumn, with chrysanthemums in full bloom. When he returned to the inn where he had stayed, he learned that troops had been called from all the provinces to put down the rebellion. It had taken five months to restore the peace, and now that the Emperor had returned to the capital, the civil examination had been postponed until spring.

Shao-yu returned to the house of Inspector Ch'in. The cool willows in the garden had faded in the cold and the colorful pavilion had been burned to the ground, leaving only scorched stones and broken roof tiles among the ashes in the empty courtyard. In the ruins of the village, there was no sound—not the crow of a cock nor the barking of a dog. Shao-yu mourned the transitory nature of human affairs, how a hundred-year pledge of marriage had ended so quickly in desolation.

He clutched the willow branches in his hands and, turning away from the setting sun, he sang the willow song that Lady Ch'in had written. He could not restrain his tears.

When he returned to the inn, he asked the innkeeper, "What has become of Inspector Ch'in and his family?"

The innkeeper frowned and answered, "Haven't you heard? The inspector went up to the capital on official business and left behind his daughter and servants to look after his home. When the rebellion was put down they found out he was in league with the traitors and he was executed. The girl was caught and taken to the capital. Some say she was executed, too. Some say she became a public slave. Just this morning the officials were marching a bunch of criminals' relatives right past the door. When I asked, I was told they were being sent off to be slaves in Ying-nan. Someone said one of them was Ch'in's daughter."

Shao-yu wept upon hearing this news. "The master of Lant'ien said that marriage to Lady Ch'in was as mysterious and dark as night. He must have meant she is dead." Lamenting, he packed his things and started his journey back home.

Meanwhile, Shao-yu's mother had heard of the war and of the attack on the capital, and fearing that her son was in danger, she called upon Heaven with all her heart and prayed until her face grew thin and her body was run-down and emaciated. It did not seem that she could physically endure for long. But now, seeing her son return safe and sound, she was so over-come with joy that she clasped him to her bosom and wept as if he had returned from the dead.

They talked together as the old year passed. When the win-ter had ended and spring came again, Shao-yu once more made ready to depart and sit for the civil examination.

His mother said: "Last year you went through many dan-gers on your way, and I still tremble when I think of it. You are still young, and there is plenty of time for great achievements, but I will not try to stop you if you wish to go now. Hsiu-chou is a remote place. No one here is your equal and there are no girls suitable to be your bride. You are fifteen now, and it is time for you to marry, before it is too late.

"At Chu-ch'ing Temple in the capital, there is a cousin of mine, Tu-ryun. She has been a Taoist priestess for countless years, but I believe she is still alive. I'm told she is a woman of great authority and wisdom. She knows all the best families in the city. Remember to go and see her, because she will treat you like a son and will help you find a good woman. Do not forget." She wrote a letter for him to take.

Shao-yu listened to his mother, then told her about his meet-ing with Ch'in's daughter in Hua-yin. Thinking of her filled him with sorrow.

His mother sighed. "Lady Ch'in must be beautiful," she said. "But it must not be the will of Heaven for you to be with her. She may not be dead, but it would be very hard to find her after the destruction and disaster that befell her family. Please, banish your vain thoughts of her and find another wife. Be a comfort to me and do what I ask."

Shao-yu said good-bye and started on his way, but just as he reached Nakyang he was caught in a sudden rainstorm and he took shelter in a wine shop outside the south gate. "This is de-cent wine," he said to the innkeeper after he'd had a drink. "But have you nothing better?"

"I have nothing better than this," the innkeeper replied. "If you want the best, you will find it at an inn called Nakyang Springtime at the entrance to T'ien-chin Bridge. That wine has an exquisite taste, but a high price. One measure will cost you a thousand cash."[15]

Shao-yu thought for a moment. "Nakyang has been the home of the Emperor since ancient times," he said. "It is a very busy and marvelous city, regarded as the greatest in the world. Last year I went by another road and so I did not get to see its sights. This time I shall stop and have a look."

MEETING CH'AN-YÜEH
AT LO-YANG

Shao-yu had his boy pay for the wine and then led his donkey toward T'ien-chin Bridge. When they passed through the gates into the city he saw that it was bustling with commerce and as beautiful as he had heard. The river Lo¹ flowed through the city like a band of gleaming silk, and the T'ien-chin Bridge— the Bridge of the Milky Way—arched over the water like a double rainbow. The brilliant red pillars and the blue tiles of the pavilion on each side rose high, reflecting the sun, and everything was reflected again below, the shadows extending onto the fragrant path. It was magnificent.

They stopped in front of one of the pavilions, where white horses with finely decorated saddles were tied up outside and grooms and servants rushed about. Shao-yu looked up—from the second story of the pavilion came sounds of music and the perfume of rich silk brocades wafting through the air. Thinking that it must be a feast for the local prefect, he sent the boy to inquire.

"All the young noblemen of the city are here," the boy said when he returned. "They are having a party with famous courtesans."

When he heard this, Shao-yu felt inspired to write poetry. He dismounted and went up the steps of the pavilion to the second floor, where he saw a dozen young men—wealthy and powerful, from the looks of their clothes—with a score of pretty girls sitting on silk cushions, laughing and chatting among tables laden with fine food and wine.

When Shao-yu stepped into their midst, they noticed his

appearance and bearing. They rose to introduce themselves and made a place for him to sit.

"I am Yang Shao-yu, a humble scholar from the country on my way to take the civil examination," said Shao-yu. "As I was passing by I heard the sound of sweet music. I could not restrain myself, and so I have come in uninvited. Please forgive me."

One of the young men, whose name was Lu, said, "If you are a scholar on your way to take the examination, you are welcome to take part in today's feast even if you were not invited. We are delighted to have a visitor, and your presence makes the party all the more interesting. You have no need to apologize."

"I see that this is not just a gathering for food and drink, but an occasion for composing poetry. Would it be presumptuous of me to join you?" he replied.

Seeing that he was young and naive, they condescended to him. "Brother Yang, since you are the last to arrive, you are not obliged to compose a poem. Just have a drink and enjoy yourself," they said. They passed him a cup and called on the women to sing and play music.

Shao-yu looked at the courtesans, his vision quickly blurred by the wine, and saw that they were all extraordinary. But there was one among them who sat there not talking, not singing, not playing. Her face was exquisite and her bearing graceful—she was beyond compare—and Shao-yu was so distracted that he forgot to pass the wine cup. She looked at him, and as their eyes met, there was a moment of recognition.

Now Shao-yu noticed that there was a pile of compositions in front of her. "I presume these are your poems," he said to the men. "May I see them?" But before they could answer, the girl rose and brought them to Shao-yu herself.

He read them one by one, some better than others, but all mediocre in the end. Not one struck him as remarkable. He thought to himself, "I have heard that the men of Lo-yang are gifted poets, but now I see that it is not true." He handed the poems back to the girl and, bowing to the men, he said, "I hail from Ch'u, and have never had the honor of reading poetry from the capital, but now that I have had the good fortune to see your beautiful compositions, I am enlightened and edified."

The party of guests had by this time become quite intoxicated, and they replied, "Brother Yang, you're only appreciating the beauty of the poems! You aren't appreciating the other beauty that goes with them!"

Shao-yu answered, "You have been so kind in your hospitality, I am sure you would not hold anything back from me. What is this other beauty of which you speak?"

One of the men, Wang, laughed and said, "Why not tell? There's a saying here that if a candidate from Lo-yang does not place first in the civil exam, then a Lo-yang man will place second. We are all great poets here, and so we cannot be our own judges. That we leave to the girl—Kuei Ch'an-yüeh. She is an unrivaled beauty, classically trained, and also an excellent critic. That is why everyone in Lo-yang submits his poems for her expert opinion. She never errs in her judgment. We ask her to choose the best and sing it for us, set to music, and then comment on the good and bad points. The *Kuei* of her name is the same *kuei* as the cinnamon tree in the moon, so to be picked by her is a good omen for taking first place in the civil exam. Isn't it wonderful?"

"There's even more," added a youth named Tu. "And it is far better. The one whose poem she chooses and sings will spend the night in her company, and we will all jealously congratulate him. Now, how about it? You are a man, too, Brother Yang. Why don't you compete with us by writing a poem?"

"It has already been some time since you all finished your poems," said Shao-yu. "Hasn't Ch'an-yüeh chosen one to sing?"

"She hasn't yet struck a note or opened her red lips. Nor has she parted her pearly teeth since we began," said Wang. "She is evidently saving her voice for the best."

"I have written some poems," said Shao-yu, "but I am from far away in Ch'u and I am afraid I may not do well in your company."

Wang said loudly, so everyone could hear, "Master Yang is

prettier than a girl! I wonder if that is why he has no manly
spirit! In *The Analects*, it is said, 'In virtue step not aside even
for your teacher; it is the duty of the superior man to do his
best.' So stop with your false modesty and show us whether or
not you can write a poem!"

Shao-yu had decided he would humbly decline, but then he
looked at Ch'an-yüeh and he was filled with such excitement
that he could not resist. He took a sheet of paper from the pile
and wrote three stanzas in what seemed like a single stroke.
His brush moved like a ship gliding over the sea in a fair wind,
or a thirsty horse galloping to water. The young men gathered
there went pale as they watched.

Finally, Shao-yu put down the brush and said to the men, "I
should be showing this to you to criticize first, but the judge
today is Ch'an-yüeh and I am anxious not to be late in submit-
ting my entry."

His verses read:

> The traveler from Ch'u comes westward to Ch'in;
> he comes to Lo-yang to get drunk on its wine.
> Who shall be first to pluck the moon's cinnamon
> but the one who can prove he is master of verse?
>
> Willow catkins float beneath T'ien-chin Bridge
> like jeweled curtains reflecting the twilight;
> Ears prick up, listening for her song
> as her silken skirts pause upon the cushions.
>
> The flowers droop in shame before her beauty,
> her lips perfumed, though she has yet to sing;
> When all the ridgepole's dust has fallen,
> her room is candlelit to greet the bridegroom.

Ch'an-yüeh read the poem with shining eyes, and then she
burst into clear song, accompanying herself on a *ch'in*. Her
voice was like cranes calling in the sky or the song of the phoenix in the bamboo grove. The flutes went silent and the pipas[2]
lost their melody.

The men in the audience were intoxicated by the music, their faces pale. They had looked upon Shao-yu with contempt, but now that Ch'an-yüeh had chosen his poem their spirits fell and they looked at each other, speechless with dismay. They resented having to give Ch'an-yüeh to this boy, but they could not go back on their promise.

Shao-yu sensed their displeasure and quickly got up. "I have enjoyed your hospitality," he said. "I have eaten my fill and I have overindulged in drink. I thank you with utmost sincerity, but I have yet a long way to go and I cannot stay. I shall look forward to your company once again at the celebration for the winners of the civil examination."

When he bid them farewell and left the pavilion, they did not try to detain him.

Shao-yu was mounting his donkey outside the pavilion when Ch'an-yüeh came running down after him. "As you go along the road you will come to a painted garden wall with a cherry tree blooming outside. That is my house. Go inside and wait for me there. I will come soon."

He nodded and rode off, whereupon Ch'an-yüeh went back up into the pavilion and said to the men, "You gentlemen have indulged me and allowed me to decide tonight's winner by singing just one song. What is your verdict?"

"Yang is an outsider," they said. "He is not one of us, and you are not obliged to concern yourself with him." Then they argued among themselves, some saying this and some saying that, but they could not arrive at an agreement.

"I have no affection for men who break a promise," said Ch'an-yüeh. "You must excuse me. I am feeling unwell and I must leave now, but do not let that spoil your good time."

The men were unhappy about her departure, but because of their agreement with her and seeing her cold smile, they dared not say a word.

Meanwhile, Shao-yu had returned to the inn for a while. Later, when he made his way to Ch'an-yüeh's house, she was already there waiting for him. He tied the donkey to the cherry tree and knocked at the gate. Ch'an-yüeh ran out so swiftly to welcome him that she did not even put on her shoes.

"You left before I did," she said. "How is it that I was here first?"

Shao-yu replied, "As it says in *The Analects*, 'It was not my intention to come late—it was that my horse was slow.'"

They embraced eagerly and went into the house. Ch'an-yüeh sang "The Gold-Embroidered Robe" as she poured him wine and offered it to him in a jade cup. Her voice was sweet and her face was like a moonlit flower. Shao-yu was enchanted. He took her by the hand and led her to the silk bedding, where they made ecstatic love.

Afterward, as they lay together, Ch'an-yüeh spoke to him. "Today I have betrothed myself to you," she said. "Let me tell you about my life, and when you hear, perhaps you will care for me.

"I come from Shao-chou. My father was a minor official in the prefecture, but he fell ill and died far away from home. We were poor and had no money for a funeral, so to bury him properly my mother sold me to be a courtesan for one hundred pieces of gold. I swallowed my pride and accepted the shame and sorrow of a life of servitude.

"But Heaven has favored me and sent you to me, the sun and moon of my life. The road to Ch'ang-an goes in front of this house, but watching all the people come and go from the capital for the past five years, I have never seen a man who is your equal. Tonight my lifelong wish has been granted. I would gladly be your servingmaid and cook your food if you think I would do. Will you have me?"

Shao-yu consoled her. "My heart is with you," he said. "But I am only a poor scholar with an elderly mother who depends on me. I would like nothing better than to marry you and grow old together, but I am not sure what she would think of it. Suppose she chose another wife and had me take you as a concubine? Even if you had no objection to it, I know I would find no one better than you. I do not know what more to say."

"You will take the top place in the examination. There is no one in the world equal to you," said Ch'an-yüeh. "You will win the ribbon seal of a minister or the insignia of a general and the most beautiful women in all the land will chase after you. How could I expect to have you only to myself? Please, when you are married to a girl from a high family and your mother is living with you, do not abandon me. I will be chaste from this day on, saving my body for you alone, and I will wait for you to come for me."

"Last year, when I went through Hua-chou, I happened to see a girl of the Ch'in family," said Shao-yu. "Her beauty and talent were like yours, but now she is gone. Where would I ever find another girl of such caliber?"

"The girl you speak of can only be Ts'ai-feng, the daughter of Inspector Ch'in," said Ch'an-yüeh. "We were best friends when her father was in charge of this province. She was a wonderful musician, with the skill of Cho Wen-chün. It is no wonder you fell in love with her. How could you not love her the way Szu-ma Hsiang-ju loved Cho Wen-chün?[3] But there is no point in thinking about her now. You must find a bride in another family."

"But truly beautiful women are rare. With you and Ts'ai-feng both living in the same age, how could I hope to meet another woman so lovely?"

Ch'an-yüeh laughed. "You talk like you are the frog in the well.[4] I will tell you about courtesans. There are three of us who are said to be of exceptional beauty: Wan Yü-yen, the Jade Swallow of Chiang-nan; Ti Ching-hung, the shy Wild Goose of Ho-pei; and myself, Kuei Ch'an-yüeh, the Moonlight of Lo-yang. I am not equal to my reputation, but Wan Yü-yen and Ti Ching-hung are the greatest beauties alive. So how can you say there is no other beauty besides T'sai-feng?

"I have never met Wan Yü-yen because she lives far away, but everyone who comes from the south sings her praises, and I am sure that what they say is true. As for Ching-hung, she is like a sister to me, so I can tell you about her. She was born to a good family in Po-chou, but she lost her parents when she was little and was sent to live with her aunt. From the time she was a teen, rumors of her beauty spread all through Ho-pei. Thousands in gold were offered for her as concubine and marriage brokers swarmed her house like bees until she asked her aunt to send them away.

"They said, 'Whom does she want that you chase us all away? Will you make her the wife of a minister or the concubine of a governor? Or will you give her to some famous scholar?'

"Ching-hung answered for herself. She said, 'If a man like Hsih An-shih, who married a courtesan of Tung-shan in the days of Ch'in, should want me, I will gladly be the wife of a minister. If someone who knows music as well as Chou Kung-chin of the Three Kingdoms comes along, I will marry a governor.

"'If there is someone who writes poetry as well as Li Po during the reign of Hsüan Tsung then I will marry a poet. And if someone as skillful as Szu-ma Hsiang-ju, who sang "The Phoenix Seeks a Mate" at the time of Han Wu-ti[5] should appear, then I will marry him. I will go where my heart goes— how can I tell you where in advance?'

"All the marriage brokers laughed derisively and went away. Ching-hung said to herself, 'How can a country girl with no worldly experience, trapped like this, ever hope to find a good husband? But a courtesan can have her pick, since she can sit with men of renown and open her gates to receive nobles and princes. She learns to recognize the quality of Ch'u-an bamboo, or jade from Lan-t'ien. She has no trouble choosing the best.' So she sold herself to be a courtesan, hoping to find a suitable man for a husband, and she was soon famous.

"Last year, renowned scholars and poets from all twelve prefectures of Shan-tung and Ho-pei had a banquet at Yeh-tu. Ching-hung sang 'The Rainbow-Feathered Robe' for them. She danced, flying like a wild goose, and she was as beautiful as a phoenix. All the other girls hung their heads in shame, so you can imagine how wonderful she was.

"After the banquet she went to the top of Bronze Bird Terrace and paced back and forth in the moonlight, recalling sad old stories and singing sentimental songs. It reminded people of the Wei emperor[6] and his cruel treatment of the pretty second daughter of the Ch'iao family. Everyone was struck by her beauty and intelligence. Do you think there are no others like her among women?

"When Ching-hung and I played together at the Hsiang-kuo

Monastery on Pien-chou, we shared our hopes and dreams with each other. She said to me, 'If either of us meets a man who would suit us both, let us recommend each other to him and both live with him as his wives.'

"I agreed, and when I met you, I immediately thought of Ching-hung. But—alas!—she is at the palace of the governor of Shan-tung now. She has a life of wealth and luxury, but that is not what she truly wants. I wish I could see her again and tell her about you. I have made up my mind."

Shao-yu replied, "There are plenty of talented courtesans. Surely there must be girls of respectable families who are just as accomplished."

"Of all the ones I know, there is no one who compares with Ts'ai-feng," said Ch'an-yüeh. "I would not dare recommend anyone who is inferior to her. But I have heard people in Ch'ang-an say that Minister Cheng's daughter is superior in beauty and virtue. They say she is the best of all. I have never seen her myself, but as they say, great fame is never undeserved. So please try to get a look at her when you reach the capital."

The east window had grown light while they were talking and they got up to wash and get dressed. "You must not stay long," said Ch'an-yüeh. "The other men who were at the party are all angry with you. You must get away quickly. We shall meet again and have many happy days together, so I will not be sad."

"Your words are like gold and jewels to me, and I shall carry them in my heart," said Shao-yu, and they parted, both in tears.

4

A MYSTERIOUS PRIESTESS

Shao-yu left Lo-yang and made his way to Ch'ang-an. He found an inn where he could stay while he waited for the examinations, which were still a few days off. He asked the inn-keeper where the Chu-ch'ing Temple was and, learning that it was outside the Ch'un-ming Gate, he took a gift of silks and went to call on his aunt Tu, the Taoist priestess who was the abbess of that temple. She was already older than sixty and highly regarded for her attainments.

Shao-yu bowed to her and gave her the letter from his mother. The priestess received his greeting, but then she wept and said, "It's been more than twenty years since I last saw your mother. And now here is her son, all grown up. Time flies, and I am an old woman tired of living in the noise and confusion of the capital. I was about to go off and retire to the Kung-tung Mountains to pursue immortality, but now that your mother's letter has reached me with this request, I will stay a while longer to help you.

"You are so handsome and have such a fine physiognomy that it will be hard to find a suitable wife for you even in the capital. You must come see me again when you have time."

"I come from a poor family, my mother is old, and I have lived in the country all my life," Shao-yu answered. "I had no chance to find a bride. It was more than my mother could do to provide me with food and clothing. But now that I have come to you with this request, I cannot tell you how sorry I am to see how much trouble it will be." He said his good-byes to her and left.

The day of the examination drew gradually nearer, but now that his aunt had agreed to help arrange his marriage, Shao-yu's dreams of fame and success began to wane. A few days later, he went to see her again.

The abbess laughed when she saw him. "I have found a girl," she said. "Her beauty and intelligence are good enough to make her a suitable wife, but her family is too high a rank for you. They have produced dukes for six generations and three of them have been prime ministers. If you win first place in the examination, it might be a possibility, but otherwise I'm afraid there is no chance of a match. So stop coming to see me and study hard for the examination."

"Whose daughter is it?" Shao-yu asked.

"She is the daughter of Minister Cheng, who lives just outside the Ch'un-ming Gate. The house is the one with the red gate topped with spikes. The daughter is more like a fairy than a girl."

Shao-yu suddenly remembered what Ch'an-yüeh had told him, and he was curious to know why Minister Cheng's daughter was praised so highly. "Have you seen her?" he asked.

"Of course I've seen her. She really is like a fairy. Her beauty is beyond words."

"I don't mean to boast," said Shao-yu, "but I am sure I will win first place in the examination. There is no need to concern yourself about that. But I have always had a special wish, though it may seem unreasonable to you. I do not wish to be engaged to a girl whom I have never seen for myself. Could you please arrange for me to see her just once?"

"How could you ever hope to see the daughter of a high minister? You do not trust what I say?"

"I do not doubt your words," Shao-yu replied. "But each sees with different eyes. How do I know that your tastes are the same as mine?"

"Han Yü[1] said that even children can distinguish between phoenix and giraffe and both the wise and foolish know when the bright sun shines in a blue sky. Only a blind man would not see her beauty."

Shao-yu returned to the inn dissatisfied. But he very much wanted to get his aunt's permission to see the girl, so he went back to the temple the following day. The abbess was laughing once again when she met with him. "You must have something weighing on your mind to come here again!" she said.

Shao-yu smiled sheepishly. "My mind will not rest until I see Minister Cheng's daughter," he said. "Please, for my mother's sake, think of some clever scheme by which I may get a look at her."

The priestess shook her head. "That would be very difficult indeed," she said. But then she ruminated in silence for a while and asked, "You are so bright and such an accomplished scholar. Have you had any time to study music?"

"I once met a Taoist master and learned some unusual tunes from him," Shao-yu replied. "And I know the five tones and the six harmonies."[2]

"It is a minister's house," said the abbess. "The walls are high and the inner quarters are secluded. There are five gates before the inner garden. You would need wings to get in. The girl has studied *The Book of Rites*, and so she follows the strictest etiquette. She never comes here to offer incense, nor does she go to Buddhist temples for the Feast of Lanterns or to celebrations for successful examination candidates. There is no occasion on which an outsider might see her. There is only one way that might work, but I have my doubts about whether you would care to try it."

Shao-yu replied, "I would go to Heaven or Hell to get a glimpse of her. I would go through fire and water. Yes, I will try it."

So the priestess explained: "Minister Cheng is old. His health is poor, and so he has little interest in matters of state. What he enjoys is watching his garden and listening to music. His wife, Madame Ts'ui,[3] also likes music, and so their daughter has studied music along with everything else. She can hear a tune once and analyze it expertly and offer criticism.

"Every time she hears something new, the mother will invite the player to the house so that she and her daughter can listen to it and discuss it in the study. Here is my idea: Since you can play the *ch'in*, practice some tunes on it. The day after tomorrow is the last day of the third month and the birthday of the Divine Emperor, Ling-fu. The Cheng family sends servants here to the temple with candles and incense on that day.

"You will dress up in the robes of a priestess and let the servants hear you play the *ch'in*. They are sure to tell their mistress about you when they return, and she will most certainly invite you to the house. Once you are inside, whether or not you will get to see the daughter is a matter of your karma. I can make no promises. I could think of no other way."

She added, "Your facial hair has not yet started to grow, so you will have no trouble being taken for a girl. Priestesses do not put up their hair as other girls do, or let it down over their ears, so your hair will also pass."

Shao-yu was delighted. He went back to the inn and, counting the days, waited impatiently for the end of the third month.

ᏩᎧ

Minister Cheng had no child but his daughter. While her mother was in a semiconscious state during childbirth, she had seen a fairy come down from Heaven into her room with a shining precious stone in her hand, and so Cheng had named his daughter Ch'iung-pei, which means "Jasper Shell." As she grew up, she became more and more beautiful and talented, most extraordinary, and her parents, who loved her dearly, had tried in vain to find her a suitable husband. Now she was sixteen and still unmarried.

One day, her mother called the nurse, Old Ch'ien, and said, "Today is the day we celebrate the feast of Ling-fu. Take incense and candles to Chu-ch'ing Temple and give them to the priestess Tu. And take some silk and fruit as presents to show that I have been thinking of her."

Old Ch'ien took a little sedan chair[4] and went to the temple as she was ordered. The abbess received the incense and can-

dles and lit them in the San-ch'ing Hall. She graciously thanked
the old servant for the presents and treated her with great hospitality. Old Ch'ien had said good-bye and was about to step
into her sedan chair to leave when she heard Shao-yu start to
play the *ch'in* in one of the halls to the west.

The sound was clear and fresh, as if it flowed down from
the clouds. Old Ch'ien told the bearers to wait while she listened, and then she went back to the abbess and said, "While
serving the Chengs, I have heard many famous *ch'in* players, but
I have never heard anything so fantastic. Who is that playing?"

"It is a young acolyte who came here from Ch'u some days
ago to see the capital," said Tu. "She often plays the *ch'in*, but
I am ignorant about music so I cannot tell good playing from
bad. But from what you say, she must be very gifted."

"When she hears of this, Madame Ts'ui will surely want to
invite her to the house," said Old Ch'ien. "Persuade her not to
leave for a while."

"Very well, I'll do so," the abbess replied. After she had sent
Old Ch'ien on her way, she told Shao-yu what had transpired.
Shao-yu was delighted, and he anxiously waited for his sum-
mons from Madame Ts'ui.

☙

When she returned to the Chengs' house, Old Ch'ien said to her
mistress, "There is a young priestess staying at Chu-ch'ing Temple who plays the *ch'in* superbly, like I have never heard before."

"I would like to hear her," said Madame Ts'ui.

The next day she sent the sedan chair and a servant girl to
the temple with a message for the abbess Tu, which read: "I
have heard that the young priestess who is staying with you
plays the *ch'in* very well. Please do your best to persuade her to
visit me at my house, even if she is reluctant."

The abbess said to Shao-yu, in front of the servant: "A great
and noble lady has invited you. You must not refuse her."

"It is not proper for a lowborn girl from the provinces to go
to the house of a noble lady," said Shao-yu. "But if you command me, then I cannot refuse."

So his aunt dressed him in the robes and hat of a Taoist priestess, and when he came out with his *ch'in* he looked just like a fairy musician of ancient times. The Chengs' servant girl was beside herself with joy.

When Shao-yu arrived at the Chengs' house, the servant girl led the way into the inner quarters. Madame Ts'ui, looking very dignified, was sitting in the main hall.

Shao-yu bowed twice at the bottom of the steps.

"I have wanted to hear you play after what my servant told me about you yesterday," said Madame Ts'ui. "Now even your very presence seems to make me feel at peace." She motioned for him to sit, but he declined.

Instead, the young priestess came up the steps. "I am only a country girl from Ch'u," said Shao-yu. "Just a traveler passing like a cloud. It is too great an honor for someone of such little talent as myself to presume to play for you."

"What can you play?"

"I learned several ancient tunes from a strange old man I met in the Lan-t'ien Mountains," said Shao-yu. "Nobody plays them anymore."

Madame Ts'ui told a servant girl to bring Shao-yu's *ch'in* to her. "What beautiful wood!" she exclaimed as she stroked it.

"It is made of paulownia wood cured for a hundred years from Lung-men Mountain," said Shao-yu. "It is as hard as rock. You could not buy it for a thousand pieces of gold."

The shadows of afternoon moved across the stone threshold as they talked, but there was still no sign of the daughter. Shao-yu grew anxious and worried. "I know many ancient tunes," he said. "But I do not know any modern ones. And I do not know the names of the old tunes I can play. I heard from the girls at Chu-ch'ing Temple that your daughter's knowledge of music is like that of Chung Tzu-ch'i. I would like to hear her comments on my playing."

The lady sent a servant girl to call her daughter. An embroidered curtain parted and a wonderful fragrance wafted into the room with the girl, who sat down at her mother's side.

Shao-yu rose, and as he bowed to her, he lifted his eyes to steal a glance. She was like the first dazzling rays of the morning sun or a lotus blossom reflected on the blue water. His eyes blinded and his mind dizzy, Shao-yu could not look for long. He was sitting so far from her that he could not see her very well in any case, so he said to Madame Ts'ui, "The room is so large I fear I will not be able to hear what the young lady says."

Madame Ts'ui told a servant girl to move Shao-yu's cushion closer. Now he was very close, but he was to the right side of the daughter and could not look directly at her. He did not dare ask to be moved again. A servant girl placed some incense in a burner as Shao-yu straightened his posture and prepared to play.

He began with "The Rainbow-Feathered Robe,"[5] and the young Lady Cheng exclaimed, "How beautiful! It comes from peaceful times. Everyone knows it, but you play it marvelously. They say of this tune:

> With thundering drums, the barbarous Yü-yang
> Drowned out the sound of "The Rainbow-Feathered Robe."

"It is associated with rebellion and brings up powerful emotions. I should not be listening to it. Please play something else."

Shao-yu played a different tune, and the girl said, "This is also beautiful. It is Ch'en Hou-chu's 'Flowers in the Jade Tree Courtyard.' It is melancholy but reckless. It is said:

> If, in Hell, you happen upon Hou-chu,
> Speak not of the flowers in the Jade Tree Courtyard.

"Hou-chu lost his kingdom to the sound of this tune. I cannot approve of it. Play something else."

Shao-yu played another tune, and the girl said, "This tune is sorrowful and happy, moving and sensitive. It is the song of Ts'ai Wen-chi, who was taken hostage by barbarians during wartime. Ts'ao Ts'ao paid her ransom so she could return to her homeland. She composed this tune when she said good-bye to the two sons she had borne during her captivity. It is said that, upon hearing it,

> The barbarians shed tears upon the grass
> And the Han envoy's heart was broken.

"It is a very beautiful tune, but it is by a woman who had forsaken her virtue. We should not discuss it. Please play another."

So Shao-yu played again, and this time the girl said, "This is 'The Song of the Distant Barbarians,' written by Wang Chaochün, who missed her king and longed for her homeland. The tune is imbued with her sorrow and her resentment of the portrait painter who was her undoing. She herself said of it,

> Who will write a tune that will move hearts
> For a thousand years to weep for me?

"But it is not a proper tune. It is from the bride of a foreign barbarian. Do you have another?"

Shao-yu played one more. The girl's expression changed, and she said, "I have not heard this tune in a long time. You are surely not of this world. This calls up the story of a great man, Hsi K'ang,[6] who had fallen on hard times and had given up all thoughts of worldly things. His loyalty brought him trouble in troubled times and he wrote this tune, called 'Kuang-ling,' or 'The Hill of the Wide Tomb.' Before he was executed in the East Market he played it, looking at his shadow. He said, 'Alas, will anyone wish to learn "The Hill of the Wide Tomb"? I have not taught it to anyone, and now it will be forgotten. What a pity.'

> Is that the direction of Kuang-ling?
> A lone bird flies southeast.

"If it was not taught to anyone, you can only have learned it by meeting the departed spirit of Hsi K'ang himself."

Still kneeling, Shao-yu replied, "The young ladyship's knowledge is beyond compare. I learned this from a great teacher, and what he told me is exactly what you have said."

He played a sixth tune, and she praised it also.

> High, high, the blue mountains,
> Wide, wide, the flowing river.

"And remarkable, the footprints of the immortals in the world of dust! That is 'The Water Fairy' by Po Ya,[7] is it not? If he had known of your great talent Po Ya would not have been quite so sorrowful at the death of Chung Tzu-ch'i."

Shao-yu played yet another tune and the girl fidgeted with her collar as she knelt. "This is the supreme sacred melody," she said. "The Sage lived in troubled times and traveled throughout the world helping the people. Who could it be except Confucius that composed a tune like this? It must be 'The Fragrant Orchid.'

> Wandering through the world
> Finding no place to settle

"—is a phrase from it. The Sage tried to save the world, but the time was not right."

Shao-yu added some incense to the burner and played again. This time the girl said, "This is a noble and beautiful tune. It expresses the joy of all things under the sun and the feeling of spring. It is the 'Song of the Southern Breeze' by the Sage King Shun,[8] almost too majestic to name.

> The fragrant southern wind
> Blows our cares away.

"There is no song in the world better or more beautiful than this. Even if you know others, I have no desire to hear them now."

Shao-yu bowed and said, "I have heard that if one plays nine tunes the spirit of Heaven will descend. I have played eight, and one is left. With your kind permission, may I play one more?"

He straightened the bridges on the *ch'in*, tightened the strings, and started. The music began softly and then became fast and lively, stimulating the spirit. The flowers in the garden all bloomed at the sound of it, swallows wove through the air in couples, and the nightingales sang to each other. The young mistress bowed her head, closed her eyes, and sat silently until he reached the part that went:

Phoenix, phoenix, come back to your home
Over the wide sea, in search of your mate.

The girl looked up at the priestess, but then she looked
down again, blushing as she pretended to adjust her dress. The
pale color of her brow reddened, as if she had been drinking
wine. She got up and went into the inner room without another word.

Startled, Shao-yu pushed away his *ch'in* and stood up, staring in the direction the girl had gone. He looked like a clay
statue.

Madame Ts'ui told him to sit down. "What was it you
played just now?" she asked.

"I learned it from my teacher, but do not know what it is
called," said Shao-yu. "I was hoping the young lady would
tell me."

When the girl did not return after a long time, Madame
Ts'ui sent a maid to ask why. She returned and said, "The
young mistress has been sitting in a draft and is not feeling
well. She cannot come out again."

Now Shao-yu was worried that he had been found out. He
dared not stay any longer, so he rose and said, "I am sorry to
hear that your daughter is feeling unwell. You will no doubt
want to look in on her. I should go now."

Madame Ts'ui presented him with gifts of money and silk,
but Shao-yu politely refused to accept them. "I studied a little
music, but it is only for my own amusement," he said. "I cannot accept payment like a professional entertainer." He bowed
and went down the stone steps.

Afterward, Madame Ts'ui asked after her daughter and
found that there was nothing to be concerned about.

&

Back in the inner quarters, the young mistress, Ch'iung-pei,
asked one of her maids, "How is Ch'un-yün feeling today?"

"She is feeling better," the servant girl said. "When she

heard that you were listening to music today, she got up and washed."

Ch'un-yün's surname was Chia and she was a native of Hsi-shu. Her father had come to the capital as a secretary some time ago and become a loyal servant of Minister Cheng. Ch'un-yün was only ten when her father died of an illness. Cheng and his wife had taken pity on her and brought her up in their own family as their daughter's playmate.

The two girls were only a month apart in age. Though Ch'un-yün was not as beautiful as Ch'iung-pei, she was still very pretty and nearly her equal in poetry, calligraphy, and embroidery. Ch'iung-pei treated her like a younger sister and they were always by each other's side, and though they were, strictly speaking, mistress and servant, they treated each other like close friends.

Originally, Ch'un-yün's name had been Ch'u-yün, "the Cloud from Ch'u," but Ch'iung-pei was so fond of her that she had called her Ch'un-yün, which means "Spring Cloud." It was an allusion to a line from a poem by Han Yü: *Beauty like a cloud in the spring sky*. Everyone in the household simply called her "Ch'un," or "Spring."

Ch'un-yün asked her mistress, "The maids all said the priestess who came to play the *ch'in* in the main hall was like a fairy and that you gave her much praise. I was so eager I forgot my pains and got up to get a look at her. But why did she leave so suddenly?"

Ch'iung-pei blushed. "I've always been careful about my thoughts and actions and observed the strictest rules of propriety and etiquette. I never stray into the outer courts of the house. I never gossip with my friends or relatives. But now I've been tricked and disgraced. How will I ever show my face again?"

"What did she do?" Ch'un-yün asked in alarm.

"She started by playing 'The Rainbow-Feathered Robe' and then went on playing one tune after another until she came to 'Song of the Southern Breeze.' I praised her playing and wanted her to stop there, but she said there was one more she wanted to play. It was 'The Phoenix Seeks a Mate,' the tune Szu-ma Hsiang-ju used to seduce Cho Wen-chün! That made me suspicious, so I got a close look at her face and it wasn't a girl's face at all! Some devious man wanting to look at girls has gotten into this house in disguise.

"If only you had been well enough, Ch'un, you could have seen him, too, and you would have known at once whether he was a man or a woman. I'm an unmarried girl of the inner quarters, and I have sat for hours talking face-to-face to a strange man! I am so ashamed I cannot tell this even to my mother. You are the only one I can tell about this."

Ch'un-yün laughed. "Why can't an unmarried girl listen to 'The Phoenix Seeks a Mate'? You are making much of nothing."

"That is not so," said Ch'iung-pei. "He played the tunes in a particular order. If there was no plan, then why did he play 'The Phoenix Seeks a Mate' at the very end? I've seen women who are delicate in their beauty and others who are homely and robust, but I've never seen anyone so handsome and confident.

"The capital is full of young scholars who have come to take the examinations. I think one of them has heard a false rumor about me and used this sly trick to see my face."

"If he is so handsome and well-mannered, and if he is such a wonderful musician, then he must be a truly remarkable man," said Ch'un-yün. "Perhaps he will be the next Szu-ma Hsiang-ju!"

"He may be the next Szu-ma Hsiang-ju, but I have no intention of becoming another Cho Wen-chün!"

"But Cho Wen-chün was a widow and you are a virgin," said Ch'un-yün. "She followed the general of her own free will, but you have been influenced unintentionally. Why are you comparing yourself to her?"

The two of them laughed together and continued talking.

❧

One morning, while Ch'iung-pei was sitting with her mother, Minister Cheng came with the list of candidates who had passed the civil examination. He gave it to his wife, saying, "We have not yet arranged a marriage for Ch'iung-pei. I am going to select a bridegroom from among these successful scholars. The top candidate on the exam was Yang Shao-yu, from Huai-nan. He is sixteen years old and everybody is speaking highly of his work. He is certainly of highest caliber. They also say he is very handsome and well-mannered and is headed for greatness. And he is not yet engaged. I would like him for a son-in-law."

"The eye perceives more truth than two ears," said Lady Cheng. "Let us see him in person before we make up our minds."

"That won't be hard to arrange," said Minister Cheng.

TRYST WITH A FAIRY
AND A GHOST

When Ch'iung-pei heard what her father had to say, she went to her room and said to Ch'un-yün, "The priestess who came here and played the *ch'in* said she was from Ch'u and she looked about sixteen. The man with the top score on the civil exam is from Huai-nan, and Huai-nan is in Ch'u. Their ages are the same. Now I am even more suspicious. That man will surely come to see my father. I want you to get a good look at him."

"I didn't see the priestess when she came," said Ch'un-yün. "I think it would be better for you to peek through the door and get a look for yourself." They giggled together.

Meanwhile, Yang Shao-yu had passed both the doctoral and the special examinations and the Emperor had appointed him imperial archivist. His name was everywhere. Every nobleman with a daughter tried to arrange a marriage with him, but he refused them all. Instead, he went to Ch'üan, the senior secretary at the Board of Rites, and requested an introduction to Minister Cheng. Ch'üan immediately wrote him a letter, which Shao-yu put away in his sleeve.

Shao-yu went straight away to Minister Cheng's house and presented his card, and Cheng, when he recognized the name, welcomed him and invited him into the guest room. Shao-yu was crowned with the cinnamon flowers that marked him as the top graduate, and official musicians followed behind him. He was handsome and modest, and everyone in the household was there to admire him with openmouthed wonder—except Ch'iung-pei.

"Come here a moment," Ch'un-yün said to one of Madame

Ts'ui's attendants. "I heard the mistress say the priestess who came and played the *ch'in* the other day is the cousin of this man. Did you notice a resemblance?"

The maid immediately answered, "Yes, it is true. How strange that two cousins could look so much like each other!"

Hearing this, Ch'un-yün went back to the inner quarters and said to Ch'iung-pei, "You were correct. They look exactly alike."

Ch'iung-pei replied, "Go back out and listen carefully to what he says."

Ch'un-yün went out again and was gone for a considerable time. "Your father suggested that you should marry Yang," she said when she returned. "Yang said that he had heard that you were graceful and modest, and that he had presumed to come here today to ask for your hand. He said he asked Secretary Ch'üan at the Board of Rites for a letter of introduction and was given one. But then he said he had not dared present it, seeing that your families are of such different stations, as unlike as bright clouds and muddy water, and your persons like a phoenix and a common crow. He still had it in his sleeve, and when he finally gave it to your father, the minister was so delighted he called for wine and refreshments."

Ch'iung-pei was upset, but before she could say anything, her mother sent a maid to fetch her.

⚬⚬⚬

"Yang Shao-yu won the top score on the government examination," said Lady Cheng. "Your father has just arranged your marriage to him, so now we will have someone to take care of us and need not worry any longer."

Ch'iung-pei said, "I just learned from a servant that Master Yang looks just like the priestess who came the other day to play the *ch'in*. Is it true?"

"Yes," said her mother. "That priestess was so beautiful I could not get her face out of my mind. I wanted to send for her again, but I did not have the chance. Come to think of it, Master Yang does look quite a bit like her. So now you will know how handsome he is."

Ch'iung-pei hung her head and said, in a small voice, "I know he is very handsome, but I do not like him and will not marry him."

"What are you saying?" exclaimed her mother. "You've been cooped up in the women's quarters all your life, while Master Yang has been living in Huai-nan. How can you possibly say you don't like him?"

"I have been so ashamed I haven't been able to speak of it," Ch'iung-pei replied. "But that priestess who came the other day was Master Yang. He disguised himself as a woman so that he could come into our house and have a look at me. I was fooled by his trick and spent half the day talking to him. Isn't that reason enough to dislike him?"

Lady Cheng was speechless.

Meanwhile, Minister Cheng, having dismissed Yang, came into the inner quarters with a delighted expression. "Ch'iung-pei!" he exclaimed. "Today, you have mounted a dragon!"

When his wife repeated to him what Ch'iung-pei had just told her, the minister asked his daughter to tell him again about how Yang had played "The Phoenix Seeks a Mate" for her. He laughed loudly and said, "That Yang is brilliant! There's an old story about Wang Wei dressing up as a musician and playing the lute in the palace for Princess T'ai-p'ing.[1] He also went on to win the top score on the government examinations. If Yang went so far as to dress as a woman to win his bride, then he is truly resourceful. For this prank you say you dislike him? In any case, what you saw was a Taoist priestess, not Yang. It's not your fault that he made a very pretty girl musician!"

"I was so humiliated, I could die of shame," said Ch'iung-pei.

The minister laughed once more. "This is not a matter I can work out for you. You settle it with Yang yourself, later." When Lady Cheng asked him what date had been set for the wedding, he became serious. "We will exchange gifts at once," he said. "But the wedding will be held in the autumn. We will pick the date once his mother arrives in Ch'ang-an."

So the minister and Lady Cheng picked a day for receiving the betrothal gifts, and when Shao-yu had sent the appropriate presents they invited him to come live in the summer house in the gardens. Yang honored them in all the ways befitting a son-in-law, and they, in return, loved him as if he were their own.

෪

One day late in the spring, Ch'iung-pei was passing by Ch'un-yün's room and saw that she had been overcome by drowsiness while embroidering a pair of silk shoes. She had used the embroidery frame as a pillow and was fast asleep. Ch'iung-pei tiptoed in to admire the beautiful work, and as she sighed over the exquisite stitchery she noticed a sheet of paper with writing on it under the frame. When she took the paper and unfolded it, she saw that it was a poem about the shoes.

> Oh, you precious companions!
> Constant, with her, step after step—
> But when the lamp's blown out and the silks slide off
> You'll be tossed under the ivory couch.

Ch'iung-pei thought to herself, "Her poetry gets better and better. She is the embroidered shoes and I am the precious one who wears them. She and I have been inseparable, but when I am married I will cast her aside. She must truly love me." Then she read the poem again and smiled. "She means that she wishes we could share the same bed. That would mean we must marry the same man."

Ch'iung-pei left quietly, so as not to wake Ch'un-yün, and went to her mother's quarters, where she was busy overseeing the maids who were preparing Yang's dinner.

"Mother," said Ch'iung-pei, "you worry yourself so much over Yang's food and clothes, I'm afraid you are exhausting yourself. It is I who should be doing these things, but there is no precedent in the classics for a girl to serve her husband while still betrothed, so I cannot perform those duties. But Ch'un-yün is grown up now and she is capable of such things. What do you think of sending her to the garden pavilion to let her look after Yang's needs?"

"Ch'un-yün's father was our most faithful attendant," said Madame Ts'ui. "She is a very beautiful and talented girl. Your father thinks the world of her and he wants to choose a good husband for her. She is not planning to look after you forever."

Ch'iung-pei replied, "I don't think she ever wants to be parted from me."

"In the old days she could go with you if you were married, but only as your husband's concubine," said Madame Ts'ui. "But Ch'un-yün is no ordinary maid. I do not think she will accompany you."

"Master Yang is sixteen and from the provinces, but he has dared to disguise himself as a girl to enter the women's quarters of an official's house to play the *ch'in* and flirt with his unmarried daughter. Can you expect such a man will be satisfied with only one wife? When he is appointed to his high post with a fat salary, how many girls like Ch'un-yün do you think he will have for himself?"

Minister Cheng came in at this point, and his wife recounted what Ch'iung-pei had just said to her. He nodded and said to his wife, "Ch'un-yün does not want to leave Ch'iung-pei before the marriage, and even afterward, it seems the two of them do not wish to be parted. So why not send Ch'un-yün ahead to Yang now? It is only a matter of time, in any case. Why not send her to comfort and entertain him in his solitude? But it may seem a bit indecorous. Perhaps we should wait until the ceremonies are over. We must be careful to do things properly. Why don't you find out what the girls think before we decide?" And with that, he left.

"I have a plan," Ch'iung-pei said to her mother. "If Ch'un-yün will offer herself to Yang, I can wash away the shame I have suffered and have my revenge on him. If cousin Thirteen will help me, I think we can succeed."

❧

Thirteen was the nickname of one of Minister Cheng's nephews. He was a fine young man—clever and full of good humor, with an appreciation for practical jokes. He and Yang Shao-yu had become great friends.

Ch'iung-pei returned to her room and said to Ch'un-yün, "You've been with me ever since the hair grew down on our foreheads. We've played together since we pelted each other with flowers. Now that I am about to be married, it is time that you were, too. Have you given any thought to what kind of husband you want?"

Ch'un-yün answered, "I have lived here happily, owing you gratitude for your great affection and all you have given me until now. What I owe you I could never repay a thousandth part, even if I were to hold your mirror to the end of my days. I shall be happy to stay with you forever."

"I have always known this," said Ch'iung-pei. "And there is something I want to ask of you. You are the only one who can help me erase the shame I have suffered because of Yang's humiliating trick. Do you know our summer pavilion in that secluded spot on Chung-nan Mountain south of the capital? It's beautiful there, almost unearthly. We will prepare you a bridal chamber there and get Thirteen to trick Yang into going there so that you can seduce him. Please say that you will do it."

"How could I possibly refuse you?" said Ch'un-yün. "But then how could I ever look Master Yang in the face afterward?"

"It is better to be the trickster than the one being tricked," said Ch'iung-pei. "Do not worry. The joke will be on him and he will be the one who feels ashamed."

"Then I will do it," said Ch'un-yün.

❧

Yang Shao-yu had many official duties in court, but that still left him with an abundance of free time and many days of leisure,[2] which he spent visiting friends or enjoying the flowers and foliage of the countryside in spring.

One day, his friend Thirteen[3] said to him, "There is a quiet and beautiful place south of the city. Let us go there together sometime soon for an outing."

"That is just what I wanted," Shao-yu replied.

They had food and wine prepared for them, and, leaving the servants, they rode their donkeys several miles to a place where the mountains were high and the streams were clear. They were alone, far from the world of dust, and the fragrance of myriad flowers and grassy meadows cleared their thoughts. They dismounted on the bank of a stream, countless flowers and trees blooming around them, and sat to compose some verses together to celebrate the onset of summer.

Suddenly, Shao-yu noticed some fallen petals drifting toward them on the water. " 'Spring, fully come, peach petals floating,' " he said, reciting the lines from Wang Wei.[4] "There must be a place like the Peach Blossom Paradise[5] of Wu Ling[6] upstream."

"This stream flows down from Tzu-ko Peak,"[7] said Thirteen. "They say, 'When the flowers bloom and the moon is full, one hears the music of the immortals among the clouds.' I myself have no affinity for the world of fairies, and I have never been among them. But today, with you, I have entered that world and I would like just once to drink their wine and taste their enchanted food."

Shao-yu was delighted. "If there are such things as fairies in this world," he said, "then surely they must be here on this mountain."

Just then one of Thirteen's servants came running. Streaming with sweat and panting for breath, he said, "I've come to tell you that the lady has suddenly taken sick."

Thirteen quickly stood up. "Hearing now that my wife is ill is just another reminder that I have no affinity for the world of fairies," he said. He mounted his donkey and rode away.

Shao-yu grew bored after Thirteen's departure. He followed the stream up the valley, looking for something more to see. The waters were crystal clear over the rocks, with no speck of dust, and his mind was tranquil as he continued slowly on.

Soon he noticed a cinnamon leaf floating on the water, and

when he had the servant boy pick it up for him, he saw that
two lines of verse had been written on it.

> The fairy's watchdog barks among the clouds,
> Knowing that Master Yang is on the way.

Shao-yu was amazed. "How could anyone possibly be living
in these mountains?" he said. "And who could possibly have
written this verse?"

As he walked on, the servant boy said, "Sir, it will soon be
dark and it will be too late to get back into the city before they
shut the gates."

Shao-yu paid no attention and continued for another seven
or eight li^8 up the steep mountain path, where he could see the
moon rising in the east. By its light, he passed through the
shadow of the pine woods and crossed the stream. He heard
the cries of startled birds and the forlorn howl of monkeys.
Stars sparkled beyond the mountain peaks and dewdrops
hung from the pine needles. He realized that night had fallen,
and he grew uneasy.

At that moment he saw a young girl dressed in green, like a
fairy, washing clothes in the stream. "My lady!" she called
out, rising up in alarm. "The master is coming!"

Shao-yu was puzzled by what he heard. He continued another dozen steps until the mountain path ended and he saw
the small pavilion rising up by the side of the stream. It seemed
to be floating above the water.

In the moonlight there appeared a woman dressed in red
standing alone under a peach tree. She bowed, saying, "Why
are you so late in coming, Master?"

Shao-yu was stunned. He observed her carefully and saw
that she was dressed in a light rose-colored silk and wore a
long pin of green jade through her hair. Her waist was girdled
in white jade, and in her hand she held a fan of phoenix feath-
ers. Hers was not the beauty of a mere human, and Shao-yu
was enchanted. "I am of the world of dust," he said, "and have
made no promise to meet you under the moon. How could I
possibly be late?"

The woman walked up toward the pavilion and invited him to talk inside. He followed her, and when they had taken their seats as hostess and guest, she called to her maidservant, "The master has come a long way and he is sure to be hungry. Bring some tea and cakes."

The servant quickly brought him a jeweled table set with delicacies. Into a cup of white jade she poured him the bright twilight wine of the fairies. Its taste was sweet and refreshing, and its bouquet filled the room. A single cup, and Shao-yu was intoxicated. "Though this mountain is high, it is still beneath Heaven. Why is it that you have left the Celestial Palace and all your companions to come down and dwell in a place like this?"

The fairy sighed. "If I tell you of my past, it will only bring back my sorrow. I was one of the ladies-in-waiting for the Queen Mother of the Western Paradise and you, Master, were an officer in the Cinnabar Court of the August Jade Emperor. Once, when the Jade Emperor gave a banquet in honor of the queen mother, and there were many officials and fairies present, you teased me by throwing a Heavenly Peach[9] at me.

"Your punishment was to be reincarnated as a human being. My punishment was less severe, and I was simply exiled to this place. You have already been blinded by the dust of the mortal world, and you have forgotten everything about your former life. My exile is nearly over, and soon I must return to the Lake of Jewels. But before leaving, I wanted to see you just once to renew our love. I asked for an extension of my time here, knowing that you would come. I have waited for so long, but now, at last, you are here and we can be together once again."

The shadow of the cinnamon tree in the moon[10] was beginning to show and the Milky Way was fading when Shao-yu embraced the beautiful fairy. Their lovemaking was like that of Liu Ch'en and Yuan Chao[11] and the two fairies on T'ient'ai-shan[12]—a dream, and yet not a dream; real, and yet not reality. When their mutual passions peaked, the mountain birds were already twittering in the trees and the east was red with dawn.

The fairy rose first. "I must return to the Heavenly Kingdom today," she said. "When the Jade Emperor's officers come

with their flags and their orders to fetch me, we shall both be
punished again if you are discovered. Please leave now and
quickly make your way down the mountain. If you remember
our love, we will surely have the chance to meet again."

Then, on a silk handkerchief, she wrote him this farewell
poem:

> When we met, the flowers bloomed to Heaven,
>   Now, as we part, each petal falls into water.
> Love in spring is just a passing dream—
>   The wide water a thousand *li* between us.

When Shao-yu read the verses he was overcome with regret
at the thought of their parting. He tore off a piece of his silk
sleeve and wrote these lines in reply:

> As Heaven's wind blows the jade flute,
>   Why must the white clouds scatter?
> On this sacred mountain, the night's torrential rain
>   Drenches my robe entirely through.

The fairy took the poem. "This will be my only connection
to you when we are separated by all of Heaven. The frost de-
scends on the cinnamon garden and the moon has set behind
the Jeweled Tree."[13] Putting the silk into the folds of her robe,
she said, urgently, "It is late, Master. Please hurry."

Shao-yu wiped his tears away with his hands as he said
good-bye. When he turned to look back toward the pavilion,
there was only the green thicket of trees and flocks of white
clouds. He felt as if he had just woken from a dream of the
Lake of Jewels.[14]

Full of regret, he made his way back to Thirteen's summer
villa. "I wish I had hidden somewhere and waited to watch the
fairies come to fetch her back to Heaven today," he thought to
himself. "Even then I would not have been very late returning.
Why did I have to hurry back?"

After a sleepless night, he rose at dawn and took his servant boy with him in search of the place where he had met the fairy. The blown peach blossoms, the flowing stream, and the empty pavilion were all that remained. The fragrance of the place was gone. He leaned against the railing, looking up into the sky full of gray clouds. "She has ridden away on a cloud to attend to the Jade Emperor. I should like to see her again, but what use is it to gaze up at the sky?"

He came down from the pavilion and stood by the peach tree where he had first met her. "These flowers know the depths of my sorrow," he said.

And he made his way back home.

※

A few days later Thirteen came to Shao-yu and said, "The other day I had to interrupt our outing together because of my wife's illness. I am still sorry about that. But the shade under the willows is still cool—how about going out together for half a day to hear the orioles sing?"

" 'The green shade is lovelier than spring flowers,' " Shao-yu replied, quoting Wang An-shih.[15]

They went out of the city gates together and found a thick grove, where they sat on the grass and made tallies of flowers to count the cups of wine each had drunk. They noticed an untended grave just to the side, overgrown with wormwood and covered in high grass that waved sadly in the wind. A few withered flowers moved to and fro beneath the trees.

Shao-yu, made mournful by the wine, pointed to the grave, saying, "Whether a man be high or low, in the end he dies and returns to the dust. In olden times Yung-men accompanied the *ch'in* by singing, 'A thousand years from now, cowherds will dance here and sing, "This is the grave of Prince Meng-ch'ang,"' and Prince Meng-ch'ang[16] wept as he listened. Let us get drunk and enjoy ourselves while we are still alive."

"Brother," said Thirteen, "do you not know this grave? It is the grave of Chang Li-hua,[17] the royal consort who was so beautiful they called her 'Lovely Flower.' She died unmarried when she was only twenty, and out of pity, they planted these flowers and willows by her grave to comfort her. Let us pour her spirit a cup of wine and compose some verses worthy of a flower."

Shao-yu was naturally kindhearted. "Yes," he said, "let us." So they poured wine at her grave and each composed a poem.[18]

When they had recited their verses, Thirteen walked around the grave and saw something in the grass where part of the mound had collapsed. It was a piece of white silk with writing on it.

"What sort of man would write such a thing and stick it in Chang Li-hua's grave?" he said.

Shao-yu picked up the scrap of silk and—lo!—it was the very piece he had torn from his sleeve and written the poem on the previous night. He was both dumbfounded and distressed. "Then, the girl I met the other night was Chang Li-hua's ghost," he thought to himself. Cold sweat ran down his back. "Meeting a fairy is governed by one's karma, but to meet a hungry ghost[19] is also karma," he thought. "So what difference does it make whether she was fairy or ghost?"

Thirteen was getting up just then, so while his back was turned, Shao-yu poured another offering and made a silent prayer. "Though the living and the dead abide in separate worlds, there is no distance in our hearts. I pray that your beautiful spirit will accept my offering and visit me again tonight to renew our love."

☙❧

That night in the pavilion, alone and sleepless, Shao-yu waited for the girl. The room was awash in moonlight and shadows of tree branches fell against the window screens. Everything was silent, until Shao-yu heard a faint voice and the sound of approaching footsteps. He opened the door to look, and there stood the fairy whom he had met on Tzu-ko Peak.

He sprang out of the room in delight and took her pale hands in his. But when he tried to lead her back into his room, she resisted.

"Now that you know what I really am, are you not repulsed?" she said. "I wanted to tell you when we first met, but

I did not want to frighten you, so I told you that I was a fairy. That night I was greatly honored to serve you in bed. Your love restored my spirit and brought life back to my decaying flesh. Today you came to my grave to pour me wine and comfort my lonely spirit. When I think of what you have done for me, I have no words deep enough to express my gratitude, and so I have come tonight to give you my thanks. But how could I dare to embrace you again with this rotting corpse?"

Shao-yu tugged at her sleeve, saying, "A man who fears ghosts is a coward. When a man dies he becomes a ghost, and when a ghost reincarnates, it becomes a man. So the man who fears a ghost is a fool, and the ghost who runs away from a living man is a foolish ghost. The two of them come from the same source, so why should we separate the world of the living and the world of the dead? Those are my thoughts, and this is my love. Why do you refuse me?"

The girl replied, "How could I possibly refuse your love? But you love me because of my dark eyebrows and rosy cheeks, and these are false. They are not my true form, but just an illusion to entice living men. If you wish to see my true self, I am just some moss-covered bones. How could you stand to touch such disgusting things?"

"The Buddha said a man's body is a transitory illusion, like foam on the water or flower petals in a gust of wind," said Shao-yu. "Who can say, then, what really exists and what does not?"

With that he led her inside and they lay together among the pillows, their love far deeper and more delightful than on the night of their first meeting. "Let us spend every night together," Shao-yu said afterward. "And let nothing keep us apart."

"Men and ghosts have different paths, but love can bring them together," said the girl. "Since your love comes from so deep in your heart, how can I not respond to it?" And then the morning gong sounded, and she disappeared among the flowering trees.

Shao-yu stood at the railing to see her off. "Let us meet again tonight," he called, but there was no reply.

She was gone.

After his meetings with the ghost, Shao-yu no longer went out to visit his friends, nor did he receive guests at home. He spent his time quietly in the pavilion. At nightfall he waited for the girl to come, and when daylight came he waited again for the night. When he tried to compel her to come more frequently, she did not, and that made him all the more preoccupied with his thoughts of her.

One day two people arrived to visit him by the side gate. He saw that one of them was his friend Thirteen, but he did not recognize the other man.

Thirteen called out to Shao-yu and introduced the stranger. "This is Master Tu from the T'ai-chi[20] Temple," he said. "He is an expert in reading physiognomy and telling fortunes, just like the ancients Li Ch'un-feng and Yuan T'ien-kang.[21] He has come with me to read your face."

Shao-yu welcomed Master Tu with clasped hands. "I have heard your venerable name, but to meet you this way is an unexpected privilege. I expect you have read Brother Cheng's face already? What do you see in it?"

Thirteen answered for himself. "I am very pleased," he said. "Master Tu read my face and told me that within three years I would pass the civil exam and be appointed an imperial inspector of the eight provinces. I think he is very accurate. Why don't you give it a try, Brother Shao-yu?"

"A virtuous man never asks about future blessings, but only about the troubles that await him," said Shao-yu. "Please tell me only the truth."

Master Tu examined Shao-yu for a long time, and said, "Your eyebrows are quite unusual and your eyes are like a phoenix's eyes, slanting toward the temples—you will surely rise to be a high minister of state. Your complexion is pale, as if you are wearing powder, and the shape of your face is round, like a pearl—your name will be known throughout the world. Your stance is that of a dragon, and you move like a tiger. This means you are destined to be a great general and your fame will span the Four Seas.[22] You will be among peers, and your name and reputation will resound as far as ten thousand *li*. But there is one unexpected flaw, and if you had not met me today, you might have fallen victim to a great danger."

"A man's good or bad fortune depends on the man himself," said Shao-yu. "But it is hard to avoid sickness if it comes. Do you see signs that I will become seriously ill?"

"Yours is not a typical misfortune," said Master Tu. "There is a blue tinge on your forehead and unhealthy shadows under your eyes.[23] Do you have a boy or girl servant in your household whose past is questionable?"

Shao-yu immediately guessed that Chang Li-hua's ghost was the source of the problem, but he did not let it show. He answered nonchalantly, "There is no such servant."

"Then have you passed an old grave—or perhaps had sexual relations with a ghost in your dreams?"

"Nothing like that."

"Master Tu is never wrong," Thirteen interjected. "Think carefully, Shao-yu."

Shao-yu said nothing, so Master Tu continued, "A man's energy is yang and a ghost's is yin—as immutably different as day and night or fire and water. Looking at your face now, it is obvious to me that some ghost has a hold on your body. In a few days it will get into your bones, and then I am afraid nothing can be done to save your life. When that comes to pass, do not complain or say that I did not warn you."

Shao-yu thought to himself: "What Tu says is amazingly accurate, but Chang Li-hua and I have promised to be together forever and our love grows deeper every day. How could she possibly hurt me? Men have married fairies and sired children with ghosts in the past. If such things have transpired, why should I be concerned?"[24]

Shao-yu said to the Taoist, "The length of a man's life, long or short, is already decided when he is born. If you see proof that I will achieve prominence and fame, how can a ghost harm me?"

"Whether you live or die is up to you. It's not for me to know," Master Tu said indignantly. When he shook his sleeves and left, Shao-yu did not try to stop him.

Thirteen comforted Shao-yu, saying, "You were born with

good fortune, Brother Shao-yu. Why should you be afraid of a ghost when Heaven favors you? Fortune-tellers often say upsetting things to trick people."

So they called for wine and spent the rest of the day getting drunk together.

That night, after Thirteen had left, Shao-yu sat alone, silently burning incense, waiting and waiting for Li-hua to appear. But there was no sign of her. He pounded on the table, saying, "The sun is about to rise and still she has not come!"

Shao-yu had blown out the candles and was trying to sleep when, suddenly, he heard the sound of weeping outside his window.

"Master," said Li-hua's voice, "the Taoist has hidden a paper talisman against demons in your topknot. I cannot come near you. I know it was not your intention, but it is done, and now our karmic bond is broken. I pray that you will be safe from harm. I have been cast from you, and I must leave you forever."

Shao-yu leaped up and opened the door, but he could not see where she had gone.[25] He felt his head and found something tied to his topknot—a talisman to repel demons. "That evil sorcerer has ruined everything!" he screamed, crumpling it in his hand. After he tore the talisman to pieces, he thought, "This must be Thirteen's handiwork from last night when he left me drunk. He has interfered with my karma! I will have some harsh words for him when I see him again!"

The next morning, when Shao-yu went to Thirteen's house, he had already gone out. He visited again for three successive days, and yet each time Thirteen was not to be seen.

Nor did Shao-yu catch even a glimpse of Chang Li-hua's shadow. He went again to the pavilion on Tzu-ko Peak to look for her, but it is hard to meet with a ghost and he did not see her again. Pining away, night and day, he lost his appetite and each successive day he ate less and less.

Minister Cheng and his wife did not fail to notice, so they prepared special dishes and invited Shao-yu to dinner. As they were sharing drinks, the minister asked, "Why is it that you are so drawn and pale these days?"

"Thirteen and I have been drinking too much lately. That must be the reason," answered Shao-yu.

It was just then that Thirteen arrived. Shao-yu gave him a sidelong glance but said nothing.

"Brother," said Thirteen, "you seem so unhappy lately. Are you so burdened with your official duties that it has affected your health? Or is it that you are so homesick you've become ill? Why do you look so worn and full of misery?"

Shao-yu could not refuse to answer. "How can a man so far from his home look otherwise?"

"I overheard the servants talking," said the minister. "They said they saw you talking to a beautiful girl in the garden pavilion. Is this true?"

"The garden has walls. How could anyone get inside?" said Shao-yu. "What they say is ridiculous."

"Brother," said Thirteen, "with all your worldly experience, why are you blushing now like a girl? You dismissed Master Tu with such bold confidence, but I can see by the pallor of your face that there is something terribly wrong. I put Master Tu's ghost talisman under your topknot while you were drunk and did not know what I was doing. That night I hid in the garden and, sure enough, I witnessed a female ghost come and cry plaintively outside your room. From this I knew that what Master Tu said was true, and that I had done you a great favor for which you should be thanking me. So why do you seem so angry?"

Shao-yu knew he could no longer conceal the matter. He addressed the minister: "The strangest things have happened to me, sir. I shall tell you all about it." And so he told the whole story, and when he concluded, he said, "I know that Thirteen did what he did for my sake, but Chang Li-hua, even though she was a ghost, had a solid form. She was full of life and good-hearted—hardly deceitful. I may be less than upright as a man, but I could never be tricked by a ghost. With his ill-placed talisman, Thirteen has severed my tie with Chang Li-hua and I cannot forgive him for it."

The minister clapped his hands and laughed. "Shao-yu, my boy," he said, "your temperament and character are like that of

Sung Yü.[26] He could invoke ghosts—surely, you must know how to conjure her up? When I was a boy, I myself met a strange fellow who taught me how to summon ghosts. I do not jest! I will invoke Chang Li-hua's ghost for you so that you can be comforted and forgive Thirteen. What do you say?"

"In the times of the Han, Shao invoked the ghost of Lady Li,"[27] said Shao-yu, "but that knowledge has been lost for many generations. I cannot believe you, sir."

Thirteen interrupted. "Brother, you called up Li-hua's ghost with no effort at all, and I drove her away with a scrap of paper. It is not obvious to you that ghosts can be controlled? Why are you so skeptical?"

"If you do not believe, then watch this," said Minister Cheng. He struck the folding screen behind him with a flywhisk and called, "Chang Li-hua, show yourself!" Immediately, a young girl came out from behind the screen, her face radiant with a smile. She went and stood demurely behind Lady Cheng.

Shao-yu could tell at a glance that she was none other than Chang Li-hua. He looked from Minister Cheng to Thirteen in astonishment. "Is this a girl or a ghost?" he said at last. "Is this a dream, or is it reality?"

The minister and Lady Cheng smiled, but Thirteen laughed so hard he could not stand up. All the servants were laughing, too. "Now I shall tell you the truth," said the minister. "This girl is neither a ghost nor a fairy. Her name is Ch'un-yün,[28] of the Chia[29] family, whom we have brought up in our own household. Since you were bound to be lonely living by yourself in the garden pavilion, we sent her to comfort you and relieve your boredom. But then the youngsters took it upon themselves to play this practical joke on you."

Thirteen, at last getting himself under control, said, "It was I who arranged both of your meetings with the fairy. You should be thanking me for doing you a favor, but you look at me as if I am loathsome. You ingrate!" He doubled up in laughter once again.

Shao-yu finally joined the laughter. "You ruined your father's gift to me!" he exclaimed. "Why should I thank you for a favor like that?"

Thirteen replied, "I am happy to take the blame, but I deserve only part of it. It is not I who hatched the plot—that credit goes to someone else."

Shao-yu looked at the minister. "If it was not you that planned the joke, then who was it?"

"I am already a gray-headed old man," said Minister Cheng. "Why would I indulge in such childish games? You are mistaken if you think it was me."

Thirteen added, "Mencius[30] said, 'What comes from you returns to you.' Think about it, brother. If a man can become a woman, then what is so strange about a human becoming a fairy or a fairy becoming a ghost?"

Only then did Shao-yu finally understand. He laughed and said to the minister, "I can see it all now, sir. I once played a trick on your daughter, and she has never forgotten it."

The minister and Lady Cheng both laughed, but said nothing. Shao-yu then turned to Ch'un-yün and said, "You are bright and clever, but to play a trick on the man you intend to marry is hardly proper, now, is it?"

Ch'un-yün knelt as she replied, "Your servant heard the general's orders but did not receive the Emperor's edict."

Shao-yu sighed. "When Prince Hsiang of olden times lay with the fairy on Wu-shan, he could not tell that she was a cloud in the morning and rain in the evening.[31] Now that I know that the girl Ch'un-yün can become both a fairy and a ghost, I have learned the principle of transmogrificaton. It is said there are no weak soldiers under a strong general. If the soldier is like you, then how great must be the wisdom of the general?"

At this, everyone laughed happily, and more refreshments were set out for a day of eating and drinking. Ch'un-yün was allowed to join them on the lowest seat.

When night had fallen Ch'un-yün carried a lantern and led her new master to the garden pavilion. Happily drunk, he took her hand and teased, "Are you truly a fairy or a ghost? I have had a fairy and I've had a ghost, and now I have a beautiful girl.[32] If you can be transformed into a fairy and a ghost, shall I turn you into Heng-o,[33] the beauty who lives in the moon? Or shall I change you into a fairy of Heng-shan?"[34]

Ch'un-yün fell to her knees and said, "Master, I have done you a terrible wrong and deceived you in so many ways. Will you ever forgive me?"

Shao-yu laughed and said, "Even when you were a ghost I did not love you any less. How could I be angry at you now?"

She rose to thank him formally.[35]

———— 夢 ————

THE BOY AT THE ROADSIDE

When Shao-yu passed the government examination and was arranging to marry Minister Cheng's daughter, he had planned to go home in the fall and return to the capital with his aged mother for the wedding celebration; but his duties as a state official had detained him from making the trip. Now he was finally about to go, but circumstances of national import intervened once again. The Tibetans[1] were making incursions along the frontier and the governors of Ho-pei, now calling themselves the kings of Yen, Chao, and Wei, had allied with their stronger neighbor, raised armies, and fomented a rebellion.

The Emperor was deeply troubled, and he gathered his counselors to discuss the logistics of putting down the rebellion, but they could not agree on a plan until Yang Shao-yu came forward and said: "In ancient times the emperor Han Wu-ti summoned the Prince of Nan-yüeh and gently reprimanded him.[2] Your Majesty should do the same. Make haste and dispatch a letter of warning to the rebels, and if they do not listen to reason, then send an army in force and destroy them."

The Emperor commanded Shao-yu to compose such a letter at once. Shao-yu kowtowed, fetched brush, ink, and paper, and wrote the letter in the Emperor's presence. "It is dignified and full of gravity," the Emperor said, delighted. "It is gracious, but it maintains a sense of our power and authority. I am certain that the foolish rebels will come to their senses."

The letter was dispatched at once to the three rebel kingdoms. Chao and Wei immediately renounced their royal titles and obeyed the Emperor's decree. They sent replies, begging the Emperor's pardon, and sent tributes of ten thousand horses and a thousand rolls of fine silk. The King of Yen, whose territory was farthest from the capital, refused, confident that his army was strong enough.

The Emperor realized that the surrender of Chao and Wei was due to Shao-yu's insight, and so he issued the following edict:

> A century ago the rebels of Ho-pei, confident of their military strength, raised an insurrection. Emperor Te Tsung sent an army of 100,000 against them, but he failed to quell the rebellion. But now, with a single letter, Yang Shao-yu has brought two entire rebel armies to surrender without the mobilization or loss of a single soldier. Imperial authority has been strengthened far and wide throughout the empire. In recognition of his service and as an expression of our satisfaction and gratitude, we award him three hundred rolls of silk and five thousand horses.[3]

The Emperor also wanted to promote his rank, but Shao-yu went before him and said, with great humility, "Your Majesty, drafting an imperial decree is merely part of my duty. The surrender of the two armies was due entirely to your imperial authority. How could I possibly accept these rewards? There is still one rebel army, and I regret that I have not been able to fight to redeem the nation's shame. How could you wish to promote me in these circumstances?

"I am not loyal to you for the sake of promotion. Since victory or defeat does not depend on the number of soldiers, I ask that you let me set out with a single regiment and, with your imperial authority, I will settle the matter with Yen by fighting them to the death. Thus would I return a ten-thousandth part of the favor you have bestowed upon me."

The Emperor considered these words and asked the opinion of his counselors, who said, "Of the three armies that were in league against the empire, two have surrendered. Little Yen is like a piece of meat in a pot or an ant in a hole. Before the imperial army he will snap like a dry twig or crumble like a rotten one. Let the army try other means before attacking. Let

Yang Shao-yu be put in charge to try his skill at negotiation, and if Yen does not surrender, then they will be destroyed."

The Emperor approved and ordered Shao-yu to set off for Yen to try persuasion with the rebels before resorting to force.

So Shao-yu went to say good-bye to Minister Cheng, who said to him, "The men of the frontier are wild and uncivilized and rebellions are an everyday occurrence. You are a scholar going off into danger. If something should happen to you, it will not be just your father-in-law, but the whole nation who would suffer from the loss. I am old now and no longer participate in affairs of the state, but I can still present a petition to the Emperor to oppose your going."

"Please," said Shao-yu, "do not worry yourself on my account. When there is discord in the capital, the people of the border states take advantage and rise up, but the Emperor has the Mandate of Heaven—his authority is strong. Chao and Wei have already surrendered and Yen is the weakest of them, so there is no need for you to be concerned."

"Then I will say no more to dissuade you. The Emperor has made his decree and the matter is settled. Just be careful. Watch out for yourself and see to it that you do not bring shame to the nation."

But the minister's wife was in tears. "When you became our son-in-law, we were much comforted in our old age. I cannot tell you how it upsets me now that you must go so far away. Please, come back quickly."

When Shao-yu went to his garden pavilion to prepare for his journey, Ch'un-yün clung to him and wept. "When you went to work in the palace, I rose early to roll up the bedding and help you into your robes. You looked at me as if you could not bear to go. But now you are going far away without saying anything at all?"

Shao-yu laughed. "A man who carries out the Emperor's orders in matters of state cannot care whether he lives or dies. He must care even less for small everyday matters. Do not mar your beauty with worry. Look after yourself and your mistress and I will return after my victory with a gold seal upon my belt."

He went out through the gate and mounted his chariot.

☙

When Shao-yu reached the city of Lo-yang, he saw that it hadn't changed since he had been there last, a poorly equipped fifteen-year-old boy riding a donkey.

Only a year had passed since then, and now he was there on an imperial mission riding in a four-horse chariot. The magistrate of Lo-yang had cleared the streets for his arrival and the governor of Ho-nan[4] obsequiously led the way. The road was lined with cheering throngs of people struggling to see the spectacle of his arrival.

The first thing Shao-yu did was to send his boy servant to find Ch'an-yüeh. But the gates of her house were locked and the pavilion doors were shut up—only the cherry trees were still in bloom along the wall. When the boy asked among the neighbors, they told him that, in the spring of the previous year, Ch'an-yüeh had spent the night with a passing scholar. Afterward, claiming she was ill, she refused to entertain any guests and stopped attending official banquets. Not long after that, she went insane, threw away all of her jewelry, put on a nun's robes, and went off on a long journey. She never came back and no one knew where she was.

The boy returned and told this to Shao-yu, who was terribly saddened by the news. He went to her house to reminisce over their meeting, and that night he was sleepless with sorrow. The governor sent him a dozen dancing girls—the most skillful—to console him. They were all beautiful, splendidly dressed, and vied for his attention, but Shao-yu showed no interest in any of them.

The next morning, just before he left, he wrote a poem on the wall.

> Rain over T'ien-chin Bridge, the willow buds green,
> The scenery unchanged since that of last spring;
> How sad my return—though I come with fame,
> The table is empty—no one here to pour my wine.

When he had finished, he threw aside his writing brush and rode away in his chariot, leaving the dancing girls to hang their heads in shame.

They eagerly copied the lines and delivered the poem to the governor. "If you had gotten even a glance from him, your reputations would have grown a hundredfold," he scolded them. "But not one of you was able to please him. You have brought disgrace upon Lo-yang."

When the governor found out who Shao-yu was referring to in the poem, he posted notices far and wide to find Ch'an-yüeh before Shao-yu returned.

☙

When Yang Shao-yu reached Yen, he saw that the inhabitants of that remote region had no inkling of the Emperor's power or splendor. Throngs surrounded his chariot, blocking his way in order to get a look at him, as if he were a fabled *ch'ilin*[5] of the Earth or a phoenix in the clouds.

When he met the King of Yen, Shao-yu's authority was like thunder and his graciousness was like spring rain. The people, in their joy, danced and sang, saying, "The Emperor will spare us!"

Shao-yu explained the position of the Emperor, the consequences of resistance, and the wisdom of submission, his words as forceful as the ocean tide and chilling as the autumn frost.

The King of Yen was deeply impressed and, realizing his folly, he bowed down and begged forgiveness. "Yen is so far from the capital that we did not know the will of the Emperor and therefore dared to disobey and oppose him. But now, hearing your words, I am enlightened and admit my wrongdoing. From now on I will do my utmost to be a loyal subject. Please, when you return, deliver my message to the imperial court to grant us peace and turn this conflict into a blessing."

A great banquet was held at the P'i-lou Palace, and Shao-yu was presented with a hundred talents[6] of gold and ten of the finest horses. He politely declined the gifts and departed from Yen.

☙

Ten days later, as he passed through Han-tan,[7] there was a boy on horseback in front of him. When the boy heard the call to clear the way, he dismounted and stood by the roadside, waiting.

"What a fine horse," said Shao-yu.

As the cavalcade drew closer, Shao-yu saw that the boy was unusually handsome, his face like a blooming flower and bright as the moonrise. His posture was straight, and he was so radiant that one could hardly look directly at him without being dazzled. "I have seen many boys at court, but never one so handsome," said Shao-yu. "Invite that boy to come see me," he told an attendant.

When Shao-yu had settled in at his lodgings for the night, the young man arrived and a servant showed him in. Shao-yu was captivated. "I was taken by your beauty and your elegance when I saw you by the road," he said. "When I sent someone after you, I feared you might refuse the invitation, so I am delighted to see you here. Tell me, what is your name?"

"I am from the north and my name is Ti Po-luan," said the boy. "As I grew up in an insignificant village, I did not have the benefit of good teachers or refined companions and so my education is lacking. I cannot write poetry, nor can I handle a sword, but my heart is strong, and I am willing to give up my life for my friends.

"When you came through Ho-pei everyone was awed by your grandeur and your goodness. I, too, was taken with you and, forgetting my low birth, I dared to imagine that I could be your companion and serve you, even if it was to be like a watchdog or a chicken in your courtyard. Now you have been so kind as to send for me and it is like two tones in harmony, two minds thinking as one."

Shao-yu was more than pleased. "How wonderful that our two minds think as one. Let us ride together and dine at the same table. When we pass through a beautiful landscape we shall talk of mountains and rivers and when the night is clear we shall recite poems to the wind and moon to forget the hardships of the long journey."

When they reached Lo-yang and were crossing the T'ien-chin Bridge in view of the pavilion, Shao-yu was reminded of the happy hours he had spent with Ch'an-yüeh. It made him melancholy. "If she knew that I had passed this way before, sad to have missed her, she would surely be waiting for me now," he said to himself. "They say she became a nun, and she must be far away at some Taoist temple or Buddhist monastery. How can I reach her, for if we do not meet now I cannot imagine how we will ever meet again."

As he looked far ahead at the pavilion, he suddenly noticed a beautiful girl standing there, with the beaded curtain rolled up, watching the approaching horses and chariots. It was Ch'an-yüeh! Shao-yu's face lit up with recognition, and as his chariot sped by, they gazed upon each other with indescribable joy and affection.

By the time he reached his lodgings, she was already there waiting, having arrived by a shortcut. Overcome with a mixture of joy and sorrow, she wept and could not speak at first.

Finally, she bowed and said to him, "You have no doubt heard what happened to me, so there is no need to repeat it for you. Last spring, I heard that you were on a mission in service of the Emperor and would pass this way, but I was too far away and I could not come to meet you. I could only weep. But the magistrate came to visit me at the temple and showed me the poem you had written on the wall. He begged my forgiveness for the wrongs he had done me and asked me to come and await your return here. I was delighted.

"I returned to my former home, happy at the thought that someone cared about me, and every day I went up to the T'ienchin Pavilion to watch for your arrival. Everyone envied me. But now that you have attained such a high position, tell me, have you not married?"

"I am engaged to the daughter of Minister Cheng," Shao-yu replied. "But we have not married yet. She is just as you said she would be. You were a wonderful matchmaker, and I owe you a great debt of gratitude."

And so they renewed their love and were inseparable for many days. Because Shao-yu was spending all of his time with Ch'an-yüeh, he did not send for the boy, Po-luan, whom he had just met. But one morning Shao-yu's servant boy came to him and quietly said to him, "That young Ti Po-luan fellow is no good. I saw him flirting with Kuei Ch'an-yüeh in the women's quarters."

"He would never do such a thing," said Shao-yu. "And Ch'an-yüeh is faithful to me. You are mistaken."

The boy left in anger, and it wasn't long before he returned. "If you don't believe me, then come see for yourself," he said, pointing to the west wing.

Now the boy led Shao-yu to the servants' quarters, and there he saw the two of them leaning over the low wall holding hands, talking and laughing together. Shao-yu drew closer to hear them more clearly, but Po-luan heard his footsteps and ran away, while Ch'an-yüeh looked at him with a guilty blush.

"Have you known him very long?" Shao-yu asked.

"I do not know him, but his sister is a good friend of mine and I was asking after her," said Ch'an-yüeh. "I am a lowborn dancing girl, as you know, and I am in the habit of flirting with young men, holding hands, and whispering in their ears. If you think what I have done is shameful, I am deeply sorry to have wronged you."

"Do not worry yourself," said Shao-yu. "I trust you completely." But he realized Po-luan was only a boy and he was ashamed to be caught flirting. Shao-yu decided to call the boy to put his mind at rest, but Po-luan could not be found anywhere.

Shao-yu was filled with regret. "In ancient times Prince Chuang of Ch'u comforted his followers by having everyone cut off their hat strings,"[8] he said to himself. "But through my carelessness I have lost my dear young friend. What shall I do now?" And he ordered his servants to search high and low for Po-luan.

Shao-yu spent the night drinking with Ch'an-yüeh, reminiscing about the past and rekindling their love, and when it grew late they put out the lights and slept together.

When the sun rose, Shao-yu awakened to see that Ch'an-yüeh was already getting dressed, but something was different about her. The delicate brows, the bright eyes, the cloudlike hair, the rosy cheeks, and the slender waist were all like Ch'an-yüeh, but it was not her. Confused and suspicious, he lay there for a time, unable to speak.

Finally, he asked, "Who are you?"

夢

7

THE IMPERIAL SON-IN-LAW

"My name is Ti Ching-hung[1] and I am from Po-chou," she said. "I have been Ch'an-yüeh's friend since childhood. We are like sisters. She was not feeling well last night, and so she asked me to sleep with you so you would not be disappointed in her. That is why I came in her place."

But even before she was finished, Ch'an-yüeh came into the room. "Now that you have a new woman to serve you, I congratulate you. I recommended Ti Ching-hung of Ho-pei to you some time ago. What do you think of her now that you've been with her?"

"She is far lovelier than you described," said Shao-yu. He studied her face again and saw that she looked exactly like the boy Ti Po-luan. "Is Po-luan your brother?" he asked. "I'm afraid I was rather harsh with him yesterday. Do you know where he is now?"

"I have no brother," said Ching-hung.

Shao-yu suddenly realized the truth. "You're the boy who followed me from the roadside near Han-tan," he said. "And it was you who was flirting with Ch'an-yüeh over the wall yesterday. But why did you dress as a boy and fool me?"

"How else could I have attracted your attention?" said Ching-hung. "Though I am lowborn and uneducated, I have always longed to serve a great man. When the King of Yen heard about me he bought me for a bag of jewels and kept me in his palace. I ate the best food and wore the finest clothes, but that is not what I wanted. I felt only sorrow like a bird in a cage. Then, when the King of Yen held a banquet in your honor, I peeked through the screen and saw you, and I knew you were the man I had been longing to serve. But how was I to escape through the nine gates of the palace unnoticed and travel so far to get to you? I thought about it for a long time until I finally had a plan, but I could not leave the same day as you, or the king would have sent his men to recapture me.

"So when you had been gone for several days, I stole one of the king's fastest horses and reached Han-tan in two days. That is where you called for me.

"I should have told you right away who I was, but there were too many people about, and I stayed in disguise to avoid being captured. What I did last night was at Ch'an-yüeh's request. If you will forgive me, I will serve you forever. Overlook my humble birth and when you are married to a noble lady, let me live with you together with Ch'an-yüeh and we will bring you happiness."

Shao-yu replied, "Even the famous Yang Chih-fu, who played the same kind of trick on Duke Li Wei when she came to him in the night, pales in comparison to you.² I only regret that I did not compare to the duke. We have gotten along so well together, what need is there of other arrangements?"

Ching-hung thanked him, and Ch'an-yüeh said, "Since Ching-hung has slept with you in my place, I should also thank you on her behalf." The two women bowed to him.

That night Shao-yu slept with the both of them, and in the morning he said to them, "You cannot accompany me now because there are too many people who will gossip about us. I will send for you as soon as I am married."

And he left for Ch'ang-an.

                                   ☙

When Shao-yu arrived back at the capital to report to the palace, King Yen's letter of surrender, along with gifts of gold, silk, and other tribute also arrived.

The Emperor was very pleased. He wanted to reward Shao-yu for his efforts by recognizing him with the title of marquis,³ but Shao-yu was shocked by the suggestion of so high an honor, and he bowed down before the throne and asked to decline.

The Emperor, moved by his modesty, took his hand and made him minister of culture, also appointing him an imperial scholar. Such a bestowal of honors, even to an emperor's favorite, was unprecedented.

When Shao-yu returned, Minister Cheng and his wife gave him a warm welcome, congratulating him on his appointment as a minister after his dangerous mission. The household was filled with happiness and rejoicing. Shao-yu went into the garden, and there he found Ch'an-yüeh. They talked of intimate things and the joy in their lovemaking was beyond description.

The Emperor was much impressed by Shao-yu's command of literature and he invited him often to his private quarters to discuss classics like the *Shu-ching*,[4] and so most days found Shao-yu in the inner palace.

One night, when he had stayed late with the Emperor, the bright moonlight made it impossible for him to sleep, and so he stepped out onto the balcony of the pavilion and, leaning over the rail, he composed a poem. Suddenly he heard the soft notes of a flute borne on the breeze. It was so ethereally beautiful it sounded like it came from another world beyond the clouds.

Shao-yu called one of the servants and asked, "Is that sound coming from outside the palace, or is that someone inside playing?"

"I cannot tell," said the servant.

So Shao-yu took his own jade flute and played several tunes, and the notes rose into the heavens and stopped the very clouds in their course. Suddenly, a pair of blue cranes came flying from the inner garden and began dancing to the melody, and all the secretaries were amazed. "It is Prince Chin of Chou!"[5] they exclaimed. "He has returned to play for us!"

Now, the Empress Dowager had two sons and a daughter. Her first son, naturally, was the Emperor, and the other, Prince Yüeh. Her daughter was Princess Lan-yang.[6]

Before the princess was born, the Empress Dowager dreamed that a fairy had placed a pearl in her bosom.

When the princess grew up, she possessed all the lovely qualities of her name, which meant "Orchid." She had excellent skill in the literary arts and embroidery, and she was her mother's favorite.

A flute of white jade had been part of the tribute presented to the court from Syria.[7] It was exquisitely crafted, but when the Empress Dowager ordered the court musicians to play it, no one could produce a sound. One night the princess dreamed that a fairy came to her and taught her how to play it. When she awakened, she took up the flute and produced a beautiful, harmonious melody.

The Empress Dowager and the Emperor were greatly surprised and pleased by this event, but no one outside the family knew of it. Whenever the princess played the jade flute, cranes would gather in the courtyard and dance to the music.

The Empress Dowager said to her son the Emperor, "In ancient times Nung-yüeh, the daughter of Duke Mu of Ch'in, could play the jade flute beautifully. Lan-yang plays just like her, and since Nung-yüeh met her husband Hsiao-shih,[8] who was also a flute player, through her music, I am sure Lan-yang will do the same."

This is why Lan-yang was of age to be married but no suitable husband had yet been found for her. That night the princess played her flute, watching the blue cranes dance under the bright moon, and when she was done the birds flew away to the garden of the Academy and danced there. After this, the people in the palace all said to each other, "The cranes are dancing to Minister Yang's flute."

When the Emperor heard of this, he realized that the princess and Yang Shao-yu were clearly destined for each other. To his mother, he said, "Minister Yang is not only the right age for our princess, he is also peerless in appearance and ability. What do you think of him marrying the princess?"

The Empress Dowager laughed. "I have been worrying about finding the right husband for Hsiao-ho," she said, calling Princess Lan-yang by her personal name, which meant "Panpipe Harmony."[9] It had been given to her because those two characters were written on the white jade flute. "But from what you have told me, it seems that Heaven has made our selection for us. Still, I will need to look at him before I decide."

"That won't be hard," said the Emperor. "In a day or two I will call him to come to discuss books with me, and then you can get a peek at him and make your decision."

The Empress Dowager was delighted.

☙❧

A few days later, from his throne in P'eng-lai Hall,[10] the Emperor sent a eunuch[11] to bring Yang Shao-yu. The eunuch first went to the Imperial Academy, only to discover that he had just left. So he went to Minister Cheng's house, only to be told that Shao-yu hadn't arrived there. Confused, the eunuch rushed about, hither and thither, trying to find him.

Shao-yu happened to be with his friend Thirteen at a drinking establishment, where they were enjoying wine and song with two famous courtesans, Chu-niang and Yü-lu.[12] When the eunuch finally found them, he informed Shao-yu of the Emperor's orders to report to the palace at once. Thirteen was frightened and immediately leaped up and made himself scarce, but Shao-yu was so drunk by then he barely understood what was happening.

The eunuch persevered, and with the help of the two girls, he got Shao-yu onto his feet, into his official dress, and to the palace. The Emperor told Shao-yu to take a seat, and he began quizzing him about past dynasties, the achievements and failures of past rulers.

Shao-yu's answers were very coherent, and the Emperor was pleased with him. "They say poetry is not an emperor's occupation," he said. "But my ancestors enjoyed composing verse and they were widely read and appreciated by the people. Tell me, who in your opinion were the best and worst poets in antiquity? Which kings wrote the best verse? And among subjects, who was the best?"

Shao-yu replied, "The dialogue between ruler and subject by means of verse began with Emperor Shun and his minister Kao Yao. Among the works of emperors, the finest are Han Kao-ti's 'Song of the Great Wind,' Han Wu-ti's 'Ode to the Autumn Wind,' and Wei Wu-ti's 'Moonlight and Starlight.'

Among ministers I would say the most notable are Li Ling of Western Han, Ts'ao Chih of Wei, and T'ao Yüan-ming and Hsieh Ling-yun of Chin.

"But through the ages, no dynasty has had literature flourish as much as ours, the T'ang, and the finest era was in the forty-year reign of Emperor HsüanTsung.[13] He was the best poet among emperors and Li Po was not only the best poet among subjects, he was the greatest of all time."

"My thoughts exactly," said the Emperor. "Whenever I read 'The Song of Ch'ing-ping' or his 'Ode on the Joy of Travel,' I regret that I could not meet Li Po, but now that I have you here, that regret is gone.

"According to an old tradition, I have picked a dozen women of the palace—female secretaries, if you will—to assist you. They are all talented and beautiful. I would like to enjoy what it must have been like to watch Li Po composing poetry while he was drunk. I hope you will not disappoint these women." He had the female secretaries set out an inkstone case made of crystal, a white jade brush holder, and a yellow jade water dropper.

Then each woman spread out a silk scarf and a silk fan as the Emperor had ordered, and Shao-yu, still happily drunk, wrote on them the verses that spontaneously came to mind, the tip of his brush flickering like lightning through wind and clouds. When at last he finished, the women knelt before the Emperor and presented each fan and scarf inscribed with Shao-yu's compositions. The Emperor regarded each fan and scarf, every poem like a jewel, and ordered the women to bring the finest wine in appreciation of Shao-yu's impressive achievement.

They carried in trays of gold with cups fashioned to look like parrots and poured them full of wine. Some knelt before Shao-yu and others stood around him, urging him to drink, a cup in each hand, and when he had downed a dozen cups in the Emperor's presence, his face flushed red and his vision grew dim.

The Emperor told the women to clear away the wine. "His poems are worth a thousand pieces of gold," he said to them. "Their true worth is beyond price. What precious things will you give him now as reward?"

The women removed their dazzling golden hairpins and jangling jade ornaments and cast them down before Shao-yu. "Gather up the paper, the brushes, the water dropper, and the secretaries' gifts," the Emperor commanded a eunuch. "Take everything and accompany the minister back to his house."

Shao-yu rose to thank the Emperor and collapsed from too much drink. The Emperor ordered the eunuchs to help Shao-yu up. They took him to the south gate of the palace, where they put him on the back of his horse and took him home to the pavilion in the garden, and there Ch'un-yün undressed him, taking him out of his court robes.

"Wherever did you get so drunk?" she asked him.

Shao-yu could only nod.

The servants piled the brushes, the jade ornaments, the water bottle, and the jewelry on the floor, and seeing it all there, Shao-yu laughed and said, "These are all the gifts the Emperor has sent to you. I am earning as much as Tung-fang Shuo!"[14]

Ch'un-yün wanted to know all the details, but Shao-yu was already fast asleep, snoring like thunder.

☙

Shao-yu woke up late the next morning. He was still washing his face when the gatekeeper rushed in and said, "Prince Yüeh is here!"

"Prince Yüeh came in person?" asked Shao-yu, startled. "It must be something important."

He quickly went out to greet the prince and showed him in to the reception room, where he extended every courtesy. The prince was about twenty years old, his features so handsome and clear that he seemed to be of another world.

Shao-yu knelt before him. "What is your command, Your Highness, that you would visit me in my humble dwelling?"

"I have known you by reputation," said the prince. "And yet I have never had occasion to meet you because of our various engagements. But now the Emperor has called upon me to deliver a message to you. The princess Lan-yang has come of age and it is time for her to marry. The Emperor was looking for a man who would suit her, and as he has a high opinion of you, he has chosen you to be his brother-in-law. He gave me the honor of delivering this news to you. The official announcement will come shortly."

Shao-yu was stunned. He prostrated himself before the prince and said, "His Majesty bestows too much favor upon me, and it is said that an excess of good fortune brings disaster. Your humble servant is engaged to the daughter of Minister Cheng. Nearly a year has gone by since wedding gifts were exchanged. Please, I beg you, convey this to His Majesty."

"I will tell him," said the prince. "But I regret that the love the Emperor shows for you is then in vain."

Shao-yu answered, "This is such an important matter for me that I dare not treat it lightly. I will prostrate myself outside the palace gate and gladly receive my punishment."

Prince Yüeh said good-bye and returned to the palace while Shao-yu went immediately to Minister Cheng and told him what the prince had said. But Ch'un-yün had already told her mother and the whole house was in an anxious uproar. Minister Cheng was so full of sorrow he could not find words to speak.

"Please, do not worry," said Shao-yu. "I know the Emperor well, and he is a wise and good man who respects the rules of ceremony and propriety. He would never force even an unworthy subject like me to go against convention. I assure you, I will not commit the crime Sung Hung refused."[15]

જ્જ

The previous day, the Empress Dowager had come into P'eng-lai Hall and peeked at Shao-yu through the bead curtain. She had taken a liking to him and said to the Emperor, "He is exactly the man I have been seeking for Lan-yang. There is no need for further discussion." And so the Emperor had sent Prince Yüeh to tell Shao-yu.

In his private rooms in the palace, the Emperor wanted to speak to Shao-yu of this matter himself. He decided to have another look at the poems from the previous day, and so he sent a eunuch to the female secretaries to collect all the poems Shao-yu had written for them.

All the other women had put their poems carefully away, but one had hidden her fan in her bosom and taken it to her bedroom, where she wept over it all night, unable to eat or sleep. She was none other than Ch'in Ts'ai-feng, the daughter of the inspector from Hua-chou.

After her father's ignominious death, she had been forced to become a servant in the palace. At one time the Emperor, hearing all the women praising her beauty, had wanted her for himself as an imperial concubine, but his mother the Empress Dowager had cautioned him against it. "The girl is indeed beautiful, but remember that you ordered her father's execution. If you are intimate with her it would violate the old convention of emperors keeping their distance from those whom they have had to punish."

The Emperor saw the reason in his mother's objections. The next day he called Ts'ai-feng and asked her if she could write, and when she modestly replied that she could, he appointed her as one of the female secretaries, putting her in charge of literary documents. She was also sent to tutor Princess Lanyang in reading and composition. The princess grew to love her, and it was only a short while before they became inseparable.

That day, Ts'ai-feng had been waiting on the Empress Dowager in P'eng-lai Hall when the Emperor called on her and the other female secretaries to receive Yang Shao-yu's poems. She recognized him immediately—how could she not? He was in her thoughts night and day, the man whose face she could not forget even in her dreams. Yet Shao-yu, not knowing that she was alive—and being in the presence of the Emperor composing poetry so furiously that he dared not look up from his work—did not recognize her.

But once Ts'ai-feng saw him, she felt as if her heart would burst. Her face flushed, and she stifled her emotions, afraid that others might notice. She could tell no one about this and there seemed to be no hope of ever seeing him again. Later, when she was alone in her room, she clutched the fan and, unable to put it down, read the poem he had written on it again and again.

Round silk fan, round as the moon;
it plays with the pale hand that holds it.
Its fragrant breeze, peace and pleasure,
restless, to and fro, across your breast.

Round silk fan, round as the moon;
it follows the pale hand that holds it.
Veiling your face, no way to move it,
no way to glimpse the beauty of spring.

She sighed, reading the first lines. "He does not know my heart," she said. "I live in the palace, but how could I possibly be intimate with the Emperor?"

She read the second stanza and lamented again. "He may not have seen my face, but surely he has not forgotten it. The poem shows how one can be so close and yet so far."

She remembered her old house and his poem about the willows and, overcome by sorrow, she burst into tears that stained her dress. Finally, she composed a poem of her own and wrote it on the fan beside Shao-yu's, and when she read it over she sighed.

Just then she heard that a eunuch was coming to collect the fans and other items on which Shao-yu had written under the Emperor's command. Ts'ai-feng trembled in fear. "What shall I do?" she cried. "I shall be killed! Surely I will be killed!"

夢

STRATEGY AND TACTICS

The eunuch said to her, "The Emperor wants to see the fans again—the ones on which Minister Yang wrote the poems."

"I am an unfortunate creature," Ts'ai-feng said through her tears. "I wrote a reply on the fan to the poem without thinking. If His Majesty sees it, he will surely order my execution. It is better that I kill myself now to avoid disgrace. When I am dead, please see that my body gets a proper burial. Do not let them leave it for the crows."

"What are you saying?" the eunuch replied. "The Emperor is kind and merciful. He will not consider it a serious crime. In any event, I will help you. Do nothing and just follow me."

So Ts'ai-feng followed the eunuch, who led her to the gate and had her wait outside while he went in alone and delivered the poems.

The Emperor looked at each piece and, by and by, he found the fan with the two poems, one of them in a different hand. "Who wrote this one?" he asked the eunuch.

The eunuch told him about Ts'ai-feng and how she had resolved to kill herself. He said he had brought her and that she was waiting outside.

When the Emperor had read her poem, he said, "Tell her there is no need to kill herself. Anyone reading this can see its quality. It would be a waste to lose such talent." He told the eunuch to fetch her, and he read the poem aloud as Ts'ai-feng prostrated herself before him.

> Round silk fan, round as the autumn moon;
> I recall our first night in the pavilion.

Had I known then that you would not know me,
I would not regret now—how I let you come too close.

"Tell me the truth behind this incident and I will forgive you," said the Emperor.

Hanging her head, Ts'ai-feng told the Emperor the story of her meeting with Shao-yu when he was on his way to the capital to sit for the state examination. She told him she had recognized the minister at the party in the palace, where they 'had written poetry, but that he had not looked at her. "Your humble servant remembered that meeting and how he promised marriage, and foolishly wrote that stanza beneath his. I deserve to die."

The Emperor took pity on her. "Can you recall the poem that led to your engagement?" he asked.

Ts'ai-feng quickly wrote it out and gave it to him.

"You have done wrong," he said. "But you have great talent and the princess loves you dearly. I will forgive you. Do not err again."

Ts'ai-feng expressed her profound gratitude and left.

❧

Meanwhile, Prince Yüeh had rushed back from Minister Cheng's house to tell the Emperor that Shao-yu had already exchanged wedding gifts with the Chengs' daughter. The Empress Dowager was there, and she was not pleased by the news. "Yang Shao-yu is a high-ranking minister of state and must know the law. How is it that he can refuse?"

"He has exchanged wedding gifts, but that does not constitute marriage," said the Emperor. "If I speak to him, I am sure he will listen to reason."

The next day, the Emperor summoned Shao-yu to the palace and he came at once.

"My sister is unusually gifted, and there is no man as suitable as you to be her husband," said the Emperor. "Prince Yüeh has already told you this, but I hear that you have declined and excused yourself, saying you have already exchanged wedding gifts with the house of Minister Cheng. Clearly, you have not thought this through. In ancient times when a woman was chosen to be the royal daughter-in-law it made no difference if she was engaged—even a married woman could be chosen. Wang Hsien-chih[1] spent his whole life regretting the women who had rejected him.

"We are not like the people, and the laws that govern them do not necessarily govern us, but I am the parent of the people and I would never ask you to behave in a way that is improper. Even if you break off your engagement now, Cheng's daughter could easily find another suitor. Since you have not yet had the marriage ceremony, how can you have failed to uphold your obligation?"

Shao-yu bowed humbly and replied, "Your Majesty has not only not punished me, but has admonished me gently, the way a father corrects a son. For this I thank you sincerely. But I can only say that my situation is not like that of other people. I am only a poor scholar from a distant corner of the country and did not even have a place to sleep when I first came to the capital. It was through Minister Cheng's kindness that I avoided loneliness.

"Not only have I sent the wedding gifts, but I have been living like Minister Cheng's son-in-law. I have already seen his daughter's face and we are already like husband and wife to each other. The only reason the wedding has not been celebrated is that I was too busy with affairs of state. Now that the border states are at peace and there are no concerns that trouble the nation, I was about to ask for a leave to go home and fetch my elderly mother so we could finally set a day for the wedding. But then, quite unexpectedly, I received your command.

"Now I do not know what to do. If I obey for fear of your punishment, Minister Cheng's daughter will never marry until her dying day. If she does not become my wife, will this not reflect badly on Your Majesty's wise reign?"

The Emperor responded, "Your argument is upright and well-intentioned, but the truth of the situation is that you and Minister Cheng's daughter are not yet married. The Empress Dowager has decided the matter herself. She wants you very badly. She insists upon it and I cannot go against her."

Shao-yu politely refused once again.

"The matter of marriage is very important and cannot be resolved in a single hurried meeting," said the Emperor. "Let us play a game of backgammon² to help pass the time."

He ordered a eunuch to bring a board and they sat down to play against each other. They did not stop until darkness had set in.

◈

When Shao-yu returned home, Minister Cheng met him with a sad countenance. "Today I received a command from the Empress Dowager ordering me to return your wedding gifts," he said, wiping tears from his eyes. "I told Ch'un-yün to get them, and now they are all piled up in the pavilion in the garden. When we consider our daughter's moral quandary, we two old people are helpless to do anything. I may manage to bear it, but my wife has fainted from the shock. She is unconscious now."

Shao-yu was terribly upset by this, and he was silent for a long while. Finally, he said, "This is unjust. If I make a sincere petition to the throne, I am sure they will listen to me."

Minister Cheng wrung his hands. "You have already defied the Emperor's orders more than once. If you petition the throne now, you will be done for. You will be severely punished for disobedience. Your only option is to submit. And you can no longer live in the garden pavilion—it is too much of an embarrassment in this circumstance. You must leave us and find somewhere else to live."

Shao-yu could not answer. He went to the garden pavilion and found Ch'un-yün crying there.

"It has been a long time since my mistress had me serve you," she said in a choked voice, giving him the wedding gifts. "You have been good to me and I am grateful. But now evil spirits are jealous of our happiness and everything has gone wrong. My mistress's marriage plans have come to naught, and now I must say good-bye to you and return to her. O blue Heaven, so far, far away, what manner of man could do such a thing?"³

"I intend to petition the throne," said Shao-yu. "Once a woman has consented to marry, she must by convention remain faithful to her husband. How can you even speak of leaving me?"

"I am not educated, but even so, I know the three relationships that govern a woman's life.[4] But my situation is different. From the time I was a little girl, I grew up with Lady Cheng with no distinction in our social status. We swore we would live and die together, through the good and the bad. I will remain with her and follow her like a shadow. How can a shadow exist by itself?"

"Your devotion is admirable," said Shao-yu. "But you and Lady Cheng are different. She can go east, west, north, and south—wherever she pleases—but can you follow her and marry another man?"

"You say that because you do not understand her heart and mine," Ch'un-yün replied. "My lady has resolved to serve her parents and when they die she will go to a Buddhist temple, cut off her hair, and become a nun. She will pray to the Buddha that she not be born a woman in her next life.[5] I have sworn to do the same. If you want to see me again, return your wedding gifts to my lady's quarters. If not, then this is our last farewell in this life. In my next life I wish I could be your dog or your horse to show my devotion to you. I wish you all happiness." She turned away and collapsed in tears against the rail of the balcony, and a moment later she stood up, bowed to him, and went into the women's quarters.

Shao-yu sat alone in the pavilion, helpless and heartsick. He looked up into the blue sky and heaved a sigh. "I must petition the throne," he said and, gathering his thoughts, he took up his brush and composed the following:

Your faithful servant, Yang Shao-yu, minister of the Board of Rites,[6] bowing before you, humbly presents this memorial to Your Imperial Majesty.

Moral law is the first principle of rule and marriage is the first of moral laws.[7] If this fundamental basis of law is disregarded, all subsequent customs and rules will fall into disorder and the nation will collapse into chaos. The institution of marriage is at the root of human ethics, and if the rules governing it are not carefully observed, then the integrity of the family will be affected, eventually to affect the welfare of the whole nation.

Your humble servant has already sent betrothal gifts to the daughter of Minister Cheng and bound himself to her family as son-in-law. It was after all this was already concluded that Your Majesty unexpectedly issued your gracious command that this unworthy commoner be chosen to be the imperial son-in-law. He is deeply distressed by this order, and fails to comprehend how this imperial command with the royal court's approval is in keeping with the accepted laws and rites.

Can this command be allowed to stand without careful review of its appropriateness and an examination of potential ridicule of the throne? Can it be permitted without investigation? Your Majesty has sent a secret order to nullify the rites that have already been performed, but your servant, as minister of the Board of Rites, cannot countenance such an action. Your servant, not wanting to be the cause of an action that compromises the virtue of Your Majesty's government, humbly begs that you rescind the command. Otherwise, the moral laws will be ignored, the honor of the throne will be marred. There will be violence and discord among the people, and the whole state will fall to ruin.

Your humble servant thus implores Your Majesty to consider the moral foundations upon which the state is built and maintain order by honoring first principles, by revoking your order and allowing your servant to return to his lowly duties in peace.

When the Emperor read the petition and showed it to his mother, the Empress Dowager was furious and demanded that Shao-yu be immediately arrested and thrown in prison. But all the ministers pleaded against it.

"I know this is too severe a punishment," said the Emperor. "But the Empress Dowager is so angry I dare not pardon him." And he ordered Shao-yu's arrest and imprisonment.

Minister Cheng, now disgraced, closed his gates and refused all visitors.

⊙⊚⊙

The Tibetans were powerful in those days, and an army of 100,000 was attacking the border regions of the empire. Their vanguard pushed as far as the bridge that spanned the Wei River not far from the northern gate of the capital.

Things grew tense in Ch'ang-an, and the Emperor called his ministers together in council. They said, "There are only a few thousand troops in the capital and those in the provinces are too far to come quickly. Your Majesty must leave for the east, for Kuan-tung, and rally the provincial troops to march and save the nation."

The Emperor found it difficult to come to a decision on his own. "Yang Shao-yu is my best strategist and his judgment has been sound," he said. "When I nearly erred in the past, it was he who brought the three rebel states into submission."

Dismissing his ministers, he appealed to his mother to release Shao-yu from prison, and summoned him to get his advice.

Shao-yu said, "The tomb of the imperial ancestors and the royal palaces are all located in the capital. If you abandon the capital, there will be great confusion throughout the empire. And if a powerful enemy were to occupy the city then, it would be very hard to drive them out again.

"In the days of your predecessor T'ai Tsung,[8] the Tibetans allied with the Uighurs and attacked the capital with a combined force of a million men. At that time, there were fewer men in the capital than now, and yet the Prince of Fen-yang, Kuo Tzu-i, drove them off with his cavalry.

"Your humble servant lacks the skill and military prowess of Kuo Tzu-i, but if you would give me a few thousand soldiers, I will do my utmost to drive out the enemy and so repay you for the great kindness you have shown me."

The Emperor gladly approved and immediately appointed Shao-yu as commanding general. He gave him thirty thousand troops from the garrison and told Shao-yu to engage the Tibetan army.

Shao-yu took leave of the Emperor and marshaled his troops, assembling them at the Wei Bridge. He beat back the vanguard and captured a Tibetan prince. The enemy was routed. Shao-yu pursued them and fought them three more times, winning all three battles, killing thirty thousand men, and capturing a thousand horses. He sent dispatches to the capital describing his victories.

The Emperor was delighted with the news and ordered the return of his armies, preparing rewards for each general according to his achievements. But Shao-yu sent the following message:

I have heard that the imperial army cannot be defeated. But I have also heard that an army that always wins does not respect the power of the enemy and cannot win unless the enemy is weak and hungry. Our enemy is strong and well-fed, but they are strangers in this land of which we are the owners, where we can wait, well-fed, while they grow hungry. They grow weaker with each passing day.

In *The Art of War*[9] it is said that one should attack the enemy when he is most vulnerable. Already their ranks are broken and they are fleeing. The outlying provinces have supplies and food for us, so there is no concern about lack of provisions, and in the flat plains and fields, they cannot find a place in which to hide from us. If we pursue them quickly, we can overrun them. I do not believe that it is wise to stop our attack and return now. I beg you—take counsel with the ministers before you come to a decision. Let me pursue the enemy as far as possible to their hideouts, set fire to their camps, and guarantee that not a suit of armor or a flight of arrows shall ever come across our borders again. Then Your Majesty can be at ease.

The Emperor was impressed by the wisdom in Shao-yu's dispatch. He promoted him to the rank of chief inspector as well as minister of war, with the title of western marshal. He sent him a sword, a red bow and arrow, a belt of water buffalo horn, a white flag made of yak tail, and a golden battle-ax. He dispatched orders for the mobilization of troops and horses to Shao-yu's army from the provinces of So-fang, Ho-tung, and Lung-hsi.

When Shao-yu received the Emperor's gifts and orders, he bowed toward the palace in thanks. Then he selected an auspicious day, offered sacrifices, and set out with twenty thousand men.

He based his strategy on *The Six Secret Teachings* of Chiang T'ai-kung[10] and his units were arranged according to the eight trigrams of the *I Ching*.[11] Discipline was strict. His army marched out like a stream of water, straight as a split bamboo. Fifty lost towns and their territories were retaken within a few months and the main body of his army arrived at the foot of the Chih-shih Mountains.[12]

A whirlwind appeared before Shao-yu's horse and blew through the camp with the cawing of crows. Shao-yu divined the meaning of this strange occurrence and learned that the enemy would attack in force, but his army would be victorious. So he made camp below the mountains, scattered caltrops[13] and posted guards, and waited for the enemy.

＊

That night, when the sentry called the third watch, Shao-yu was sitting in his tent reading dispatches by candlelight. Suddenly, a cold gust of air blew out the candle and a young woman materialized in the middle of the tent as if she had come out of the very air. In her hand she wielded a double-edged sword that gleamed like frost.

Shao-yu realized she was an assassin, but his voice did not waver, and he said to her, calmly and sternly, "What manner of woman are you that you come in the night air to the middle of my camp? What is your purpose?"

"I have been sent by Tsen-po, King of Tibet,"[14] she said. "I am to return with your head."

Shao-yu laughed. "The superior man never fears death. Take it—quickly—and go."

But the girl threw down her sword and bowed her head, saying, "Do not worry. I could not do such a thing."

"You come bearing a sword and infiltrated my camp, and yet you will not harm me? So what is your purpose, then?"

"I want to tell you my story, but I cannot give you all the details now," she said.

Shao-yu asked her to sit down. "You faced great danger to find me. Now tell me why you came."

"I have been trained as an assassin, but I do not have the heart of one. I will tell you what is in my heart." She rose, relit the candle, and sat down in front of him.

Looking at her again in the light, Shao-yu saw that her hair, fastened high with a golden hairpin, was like a dark cloud. She wore a military jacket with narrow sleeves embroidered with small pink flowers. Her boots were high-backed, shaped like a phoenix tail, and she wore a dragon scabbard for her sword. Her face was like a wild rose covered in morning dew, and when she spoke with cherry-red lips her voice was like an oriole's.

"I am originally from Yang-chou from a family that has been T'ang subjects for generations. I lost my parents when I was a child, but I was found by a woman who became my teacher and I her disciple. She was a master of the sword, and of her disciples, three were the best: Chen Hai-yüeh, Chin Ts'ai-hung, and me—Shen Niao-yen.[15]

"After devoting myself for three years to the art of the sword, I also learned the art of transformation. I can ride the wind, follow the lightning, and traverse a thousand *li* in an instant. The three of us were equally matched in our swordsmanship, but whenever our teacher wanted to destroy an enemy or kill some evil person, she would always send Hai-yüeh or Ts'ai-hung. She never once sent me.

"I could not get over my anger at this, and I asked my teacher, 'The three of us have studied under you together, but I am the only one who never gets to repay your kindness. I do not understand. Is it that my skill is inferior, or do you not trust me?'

"My teacher answered, 'You are not really one of us. In time you will learn your proper path and achieve perfection. It would mar your virtue if I sent you to kill men like the others, and that is why I have never sent you.'

" 'Then what is the use of teaching me how to use the sword?'
I asked.

" 'Your destiny lies in the empire of T'ang, where you will
meet your master,' she said. 'He is a superior man. I have
taught you that humble skill so that you will be able to meet
him. You will have to enter a camp of thousands of men, where
you will find him among the swords and spears. The T'ang
emperor will send a great general against the Tibetan army,
and the king, Tsen-po, has advertised for an assassin to kill
that general. Take this opportunity. Go down from this mountain and go to Tibet and show off your skill as an assassin.
With one edge you apply your training, with the other you
meet the man for whom you are destined.'

"I did as my teacher said and went immediately to Tibet,
where I tore down the notice on the city gate and took it to the
king. He summoned me and tested my skill against the other
assassins. After I cut off the topknots of a dozen men, he decided I was the best and he chose me, saying, 'Bring me the
head of the T'ang general and I will make you my first consort.'

"But now I have met you, and it is as my teacher said. Please,
my only wish is to be with you, even if I must serve as a companion to your ladies-in-waiting. Will you take me?"

Shao-yu was very pleased. "I was condemned to die, but you
have saved my life and now you wish to belong to me? How
can I ever repay you? I wish we could marry and be together
for a hundred years."

And so they consummated their meeting. The gleam of the
sword served as nuptial candles and the boom of battle gongs
replaced the sound of lutes. Bathed in soft moonlight, that distant tent was more joyful than a silk-curtained bridal chamber. Their ecstasy soared like the mountains and thundered
like the ocean surf.

For three days, Shao-yu was under Niao-yen's spell and did
not bother to see his officers or troops. Niao-yen finally said to

him, "An army camp is no place for a woman. Your soldiers will be demoralized. I must go."

"But you are no ordinary woman," Shao-yu replied. "Why not stay and teach me some tactics by which I may destroy my enemy?"

"You do not need me," she said. "You are strong enough. You will cut them down like rotten tree trunks. I came here on my teacher's orders, but I have not said a proper good-bye. I must go back to her, and then I will await your return from the campaign and meet you again in the capital.

"If Tsen-po sends another assassin, I will let you know. They are not my equal, and since you have accepted me as yours, there will be no danger from them. Do not worry." She drew a jewel out of her belt. "This is called Miao-ya-wan, the Mystic Trinket," she explained. "King Tsen-po wore it as an ornament over his topknot. Please send it back with a message so he will know that I have no intention of returning."

"Do you have any other instructions?" Shao-yu asked.

"As you continue your advance, you will reach a place called P'an-she Valley. The water there is not drinkable. Be sure to have your men dig wells there so that they may drink." Then she threw down the jewel, leaped into the air, and was gone.

Shao-yu called his men together and told them what she had said. They all agreed that she would be good luck and a source of power to strike fear into the enemy. "Surely," they said, "she was sent by the gods."

PART II

AMONG THE
DRAGON FOLK

Shao-yu immediately sent a man to the enemy camp to deliver the jeweled pin to King Tsen-po. Meanwhile his army marched to T'ai-shan, where the path through the gorge was so narrow that only one rider at a time could pass. They followed the edge of a stream along the base of a cliff for many miles before they found a place open enough to pitch camp and rest.

The soldiers were exhausted and thirsty and went searching for drinking water but could not find any. They searched until they discovered a large lake under the mountain, but when they eagerly drank from it, they turned green and they gasped for breath, unable to speak.

Shao-yu was disturbed by this news and went to investigate in person. The water was dark and too deep to measure, as cold as autumn frost. He realized this must be the P'an-she Valley of which Niao-yen had warned him. He ordered the other soldiers to dig wells, but though they dug in a hundred different places, they found no fresh water.

Discouraged, Shao-yu ordered his men to move the camp. Suddenly, the valley shook with the sound of war drums from the cliffs. The Tibetans, hiding in the gorge, had cut off the narrow path and any means of escape.

With his soldiers dying of thirst and now trapped by the Tibetan army, Shao-yu sat in his tent trying to think of a way out of the predicament. He was exhausted, dozing off against the table, when, suddenly, the tent was filled with strange fragrances. Two young girls stood before him, looking as if they could be fairies or ghosts. "We have come to deliver a message from our mistress," they said. "Please accept her invitation to visit her."

"Who is your mistress?" Shao-yu asked. "And where does she abide?"

"She is the youngest daughter of the Dragon King of Lake Tung-t'ing," they answered. "She left her father's palace for a time and now lives nearby."

"The Dragon King lives underwater and I am only a man," said Shao-yu. "By what magic could I make a visit?"

They replied, "There is a heavenly horse already waiting for you. You may ride it safely to the Underwater Palace."

So Shao-yu followed the girls to the gate of the camp, where he found the Dragon King's retinue assembled outside in strange garb. One of them held a spotted horse with a golden saddle. They helped him mount the horse, and it glided through the air, its hooves never raising dust, and they arrived under the water—as if it were perfectly natural—to a regal palace constructed of pearls and shells.

The guards had heads like fish and were bearded like shrimp. Maidens came out to open the gate and guide Shao-yu inside. In the middle of the throne hall one of the maidens asked him to sit in a chair of white jade facing south. They put a silken cushion on the floor at the foot of the steps and withdrew.

Then a dozen attendants entered, accompanying a lady from a room on the left side of the hall. Her beauty and the finery she wore were beyond description.

One of the ladies-in-waiting stepped forward and announced, "The daughter of the Dragon King requests the marshal's audience."

Shao-yu was struck with fear and indecision, but the maiden did not let him rise from his seat. In a moment the Dragon Princess bowed to him four times, her jade ornaments tinkling, the air imbued with the wonderful fragrance of flowers. Shao-yu bowed in return and asked her to sit beside him, but she declined and sat instead on the cushions on the floor.

Shao-yu objected, "I am a mere mortal and you are a Dragon Princess of the underwater realm. Why do you treat me with such exaggerated respect?"

She replied, "I am Po Ling-po,[1] the youngest daughter of the Dragon King of Lake Tung-t'ing. After I was born my father went before the Jade Emperor in Heaven² and asked Chang the Fortune-Teller to cast my horoscope. Chang said that I had been a fairy in a former life but that, for a crime, I had been banished from Heaven to be born the Dragon King's daughter. In time I would become human and marry a superior man with whom I would enjoy fame and fortune until, finally, I would dedicate myself to the Buddha and become a distinguished nun.

"We dragon folk belong in the underwater realms, but to be human is a great honor for us and we long to attain Taoist immortality or Buddhahood. My elder sister became daughter-in-law to the Dragon King of Ch'ing-shui, but she did not get along with her husband and our two families had a falling-out. She remarried, this time to Liu I, a mortal man, and my family and relatives admire and respect her more than the other sisters. But if I meet the one for whom I was destined, my honor will be greater than hers.

"After hearing what Chang the Fortune-Teller said, my father loved me more and the palace women treated me as if I were a heavenly creature.

"When I came of age, Wu-hsien, the son of the Dragon King of the Southern Sea, heard of my beauty and asked my father for my hand in marriage. Since we are subjects of the Southern Sea, my father could not refuse offhand—it would have been rash. But he went to the Dragon King of the Southern Sea in person to explain what Chang the Fortune-Teller had said and why he thus had to refuse the proposal.

"But the Dragon King spoke up for his prideful son, saying he did not believe such nonsense. He rebuked my father and hastened the marriage. I thought to myself that I would be disgraced if I stayed with my parents, so I ran away. I cleared some brush and built a house for myself in a remote place, and I lived a humble life, but the Southern Sea king only renewed his pursuit of me.

"My parents said to him, 'Our daughter does not want to marry. She has run away and now she lives alone in hiding.' Wu-hsien had no regard for my determination and he came at the head of an army to take me by force.

"But Heaven and Earth were moved by sympathy for me and the waters of the lake were transformed—they became cold as ice and dark as Hell and his troops were unable to enter. I was encouraged by this and have persevered until now.

"When I asked you here, it was not just to tell you my story. I know that your soldiers dug wells because they had no water to drink, but no matter how many they dug, they could not find any water, and now they are too weak to fight. This lake was originally called Ch'ing-shui-t'an, Clearwater Pool, but since I have lived here they call it Po-lung-t'an, the White Dragon Pool. The water has turned brackish, and anyone who drinks it becomes sick.

"But now that you are here, I have a man upon whom I can rely, who will care for me. It is like spring sun on the shadowed side of a hill. I have already promised myself to you, so now your troubles are my troubles, and I will do everything in my humble power to help the Emperor's army. From now on, the water will taste sweet, as it did in the past, and your soldiers may safely drink it. Those who became ill from it will recover once they drink it again."

"Now that I have heard your story, I realize we were destined for each other by the will of Heaven," said Shao-yu. "We must give ourselves over to the silken bonds of the old man under the moon.³ I understand what is in your heart."

The Dragon Princess answered, "I have promised myself to you, but there are still three things that make it wrong for me to marry you. First, I have not yet told my parents. Second, I cannot think of being intimate with you until I have changed my form. I am covered in scales, and I do not want to defile your bed with my fins and my repulsive fishy smell. And finally, Prince Wu-hsien is always sending his spies to watch me, and if he learns of our meeting, he will be furious and I am afraid of what he will do in his fit of anger.

"Quickly—return to your camp. Marshal your troops and destroy the enemy. Then you can return to the capital with honor, singing victory songs, and I will pull up my skirts and follow you across the river to Ch'ang-an."

"What you say is all very reasonable," said Shao-yu. "But

by my reckoning, you came here not only for yourself, but because your father told you to wait until I appeared in your life. So our meeting each other today is in keeping with your parents' wishes. And since your original form was that of a fairy—an ethereal creature—and there is no rule that prohibits relations between humans and spirits, why should I be repulsed by your scales and fins?

"Though I am not very wise, I command tens of thousands of soldiers serving the Emperor's will. The god of the winds is my vanguard and my rear guard is the god of the sea, so the Dragon Prince to me is naught but a mosquito or an ant. If he cannot see the grave error of his ways and continues to pester you, I will be forced to stain my sword with his blood.

"Our meeting tonight has been so auspicious it would be a shame to let it pass without consummating our beautiful new relationship." And so saying, he took her to her bedchamber, and their union was so ecstatic they did not know whether it happened in reality or dream.

❧

Just as the next day was dawning, the Dragon Princess was startled awake by thunderous sounds that shook the Underwater Palace. One of her ladies-in-waiting rushed into her chamber and said, "The Dragon Prince of the Southern Sea has assembled his army at the foot of the mountain! He demands a fight to the finish with Marshal Yang!"

"I was afraid of this," said the princess to Shao-yu. "This is why I said you had to leave."

"How bold of that madman to dare come here," said Shao-yu. He got up without hesitation and rushed to the riverbank to find that Wu-hsien's soldiers had already surrounded Po-lung Lake.

The earth shook with the sound of their clamor and they exuded their stench into the four directions. The Dragon Prince of the Southern Sea rode forward on his mount and challenged, "How dare you steal my wife! For that I will remove you from the face of the Earth!"

Shao-yu mounted his own horse and laughed in response. "My marriage with the Dragon Princess was the will of Heaven. Chang the Fortune-Teller foresaw it. I obey only the will of Heaven. How can you oppose it, you spawn of a fish?" He called his troops into attack formation.

Wu-hsien, in a rage, called upon every manner of fish.[4] His carp general and his turtle commander rushed forward, leading a brave and savage attack, but Shao-yu led the counterattack wielding his whip of white jade, killing them by the thousands until the ground was littered with their crushed fish scales and shattered turtle shells.

Wu-hsien himself was wounded several times by spear thrusts and could not transform himself.[5] He was captured and bound by Shao-yu's soldiers.

Shao-yu was pleased, and he called his army back by sounding the battle gong.

A sentry came and pronounced, "The Dragon Princess of Po-lung has come to congratulate you and she has brought wine so the troops may celebrate."

Shao-yu sent someone to escort her in. She congratulated him on his victory and had a feast prepared for the soldiers with a hundred barrels of wine and a hundred head of cattle. The soldiers ate their fill, thumped their bellies, and sang and danced, their courage a hundredfold greater than before the battle. Shao-yu sat beside the Dragon Princess and admonished Wu-hsien, who had been brought before them.

"By the Emperor's command I have defeated our enemies in the four directions. Ten thousand demons dared not oppose me, but you, naughty boy, not knowing the will of Heaven, fought boldly against my forces. It was suicidal of you. I have here the great sword that Wei Cheng, the minister of state, used to cut off the head of the dragon of the Ching River.[6] I should cut off *your* head with it for the honor of my soldiers, but the realm of the Southern Sea is a peaceful one and you provide rain that benefits the people, and so it is respected. Therefore I pardon you, but from this day on you must mend your ways and never trouble the princess again."

They sent him away, and he ran like a mouse to its hole, hardly drawing breath.

Suddenly, the sky in the southeast was infused with a bright glow and multicolored clouds, a glorious air. A messenger in red, bearing a flag and a halberd, descended from the sky and announced, "The Dragon King of Tung-t'ing, hearing that you have destroyed the army of the Southern Sea and saved the princess, desires to come to your camp to congratulate you. But being unable to leave his official duties, he has, instead, prepared a great celebratory feast at his summer palace and sends you this invitation. Please come. His Majesty has also instructed me to tell the princess to accompany you."

Shao-yu replied, "The Tibetans have withdrawn, but their camp is still here. Tung-t'ing is very far, and it will take a long time to make the trip there and back. How could I possibly go so far without deserting my command?"

"We have prepared a chariot for you drawn by eight dragons," the messenger replied. "You can be back in half a day."

STRANGE DREAMS

Shao-yu and the princess got onto the chariot together and it rolled into the air on a magical wind until they could see the clouds below them shading the earth like a parasol. Then the chariot descended lower and lower, and they were in Lake Tung-t'ing.

The Dragon King came all the way out to welcome them, receiving them as honored guests, and he treated Shao-yu like a son-in-law. Leading them to the great banquet, the Dragon King praised Shao-yu.

"As I am of little virtue, I was unable to make my own daughter happy," he said. "But you, with great dignity and skill, have captured the arrogant son of the Southern Sea and saved my daughter's honor. Your merit is higher than the sky and deeper than the earth."

"It was all made possible by the virtue of the Emperor," said Shao-yu. "What merit have I to claim?"

They imbibed together, at length, until they were both drunk. The Dragon King called on his musicians to play and sing for them, and their melodies were unlike anything in the world of men. A thousand warriors were lined up on either side of the hall with swords and spears beating drums, and six pairs of beautiful girls in lotus dresses with girdles of moonlight pearls danced in their flowing, long sleeves. It was a spectacular sight.

"What is that tune?" Shao-yu asked as he listened to the music.

"There was no such tune in the old days," said the Dragon King. "But when my daughter married the son of the Dragon

King of the Ching River, they did not suit each other. Liu I's writings foretold that she would have a hard life like that of a shepherd. My younger brother, the Prince of Ch'ien-t'ang, fought the Dragon King of the Ching River and defeated him after a fierce battle to bring her back. That is when the palace musicians composed this piece. They call it 'The Victory of the Prince of Ch'ien-t'ang.' Sometimes it is called 'The Return of the Princess.' They often play it during festivities in the palace. Now that you have defeated Wu-hsien and brought my daughter back to me again, it is so much like the story of Ch'ien-t'ang that we should call the tune 'The Marshal's Triumph' from now on."

Shao-yu asked, "Where is Liu I? Could I meet him?"

"Master Liu lives in the realm of the immortals and he cannot leave his duties there," said the Dragon King.

After nine rounds of drink, Shao-yu said, "There are many things I must attend to in my camp and I cannot stay longer. I wish Your Majesty a long and healthy life." Looking at the princess, he said, "Do not forget what we promised each other."

The Dragon King answered for her. "Do not worry. Her promises will be kept." And he came out of the palace in person to see Shao-yu off.

Shao-yu suddenly saw a mountain with five peaks looming above the clouds. He asked the Dragon King, "What is the name of that mountain? I have seen all the mountains in China except for Heng-shan and Pa-shan."[1]

"You don't know this mountain?" said the Dragon King. "It is the southernmost peak of Heng-shan. Haven't you heard of its strange wonders?"

"How could I get there?" Shao-yu asked.

"It is not yet late," the Dragon King replied. "You have time for a short hike up to it before the sun goes down."

Shao-yu thanked him and mounted the chariot, which took him to the mountain in almost no time. He found a trail that wound over a ridge and through a valley. The mountain was even higher than it had appeared. Its beautiful vistas were more than he could take in with a single visit. He recalled: *A thousand peaks compete for splendor and in the myriad ra-vines, the clamor of streams.*[2]

As he looked around, he was filled with melancholy thoughts, and he sighed. "My mind is tired and my nerves are frayed from the war. Why must I be so engaged with worldly troubles? After I have fulfilled my duties I will retire and live in nature, detached from the cares of this world of dust."

Just then, he heard the sound of bells ringing through the trees. "There must be a temple nearby," he said. Climbing to the top of the next ridge, he saw a secluded temple where an old Buddhist monk was sitting on a high seat giving a teaching from the sutras. He was thin and his pale skin nearly translucent. His eyebrows were long and white—he was obviously very old.

When the old monk saw Shao-yu, he stepped down from his seat and, with his disciples, came to welcome him. "Those who live in the mountains hear very little, and so we did not know you were coming," he said. "Please forgive us. This is not the time when you can stay, so visit the shrine room and make your offering to the Buddha there before you return."

Shao-yu went into the shrine room, burned some incense, and bowed to the image of the Buddha, but as he came down the steps afterward he stumbled and suddenly startled awake back at his camp, his head resting on the writing table. The sun was just coming up. He was confused, and he went out of the tent to ask his officers, "Have any of you had strange dreams?"

They answered in unison that they had all dreamed that they had followed him and fought a great battle against demon soldiers. "We routed them and took their leader captive," they said. "It must be a good omen meaning that we will defeat the Tibetans and take prisoners."

Shao-yu told them about his own dream and then went to Po-tung Lake with them. Crushed fish scales and smashed turtle shells were scattered everywhere and there was so much blood it flowed in streams. He took a gourd and drank some water from the lake and gave some to the sick soldiers, who quickly became well again. Then all the soldiers and their horses came to the lake and drank their fill. Their shouts of joy echoed through the hills, and the Tibetans were so scared by the sound they were ready to surrender at once.

∞

From the time he set out for the front, Shao-yu had sent regular dispatches to the Emperor, who was delighted to hear about his victories. One day, as he paid a visit to the Empress Dowager, the Emperor praised Shao-yu.

"Yang Shao-yu is like the great general Kuo of Fen-yang,"[3] he said. "When he returns, I will make him prime minister to reward him for his merits and his value to us. But we have not yet resolved the issue of the princess's marriage. If Marshal Yang changes his mind and obeys us, all will be well, but if he is obstinate and continues to resist, we cannot punish him because he has done so much for us. I am sorry, but I am at a loss as to how to deal with him now."

The Empress Dowager replied, "I have heard that Minister Cheng has a very beautiful daughter whom Yang has already met. I do not see how he will refuse her now. But if we order the Chengs to marry their daughter to someone else while Yang is still away, then he will give up hope. And then he will have no reason not to obey your command."

The Emperor said nothing, and after a long silence, he left the room. The princess Lan-yang had been standing by her mother, and she said, "Your plan is not proper, Mother. Lady Cheng's marriage is something that should be decided by her father—it is not the business of the royal court."

"This matter is very important for you and it is also an important matter of state," said the Empress Dowager. "I must discuss it with you. Yang Shao-yu is superior to all other men in both appearance and achievement. He is the minister of war. And I know he was predestined to be your husband when I heard of his flute playing. You cannot possibly pass him by and marry someone else.

"But for his part, he has become close to the Cheng household and neither party desires to break off the engagement. It has become a complicated matter. If we allow him to take the

Cheng girl as a concubine, Yang cannot refuse if we order him to marry you upon his return. However, I hesitate to do this without hearing your thoughts."

"All my life I have never known jealousy," said the princess. "There is no reason I should be jealous of the Chengs' daughter now. Yang was betrothed to her first, so it is not proper for him to take her as a concubine. The Cheng family is well respected and they have been ministers for many generations. It would be humiliating for them if their daughter were to be taken as a concubine. That would be unjust."

"Then what do you suggest is the right thing to do?" asked the Empress Dowager.

The princess replied, "The law permits all noblemen three wives. When Marshal Yang returns, he may be made a prince—a high-level retainer,[4] at the least. There is no reason for him then not to have two wives. Why not allow him to have the Chengs' daughter as a wife, too?"

"Impossible!" said the Empress Dowager. "You are the beloved daughter of the late emperor and the beloved sister of the current emperor. How can you suggest that someone of your elevated status share a husband with a commoner?"

The princess replied, "In the old days a wise and upright ruler held virtue in highest esteem and honored good scholars regardless of their social position. What they loved was virtue, and an emperor with ten thousand chariots at his beck and call would have a lowborn man as a friend. So how can we make an issue of who is high and who is low?

"From what I have heard, Lady Cheng surpasses all other women in her physiognomy and manner. If that is true, to be compared to her would not be a disgrace, but an honor. But, since hearsay is not to be trusted and is usually contrary to reality, I will arrange to see her myself. If her looks, talent, and virtue are superior to mine, I will be happy to serve her. And if not, then I will not mind her being made a concubine or a servant."

The Empress Dowager was impressed. "It is natural for women to be jealous of another woman's talent and looks. But as your mother, I am happy to see that you love another girl's qualities as if you are thirsty and searching for water. Tomorrow,

I will meet the Cheng girl and I will have an edict sent to her father."

The princess said, "Even if the Emperor orders it, Lady Cheng is likely to feign illness and not come. And we cannot force her to come—she is the daughter of a minister, after all. But if you tell a priestess or a nun to inform us when she will go to burn incense next, it should be easy to meet her then."

The Empress Dowager agreed to the plan and immediately sent a eunuch to the local temples.

At the Ting-hui-yuan Temple, a Buddhist nun told him, "Lady Cheng never comes here herself, but her servant, Chia Ch'un-yün, who is Marshal Yang's concubine, brings her prayers in writing and leaves them on the shrine."

The eunuch took the prayer from the shrine and delivered it to the Empress Dowager.

"It sounds as if it will be very difficult to see the Cheng girl," she said, and she unfolded the prayer and read it together with the princess.

The humble disciple Cheng Ch'iung-pei respectfully prays at your shrine, sending my servant, Ch'un-yün, who has fasted and purified herself, to offer my prayers to the Lord Buddha. I have many sins and my accomplishments are few. I was born into this life a girl with no brothers or sisters. Recently, I received be-trothal gifts from Yang Shao-yu and sincerely desired to marry him, but then he was chosen to be the husband of the royal prin-cess by imperial command, and now I do not know what to do. I can only lament that the will of Heaven is contrary to the ways of man. I have no hope. I have given him my heart, though not yet my body, and so I will remain with my parents and devote the rest of my life to them.

As I have received refuge from my life of suffering, I offer my de-votion to the Buddhas, revealing what is in my heart of hearts. I pray that the Bodhisattva of Compassion will look into my heart and have mercy on me. Let my elderly parents live long lives free from sickness and suffering, and let me serve them with a joyful heart. When they have departed this world, I will return to the

Buddha, renouncing this world, repaying the kindness of the bod-hisattvas with devotion, reciting sutras, maintaining my chastity.

Since Ch'un-yün's karma is bound to mine, though we are mistress and servant, in our hearts we are sisters. She has already become Minister Yang's concubine in obedience to my father. But things have not gone according to our wishes and she has left him to return once again to me in order that we may share our fates together.

I pray the Buddha will look into our hearts and grant that we not be reborn as women again, and cleanse us of the sins of our former lives. Bless us that we may be reborn into a better world and have good fortune, peace, and happiness forevermore.

When the princess finished reading, she frowned and said to her mother, "To ruin the lives of two women for the sake of my marriage is not proper."

The Empress Dowager said nothing.

಄

At this time, Ch'iung-pei looked as if she were cheerfully attending to her parents, showing no sign of unhappiness, but whenever her mother saw her, she felt sorry for her daughter. And Ch'un-yün, who had served her faithfully and long as her companion, tried her best to distract her with literature and embroidery, pretending nothing was amiss. But Ch'iung-pei's heart was heavy, and she could find no peace. She was thinking of her parents and of Ch'un-yün, and her heart was troubled.

One day, a girl came to the house with two embroidered scrolls for sale. When Ch'un-yün unrolled them, she saw that one showed a peacock among flowers and the other was a partridge in a bamboo grove. Ch'un-yün was impressed by the scrolls, and she asked the girl to wait while she showed them to Ch'iung-pei and her mother. "You always praise my embroidery," she said to them, "but look at these! They must have come from the hands of a fairy or a ghost!"

Ch'iung-pei looked at the scrolls with her mother, exclaiming, "No one in this world could be so exquisitely skilled! It's strange—it looks like old traditional work, but the colors and decorative touches are fresh." She made Ch'un-yün ask the girl where she had gotten the scrolls.

The girl answered, "My mistress did them. She is living away from home and she desperately needs the money, so I am to sell them without quibbling about the price."

"What is your mistress's family?" Ch'un-yün asked. "And why is she living away from home?"

The girl said, "My mistress is the sister of Subprefect[5] Li. He took their mother with him to his post in Che-tung, but my mistress could not go because she was ill. She had to stay behind at the house of her mother's brother, Subprefect Chang. But there were problems in the Changs' household, so she moved to a cosmetics shop across the way, where she is staying in the home of Hsieh San-niang while she waits for a carriage to come from Che-tung to take her home."

Ch'un-yün went in and told the story to Ch'iung-pei, who gave her a long hairpin and other jewelry—enough to pay for the scrolls, which she hung in the main hall. They admired them all day, praising them until the sun went down. Afterward, the girl who sold the pictures visited the Chengs' household frequently and became friendly with the servants.

"If Miss Li's embroidery is this good, she must be an extraordinary person," Ch'iung-pei said to Ch'un-yün. "I will send one of the maids to follow that girl to get a look at her."

She sent her most clever maid, who followed the girl to a common house, very small, and with no separate quarters for the men and women, just the way the girl had described.

When Miss Li learned that the maid had come from the Chengs' house, she gave her something good to eat before she sent her back. And upon her return, the maid reported to Ch'un-yün that Miss Li was as beautiful and well-mannered as her own mistress.

But Ch'un-yün was doubtful. "I can see from her embroidery that she is hardly stupid, but why do you make up such a story? I cannot believe there is anyone in the world as beautiful as our mistress."

The girl replied, "If you do not believe me, then send someone else to confirm that what I said is true."

So Ch'un-yün secretly sent another girl to the house, and when she returned, she said, "Her beauty is unearthly! What you heard yesterday is true. If you doubt me, go and see for yourself."

"I don't believe either of you," said Ch'un-yün. "Don't you have eyes to see?" They all had a laugh together.

A few days later, Madame Hsieh from the cosmetics shop came to see Lady Cheng. "A young woman, Subprefect Li's sister, has been living in my house of late," she said. "I have never seen such a talented and beautiful girl before. She has heard of your daughter and deeply admires her. She would like to meet her and chat, but she has never been introduced and is too shy to ask. She knows I often come to see you, so she asked me to tell you."

Ch'iung-pei's mother immediately called for her and told her. Ch'iung-pei said, "I am fortunate not to want to see anyone, but I've heard that her personality is as wonderful as her embroidery, so I would like to meet her."

Madame Hsieh returned, delighted, and the next day, Miss Li sent a servant ahead to say she was coming. She arrived later, accompanied by several of her maids in a curtained sedan chair.

Ch'iung-pei received her in her bedroom, and they sat, regarding each other, hostess and guest, one facing east and the other west, like the Weaver Girl visiting the Palace of the Moon or Lady Shang Yuan at Jewel Lake. Like mirror images reflecting the other's beauty and radiance, they were amazed at each other.

Ch'iung-pei spoke first. "I heard from the servants that you've been living nearby, and I am sorry I was not able to visit you. And now that you've come in person, I don't know how I can thank you."

"I am an uneducated person," said Miss Li. "I lost my father when I was little and my mother doted on me. I never learned anything in my life, and have no talent to speak of. I've often regretfully said to myself, 'A girl is shut up in the inner quarters, seeing no one but her household servants. A boy is free to go where he pleases, make friends, and watch and learn from other boys.'

"I've heard that you write as well as Pan Chao, the woman who finished her brother's writings,[6] and your virtue is like that of Meng Kuang, the paragon of womanhood.[7] And though you have never ventured out of your house, your reputation is known in the palace. So, not considering my own lack of worthiness, I wanted to come and meet you. And now that you have not denied me, I feel my life's wish has been fulfilled."

Ch'iung-pei replied, "What you say is exactly how I feel myself. Confined as I am in the inner quarters, I am in the shadows, not seen by the eyes of others. I have never seen the water in the ocean or the clouds on the mountaintops. I am like the jade of Ching-shan,[8] its beauty hidden for fear of vanity, or an old oyster shell that hides the luster of its pearl inside. I know so little, really, that I am ashamed to be so highly praised by you."

Tea and cakes were brought out, and as they continued to chat, Miss Li asked, "I've heard that you have a woman named Chia in your house. Is it possible for me to meet her?"

"I was going to introduce you," said Ch'iung-pei, and she sent for Ch'un-yün. When Miss Li stood up to greet her as she entered, Ch'un-yün was stunned. "What the maids said the other day is true," she thought to herself. "Heaven created my mistress and also Miss Li. Its will is truly a mystery."

Miss Li was also thinking to herself, "I have heard much about this girl, but she is far more beautiful than they say. It is no wonder that Minister Yang loves her. She would be the perfect partner for Lady Ch'in. If she could only meet her! How can Yang be expected to give up either of them when they are both so beautiful and talented?"

As they talked, she told Ch'un-yün what was in her heart, and thus Ch'un-yün could see that her heart was the same as Ch'iung-pei's. When it was time to go, Miss Li said, "The sun is setting and I am sorry we cannot talk any longer. But my house is only just across the street, and I will come out again when I have a chance and continue our chat."

"I am glad to have met you and I have enjoyed our talk," said Ch'iung-pei. "I should come out to see you off, but my situation is not like that of other people, so I dare not take even one step outside the house. I hope you understand and will forgive me."

When they said good-bye, they could not bear to let go of each other's hands. After Miss Li finally left, Ch'iung-pei said to Ch'un-yün, "The jeweled sword was hidden in its scabbard, and yet its light shone to the seven stars,[9] and though the oyster is buried deep in the bed of the sea, the light of its pearl rises up like a high tower. How strange that we have been living in the same city all this time without being aware of each other."

"I am suspicious," said Ch'un-yün. "Minister Yang said he met the daughter of an Inspector Ch'in at a pavilion in Huachou and he made a marriage contract with her after exchanging poems.

"But the Ch'in family came to grief and the marriage came to nothing. He said she was beautiful, and the poem she wrote shows she had great talent. I fear she has changed her name and is trying to revive an old relationship by getting close to you."

"I've also heard how beautiful Ch'in's daughter is," said Ch'iung-pei. "She must be very much like this woman. But didn't Yang say that she became a lady-in-waiting at court after her family was ruined? So how can it be her?" With that, Ch'iung-pei went to see her mother and had nothing but praise for Miss Li.

"Then I must invite her again so I can see her for myself," said Madame Ts'ui.

෧෨

A few days later, Madame Ts'ui sent for Miss Li to come visit her. When Miss Li came over, delighted with the invitation, Madame Ts'ui came out and received her in the front courtyard. Miss Li bowed politely as if she were a niece. This made

Madame Ts'ui happy, and she said, "Thank you for coming to visit my daughter the other day. It is very kind of you to be a friend to her. I am truly grateful, and it shames me that I have been ill and was unable to meet you then. I have been regretting it ever since."

Miss Li bowed on the floor. "I wanted so much to meet your daughter. She is like a fairy, and I was afraid she would refuse me. But when I met her, she treated me like a sister and now you treat me like your own child. It is an undeserved honor and more than I dared to hope for. I will visit you as long as I live and serve you as I would my own mother."

Madame Ts'ui declared again and again that it was too much. Her daughter and Miss Li sat with her for half the day and then Ch'iung-pei invited Miss Li and Ch'un-yün into her bedroom, where they sat like three legs of an incense burner, laughing and chatting happily, already good friends, discussing ancient and new literature, and the lives of virtuous women, not noticing that the sun was slanting through the west-facing windows.

夢

THE TAKING OF CH'IUNG-PEI

After Miss Li left, Madame Ts'ui said to Ch'iung-pei and Ch'un-yün, "Between our families on my husband's side and mine, we must have a thousand relations, but never in my life until now have I come across a woman as beautiful as Miss Li. She is as beautiful as you, Ch'iung-pei. It would be wonderful if you considered each other sisters."

Ch'iung-pei recollected what Ch'un-yün had said earlier about the Ch'in girl. "Ch'un-yün said she was suspicious, but I can't help but disagree. Miss Li is not only beautiful and well-mannered, she has a dignified bearing that sets her apart from women of a common background. The Ch'in girl would not be like that. However, I've heard that the princess Lan-yang is beautiful and gracious, and I dare to suspect Miss Li may actually be the princess."

"I have never seen the princess, so I will not presume to guess," said her mother. "But she is royalty—of the Emperor's family. How could we possibly mistake her for Miss Li?"

"When I think of Miss Li, I cannot help but wonder," said Ch'iung-pei. "I think it makes sense to send Ch'un-yün to find out more about her."

Ch'iung-pei and Ch'un-yün were still talking about this the next day when Miss Li's maid came to the house to deliver a message. "My mistress had the good fortune of finding a boat bound for Che-tung. She will be leaving on it tomorrow, and she asks if she may come and say good-bye to you all today."

Ch'iung-pei had the main room readied and waited for Miss Li. When she arrived to say her good-byes, her affection was so deep it was as if she were an older sister lingering in parting from her younger sister, or even a lover parting with his sweetheart.

Finally, she got up, bowed, and said, "It has already been a whole year since I last saw my mother and my brother. I am so eager to see them my heart flies to them like an arrow. I cannot stay longer, but your ladyship's kindness and your daughter's affection have tied me to you with thread that tightens the more you try to loosen it." She hesitated. "There is a request I would like to make of your daughter, but I am afraid she may not want to grant it, so I am telling you, first."

"What is it you want to ask her?" Madame Ts'ui asked.

"I have almost finished embroidering an image of the Bodhisattva of Mercy in memory of my dead father. My brother is in Che-tung now and I am a woman, so I cannot ask any other learned man to write a few lines to go with it. Without a proper inscription, the embroidery will have been in vain. This would be such a shame, so I wish your daughter would write something on it for me. It is too big to fold up, and I dared not bring it with me for fear of damaging it. I want to fulfill my filial duties and make our parting less sorrowful, but since I do not know what she will think, I hesitated to ask her directly. That is why I am first confiding in you."

Madame Ts'ui turned to her daughter and said, "You do not visit even your close relations. But her request is sincere and comes from her devotion to her father. Her house is nearby—it shouldn't be hard for you to go over for a little while."

Ch'iung-pei had misgivings at first, but she soon changed her mind. She thought to herself, "She is leaving very soon, so I cannot send Ch'un-yün. I shall take this opportunity to visit her." To her mother, she said, "If Miss Li's request was a casual one, I would never do this, but how can anyone not be moved by such filial devotion? I cannot refuse her, but I will go after it is dark."

Miss Li was very pleased and thanked her. "It will be hard to write after the sun goes down," she said. "If it's the crowds in the street that make you anxious, you can ride with me in

my palanquin. There is room enough for two, and you could
return this evening."

"That seems reasonable," said Ch'iung-pei.

Miss Li bowed to Madame Ts'ui, held Ch'un-yün's hands in
good-bye, and got into her palanquin with Ch'iung-pei. They
left, followed by several of the Chengs' maids.

When they were in Miss Li's bedroom, Ch'iung-pei noticed
that though she had few possessions, what she did have was
exquisite, and the food served to them was simple but deli-
cious. The more she saw, the more curious she became, and
she began to wonder. Miss Li did not seem to be in any hurry
to get the inscription, and the sun was going down, so Ch'iung-
pei asked, "Where do you keep the portrait of the Bodhisattva? I would like to honor it."

"I'll show it to you now," said Miss Li.

Just as she said this, there was a commotion outside and the
street was crowded with flags. A maid from the Cheng house
rushed in, terribly anxious, and said, "A company of soldiers
has surrounded the house! What are we to do?"

Ch'iung-pei immediately knew that her suspicions had been
correct, and she said nothing. It was Miss Li who spoke. "Please
do not worry," she said. "I am none other than Princess Lan-
yang, Hsiao-ho. Hsiao-ho is my given name. They have come
for me on the orders of the Empress Dowager."

Ch'iung-pei rose from her seat. "I am just an ignorant commoner and know nothing," she said. "But I could see that you
were of royal blood and not like ordinary people. To be visited
by Your Majesty was beyond my wildest dreams, and I did not
respect you properly. I fear I have greatly offended you and
humbly bow my head to receive the punishment I deserve."

Before the princess could answer, a servant girl came in to
announce the arrival of three court ladies, Hseuh, Wang, and
Ho, sent by the Empress Dowager.

"Sister, wait here a while," the princess said, and she went
out into the main hall and sat down on a chair to receive the
three women. They came in, and one by one they bowed and
prostrated themselves before her.

"It has been several days since Your Highness left the palace," they said. "Your mother the Empress Dowager is anxious to see you, and the Emperor is concerned about your welfare. You are to return to the palace today. We have come with your royal palanquin and guards to accompany you. They are waiting outside with the eunuch Chao, whom the Emperor has sent to escort you." They added, "The Empress Dowager has ordered that young Lady Cheng return with you to the palace in your royal palanquin."

The princess returned to the bedroom and said to Ch'iung-pei, "I will explain everything later when there is time, but the Empress Dowager is waiting to see you, so please do not refuse. Come with me, and we will see her together."

Ch'iung-pei already knew that she could not refuse. "I am just a lowly commoner," she repeated. "I know how much you love me, but I have never been presented at court and I am afraid I will make some terrible mistake in etiquette."

"My mother wishes to see you for the same reason I love you so dearly," said the princess. "There is no reason for you to worry."

Ch'iung-pei replied, "If Your Highness will go first, I will humbly return to my house and inform my elderly mother, then I will follow you right away."

"Please do not be uncooperative," said the princess. "The Empress Dowager has made her orders clear and she has already sent the royal palanquin for the two of us to ride together. You must come with me now."

"But I am a commoner! How could I possibly ride in the same palanquin with Your Highness?"

The princess reassured her. "In the old days, Chang T'ai-kung was fishing in the river Wei at the same time as King Wu. Though Chang was just a lowly fisherman, he rode in the same carriage as the king. Old Hou Ying was just a gatekeeper, but he once held the bridle of Prince Hsin-ling's horse. Those who are sincere and of good character deserve to be treated with respect regardless of status, so how can I consider myself a more important person? Sister, you are the daughter of a minister from a respected family. Why should you not ride with

me?" She took Ch'iung-pei by the hand to the palanquin and they got in together.

Ch'iung-pei sent one of her maids back to her mother to let her know where she was going, and she took the other maid with her to the palace.

The princess and Ch'iung-pei rode together through the east gate until they reached the Chang-hsin-kung, where the Empress Dowager had her quarters. The princess stepped out of the palanquin and instructed Lady Wang, "Wait here for a little while with Lady Cheng."

"The Empress Dowager has already ordered that a place be made ready for her," said Lady Wang.

The princess was made happy by this news. They had set up a canopy, and Ch'iung-pei went in to wait until it was time for her to see the Empress Dowager.[1]

After Ch'iung-pei had waited a while under the canopy, two court ladies came to her with a box containing new clothes and instructions from the Empress Dowager, which they read to her.

> Lady Cheng is the daughter of a minister and has received her gifts of marriage, but she is still dressed in the clothes of an unmarried girl. She cannot come before me dressed in that fashion, so I am sending her the ceremonial clothes of a wife of the first rank. She is to wear those when she presents herself.

Ch'iung-pei bowed low and said, "I am yet an unmarried girl. How could I presume to wear the robes of a wife of the first rank? The clothes I wear now are not ceremonial robes, but these are what I wear before my parents. Since Her Majesty is the mother of us all, I hope she will permit me to wear these clothes when I meet her."

The ladies went in and reported this to the Empress Dowager, who was much impressed and had them bring Ch'iung-pei into her room right away. The ladies-in-waiting on either side of the hall admired her and made much of her. "We thought only our princess was so beautiful," she exclaimed. "How could we not have known about such a beauty as Lady Cheng?"

When Ch'iung-pei had made her prostrations, the court ladies guided her up to the dais and the Empress Dowager told her to sit down. "You were made to break off your engagement with Marshal Yang because he was to marry my daughter the princess," she began. "It was a matter of state, a decision I did not make on my own. Indeed, the princess argued that to break one engagement to make another was unethical conduct, even for royalty. She suggested that both of you should marry Yang Shao-yu. I spoke with my son the Emperor about this, and we both agreed to accept the princess's suggestion.

"When Marshal Yang returns to the capital, we shall have him send the betrothal gifts to you once more and renew the plans for your marriage. This special dispensation has never occurred before in the history of this nation and is not likely to be given again. That is why I tell you this myself."

Ch'iung-pei prostrated herself in gratitude for this great favor. "Your Majesty's grace is too much for me and beyond my greatest expectation," she said. "This lowly being is unable to repay you. I am the daughter of a humble subject—how can I presume to accept the same status as Her Royal Highness the princess? And even if I did obey your command, my parents would regard it too great an honor and make me refuse it."

"Even your humility is admirable," said the Empress Dowager. "Your family has been renowned for generations. On your father's side it has been famous since the beginning of the dynasty. Your father was a minister who advised the late emperor. We need not concern ourselves about your status."

"A subject should obey the ruler the way nature follows the way of Heaven," said Ch'iung-pei. "Whether you make me a lady-in-waiting or allow me to remain in my low status and serve as a maid, I will obey. But what about Marshal Yang? Surely he will not be agreeable to your plan. I have no brothers or sisters, and my parents are old. My only wish is to serve them so they may live in comfort the rest of their days."

"I appreciate your devotion to your parents," the Empress Dowager replied. "But to sacrifice your future is not the only way you may be filial. You are beautiful and there is no fault in you. Marshal Yang will not want to give you up, and his destiny to marry the princess was clear from a single note blown on his flute. It is the will of Heaven. Yang is a hero whose like has not been seen in a hundred years, so I see nothing wrong in his having two wives.

"Once I had two daughters, but Lan-yang's sister died at the age of ten, and I have always worried that Lan-yang would be lonely. But seeing you, I see my dead daughter. I would like to adopt you. I will tell the Emperor to give you a royal title. It will be a sign of my love for my first daughter, and it will allow Lan-yang to be with you as she wishes. And it will permit you to marry Yang with her. What do you think?"

But Ch'iung-pei bowed her head once again and said, "If that is what you decide, I do not know if I can bear it. Please—change your mind and let me go on in peace as I was."

"I shall tell the Emperor of this and leave the final decision to him. Do not be obstinate!" The Empress Dowager sent for the princess, who came dressed in her ceremonial robes and stood next to Ch'iung-pei. That brought a smile to the Empress Dowager's face. "You wanted Lady Cheng as your sister and now I cannot tell which of you is the younger! Did you get what you wished for?" The Empress Dowager took Ch'iung-pei by the hands to show that she had become an adopted daughter.

The princess was overjoyed and, bowing to her mother, she said, "What you did is most appropriate and just. I cannot tell you how happy it makes me."

The Empress Dowager now treated Ch'iung-pei with a respectful affection and turned their conversation to classical poetry. "I have heard from the princess that you are a very gifted poet. The palace is beautiful and peaceful in the spring. Would you compose a poem for my pleasure? In the old days there was a tradition of the seven-character line. Could you do that?"

Ch'iung-pei bowed. "Since it is your wish, I will write one, but the result may only amuse you."

The Empress Dowager made one of the court ladies go and stand at the front of the hall. She was about to announce the theme for the poem when Princess Lan-yang interrupted. "How can you ask my sister to stand there and write one all by herself? I would like to write one, too."

The Empress Dowager was very happy. "What an excellent idea," she said. "I shall propose something fresh and new."

It was late spring, and beyond the railing of the pavilion, the peach trees were covered in blossoms. All at once, a magpie sang out from its perch in the branches. The Empress Dowager pointed to it. "I have just decided on the issue of your marriages and now the magpie marks the happy occasion. How auspicious! So that will be the theme. You must use seven characters in a four-line stanza, and conclude with an allusion to the betrothal.

She ordered the ladies-in-waiting to prepare paper and brushes.

When the princess and Ch'iung-pei lifted their brushes to begin, the lady at the front of the hall began to take her seven measured steps. The brushes flickered like a sudden cloudburst, and they were finished before the lady had gone more than five.

The Empress Dowager read Ch'iung-pei's poem first.

> A happy magpie circles the inner palace
> As spring breathes over the peach blossoms.
> Come—nest in comfort—fly not south;
> A pair of stars twinkles in the eastern sky.

Then she read the one composed by the princess.

> Myriad peach blossoms in the deepening spring,
> A happy magpie, bringing good news,
> With a great push, bridges the Milky Way,
> And two of Heaven's children—their timely joining.

"I have two daughters who are like Li T'ai Po and Ts'ao Chih,"[2] she declared, surprised by their talent. "If the court were to choose officials from among women, you two would be the best." She showed each poem to the other girl and they sighed in mutual admiration.

The princess said to her mother, "My stanza could have been written by anyone, but Ch'iung-pei's poem is so refined that mine does not even bear comparison."

"That is true," said the Empress Dowager. "But yours is also neatly structured and quite delightful."

SHAO-YU'S REGRET

At that moment, the Emperor came to see his mother.

The Empress Dowager sent the princess and Ch'iung-pei into the next room. "For the sake of the princess's marriage, I have had Marshal Yang return his betrothal gifts so as not to violate our customs," she said to the Emperor. "The Chengs would not find it acceptable for their daughter to be made a wife of equal status to the princess, and I simply cannot ask her to be a concubine. I had Lady Cheng here today, and she is beautiful and talented, worthy of being a sister to the princess. So I would like to make her my daughter and have her marry Yang together with the princess. What do you think of this?"

The Emperor was pleased. "It appears to be the blessing of Heaven," he replied. "Your grace is like that of ancient times, imbued with profound virtue, and I have no qualms about your decision."

The Empress Dowager called Ch'iung-pei to meet the Emperor, who told her to come up to the dais. "Now that Lady Cheng is the princess's older sister, how can it be that she is still wearing the clothes of a commoner?" he asked.

"It is because you have not said otherwise, but we will find her clothes appropriate for court," said the Empress Dowager, and she ordered the ladies-in-waiting to bring a bolt of crimson silk decorated with two phoenixes.

When it was brought in by Ch'in Ts'ai-feng, the Emperor took it, and as he raised his brush to write the royal edict, he asked his mother, "If we make her a princess, should we not also give her our family name?"

"That was my original intention," said the Empress Dowager.

"But the Chengs are elderly and she is their only child. It would be a shame if there was no one to carry on the family name. It troubles me. So, for their sake, and to show our generosity, let us allow her to keep her own surname."

The Emperor dipped his brush in black ink and wrote in bold characters:

Honoring the wish of Her Majesty the Empress Dowager, I hereby declare Cheng Ch'iung-pei to be the adopted daughter of Her Imperial Majesty and decree that she shall henceforth be called Princess Ying-yang.

When he was finished writing, he and the Empress Dowager stamped it with their royal seals. It was given to Ch'iung-pei, and the ladies-in-waiting were told to dress her in royal robes.

Ch'iung-pei came down from the dais and bowed to express her thanks. The Emperor determined the order of their seats in court, but Ying-yang, though she was a year older than Princess Lan-yang, declined to take the seat closer to the throne.

The Empress Dowager said to her, "You are now my daughter, the princess Ying-yang. The elder sits above and the younger below. That is the prescribed relationship for both brothers and sisters. How can you refuse it for the sake of humility?"

Ying-yang bowed and said, "Let us decide the order of sitting at another time. How could I not be humble?"

Princess Lan-yang said, "In the time of *The Annals of Spring and Autumn*, Chao Shuai's wife, who was the daughter of Duke Wen of Chin, gave up the first seat to the senior wife. We are sisters and you are older. What misgivings could you possibly have?"

But Princess Ying-yang persisted, and in the end the Empress Dowager had to order the matter to be settled according to age. Afterward, Ch'iung-pei was known as Princess Ying-yang and the court ladies served her faithfully.

The Empress Dowager showed the poems the two princesses had written to the Emperor, and he praised them both. "They are exquisite," he said. "But Ying-yang's poem alludes to the ancient *Book of Songs* and also pays homage to Lan-yang's poem."

"True," said the Empress Dowager.

"You love Ying-yang so much," said the Emperor. "I have never seen you like this before. Now it is my turn to ask a favor of you." He told the Empress Dowager about the lady secretary Ch'in Ts'ai-feng. "Her father was executed for his offense," he said. "But her ancestors were all loyal subjects. Let us be sympathetic to her situation and allow her to marry Marshal Yang and be his concubine after the two princesses are married to him. Would you be kind enough to permit this?"

The Empress Dowager turned to the princesses.

"Lady Ch'in told me her story long ago," said Princess Lan-yang. "I am very close to her and neither of us wishes to be separated from the other. Even if I do not order it, it is what I would want."

So the Empress Dowager called Ch'in Ts'ai-feng before her and said, "The princess wants to live with you through life and death, so I am ordering you to become Marshal Yang's concubine. From now on you must do your utmost to repay the kindness she has shown you."

Ts'ai-feng was so deeply moved she burst into tears as she expressed her gratitude.

The Empress Dowager said, "The marriages of the two princesses has been decided and a happy magpie has come to mark the occasion as auspicious. Both of the princesses have written poems about it, and now you must write one, too, for this momentous occasion."

Ts'ai-feng immediately wrote a poem and presented it to the Empress Dowager.

> Happy magpie, circling the inner palace
> As spring breathes over the peach blossoms.
> Come rest in comfort—do not fly away south—
> Stars twinkle in the eastern heavens.

"The theme given for this poem is very constraining, and we two princesses left hardly anything that could be said," Princess Lan-yang explained. "A new one was very hard to write, but her poem is beautiful. It alludes to the works of the masters, and there is not a fault to be found even in a single phrase—it is as if the ancient poets themselves had written it through Lady Ch'in."

The Empress Dowager answered, "In ancient times there were only four great women poets. Pan Chieh-yü the royal concubine, Ts'ai Yen, Cho We-chün, and Hsieh Tao-yün. But today we have three extraordinary poets here before us. It is truly a rare occasion!"

Princess Lan-yang remarked, "Ying-yang's servant Chia Ch'un-yün is an extraordinary poet, too."

By now it was getting dark and the Emperor took his leave. The two princesses retired to their bedchambers to sleep.

ॐ

The next morning at first cockcrow, Princess Ying-yang went to the Empress Dowager and asked permission to visit her old home. She prostrated herself and said, "When I came to the palace, my parents must have been anxious and awestricken. Please—would you allow me to go and see them today? I will tell them of your graciousness and my good fortune."

"It is not an easy matter for a woman to leave the palace," said the Empress Dowager. "I will invite your mother to come here instead so I may talk to her." And she sent for Madame Ts'ui.

The previous day, one of the maids the Chengs had sent with their daughter had returned to tell them that she had been taken to court and that she had been made the Empress Dowager's adopted daughter. They had been much relieved and grateful.

Madame Ts'ui, taken aback by the sudden royal summons, went quickly to the palace and was received by the Empress Dowager.

"I took your daughter for the sake of Princess Lan-yang's marriage," she said. "But once I saw her loveliness was like a flower and her intelligence was incomparable, I adopted her as my own daughter, and now she is Lan-yang's older sister. I think that she may have been my daughter in a previous incarnation, but in this one she was born into your household. Now she is the princess Ying-yang. We were going to give her the proper royal surname, but I realized that would end your lineage, so I did not have her change her surname. You have been very fortunate."

Madame Ts'ui bowed her head. "I had my daughter late in life," she said. "The arrangements for her marriage failed and I wronged her so terribly that, in my shame, I did not even know where I should go to die. Then Princess Lan-yang came to our house and became friends with her, and now you have brought her to the palace. How on Earth could this be? Even by doing everything in our power, with utmost devotion, we could not hope to repay one ten-thousandth of your graciousness.

"My husband is old and his health is failing. He has already resigned his position, but I could serve as a sweeper in the palace garden. Is there any way in Heaven and Earth to repay the Emperor for showing us such favor? I can only show my gratitude through these tears of joy." She rose and bowed deeply, then prostrated herself again, soaking her sleeves with her tears.

"Princess Ying-yang is my daughter now," responded the Empress Dowager. "You cannot take her with you again."

Madame Ts'ui replied, still on the floor, "I wish only that I could meet with her so that I may speak to her, praising you for your grace."[1]

The Empress Dowager smiled and said, "After the wedding, Princess Lan-yang will also come to you. Care for her just as you would Ying-yang."

Then the Empress Dowager called for Lan-yang, and when she came, Madame Ts'ui repeatedly begged the princess to forgive her for treating her with such a lack of courtesy when she had visited.

"I have heard there is a maid named Chia Ch'un-yün in your house," said the Empress Dowager. "I would like to see her at once."

Madame Ts'ui immediately sent for Ch'un-yün, and after a short while she arrived and presented herself before the Empress Dowager. She was praised for her beauty and told to come forward.

"Princess Lan-yang tells me you are a talented poet," said the Empress Dowager. "Would you write a poem for me now?"

Ch'un-yün prostrated herself, saying, "How could I possibly write a poem for Your Majesty when I am trembling so? But I will try my best if you will tell me the theme."

The Empress Dowager showed her the poems written earlier by the three girls and Ch'un-yün quickly composed hers and presented it.

> To express my joy, in humble devotion,
> I'll follow the phoenixes in the palace courtyard.
> As spring's myriad blossoms fill the Ch'in pavilion
> Is there a twig where the circling magpie may alight?

The Empress Dowager read it and gave it to the princesses, saying, "I would never have guessed she was this talented."

"The magpie in the poem is her and we princesses are the phoenixes," said Princess Lan-yang. "She has made the comparison very clear. Fearing I might not permit her to join us, she added a subtle hint in the last line, and she alludes to *The Book of Songs*[2] and the poems of Ts'ao Ts'ao,[3] merging them beautifully. The emotion in her poem is like the old saying, 'The birds of the air rely on man—how can man not pity the birds?'"

The princess took Ch'un-yün to meet Ts'ai-feng, explaining, "She is the daughter of Inspector Ch'in of Hua-yin, and you will grow old together."

"Then you must be the Lady Ch'in who wrote the willow poem?" said Ch'un-yün.

Ts'ai-feng was shocked. "Who could have told you about my willow poem?" she asked.

Ch'un-yün answered, "Marshal Yang thought of you constantly and would recite that poem from memory when he reminisced about you. That is where I heard it."

Ts'ai-feng was deeply moved. "Then he hasn't forgotten me." She sighed.

"How could you think such a thing?" said Ch'un-yün. "He carries that poem with him everywhere. He is in tears when he reads it, and he sighs when he recites it."

"If he still loves me as he did, I will die happy even if I should never see him again," said Ts'ai-feng. And she told them about how Yang Shao-yu had written the poem on her silk fan, and Ch'un-yün said, "I am wearing some of the jewelry he won that day." They began to tell each other stories, but a eunuch came to announce that Madame Ts'ui was leaving and the two princesses had to go back to say good-bye.

When they returned to the audience chamber, the Empress Dowager was saying to Madame Ts'ui, "Marshal Yang will return shortly and the betrothal gifts will be returned to your home. But now that Princess Ying-yang is my daughter, I want my two daughters to have a double wedding. Do you find this agreeable?"

Madame Ts'ui bowed to the ground and replied, "I will abide by Your Majesty's decision."

The Empress Dowager laughed. "Marshal Yang has resisted me three times for the sake of Princess Ying-yang. So I would like to play a trick on him. There is an old saying: 'Bad news turns out to be good news.' When he returns, tell him that your daughter took sick and died. In his letter to the Emperor, he described his meeting with her. Let us see if he can recognize her on his wedding day!"

Madame Ts'ui, having received the Empress Dowager's instructions, took her leave and returned home. Princess Ying-yang went out to the palace gates to see her off and then she called Ch'un-yün and told her about the Empress Dowager's plan to fool Shao-yu.

"I already pretended to be a fairy and ghost and fooled Marshal Yang. I feel bad about it. Isn't another trick like this too much?"

"It's not our idea," said Ying-yang. "It's my mother's."

Ch'un-yün could not restrain her laughter as she left the palace.

◈

Meanwhile, Shao-yu let his soldiers drink the waters of Po-tung Lake and they were getting well, raring to fight again. He assembled his officers, issued them orders, and mobilized his army to the sound of beating drums.

The Tibetan king, Tsen-po, had just received the jewel sent by the assassin Shen Niao-yen. When he learned that Marshal Yang's army had marched out of P'an-she Valley, he was on his way to discuss terms, but his own generals bound him and took him to Shao-yu's camp, where they surrendered.

Yang marched his soldiers into the Tibetan city, put an end to the looting, and pacified the people. Then he went up into the Koul Kun Mountains[4] and erected a commemorative stone with an inscription that celebrated the authority and benevolence of T'ang, and then the army marched back to the capital singing songs of victory.

It was already autumn when they reached Chen-chou. The land was bleak, the air chilly, the flowers wilted. The mournful honking of departing geese made the men long for home. Shao-yu retired to the guest house, but the night was long and quiet and he could not sleep.

"It's been more than three years since I left home," he thought. "My mother's health must be declining. Who will take care of her if she is sick, and who will look in on her every morning and every night? I have repulsed an invasion and achieved victory, but I have yet to fulfill my filial duty to her.

"I have failed her as a son. For years I have been so busy with my state duties that I haven't yet married, and it has been very hard to keep my promise of betrothal to Cheng Ch'iung-pei. Now I have reclaimed five thousand *li* of territory and pacified a million rebels, and the Emperor will surely reward me with a position of high rank to show his gratitude. Yet I would rather decline those rewards and ask instead that he allow me to marry Minister Cheng's daughter. But will he permit it?"

Somewhat comforted by these thoughts and feeling more at ease, he fell asleep with his head on the pillow. And he dreamed that his body flew high up into the heavens and entered the Palace of Seven Treasures surrounded by rainbow-colored clouds. There, two ladies-in-waiting met him and said, "Lady Cheng is asking for you."

He followed them into the palace to a wide courtyard full of flowers blooming. Three fairies were sitting in a white jade pavilion. They looked like royalty, and the brilliant light around them dazzled his eyes. They were leaning on the railing playing with flowering branches, and when they saw him enter they stood up to greet him.

When he was seated, the oldest of the fairies asked, "Have you been well since you left us?"

Looking closely at her, he realized that she was Ch'iung-pei, the girl whose inner chambers he had entered, with whom he had talked of music as he played on the *ch'in*! Amazed and delighted, he tried to say something, but he was unable to speak.

"I have left the world of humans and entered the Heavenly Kingdom," said the fairy. "It makes me sad when I am reminded of the past, and if you are to meet my parents, you will have no news of me."

Then she introduced the two other fairies. "This is the Weaver Girl and that is the Jade Fairy of the Incense. You are connected to them by your previous life. Please seek them out, reunite with them, and I shall be comforted."

Shao-yu looked at them—they seemed familiar, but he could not remember who they were. Suddenly, he was startled awake by the pounding of drums and he realized he had been dreaming. When he paused, trying to recall it, he knew it was not at all a good omen.

"Ch'iung-pei must be dead." He sighed to himself. "Ch'un-yün's recommendation and my aunt's matchmaking were all for nothing. Our betrothal is a failure and she is dead. Is this my karma? But they say a bad dream can be a good omen. I wonder if it is true of my dream."

☙❧

Months later, Shao-yu's vanguard marched triumphantly into the capital, and the Emperor himself came out as far as the Wei Bridge to welcome them. Shao-yu wore a golden helmet and golden armor, and he rode a majestic horse that could gallop a thousand *li*. He carried the long yak-tail spear the Emperor had given him, and all around him flew dragon and phoenix flags. Near the front of the procession was the cart that held the caged Tsen-po, the Tibetan king, followed by carts loaded with tribute from the thirty-six provinces of Tibet. Nothing like it had been seen before under Heaven.

Shao-yu dismounted and bowed low to the ground to greet the Emperor, who took him by the hands and raised him up, praising him for his victories.

An edict was immediately issued, just as had been done in the past when Kuo Tzŭ-i of Fen-yang had been given many awards along with his own territory over which he was made a prince. But Shao-yu insisted on declining these honors, and in the end the Emperor relented and issued an edict making him the prime minister and the Duke of Wei, giving him a town of thirty thousand households and other rewards too numerous to recount here.

Shao-yu followed the Emperor's carriage into the palace, and there he formally expressed his thanks for the gifts and titles. The Emperor held a great victory banquet and ordered a portrait of Shao-yu to be made and placed in the Ch'ilin Pavilion where the portraits of famous men were hung.

Afterward, Shao-yu left the palace and went to Minister Cheng's house, where the entire household—except for the minister and his wife—came out to the courtyard and bowed to welcome and congratulate him.

When Shao-yu asked after the health of the minister and his wife, his friend Thirteen replied, "My uncle and aunt were well until my cousin left this world. They were so grief-stricken they lost the will to live and are unable to come out to welcome you. Please—will you come with me to the inner quarters?"

When Shao-yu heard this he was dumbstruck. When he had recovered his wits, he asked, "Which of your cousins is it who died?"

"My uncle had no son and only one daughter," said Thirteen. "Heaven has neglected her. Isn't it tragic? What can one do but be sorrowful? But please—when you go in to see my uncle, try not to show your sadness."

Shao-yu wept until his collars were soaked with his tears.

Thirteen comforted him. "Your marriage contract was like

a dream come true, but this family's karmà is so bad that your engagement was hopeless from the start. So get ahold of yourself and do not be so sorrowful."

Shao-yu dried his tears and thanked Thirteen, and they went together into the inner quarters to meet Minister Cheng and his wife.

They were happy to see Shao-yu and congratulated him on his triumphant return, but they mentioned nothing about their daughter.

"I had the good fortune to save the nation from invasion and I have achieved great success and received the Emperor's favor. I have declined most of it, asking him only to change his mind and let me keep my marriage promise. But already the dew of morning has dried and the splendor of spring is faded. How can the living conceal their sorrow for one who has died?"

Minister Cheng frowned. "Today we are all gathered to celebrate your success," he said sternly. "We are not here to mourn—let us not speak of sad things."

Noticing Thirteen's sideways glance, Shao-yu followed him out into the garden. Just then, Ch'un-yün came down from the pavilion to meet them, and seeing her Shao-yu was reminded so much of Ch'iung-pei that he began to weep again.

Ch'un-yün knelt in front of him. "My lord, please do not be sad," she said, trying to comfort him. "Please dry your tears and listen with an open heart to what I have to say. From the beginning, my mistress was a heavenly being who was temporarily exiled in the world of mortals. On the day she reascended, she said to me, 'You once left Minister Yang to be with me, but now that I am leaving this world you must go back to him and serve him. He will return soon, and when he thinks of me and with sadness, tell him this to comfort him: Since the wedding gifts were returned, I am like a stranger to him, and if he is sad remembering the time when I listened to him playing the *ch'in*, tell him it is against the orders of the Emperor for him to be so self-indulgent. It is also not what I would wish.

"'And it is not a good thing. Also tell him that we should

not have any memorial service at my grave, nor should he weep for me after my death, and that if he does not follow my last wishes he would be insulting my memory. I would suffer for it in the next world. The Emperor is waiting for his return to discuss his marriage with the princess. Her virtue is like the devotion of the osprey as it says in *The Book of Songs*. That is what I want—for him to do as the Emperor says.' "

Hearing this, Shao-yu was even more grief-stricken, and he said, "Even if she left those words for me, how can I possibly help but be sad? If I died ten times over, I could still never repay her for such generosity." Then he told Ch'un-yün about the dream he'd had at the guest house on his way back to the capital.

It made Ch'un-yün cry. "Lady Cheng is in the Heavenly Kingdom, and you are sure to meet her there. Do not grieve so—it will make you sick."

"Did she say anything else?"

"There is something else," said Ch'un-yün. "But I hesitate to tell you."

"Tell me everything she said," Shao-yu replied.

"She said to me, 'You and I are of the same body. If he cannot forget me and he desires you as he desired me, if he would not desert you, I would still be loved by him.' "

Shao-yu became even sadder at this. "How could I possibly desert you?" he asked. "Especially now that I know she wanted me, in her last request, to keep you? Even if I were to marry the Weaver Girl in the night sky or have Fu-fei of the river Lo[5] as my concubine, I would never dream of deserting you."

梦

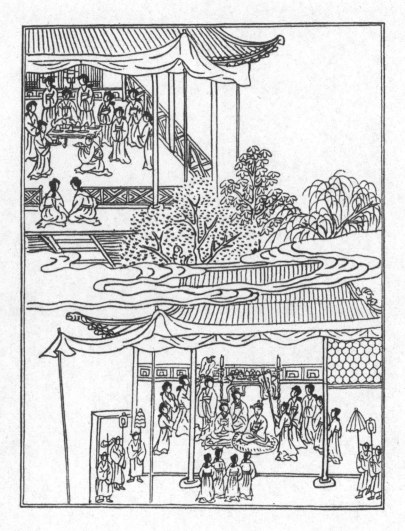

TWO PRINCESSES, TWO WIVES

The next day, the Emperor called Shao-yu and said to him, "Regarding the princess's marriage, the Empress Dowager issued a strict edict, and I was concerned. But now young Lady Cheng is dead and the situation is resolved. We had decided to hold the wedding as soon as you returned. You are at the peak of youth, with a high rank, and the time is nigh for your marriage. Your mother is still living, after all—how is she to perform all of her many duties on her own?

"The wedding will be held at your home, and as Duke of Wei you will need to hold a memorial service at the proper shrine. I have already prepared a place for you to live in the palace and now await the day of the ceremony to be decided. Do you agree to all of this?"

Shao-yu bowed and answered, "My crime of refusal deserves ten thousand deaths and yet you are so gracious and merciful that I know not where to crawl and die. I have presumed to agree to your plans, but I am of low birth, ignorant, and unskilled. I cannot possibly be worthy of being the princess's husband."

The Emperor was pleased, and he ordered the minister of rites to set the best date for the ceremony, and the court astrologer chose the middle of the ninth month as the most auspicious time. The Emperor said to Shao-yu: "I did not tell you before, because no firm time had been set for the wedding, but I have two sisters. They are both educated and superior in every way. I was looking for a husband like you for my second sister, but it turns out to be impossible. So I am going to follow the Empress Dowager's advice and ask you to marry them both."

Shao-yu suddenly remembered the dream he'd had at the guest house at Chen-chou. It was decidedly strange. Bowing to the Emperor, he said, "I was uneasy when you chose me to be the princess's husband, and now you say I am to marry two princesses? I have never heard of such a thing. How could I possibly agree to it?"

"Your accomplishments are the most distinguished in the history of our nation," said the Emperor. "I cannot reward you adequately, but I can give you both of my sisters in marriage.

"The two princesses are so close that when one stands the other sits, and when one comes the other follows. They cannot bear to be separated and want to grow old together. The Empress Dowager wants them to share a husband—you cannot refuse.

"There is also a lady secretary, Ch'in Ts'ai-feng, who is from a distinguished family. She is beautiful and intelligent, and the princess Lan-yang loves her very much. I suggest you take her as a concubine.

"I wanted to tell you all of this ahead of time," said the Emperor.

Shao-yu stood and bowed, and he thanked the Emperor before he took his leave.

❧

Princess Ying-yang had been in the palace for many months, serving loyally, getting along with Princess Lan-yang and Ts'ai-feng as if they were sisters, which pleased the Empress Dowager very much.

As the day of the wedding drew closer, Princess Ying-yang confided to the Empress Dowager, "When you decided on the seating order and put me ahead of Princess Lan-yang, I reluctantly accepted, though it was presumptuous of me, because I thought I might offend you if I was stubborn in my refusal. But now when we marry the prime minister, it is not proper for Lan-yang to relinquish her place again. It is my sincere hope that you and the Emperor will give careful thought to this issue so that I may have my proper position in the family and there will be no disharmony."

In a moment, Princess Lan-yang, who was with the Empress Dowager, said, "Ying-yang's virtue and talent have been like teachers to me. Even though she is of the Cheng household, I believe I should still yield my place to her like the wife of Chao Shuai. Now that she is the Emperor's sister and my older sister, how can there be a difference in status between us? Even if I am the second wife, that does not change my status as the Emperor's sister. If I was going to be the first wife all along, what was the point of adopting Ying-yang in the first place?"

The Empress Dowager asked the Emperor what he thought of the matter.

"Lan-yang is entirely sincere, but I have never heard of a princess doing such a thing even in ancient times," he said. "I say we should recognize the beauty in this humility and let things be as she wishes."

"You are right," said the Empress Dowager. And she ordered that Princess Ying-yang be made the first wife of the Duke of Wei and Princess Lan-yang the second wife. Ts'ai-feng, being of a distinguished family, was made a concubine of the first rank.

According to custom, the wedding of a princess had always been celebrated outside the inner palace, but this one, by the Empress Dowager's order, was to be held inside.

On the auspicious day, Shao-yu, wearing his jade belt and *ch'ilin*[1] robe, married the two princesses in a ceremony so splendid and ritual so solemn that words fail to describe them. When the ceremony had concluded and everyone was at ease, Ts'ai-feng came to join the princesses.

To Shao-yu, they appeared so radiant and serene it was as if they were three fairies come down from Heaven, and he could not help wondering if it was all a dream.

⁂

That night Shao-yu shared his pillow with Princess Ying-yang side by side in his bed. The next morning the Empress Dowager held a banquet in their honor, and she and the Emperor and the Emperor's concubine spent the whole day celebrating.

The next night, Shao-yu slept under the same quilt as Princess Lan-yang. And on the third night he came into Ts'ai-feng's room. It made her cry, remembering the old days. Shao-yu said to her in surprise, "Today is a day to be happy. You should not be crying. Please tell me why, whatever the reason."

"It is because you do not remember me," she said. "You have forgotten who I am."

He took her hand, pale as white jade and, looking into her face, he said, "You are the daughter of Inspector Ch'in of Hua-yin. I have not forgotten you even in my dreams."

She was so choked up, all she could say was, "Prime Minister . . ."

"I thought you were dead," he said. "But here you are in the palace alive! I am so happy you are here. After we parted at Hua-chou, I could not bear to think of the tragedy that befell your family, and since the time I fled from that place, not a day has gone by when I did not think of you. Today we are fulfilling our old promise, though I had given up hope and you, too, could never have imagined we would be together again like this."

Then he took her poem—the willow poem—out of his pocket and Ts'ai-feng took out the poem he had written and gave it to him. And they recited them together as they had the day they first composed them.

"This poem was what brought us together," Ts'ai-feng said. "But do you know how the silk fan has connected us?" She produced a box and opened it, taking out a painted fan. She showed it to him and told him the story behind it.

Shao-yu comforted her, saying, "When I returned from my refuge at Lan-t'ien-shan I asked the innkeeper what had happened to you, whether you had escaped the disaster. But I could find no reliable news about you and I lost hope. When I passed between Hua-shan and the river Wei, I felt like a wild goose without a mate or a fish caught on a hook. Now, thanks to the Emperor's favor, we are together again, and yet I am still regretful. When we met at the inn you could not have dreamed that one day I would be taking you as my concubine. It embarrasses me that I could not take you as my wife."

Ts'ai-feng replied, "I knew my fortunes were meager. When I sent my nurse to you at the inn I had already decided that if you were married I would gladly be your concubine. But now I am with the two princesses, and it is my great good fortune to serve them faithfully. If I sigh about my fate now, Heaven will forsake me."

And that night, awash in nostalgia and newfound love, their union was more ecstatic than on the previous two.

ᗦᖬᗦ

The next day, Shao-yu sat with Princess Lan-yang and Princess Ying-yang talking and drinking wine together in Ying-yang's room.

Princess Ying-yang whispered to a maid and ordered her to invite Ts'ai-feng to join them. But the moment he heard Ying-yang's voice in that tone, Shao-yu became melancholy, recalling the time he had disguised himself as a woman and gone to Minister Cheng's house to play the *ch'in* and listen to Ch'iung-pei's criticisms. He vividly recalled her face. Now he suddenly realized that Princess Ying-yang spoke like Ch'iung-pei and also looked like her. He thought to himself, "How remarkable that there is someone else in the world who looks like her. When I promised to marry Ch'iung-pei I intended to be with her in life and death, but now I am happily married to two other women. What must her lonely spirit be doing? To avoid jealousy, I have not even looked for her grave or offered a cup of wine or wept there even once. With her heart as fragile as glass, how could I not be distraught?"

Princess Ying-yang adjusted her clothes. "You are holding the glass and it is your turn to drink, but you look sad. What is the matter?"

"I cannot hide my thoughts from you," said Shao-yu. "I once went to Minister Cheng's house and saw his daughter. Strange, isn't it, that your voice and face are so much like hers? That is what made me sad."

Hearing this, Ying-yang's cheeks flushed red and she rose and rushed into the inner rooms. When she did not return after a long while, Shao-yu sent a maid to fetch her, but the maid, too, did not return.

"She is the Empress Dowager's favorite, so she is temperamental, unlike me," said Lan-yang. "When you compared her to the Cheng girl, I think you broke her heart."

Shao-yu immediately sent Ts'ai-feng in to apologize for him. "Tell her she may imprison me like Duke Wen of Chin," he told her.

When Ts'ai-feng returned after some time and was silent, Shao-yu asked, "What did she say?"

Ts'ai-feng answered, "She said, 'I may not be an important personage, but I am still the Empress Dowager's favorite daughter, and that Cheng girl may have been wonderful, but she was only a commoner. *The Book of Rites* says one bows to the king's horse not for its sake but because the king is riding it. I am the Emperor's sister.

"'That Cheng girl didn't know her place and had no modesty, proud of her looks and gabbing with him about music and rudely criticizing his playing. And I know she got sick and died because she was so peeved about her wedding being called off. What an unlucky person! How could he compare me to someone like her? In the old days, Ch'iu Hu of Lu seduced a girl who was picking mulberries by bribing her with gold and she drowned herself.[2] That's a true story. How can I just sit there and not feel shame when he's reminiscing about her after she's dead and tells me how he remembers her voice?[3] I am staying in this room now and won't come out again until I'm dead! Lan-yang can put up with him. Let him live the rest of his life with her!'"

Shao-yu was furious, and in his mind, he thought, "I did not think any woman under Heaven could be so proud of her position. Now I understand what a terrible thing it is to be the husband of a princess." To Lan-yang, he said, "I had my reasons for the way I talked with Ch'iung-pei, but Ying-yang is accusing me of shameful intentions. It is not important to me, but it is not right for her to be blaming the dead."

"I will try to calm her down," said Lan-yang, going into the inner rooms. But even when the sun had set, she did not return, and the candles and lamps had been lit by the time a maid came with a message from her.

I tried my best to convince her, but the princess would not change her mind. And since I made a promise to her that I would spend the rest of my life with her, I must do as she does and shut myself away in some corner of the inner palace. Please enjoy the night with Ts'ai-feng.

At this, Shao-yu's temper flared, but he restrained himself and did not let it show. The silence was long and the screens looked frigid. He reclined on the bed, gazing at Ts'ai-feng, who took up a candle and guided him into her bedchamber. She put incense into the golden brazier and turned down the silken bedding.

"I am not very learned," she said. "But I know some manners, and in *The Book of Rites*, it says, 'A concubine must not share her master's bed when his wife is away.' And since the two princesses have closed themselves up in their inner rooms, I wish you a good night." And she withdrew.

Shao-yu did not stop her, but his mood was foul. After a while, he went to bed, but he wrestled with his thoughts and he could not sleep. "They have put their heads together and conspired to taunt me," he thought. "I cannot go down on my knees for them. In the old days I lived in the Chengs' flower garden drinking with Thirteen by day and playing with Ch'un-yün by night. Not a day was unhappy. And now, after only three days being married, I am thoroughly frustrated!"

He raised his hand and opened the gauze window to see the Milky Way arching across the sky and the courtyard flooded with moonlight. He went out and wandered in the garden until he saw the lights in Princess Ying-yang's room, the candlelight so bright against the gauze of the windows. "The night is far gone," he thought. "Why are they not asleep? Ying-yang was furious and she abandoned me to go to her bedroom."

Quietly, he walked up to the window. He could hear the two princesses talking and laughing as they played backgammon. He peeped through the blind and saw Ts'ai-feng and another girl sitting in front of the princesses moving the pieces on the board. When the girl turned her body to adjust the candle, Shao-yu was shocked to see that she was Ch'un-yün. "How can this be?" he thought.

Ch'un-yün had come to the palace on the day the princesses were married, but she had hidden herself so that Shao-yu could not see her, and so he had not known she was there. He was surprised, but also suspicious that something was afoot. "The princesses must have brought Ch'un-yün to the palace so they could have a look at her," he thought.

Now Ts'ai-feng began another kind of game. "It's no fun unless there's something at stake," she said. "So I will make a bet with you, Ch'un-yün."

"I'm from a poor family, so I would be happy to win a bowl of rice with some vegetables," said Ch'un-yün. "Whereas you are with the princesses, and thus you have silks and jewels and many other things. I have nothing like that, so why would you want to make a bet with me?"

Ts'ai-feng replied, "If I lose, I will give you any of the jewels or trinkets I am wearing on my girdle, but if I win you must do whatever I ask as a penalty. I will not be too harsh."

"First I want to know what you will ask of me," said Ch'un-yün.

"I heard the two princesses talking once about how you pretended to be a fairy and then a ghost to fool Minister Yang, but I never heard all the details, so if you lose you will have to tell me the whole story."

Ch'un-yün pushed the backgammon board aside, saying, "Sister! You used to love me so much, but now that you have told that story to Ts'ai-feng, who in the palace will not have heard about it? How will I ever show my face?"

"Watch yourself, Ch'un-yün," said Ts'ai-feng. "How dare you call the princess your sister? She may be young, but her status is high. You should not be calling her sister."

Ch'un-yün apologized. "My lips have been calling her that for ten years. It is hard to retrain them in one morning. It seems just yesterday that we were fighting with each other while picking flowers, so I am not afraid to call her sister." She laughed brightly.

Lan-yang asked Ying-yang, "This little sister hasn't heard all of the story. Did Ch'un-yün really make a fool of him?"

"There's no smoke in the chimney without a fire," said Ying-yang. "She only wanted to give him a scare, but he was so smitten he wasn't even afraid. It's true what *The Book of Rites* says—'The lustful man is a hungry ghost for women.' He was so hungry for the ghost, why would he be afraid of her?"

This time they all laughed.

Listening to them, Shao-yu finally realized that Princess Ying-yang was Ch'iung-pei. He was surprised and overjoyed, and he was just about to open the door and burst into the room when he changed his mind. "They fooled me," he said to himself instead. "So I shall have to make fools of them." And he went back to Ts'ai-feng's room, quietly opened the door, and went to bed.

The next morning, Ts'ai-feng came early and asked the maid, "Is the master up?"

"Not yet," the maid replied.

Ts'ai-feng waited outside for a long while. From time to time she could hear him groaning and moaning inside, but even by breakfast time, Shao-yu had not gotten up. Finally, she opened the door and went in.

"Are you not feeling well?" she asked.

He stared at her with open eyes but did not seem to recognize her, and he mumbled incoherently, as if he were talking in his sleep.

"Are you having a dream?" she asked.

He looked like he might be in a trance. "Who are you?" he asked suddenly.

"Don't you recognize me?" she said. "I'm Ts'ai-feng."

He only nodded his head, whispering, "Ts'ai-feng. Ts'ai-feng. Who is she?"

Ts'ai-feng became greatly concerned and put a hand to his forehead. "You have a fever," she said. "How did you get so sick overnight?"

Now he opened his eyes as if he were coming to his senses.

"Ch'iung-pei has been tormenting me all night," he said. "What shall I do?"

When she asked him to explain, he simply turned over and went back to sleep. Ts'ai-feng was terribly upset. She sent a maid with a message to the princesses telling them that he was sick and they should come at once.

"He was drinking last night," said Princess Ying-yang. "He isn't sick. It's just a ploy to make us to come to him."

So Ts'ai-feng went to the princesses herself and said, "He is in a daze and he does not recognize anyone. He turned over to face the dark and he seemed delirious. Tell His Majesty to send for a doctor."

When the Empress Dowager heard, she summoned the princesses and reprimanded them. "You have taken this too far. You hear he is sick and yet do not go to see him? Go look in on him at once, and if he is actually ill, call the court physician."

So they went to his bedroom, and Princess Ying-yang let Lan-yang and Ts'ai-feng go in first. Shao-yu clawed at the air, staring wide-eyed, unable to understand what Lan-yang said to him. Eventually, he said in a whisper, "I have not long to live. I want to say good-bye to Ying-yang. Where is she?"

Princess Lan-yang said, "Please—do not say such things. Why are you speaking like that?"

"Last night I had a dream and yet it was not a dream," said Shao-yu. "Ch'iung-pei appeared to me and said, 'How could you forget our promise?' And she gave me a handful of pearls, which are a terrible omen. Now, when I close my eyes she presses down on my body and when I open them she is standing before me. How can I continue living?" Before he had even finished speaking, he made a strange expression and turned his face to the wall again, mumbling.

Lan-yang was very upset to see this and went out to Ying-yang. "The prime minister's symptoms are not normal," she said. "There is no doctor skilled enough to cure him—you are the only one who can help." She described his condition, but Ying-yang, still half-suspicious, was hesitant. Lan-yang took her by the hand into the bedroom.

"My lord," said Lan-yang. "Ying-yang is here. Please open your eyes and look at her."

Shao-yu lifted his head momentarily and opened his eyes. He struggled to get up until Ts'ai-feng finally helped him, and then he sat up in bed facing the two princesses. He sighed. "I have received the Emperor's special favor and married you two princesses to live happily together for a hundred years. But there is someone coming to take me, and it makes me sad that I cannot live much longer in this world."

"How can a learned and rational man like you speak such nonsense?" demanded Ying-yang. "Even if Ch'iung-pei's hungry ghost is lingering, the gods of Heaven and Earth watch over the palace. She could never get in. How could she come near my lord's precious body?"

"She's here—right beside me!" Shao-yu shouted. "What do you mean she can't get in?"

"In ancient times there was a man who drank a snake that was in his wine cup and got sick. But then he saw a bow hanging on the wall reflected in his wine cup and it looked like a snake. When he realized the snake he'd drunk was only the reflection of the bow, he got better. That is what your sickness is like. I'm sure you will get better."

Shao-yu just closed his eyes and waved her off. Princess Ying-yang could see then that this was no ordinary sickness. "You are only thinking of Ch'iung-pei as dead," she said. "Don't you want to see the living Ch'iung-pei? Here I am. It's me."

Shao-yu pretended he did not understand. "What are you saying? Why are you saying this? Minister Cheng had only one daughter, and she is dead! Her ghost is with me now so how can she be alive? The dead are dead and the living are living. There is no shame in death and the dead do not come back to life. I cannot trust what you say."

"The Empress Dowager adopted Ch'iung-pei as her daughter and gave her the name Ying-yang before the two of us were married to you," said Lan-yang. "But Princess Ying-yang is the one who listened to you playing the *ch'in*. She is Ch'iung-pei! How else could she look exactly like her?"

Shao-yu did not answer. He groaned and raised up his head, gasping for breath. "When I lived at the Chengs' house, Ch'iung-pei's maid Ch'un-yün took care of me. So I ask you now, where is she? I long to see her, but it is not possible and I am full of regret."

"Ch'un-yün is here in the palace," said Lan-yang. "She came to see Ying-yang."

Just then, Ch'un-yün came into the room, asking, "My lord, what is the matter?"

"All of you get out!" Shao-yu commanded. "Ch'un-yün, you stay in the room with me. I have something to ask you."

The two princesses and Ts'ai-feng went and stood outside at the railing in the hall. Shao-yu got up, washed his face, tidied himself, and dressed with Ch'un-yün's assistance, and when he was properly attired, he told Ch'un-yün to bring the others back in.

She went out, smiling, and told them, "He says you are invited back in." And so the four of them went back inside.

Shao-yu, wearing his white cap and robe of silver and gold, was sitting in his chair holding the white jade rod that was the symbol of his official rank. His face was fresh as spring, with not a trace of his illness.

Ying-yang smiled, realizing she had been fooled, and did not ask about his condition, but Lan-yang bowed and inquired, "Are you feeling better now?"

"I have been witness to outrageous behavior," Shao-yu said solemnly. "Women trying to fool their lord by the guile of their beauty. What happened to all the proper and well-mannered women of virtue?"

Lan-yang and Ts'ai-feng giggled, but said nothing. It was Ying-yang who replied, "We do not know of what you are speaking, my lord. If you want to know the whole story, perhaps you should begin by apologizing for your own trickery and then go and ask the Empress Dowager?" And then she told him how she had come to court with the princess.

Shao-yu could not restrain himself any longer and he burst into laughter. "I have examined this back and forth, playing it out with divine strategy, discovering how you beauties hatched your plot. Now I respect and admire even more the way the Empress Dowager shows her love for you, nurturing you like her own daughters, showing appreciation for your virtue and the friendship between you two princesses. I will do my best to keep our lives together happy."

The princesses and Ts'ai-feng, abashed, listened to him in respectful silence.

⨾⨾⨾

When the Empress Dowager heard from the court ladies about Shao-yu's feigned illness, she had a good laugh. "I suspected as much," she said, and she summoned Shao-yu to her room. When he arrived, followed by the two princesses, she asked, "Is it true? You have renewed the broken marriage contract you made with the dead Ch'iung-pei?"

Shao-yu bowed and answered, "Your grace is as great as the harmony of Heaven and Earth, and I could never possibly repay you."

"No need to flatter me for my graciousness," said the Empress Dowager. "It was all just a practical joke, after all."

Later that day, when the Emperor was in the main hall holding court, his ministers reported: "A bright new star has appeared, sweet dew falls each morning, the Yellow River flows clear, and the crops are abundant for harvest. The people are tranquil now that the barbarian tribes have surrendered—all due to Your Majesty's great virtue."

The Emperor received all of this with due modesty. And then they told him, "Prime Minister Yang Shao-yu has been dallying a long time in the inner palace and he is delaying matters of state that require his attention."

The Emperor laughed loudly at this. "The Empress Dowager has been summoning him every day—that is why he has not emerged. I will tell him myself to come out and get back to work."

The next day Shao-yu came out to his offices and saw to some of his official duties, and afterward he composed a letter to the Emperor asking if he could bring his mother to the capital.

Prime Minister, Duke of Wei, and Imperial Son-in-Law Yang Shao-yu humbly addresses Your Imperial Majesty. I am originally a lowly subject from Ch'u, without rank and of little talent. I sat for the national civil examination in order to provide for my aging mother, and after being favored with success, I have spent several years in the service of the court.

By your order, I fought and subdued powerful enemies until all of the barbarians of the west and the Tibetans were conquered. But I take no credit for this because it was all due to your virtue and imperial authority that my generals were willing to give up their lives. And yet you bestowed such high honors upon me that I was overwhelmed, and you chose me as your imperial brother-in-law, showering me with such grace and love that I know not how ever to thank you.

My old mother hoped for no more than a handful of rice, and I dreamed of nothing more than a lowly clerkship in a government office, but now I find myself prime minister and Duke of Wei, and preoccupied with my duties, I have had no time to fetch my aging mother. Now my circumstances and hers are profoundly different—while I enjoy luxuries and honor, she still struggles in poverty, and I fail in my filial duty to her. My mother is growing older, her health is failing, and she has no other children who can look after her. She lives far away, and news is slow and scarce; it breaks my heart to think of her.

Now that we are at peace I humbly bow to Your Majesty and hope that you will grant my sentimental request. Please give me leave to visit my ancestral graves and bring my mother back, so that I may do my filial duty and my duty to the throne. Then we may both pay our respects and receive Your Majesty's grace, and I will do my utmost to repay Your Majesty's favor.

When the Emperor finished reading the letter, he said, "I am moved by your filial piety, Shao-yu." He gave him a thousand gold ingots and eight hundred bolts of silk and told him to go see his mother right away. And when Shao-yu bowed thanks to him and went to the Empress Dowager to take his leave, she gave him more gold and silk. He thanked her also, bade goodbye to his wives and concubines, and left the palace.

When he reached the T'ien-chin Bridge at Lo-yang, the two courtesans Kuei Ch'an-yüeh and Ti Ching-hung had been alerted by the governor and were awaiting him at the guest house. Shao-yu met them with a smile, and he asked, "I am on a personal trip not ordered by the Emperor. How did you know I would be coming?"

They replied, "When the prime minister, Duke of Wei, and brother-in-law of the Emperor goes on a journey, it is known in the deepest mountains and the lowest valleys, so how could we not have heard of your coming? And, of course, the local governor respects us. He told us, but why didn't you let us know yourself? Last year we were very happy when you passed this way on your mission. Now that you have risen higher in rank and your official title is even grander, our reputations will also be a hundred times greater. We have heard that you married two princesses during that time. We wonder if you will accept us now?"

"One of them is the Emperor's sister and the other is the daughter of Minister Cheng, who was adopted by the Empress Dowager as her daughter," said Shao-yu. "She is the one you recommended to me, Ch'an-yüeh, so how could she not accept you? Lady Cheng and her sister have the great virtue of loving and tolerating everyone. It will surely please them to accept the two of you."

So Shao-yu spent the night with the two of them and started for his home village the next day.

ᏻᏻ

Shao-yu left his mother when he was fifteen years old, a student, and now, only four years later, he returned wearing the robes of the Duke of Wei, riding in a carriage befitting only those of the highest rank, as the Emperor's brother-in-law.

When he went in to see his mother she clasped his hands and shed tears of joy, exclaiming, "Are you really my son Shao-yu? I can hardly believe it. Only yesterday you were learning your numbers and characters. Who would have dreamed of such glory?"

Shao-yu told her about his achievements and how he now had two wives and concubines.

"Your father said you would bring honor to us," his mother replied. "I wish he were with us to see for himself."

Shao-yu visited his ancestral graves and held a great feast at home for his mother, celebrating with the gold and silks he had received on her behalf. He invited all his friends and relatives and the feasting went on for ten days. Afterward, he left for the capital with his mother, and all along the road, the local officials and the people came to participate in the glorious procession.

As they passed through Lo-yang, Shao-yu asked for Ti Ching-hung and Kuei Ch'an-yüeh, but was told by the governor that they had already set out for the capital several days earlier. Shao-yu was sorry to have missed them and immediately continued onward.

When he finally reached the capital, he took his mother through the palace grounds to his official residence, and then he went to the main audience hall to make obeisance to the Emperor.

The Emperor and his mother the Empress Dowager called for Shao-yu's mother, and when she presented herself they gave her ten carts loaded with gold and silver and bolts of silk. They moved her into a grand new mansion with large pavilions surrounded by great gardens dotted with lotus ponds.

The two princesses came to make their bows, and ceremonially introduced themselves to their mother-in-law as Shao-yu's new wives. Ts'ai-feng and Ch'un-yün also introduced themselves. Shao-yu's mother was overjoyed and her countenance was peaceful and content.

Following the Emperor's orders, Shao-yu used the gifts he had received and held a three-day feast, which was attended by the whole court. As the royal musicians played, Shao-yu sat in his colorful robes, attended by the two princesses. He passed the jade wine cup to his mother in the ceremony that introduced the new brides to his ancestors. Everyone rejoiced at the happy occasion.

In the middle of the banquet, a gate guard came in and said,

"There are two ladies outside who wish to see the prime minister and his mother. They have presented their name cards."

Shao-yu looked at the cards and saw they were from Ch'an-yüeh and Ching-hung. He told his mother who they were and had the guard bring them in, and when the two courtesans bowed in the courtyard beneath the stone steps, all the guests were impressed.

"Ch'an-yüeh is from Lo-yang and Ching-hung is from Ho-pei," his mother announced. "These names are famous and widely known. Now we see them here for the first time and they are exquisite beauties. This could only happen for a man like the prime minister!"

When Shao-yu asked them to show off their talents, the two courtesans put on their beaded shoes. Stepping up to the platform and facing each other, they performed a dance to the tune of "The Rainbow-Feathered Robe."

It was like flower petals floating in a spring breeze and the shadows of clouds against a screen. It seemed as if Fei-yen, the dancer of Han, had appeared in Shao-yu's garden, or Lu-chu, the beauty of Chin-ku, were standing on the duke's dais.

The two princesses gave them brocade and silk for their wonderful performance. Ts'ai-feng was an old friend of Ch'an-yüeh, and they reminisced together about the past. Princess Ying-yang personally offered a cup of wine to Ch'an-yüeh to thank her for the kindness of recommending her to Shao-yu.

"Why are you only thanking Ch'an-yüeh?" asked Shao-yu's mother. "Have you forgotten about my cousin the priestess?"

"For all I am now, I am in priestess Tu's debt," said Shao-yu. "And now that you are here, I shall invite her here also, even without an imperial edict."

He sent a messenger immediately to Chu-ch'ing Temple, but the priestess there sent back a message saying she had departed for the land of Shu[4] three years earlier.

Shao-yu's mother was sad to hear the news.

THE CONTEST OF BEAUTIES

Shao-yu arranged for each of his women to have a place to live in his palace compound. His main hall was Ching-fu-t'ang, the Hall of Great Happiness, and that was where his mother lived. In front of that hall was Yen-hsi-t'ang, the Hall of Feasting and Celebration, where Princess Ying-yang, his senior wife, lived. To the west was Feng-sho-kung, the Palace of the Dancing Phoenix, where Princess Lan-yang lived.

South of Yen-hsi-t'ang stood two buildings: Ning-hsiang-ko, or the Frozen Fragrance Hall, and Ch'ing-ho-lu, the Clear Harmony Pavilion, where Shao-yu himself stayed and sometimes entertained. In front of these was Yen-hsien-t'ang, the Hall for the Welcoming of Virtues, where Shao-yu received guests and took care of his official business.

Hsin-hsing-yüan, the House of New Delights, was where Ts'ai-feng lived, and it stood to the south of Lan-yang's palace; and to its east, next to Shao-yu's quarters, was Ying-ch'un-ko, the Hall of Welcome Spring, whose position was fitting because that is the direction of spring.[1] Ch'un-yün, whose name means "Spring Cloud," lived there.

South of Shao-yu's quarters there was a small, shining pavilion with blue tiles and red balustrades, and in it were rooms for the servants from both sides of the gate that led to Shao-yu's quarters. To the east of Frozen Fragrance Hall was Shang-hua-lu, the Flower-Viewing Pavilion, where Ch'an-yüeh lived, and on the west was Wang-yüeh-lu, the Full Moon Pavilion, where Ching-hung lived.

Of the eighty most talented and beautiful female musicians in the empire, forty lived on the east side under Ch'an-yüeh's direction and the other forty lived on the west under Ching-hung's. They were instructed in singing, dancing, and music.

Once a month, the two groups met at Ch'ing-ho-lu and would compete against each other, with the princesses leading them. Shao-yu would preside over the judging and the winners were celebrated with wine and crowned with flowers. The losers were served cold water and a spot of ink was put on their foreheads to mark their shame. Thus, all of the courtesans strove, every day, to perfect their skills.

The most famous lady musicians in the world were those of the court of Wei and those of Prince Yüeh. Even the musicians of the imperial opera, the Pear Orchard, could not compare.

One day, when the two princesses were with Shao-yu's mother and the other ladies, Shao-yu brought a letter and gave it to Princess Lan-yang, saying, "I have a letter from Prince Yüeh."

The princesses opened it and read:

How fares my dearest prime minister on this bright and lovely spring day? I trust the ten thousand happinesses are with you. Until recently, you have been so busy with affairs of state that you have not enjoyed any leisure. No time to enjoy the green hills or to watch the people parading by. No horses on Lo-yu-yüan. No boating parties on K'un-ming Lake. The dancing ground is overgrown with weeds.

Now the old people in the capital are waxing nostalgic about days gone by, fondly recalling the virtue and character of the old emperor until it makes them cry to remember the glory of former times. In these times of peace and security, it is appropriate to bring back those old pleasures as in the reign of Hsüan Tsung when life in the palace was full of delight. The spring sun still sets late, the weather is pleasant, and tender willows put our hearts at ease. There is no better time to enjoy the outdoors.

Let us get together at Lo-yu-yüan and we can hunt and enjoy some music to appreciate these times of peace and prosperity. If you find this agreeable, choose a date and let me know, for I would be delighted to be with you there.

When Princess Lan-yang finished reading the letter, she asked Shao-yu, "Do you know what he is really getting at?"

"I'm not sure," said Shao-yu. "Perhaps he merely wants to enjoy the flowers and willows with me because he enjoys the pleasure of such things as a prince."

"I don't think you quite understand," said the princess. "My brother likes women and music. He has to have the most beautiful women in the palace, but once those beauties of his got a look at Wan Yü-yen, the dancer from Wu-ch'ang, they all lost face.

"When she appeared at his palace, his women were stunned, and now they are depressed, comparing themselves to the homely Mo-mu and Wu-yen.[2] Wan Yü-yen's beauty is beyond compare.

"My brother has heard that you have many beauties of your own, so he wants to be like Wang Kai and Shih Ch'ung and hold a contest to compare them."

Shao-yu laughed. "I thought his letter was perfectly straightforward, but I see now that you know your brother better than I do."

"Even if it's only a game, we must be sure not to lose," said Ying-yang, and she gestured at Ching-hung and Ch'an-yüeh to come closer. "An army trains for ten years for a single morning of battle. Winning or losing will depend entirely on the two of you as teachers. You must do your best."

"I'm afraid we can't compete with them," said Ch'an-yüeh. "The music of the prince's palace is known everywhere, and so is Wan Yü-yen's reputation as a dancer. With both Wan Yü-yen and his musicians, he will be unbeatable, and we are an army with little training. We lack discipline and are ignorant of tactics, and I'm afraid we may run away in the face of combat.

"We two don't mind being laughed at ourselves, but we cannot bring shame on this entire household."

"When I first met Ch'an-yüeh at Lo-yang, she told me there were three great beauties in dancing. Yü-yen was one of them. I have the other two here, so why should I be afraid of her? Like the first emperor of Han, I already have my Chang Liang and Chen P'ing, so why should I worry about Fan Tseng on Hsiang Yü's side?"

"There are beautiful girls in Prince Yüeh's palace like there are blades of grass on the Pa-kung hillside," said Ch'an-yüeh. "Our army can only run away—we cannot compare with them. Please—I hope the two princesses will ask Ching-hung to be our strategist. I am cowardly, and even listening to myself say this makes my throat choke up and I won't be able to sing a single note."

"Do you really mean that?" Ching-hung said. "We are known among the seventy towns of Kuan-tung, so how can our talent be inferior to Yü-yen's? If we were like the women of Han or the fairies of Wu-shan, who ruined nations and cities, it would be one thing, but why should we be afraid of Yü-yen?"

Ch'an-yüeh responded, "How can you make it sound so easy? In Kuan-tung we performed in small towns at parties for interested nobility and adventurous gentlemen and scholars. But Prince Yüeh was born and raised in the palace and so he has a discerning and critical eye. You are mistaking a mountain for a stone, Ching-hung. You are underestimating Prince Yüeh. Yü-yen is the mastermind of this plan. She is like Chang Liang, who could sit in his tent and win a battle a thousand *li* away. Ching-hung is bragging like Chao-kuo—she is foreseeing her own defeat. If we take this matter lightly, we are sure to lose."

She continued, "Ching-hung likes to brag, so I will tell you about her shortcomings. She once stole a horse from the Prince of Yen and pretended to be a boy from Ho-pei to trick you at the roadside in Han-tan. If she were truly so beautiful and delicate, how could you think she was a boy? The first night she was with you, she took my place in the dark to make her dreams come true. And now she brags to me about it. It's funny, isn't it?"

Ching-hung laughed. "I cannot fathom her jealous heart," she said. "Before I came to live with you, she praised me like I was the Maiden in the Moon. But now she is belittling me, and do you know why? It's because she wants you all to herself."

Ch'an-yüeh and the others all laughed out loud.

"Ching-hung, you are so delicate and beautiful, how could

he ever take you for a boy?" said Ying-yang. "There must be something wrong with his eyes. It is no shame to you that he mistook you for a boy. But Ch'an-yüeh is also right. It isn't ladylike to disguise yourself as a boy to fool someone, just as it would be unmanly for a man to disguise himself as a girl. Those who disguise themselves like that are usually trying to cover something up."

Now it was Shao-yu's turn to laugh. "You are quite right, Princess. My eyes must be dim. But you yourself could discern the tunes played on the *ch'in*, and yet you couldn't tell a man from a woman, so you have excellent ears but terrible eyes. All one needs is one working hole to be a human being. The princess may belittle me, but all who see my portrait in the Ch'ilin Pavilion praise me for my imposing stature and my serious dignity." And now everyone joined in the laughter.

"Now that we are facing our archenemy, it is no time to be joking with each other," said Ch'an-yüeh. "We cannot rely on just the two of us. We would like Ch'un-yün to help. And since Prince Yüeh is not an outsider, I hope Ts'ai-feng will also join us."

"If the two of you were going to sit for the national civil exam, I would surely go with you to offer my support," said Ts'ai-feng. "But how can I be of any help when this is all about singing and dancing? It would be like asking me to help in a boxing match. I would be no use at all."

Ch'un-yün also declined. "People will make fun of me because I cannot sing and dance. People will point their fingers at me and say, 'That's the prime minister's concubine.' They will laugh and bring shame on my lord and the two princesses. There is no way I can participate."

But Princess Ying-yang reassured her. "There won't be any ridiculing of the prime minister if you participate, Ch'un-yün. And we would not be upset at all."

Ch'un-yün answered, "If we spread out the silk cushions and pitch a tent as high as the clouds, people will come and say, 'Here comes the prime minister's concubine!' They'll shove at each other and stand on tiptoes to gawk at me. And once I sit down with my shaggy hair and ghostly pale face, they'll be shocked and they'll say, 'The prime minister must be a letch like Teng Tu-tzu.' And that will bring disgrace upon him. As for Prince Yüeh, he's never seen anything so ugly as me, and if he does, it would make him sick. Doesn't that concern you?"

"That is too much," said Princess Lan-yang. "Now you are going overboard with your modesty. Once you transformed yourself into a ghost, but now a beauty like you is trying to change from the irresistible Hsi into the homely Wu-yen—I can't believe it!" Then she asked Shao-yu, "What date have you picked?"

"Tomorrow," said Shao-yu.

Ching-hung and Ch'an-yüeh were stunned to hear this. "We haven't even begun training the two groups yet," they said. "It is not enough time!" They called the lead dancers and told them, "The prime minister and Prince Yüeh have arranged to meet tomorrow at Lo-yu-yüan. All of you must be ready at dawn with your instruments tuned and wearing your best dresses to accompany the prime minister."

The eighty girls, receiving these orders, put on their makeup, redrew their eyebrows, and practiced on their instruments to get ready for the next day's contest.

❧

Shao-yu rose early the next morning, put on his armor, slung his quiver on his back, and with his bow in hand he mounted his white battle horse. With three hundred huntsmen, he left his walled compound and rode to the south of the capital.

Ching-hung and Ch'an-yüeh, in their embroidered dresses decorated with golden ornaments, jade, and flowers, led their dancers, and rode right behind Shao-yu on horses bedecked with flowers, with gilded saddles and reins threaded with jade and pearls. The eighty dancers, on smaller horses, rode in two lines on either side.

On their way, they met Prince Yüeh, whose huntsmen, dancers, and musicians were a match for Shao-yu's. The prince and Shao-yu met up and rode side by side.

"What breed of horse is that?" Prince Yüeh asked.

"He comes from Afghanistan. Yours must also be from there," said Shao-yu.

"Yes," said the prince. "Its name is Thousand Li Floating Cloud. Last fall when I took the Emperor hunting up in Shanglin, a thousand horses from the imperial stable were there, all of them with legs as swift as the wind, but none of them were as swift as this one, not even my nephew Chang's Peach Blossom or General Li's Black Brocade. People say those horses are like dragons, but compared to mine they are just sacks of bones."

Shao-yu replied, "Last year when I fought the Tibetans, this horse crossed rough waters and scaled steep cliffs that even my brave men dared not try, taking them like level ground and never once losing his footing. My victories were thanks to this horse. Tu Fu[3] wrote: 'Of one mind with man, he achieves great things.'

"Since I left my troops and was promoted in rank, I now lounge around in a palanquin and walk on level roads. The horse and I have both become lazy and our health has suffered, so let us snap our whips and test our skill in a race that goes to the swiftest."

Prince Yüeh was delighted. "That is just what I was thinking myself," he said. He told his servants to have the guests, the dancers, and the musicians from both sides wait in the tents.

Just as Prince Yüeh was about to whip his horse, a stag leaped out in front of him, chased by his huntsmen. He ordered one of his best hunters to shoot it, but then, even with all of his best men shooting at the same time, they missed. Prince Yüeh was furious. He galloped forward and killed the stag himself, shooting it in the flank.

All of the soldiers cheered and Shao-yu praised him. "You are a better archer than Prince Ju-yang," he said.

Prince Yüeh replied, "Why bother complimenting such modest skill? I am looking forward to watching you shoot."

As he was still speaking, a pair of swans flew between the clouds, and the soldiers exclaimed, "Those are the hardest birds to hit. We will need to use the Hai-tung falcons to catch those."

"Hold off," said Shao-yu. He nocked an arrow and shot it

straight up, hitting one of the swans, the shaft piercing its eye, and it fell out of the sky, hitting the ground before their horses.

Prince Yüeh was duly impressed. "Your shooting is as skillful as Yang Yu-chi's,"[4] he said.

Now they flicked their whips and their horses leaped forward like shooting stars, flashing like lightning, flying like pale ghosts. Within minutes they had traversed a wide plain and climbed the high slope of a hill. They pulled their reins and stood side by side.

For a while they looked out across the landscape and spoke of archery and swordsmanship. And then the grooms caught up to them with the meat of the stag and the swan prepared on standing silver trays. The prince and Shao-yu dismounted and sat in the grass. Drawing their swords from their belts, they cut some of the meat and roasted and ate it, offering each other wine to drink.

In the distance they saw two red-robed officials hurrying toward them, a host of people following behind. They appeared to be coming from the palace, and in a little while, one of them came running up, breathless, and said, "The Emperor and Empress Dowager have sent wine for you."

Prince Yüeh went back to the tent, where two eunuchs poured the wine and laid out ruled writing paper. The prince and Shao-yu washed their hands before kneeling and unrolling the paper, on which they found the order: "Compose a poem using this theme: The Great Hunt in the Hills."

Shao-yu and the prince both bowed their heads four times in salute. Then they each separately composed a poem and gave it to the eunuchs.

Shao-yu wrote:

Warriors set out to the field at the break of dawn
Swords glistening like the autumn lotus; arrows fly like falling
   stars.
The beautiful ladies flock in the tents,
And before the horses, two mighty-winged falcons.
We share cups of the Emperor's wine,
Our reflections bowing our gratitude,

And drunk, we draw our golden blades to cut the blood-fresh
    meat.
I remember last year, beyond the west frontier
When we hunted in bleak snow at Ta-huang Preserve.[5]

And Prince Yüeh wrote:

Lightning flashes—horses flying like dragons,
With high saddles, to the thundering drums on the hilltop.
The leaping stag cut down by a shooting star,
The white swan felled from Heaven like the bright moon—
A wild blood thirst spurs the hunting spirit.
With royal wine, our visages red with joy,
No need to speak of Ju-yang's fabled bow.

The eunuchs took the poems back to the capital with them.

෴

One after the other, each of the guests from the two sides was
seated, and tables laden with food and wine were brought in.
Grilled camel and delicate orangutan lips were served on silver
trays and green jade platters were piled with lychees from
Tongking and tangerines from Ying-chia. The feast was like
one thrown by the Queen Mother of the West in Jewel Lake or
the lavish parties of Emperor Han Wu-ti at the Cypress Beam
Terrace.

Hundreds of musicians sat in circles, row upon row, under
silken awnings. The sound of jade ornaments jangling was like
thunder and their beautiful faces were as lovely as flowers. The
sound of their music made ripples in the waters of the Ch'ü River
and the sound of their singing shook Chung-nan Mountain.

Prince Yüeh was already half-drunk. "In appreciation of
your great friendship, I would like you to have some of the
dancing girls I brought today," he said. "Pick some of them
and enjoy yourself with singing and dancing."

"How could I dare to take your beauties?" asked Shao-yu.

"But since we are brothers-in-law, I will indulge myself. Some of my women are here to enjoy the forest. Let me call them and have them join with yours to entertain us with their skills."

"Agreed," said the prince.

Then Ch'an-yüeh and Ching-hung and four of Prince Yüeh's beauties stood up one by one and came to bow in front of the tent.

Shao-yu said, "In ancient times, the Prince of Ning had a beautiful dancing girl named Fu-yung, the Lotus Flower, and Li Po, the great poet, begged him to be allowed to hear her sing, but he was never permitted to see her face. But I can see your faces now, so I have been far more favored than Li Po. What are your names?"

The four girls rose and gave their names: Tu Yün-hsien, Cloud Fairy of Chin-ling; Su Ts'ai-o, Painted Moth of Chen-liu; Wan Yü-yen, Jade Swallow of Wu-ch'ang; and Hu Ying-ying, Lovely Flower of Ch'ang-an.

To the prince, Shao-yu said, "I had heard of Yü-yen when I traveled as a young scholar, but now that I see her, she is far more lovely than her reputation."

The prince already knew the names of Ch'an-yüeh and Ching-hung. "The whole empire sings your praises," he said to Shao-yu. "They are fortunate to serve a master like you. How did you meet them?"

"I met Ch'an-yüeh when I stayed in Lo-yang on my way to take the civil exams and she followed me on her own. Ching-hung used to be in the palace of the Prince of Yen. When I was sent there as an envoy, she ran away to follow me."

The prince had a hearty laugh. "She is like the famous Girl in Purple who sneaked out of the house of Yan," he said. "But when she followed you, you were already famous. On the other hand, when Ch'an-yüeh followed you, you were only a common scholar with no inkling of your future fame and fortune. She is truly special. How did you happen to meet her?"

Shao-yu told him the whole story of their first meeting at the poetry contest on T'ien-chin Bridge and how Ch'an-yüeh had picked his poem and sung it. "They had agreed that she would spend the night with the one whose poem she sang, so there was no argument about it," he said. "It was karma."

"Well, that is a happier outcome than placing first in the exam," the prince said, laughing. "It must have been a wonderful composition you wrote in Lo-yang. Could I hear it, perhaps?"

"Oh, I cannot recall it now," said Shao-yu. "I was drunk when I wrote it."

So the prince said to Ch'an-yüeh, "He may have forgotten it, but surely, you must remember."

"Of course I remember," she replied. "Shall I write it out for you later, or shall I sing it now?"

"I would prefer to hear you sing it first," the prince said.

When she came forward and sang, everyone was filled with wonderment and the prince praised her extravagantly. "Your poem and her singing are beyond compare," he said. "The lines—

> The flowers droop in shame before her beauty,
> her lips perfumed, though she has yet to sing

"—well describe her talent and her beauty. Even Li Po himself could not have done better."

Showering her with more praise, the prince poured wine for her and Ching-hung in cups of gold. Then he ordered his four women to sing and dance in honor of the two. Host and guest were in harmony.

The prince was very pleased, and now he went out of the tent with all the guests to watch a demonstration of the martial arts by his soldiers. "It is also worth seeing archery and horsemanship by beautiful girls," he said. "I have several girls who are good at it, and I hear some of yours are from the north. Why don't we have them shoot some rabbits and pheasants to amuse us?"

When Shao-yu agreed and picked a dozen of his beautiful girls to join the palace girls for a competition, Ching-hung stood up and said, "I am not very good with a bow or a sword, but I want to compete today."

Shao-yu gave her his own bow with a smile. Ching-hung held it up and said to the other girls, "Don't laugh at me if I miss!"

She leaped into the saddle of one of the best horses and galloped from the tents just as a pheasant flew up out of the tall grass.

Ching-hung arched her body backward, drew back the bow, and let loose an arrow that dropped the many-hued bird right in front of the horse where everyone could see.

The prince and Shao-yu guffawed in delight.

Ching-hung nimbly dismounted in front of the tent and slowly made her way back to her seat, where all the other girls showered her with praise. "We have trained for many years in vain!" they said to her.[6]

"We did not lose the contest to the prince's women," said Ch'an-yüeh. "But still, they are too much for us because there are four of them and only two of us. I'm sorry that we didn't bring Ch'un-yün with us. Singing and dancing are not her strengths, but her beauty and her repartee would easily surpass Tu Yün-hsien's." Even as she sighed, she saw a carriage approaching in the distance, and in it, two beautiful girls.

꧁꧂

When they arrived at the tent in their lacquered carriage, the guard asked, "Do you come from Prince Yüeh's palace?"

"These two ladies are concubines of the Duke of Wei," the driver answered. "They were delayed and unable to come here with him."

When the guard reported this to Shao-yu, he thought it must be Ch'un-yün coming to watch. He thought it rather impulsive of her, but he told the guard to bring them in.

But to his surprise, *two* girls got out of the carriage. The first was Shen Niao-yen and then, behind her, Po Ling-po, whom he had met in his dream at camp—the daughter of the Dragon King of Tung-t'ing Lake.

They bowed to Shao-yu and, gesturing to the prince, he said to them, "This is His Highness Prince Yüeh. Pay your respects to him as well."

After they bowed to the prince, Shao-yu had them sit beside Ching-hung and Ch'an-yüeh. He said to the prince, "I met these two girls during my campaign against the Tibetans. I have been so busy I was not able to bring them with me, but they have come to the capital on their own. They must have come here after hearing about our contest."

The prince looked at them again and saw that they were as beautiful as Ching-hung and Ch'an-yüeh, perhaps even more so, and they looked as if they might be sisters. And all the girls of his palace now seemed bland by comparison.

"What are your names?" he asked them. "Where did you come from?"

"I am Shen Niao-yen from Hsi-liang," said one.

"I am Po Ling-po," said the other. "I lived in the Hsiao-hsiang River but fled to the west because of the war, and then I followed Yang Shao-yu."

"You are not of this Earth," the prince said to them. "Could you play some of your music for us?"

"I come from the borderlands, and I do not know the kind of thing that might entertain you," said Niao-yen. "I did learn the sword dance when I was a child. But that is to perform for soldiers and not worthy of showing to men of your stature."

But the prince was enthused, and he said to Shao-yu, "During Hsüan Tsung's reign the sword dance of Kung-sun Ta-hiang was famous throughout the empire, but no one carried on the art after her and it has been lost. Ever since I read Tu Fu's[7] description of her dance, I was sorry I could not see it. So I am glad to learn that she knows it."

The prince and Shao-yu drew their swords and gave them to Niao-yen. She folded up her sleeves, took off her sash, and began her dance, moving so lightly it seemed as if she were flying. The swirling of her bright dress and the flashing steel of the swords blurred together like spring snow falling on peach blossoms. Soon the tent was filled with a frosty light so dazzling she could no longer be seen, and then, suddenly, a blue rainbow arched across the sky and an icy wind blew between the tables. The spectators froze in fear.

Niao-yen had wanted to show off the full extent of her skill, but she stopped because she did not want to frighten the prince. She threw down the swords, bowed twice, and returned to her seat.

The prince took a while composing himself. "No earthly being could be so marvelous," he said when he had finally caught his breath. "I have heard there are those among the fairies who are experts at the sword dance. Are you one of them?"

"I learned it as a child because we of the west play with weapons," Niao-yen answered. "There is nothing to marvel at, and I am not a fairy."

"When I return to my palace, I will pick some of my best dancing girls and send them to you for instruction. Please do not refuse them."

Niao-yen bowed and accepted his request.

Now the prince turned to Ling-po. "And what is your special talent?" he asked.

"My home was near the Hsiao-hsiang River at Huang-ling-miao, where O-huang and Nü-ying[8] would play. On clear moonlit nights when the wind was calm, the sound of lutes would echo among the clouds. From the time I was very young, I imitated that sound for my own pleasure. I fear my skill is not worthy of your ears."

"I did not know the music of O-huang and Nü-ying were ever passed down to posterity," said the prince. "Surely, if you know that music, there is nothing in this world that can compare."

Ling-po drew a small lute from her sleeve and began to play. The sound was clear and plaintive, like water flowing deep in a valley or wild geese crying far off in the sky. The guests shed tears without knowing why. Reedy grasses trembled and leaves fell from the trees.

The prince was mystified. "I did not believe earthly music could change the way of Heaven," he said. "But you have changed spring into autumn and made the leaves fall. Could an ordinary human being possibly learn to play like this?"

"It is only the remnants of old melodies," said Ling-po. "There is nothing marvelous about it that anyone could not also learn."

Yü-yen said to the prince, "Though I have no skill to speak of, I will play for you a tune I learned in the past. It is called 'The White Lotus.'" And taking up a ch'in *cheng*, she played on the twenty-five strings, her music clear and pleasurable. Shao-yu, Ch'an-yüeh, and Ching-hung gave her high praise, and that pleased Prince Yüeh very much.

THE WINE PUNISHMENT

Though they were enjoying themselves and there were many amusements yet in the Shang-lin Preserve, they ended the feasting when it became dark. Rewards of gold, silver, and silk were given to the performers, and the prince and Shao-yu returned to the capital and entered the gate under moonlight.

Bells rang, and as the musicians and the dancing girls hurried to return home, their tinkling ornaments caused a din and the streets were thick with perfume. Fallen hairpins and jewelry crunched under the horses' hooves, sounding like a distant rainstorm.

The people of the capital thronged to watch the returning company. An old man said, through his tears, "When I was young I saw the Emperor Hsüan Tsung's procession to Hua-ch'ing Palace, and it was as stately as this. It brings me joy to live long enough to see such things again."

❧

Meanwhile, the two princesses and Shao-yu's mother were awaiting him with Ts'ai-feng and Ch'un-yün. When he returned, he introduced Niao-yen and Ling-po to all of them. The two bowed at the stone steps, and Princess Ying-yang said, "The minister has told me many times that it was because of you two girls that he was able to win back two thousand *li* of territory. I worried that I would never meet you. Why did you come so late?"

They replied, "We are lowborn and from the frontier regions. The minister loved us once, but we worried that Your Royal

Highnesses would never accept us, and so we did not dare to come."

"But then we heard that you were kind to all the concubines and favored everyone equally without regard to rank, so we presumed to come and meet you. We happened to arrive when the minister was having his hunting party at Lo-yu-yüan, so we joined him there for the festivities. We are very fortunate to be received with such kindness."

"The palace is full of beautiful flowers today," the prince said to Shao-yu with a proud smile. "You are probably full of yourself thinking the credit is all yours, but you do realize this is all *our* doing, don't you?"

Shao-yu laughed. "These two are newcomers in the palace. They were only flattering you because of your regal air. Do you really think you deserve all the credit?"

Now everybody laughed, and Ts'ai-feng and Ch'un-yün asked Ch'an-yüeh, "Who won at the contests today?"

Ching-hung answered first. "Ch'an-yüeh laughed at my bragging, but I put the prince and his people in their place. I was like Chu-ko who sailed to Chiang-tung in a small boat and silenced Chou Kung-chin and Lu Tzu-ching with just a few words of admonishment.[1] Because my heart is big, sometimes I have a big mouth. But there is truth in boasting, and you can ask Ch'an-yüeh to confirm it."

Then Ch'an-yüeh said, "Her archery and horsemanship are certainly amazing and praiseworthy at a feast, but I doubt she would be able to ride a single stride or shoot a single arrow in a battlefield under a storm of arrows and stones. What showed the prince up was the two newcomers and their fairylike beauty and talent, not Ching-hung's doing. There is something I must remind her about.

"Long ago, in the time of Spring and Autumn, the minister of state, Chia, was very ugly. His wife had not smiled once in the three years following their marriage. One day, he went out into the fields with his wife and shot a pheasant with a bow and arrow. And his wife laughed for the first time. Ching-hung's hitting the pheasant was just that kind of luck."

Ching-hung responded, "He might have had an ugly face,

but he did make his wife laugh with his skill in archery and horsemanship. But imagine if he had been a beautiful and articulate girl hitting a pheasant with that arrow. Don't you think he would have been loved and praised even more?"

Ch'an-yüeh laughed and said to Shao-yu, "She brags about herself even more! You paid her too much attention, and now she is full of herself!"

Shao-yu joined in the laughter. "I knew you had many talents," he said to Ch'an-yüeh. "But I had no idea you were so well versed in the classics. Now I see you can quote from *The Annals of Spring and Autumn*!"[2]

"I only read histories in my spare time," Ch'an-yüeh said with a smile. "I really don't think I'm well versed."

The next morning, Shao-yu went to the palace for an audience with the Emperor, and afterward, the Empress Dowager sent for him and Prince Yüeh. The two princesses were already with her when they arrived.

"I heard you two had a contest with your pretty girls," the Empress Dowager said to Prince Yüeh. "Who won?"

"The prime minister has so many beauties and is so blessed, no one could possibly beat him," said the prince. "Ask him how the two princesses enjoyed it."

Shao-yu replied, "His Highness saying that I could not be beaten is like Li Po turning pale at the sight of Ts'ui Hao's[3] inferior poems. I cannot say how the princesses enjoyed themselves. You must ask them yourself."

The Empress Dowager looked at the two princesses, who said, "A husband and his wives are of one flesh. If he is blessed, we are blessed. If he is beaten, we are beaten, and if he is happy, then we are happy, too."

"They do not mean what they say!" exclaimed the prince. "There has never been such a degenerate imperial son-in-law! The moral laws of society are corrupted because of him. You should have him prosecuted by the Ministry of Justice and punished for his contempt for the laws of the state."

The Empress Dowager took all this to be a joke. "Well, he may scoff at the law," she said. "But if there is a trial it will cause undue worry for my daughters and for me in my old age. Let us deal with it privately."

But the prince persisted. "Then let him be examined in front of you, and once a verdict has been reached, we can deal with him appropriately." He quickly dashed off a list of charges and signed his mother's name to them.

No imperial son-in-law has ever dared to take concubines, not because he did not desire it, nor because he could not support them, but to maintain the imperial prestige and to show reverence for the state. The two princesses Ying-yang and Lan-yang are my own daughters. They are as regal as Jen and Szu of ancient times. And yet you, Yang Shao-yu, have shown no regard for any of this.

You have collected pretty girls. You have fed your hungry eyes with the beautiful women of Yen and Chao and your hungry ears with the sensual songs of Chen and Wei. You have made girls swarm like ants in my daughters' pavilions and terraces and buzz in their chambers like bees.

Through virtue of good breeding and generosity they have shown no jealousy, but how could you presume to abuse the princesses in this way? Your sins of pride and debauchery must not go unpunished, and therefore you will refrain from prevarication and confess everything before receiving your sentence.

Shao-yu stepped down from the dais and took off his official headdress as he listened to the charges leveled against him, read out loud by the prince. Then he began his confession.

"I have insinuated myself into Your Majesties' favor and thus risen to the rank of prime minister, received numerous undeserved honors, and married two princesses of incomparable beauty. I had all a man could dream to have, and yet, full of covetousness, I acquired second wives, concubines, and many singing and dancing girls.

"I married Princess Lan-yang by order of the Emperor, and

according to the laws of the state, as I understand them, the imperial son-in-law may take concubines before marrying the princess. I did take concubines, but only before my marriage or while I was out on my military campaigns on the frontier. I have not violated the law or failed in my duty as a subject, and it is my hope that you will take this into account when you deliver your judgment. I humbly await your sentence."

Hearing this, the Empress Dowager laughed and said, "Having many concubines is an easy thing for me to forgive. What concerns me is his excessive drinking."

"You must investigate this further," said Prince Yüeh.

Shao-yu hung his head in shame, causing the Empress Dowager to burst into laughter once again. "He is the prime minister," she said. "I can hardly go on treating him like a little boy!" She made him put his headdress back on and come up onto the dais.

"His high rank makes it difficult to punish him," said Prince Yüeh. "But the law must be upheld, so I suggest you condemn him to the wine punishment."[4]

When the Empress Dowager agreed, the court ladies brought a cup.

"The prime minister drinks like a whale!" exclaimed the prince. "What use is a small cup like this?"

So they brought a huge golden bowl and filled it to the brim with strong wine, and though he could hold his liquor well, Shao-yu could not help but be drunk by the time he had drained it.

"The Herder Boy was scolded by his father-in-law because he loved the Weaver Girl too much,"[5] he said. "And me—because I have so much love, I am being punished by my mother-in-law. It is hard being the son-in-law to the Empress Dowager. Now that I am drunk, please let me go." He collapsed as he tried to get up.

The Empress Dowager laughed. "Help him to the gate," she told the court ladies. To the two princesses, she said, "He will have a terrible headache in the morning. Go take care of him."

They protested that he had more than enough women to take care of him, but they did as they were told.

Shao-yu's mother was waiting for him, with candles lit, in the main hall. When he returned in his drunken state, she exclaimed, "What happened? I've seen you drinking plenty of times, but I've never seen you so intoxicated before."

"It was my punishment," Shao-yu said. After glowering at the princesses a while with his drunken eyes, he spoke again. "Their brother, Prince Yüeh, made accusations against me to the Empress Dowager. All fabricated! I spoke well in my defense. I proved myself innocent. But the prince insisted I was guilty and made the Empress Dowager give me the wine punishment! If I couldn't hold so much liquor, I would be dead now! All because I beat him yesterday. He wanted revenge!

"And Lan-yang is jealous because I have so many concubines, so she and the prince hatched this plot to get back at me. So don't believe a thing she says—now or in the past! Make her drink a glass of wine, too, to show my displeasure."

"You can't be sure she's guilty," Shao-yu's mother replied. "And she's never had a glass of wine in all her life. If you insist on my punishing her, I will make her drink tea instead."

"No!" said Shao-yu. "It has to be *wine*!"

His mother said to the princess, "If you do not drink the wine, his offended heart will never be satisfied." She called a maid to serve a cup of wine to Lan-yang. The princess took the cup and was about to put it to her lips when Shao-yu suddenly tried to snatch it away from her. She quickly threw the cup to the floor.

Shao-yu dipped his finger in the overturned cup and tasted what was left. It was honeyed water.

"If the Empress Dowager had given me honeyed water as my punishment, you could have given her the same," Shao-yu said to his mother. "But what I drank was wine, so the princess must drink wine, too."

This time he poured the wine himself and gave it to Lan-yang to drink. Having no choice, she drank it all.

"She was the one who urged the Empress Dowager to punish me," Shao-yu said. "But Princess Ying-yang was also in on

it. She sat next to the Empress Dowager and watched me hu-
miliate myself, and all she did was laugh and wink at Lan-
yang. I cannot trust her, either. So punish *her*, too."

Now Shao-yu's mother laughed, and she had a cup of wine
sent to Ying-yang, who moved to another seat and drank it all
down.

"The Empress Dowager punished you because you have too
many concubines," said Shao-yu's mother. "Now that the two
princesses have been punished with you, how can you leave
your concubines alone?"

Shao-yu answered, "Prince Yüeh held the contest to have a
look at our beauties and compare them. But my four concubines did well and defeated him. He was furious, and felt
obliged to retaliate. That is why he had me punished today, so
they must also be punished."

"You mean to punish the ones who helped you win?" his
mother said. "That's ridiculous drunken talk." But she went
ahead and gave each of the four girls a cup of wine.

After they had all drunk, Ching-hung and Ch'an-yüeh knelt
in front of Shao-yu's mother. "The Empress Dowager punished
him because he has many wives, not because we won the contest," they said. "Niao-yen and Ling-po took the wine punishment. Won't they feel it's unfair? But Ch'un-yün has been with
him for a long time and he loves her too much. She wasn't punished only because she didn't take part in the contest! How can
we not be resentful?"

"You are right," said Shao-yu's mother, and she gave a large
cup of wine to Ch'un-yün, who drank it between fits of laughter.

Now they had all endured the wine punishment and they
were all drunk. Lan-yang was quite sick and Ts'ai-feng sat silently in a corner without even a smile.

"Ts'ai-feng is the only one not affected by the wine," said
Shao-yu, and he poured another cup and gave it to her. She
cracked a smile and drank it down.

Shao-yu's mother said to Lan-yang, "You aren't used to
drinking. Are you all right?"

"I feel sick," said the princess.

Shao-yu's mother had Ts'ai-feng help the princess to her

bedroom, and she had Ch'un-yün fill another cup. She took it and said, "My two daughters-in-law are imperial princesses. I will worry constantly that we will lose all our blessings because Shao-yu has offended them with his drunken debauchery. If the Empress Dowager hears of this, she is bound to be upset. I have failed in my duty of raising a son, and it has led to this disgrace. I cannot deny responsibility or claim that I have not sinned, and so I shall drink this cup as punishment." And she drank it all.

Shao-yu knelt before her in shock. "You have punished yourself because of me," he said. "How can I ever live down this humiliation? I deserve more punishment than the spankings you gave me when I was little."[6] He told Ching-hung to fill another large cup up to the brim. "I have not lived as you taught me, Mother, and I have caused you nothing but grief. So I make this confession and receive this punishment." And he drained the cup.

Soon Shao-yu was so drunk he could no longer sit up. He could only gesture to Ch'un-yün's quarters. Shao-yu's mother asked Ch'un-yün to take him there, but she protested, "I can't take him because Ch'an-yüeh and Ching-hung would be too jealous."

So Shao-yu's mother asked the other two girls instead, but Ch'an-yüeh said, "Ch'un-yün refused because of what I said, so I won't do it, either."

Ching-hung laughed and helped Shao-yu back to his feet, and soon afterward they all went off to bed.

෴

Shao-yu knew that Niao-yen and Ling-po loved beautiful landscapes. In the corner of one of his palace gardens there was a lotus pond with water as clear as a natural lake, and in the middle of it stood a pavilion called Ying-o-lu, Radiant Beauty. That was where Ling-po lived. On the south side of the lotus pond there was a formation of rocks with pointed peaks like cut jade and stone walls so sheer and smooth they looked like stacked plates of metal. There, in the shadows of old pines and bamboo, stood a small pavilion called Ping-hsüeh-hsüan, the Hall of Ice and Snow,[7] and this was Niao-yen's home. When Shao-yu's wives or concubines came to the mountains in the garden, Niao-yen and Ling-po were the hostesses.

The other women asked Ling-po how she was able to magically transform herself, and she replied, "That belongs to my former life. I drew on the powers of Heaven and Earth and their harmony in order to become a human being. I cast off my scales and hide and piled them in a heap. Like a sparrow that has changed into a clam, how can I fly when I no longer have wings?"[8]

The women accepted her explanation and didn't ask anymore. Sometimes Niao-yen would perform the sword dance for Shao-yu, his mother, and the two princesses, but she did not like to do it very often. "I met the minister by virtue of my skill with the sword, but it is associated with death and it should not be performed too much," she said.

As time passed, the two princesses and six concubines enjoyed each other's company like fish in a stream or birds in the clouds. They spent their time together and relied on each other like real sisters, and though Shao-yu loved them all equally, it was their wifely virtue that made the household peaceful and happy. And all of this was a result of the karma they carried from their former lives together.

One day, when the two princesses were together, they said to each other, "Now the two of us and the six concubines are closer to each other than sisters of the same flesh and blood. How can this be if it isn't by the mandate of Heaven? It is only proper then that we not distinguish our social rank, so let us all just call each other sister."

But when they suggested this to the six concubines, they all protested, especially Ch'un-yün, Ching-hung, and Ch'an-yüeh.

Princess Ying-yang said to them, "In ancient times, Liu Pei, Kuan Yü, and Chang Fei were all loyal courtiers to the emperor, and they swore an oath in the peach garden to treat each other as brothers. Ch'un-yün and I grew up together like best friends, so why should we not be sisters? The wife of the

Shakyamuni Buddha and Matangi[9] the courtesan were from
different castes and their virtue and chastity were hardly alike,
but after they became disciples of the Buddha, they shared the
same fate. What has high or low birth to do with ultimate ful-
fillment?"

In the end, the two princesses and the six concubines left the
palace and went to a shrine of the bodhisattva Kwan Yin.[10]
They burned incense, prostrated themselves, and offered a solemn promise which they had written:

On this day of this year, the disciples Cheng Ch'iung-pei, Li
Hsiao-ho, Ch'in Ts'ai-feng, Chia Ch'un-yün, Kuei Ch'an-yüeh,
Ti Ching-hung, Shen Niao-yen, and Po Ling-po, having purified
our bodies and minds, bow before the merciful Bodhisattva.

It is said in the *Tripitaka*[11] that all people are related through
understanding because they share the same desires. We disciples
were born in different places in the south and north and we have
been scattered east and west. But now we all serve one husband,
abide in one place, and have come to appreciate and bond with
one another.

We are like flowers on a branch blown by the wind and
rain, one into a courtyard, one down the hillside, one into a
deep mountain stream, yet all born of one root and one source.
Likewise, men born into one family sharing the same siblings
and the same spirit, though they be scattered far and wide, must
come together again in the end. Though the past is long gone,
we have come together at this one time, and though the world is
vast, we live together in one house.

Surely, this is our karma from a previous life, and it explains
our happiness now. And so we take this vow of sisterhood and
swear to share our joys and sorrows through life and death.
Should any one of us break this vow or change her mind, may
Heaven strike her dead and the spirits of Heaven abandon her.
We beseech you as we prostrate ourselves here before you that
you will give us your blessings, deliver us from sorrow, and after
a life of a hundred years, we may be enlightened and delivered
to Paradise.

Afterward, the two princesses called the concubines "sister," and although the concubines maintained their humility and dared not presume to refer to the princesses in the same way, their affection for each other grew deeper.

All of the women had children, each of them bearing sons except for Ts'ai-feng and Ling-po, who each bore a daughter. They raised their children well, never having to witness any poor behavior. And this was entirely unlike the common people.

இ&

It was a time of peace and prosperity and bountiful harvest. The people were content and there was little work to keep ministers busy. Shao-yu accompanied the Emperor on hunting parties in the Shang-lin Preserve[12] and returned to his mother and family to banquets with singing and dancing. He was happy to remove himself from the outside world and enjoy the changing seasons and, having served many years as prime minister, he also appreciated the many rewards of his success.

But when all is happiness, pain and sorrow are wont to follow, and Shao-yu's mother fell ill and died at the age of ninety-nine. Her son's grief and anguish were so profound that the Emperor and Empress Dowager worried. They sent a eunuch from the palace to convey their condolences and saw to it that his mother was buried like a queen.

Minister Cheng, the father of Ying-yang, also lived to enjoy a long and honorable life, and when he and his wife passed away, Shao-yu grieved for them as much as Ying-yang did herself.

Shao-yu's six sons and two daughters were all like their parents in appearance and temperament, the sons like dragons and tigers and the daughters like the fairies of the moon.[13] Princess Ying-yang's son Ta-ch'ing, the eldest, grew up to become the minister of foreign affairs. The second son, Tzu-ch'ing, who was Ching-hung's, became the major of the capital.[14] The third son, Shu-ch'ing, was Ch'un-yün's, and he became chief justice. The fourth son, Princess Lan-yang's Chi ch'ing, became minister of defense; the fifth, Wu-ch'ing, Ch'an-yüeh's son, became chancellor of the Academy. Chih-ch'ing, the youngest and the son of Niao-yen, was already stronger than any man by the time he was fifteen. He was also as wise as a deva and much beloved by the Emperor, who made him the marshal of the Imperial Guard and gave him command of forty thousand soldiers to protect the royal palace.[15]

The elder of Shao-yu's two girls was Fu-tan, Ts'ai-feng's daughter, and she grew up to marry Prince Yüeh's son, Langyeh. The younger girl, Ling-po's daughter, Ying-lo, became a concubine of the prince.

One day, Shao-yu said to himself, "Ripe fruit soon decays and a full cup will soon overflow." And he wrote a letter to the Emperor asking permission to retire.

I, Yang Shao-yu, bow before you a hundred times and humbly submit this petition to Your Majesty. When a man born into this world has attained the highest rank and fulfilled all his desires, there is nothing left for him to want. Parents wish for their children to have riches and status, believing that once they attain these there will be nothing left to desire. Is it not the happiness that long life, fame, and wealth bring that make people envious? And yet men continue to desire more and more, not having the wisdom to know when to say enough is enough.

And knowing how to be satisfied with worldly wealth and glory, should we not also know when to be dissatisfied? I am a man of ordinary talents and little promise, but I have risen to the highest ranks. I have received every conceivable honor and held an important office for many years. I have been showered with wealth and glory beyond my dreams and my mother, too, has basked in it. My original ambition was not a ten-thousandth of what I received.

I reluctantly became the imperial son-in-law, and gifts and favors were bestowed upon me far beyond what was received by your other loyal subjects. As a child I ate weeds and scraps, and I have since been filled with delicacies. I was a peasant and now I live in the imperial palace. But I fear all this has been contrary to my proper station and I will bring shame upon Your Majesty for not knowing my proper place.

When I was younger I wished to flee my position and retire from the world, lock my gates, refuse all favor, and beg pardon from Heaven and Earth and the spirits. But Your Majesty was so gracious that I could not refuse you, and I stayed, accepting your generosity, hoping—since I was strong of body—to repay you in some measure.

Now I propose to spend the remainder of my days tending my ancestral graves. I have grown old, and my hair has turned gray before I have had the chance to fulfill my many duties, and I am unable to repay all of the favor you have heaped upon me. Like a loyal horse or dog, I want to return your faith in me, which was as great as a mountain, but I have not the strength.

Your Majesty, the frontier regions are peaceful and there is no longer need for military force. The people are content, and there is no longer a need to sound the drums. Please consider my petition. The Mandate of Heaven is with us as it was in the times of the three great kingdoms of Hsia, Ying, and Chou. If you keep me in office, it would only be at an unnecessary expense to the state, while I spend my days listening to happy songs.

The regent is like a parent and the subject is like a child. A parent loves even an undutiful child and worries when he leaves home. Now I bow to you, praying you will see that I am old and of little use, and though you may not wish me to retire, I ask that you treat me as a loving parent treats a child. Having received a surfeit of favor, how can I leave you and seclude myself in some far mountain, away from a ruler as benevolent as Yao or Shun?[16] But let not this vessel overflow, as spilled water cannot be poured back in, nor can a broken yoke still be useful upon the ox.[17]

I bow to you and ask that you understand—I can no longer bear the burden of my duties to the state. Consider that I no longer wish to live in a place of luxury. Please allow me to retire to my native province and live out my years there remembering your great benevolence and singing your praises.

After the Emperor read Shao-yu's petition, he wrote a reply in his own hand:

You and your work have been of great benefit to the people, and you have been of great service to the state. In ancient times the duke Chiang was almost a hundred years old but he continued to serve the kingdom of Chou and helped to maintain peace. You have not yet reached the age which, according to *The Book of Rites*, is the proper time for retirement, and though you wish to retire from your office early, I cannot allow it. The pine tree in the forest looks with contempt upon the winter snow because its spirit is strong. You are that pine.

To my eyes you seem as youthful and as strong as the day you took up your position in the Imperial Academy or the day you crossed the bridge at Wei on your way to fight the rebels. I cannot agree with your claim that you are old, and I do not believe that you can no longer bear the burden of your duties to the state. And though Ch'ao-fu[18] refused to rule when Emperor Yao asked him, I hope you will change your mind and continue, with your exemplary integrity, to help maintain this peaceful reign.

Though Shao-yu was old, he still appeared to be in robust health, and so he was often compared to the immortals. That was why the Emperor had replied in this way. But Shao-yu sent another petition, asking again for permission to retire, and this time the Emperor summoned him.

"If you truly wish to retire, I will not refuse your request," he said. "But if you go to your fiefdom of Wei, it will be difficult to consult with you for urgent matters of state. And since my mother the Empress Dowager has left this world, I cannot bear to be far from my sister, Princess Lan-yang.

"There is a palace four hundred *li* south of the capital. It is called Ts'ui-wei-kung, the Mountain Mist Palace, formerly used by the emperor Hsüan Tsung[19] in the summertime. It is a good place to relax and enjoy old age, and I will give it to you."

The Emperor issued an edict appointing Shao-yu to the post of chief preceptor[20] and had him turn in his official prime minister's seal. He remained Duke of Wei, and was given five thousand additional households to his fief.[21]

Shao-yu was moved by the Emperor's generosity, and he bowed deeply and gave his thanks. He moved his household to

Ts'ui-wei-kung, which was located in the greenery of Chung-nan Mountain to the south. The graceful and stately lines of the pavilion roofs and the vistas of the landscape reminded him of the unearthly beauty of Mount P'eng-lai, the abode of the immortals. Even fairies could not live in a place more beautiful. Who would play his flute here and ascend to Heaven?

Shao-yu treasured the Emperor's edicts, keeping them on display in the main hall. He assigned the other pavilions as residences for the two princesses and six concubines.

Every evening, they enjoyed the moonlit mountain streams, and in the day they explored the valleys, searching for plum blossoms. When they happened upon a sheer cliff face they would compose poems and play the lute in the shade of pine trees.

As he grew older, Shao-yu's once-bright future became even brighter, and there came a time when everyone envied his happiness, and Shao-yu, jealously guarding his quiet life, stopped receiving visitors.

And thus did several years pass by.

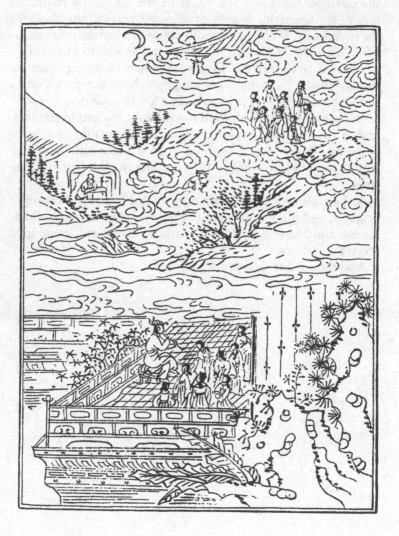

RETURNING TO
THE SOURCE

Shao-yu's birthday was around the twentieth day of the eighth month, and the great feast that was held to celebrate his long life—with his entire family and his children's families in attendance—lasted more than ten days. Its scale was impossible to describe, and when it was finally over, all the sons and daughters and their children returned to their homes and it was peaceful in his palace once again.

Late in the ninth month of the year, autumn was at its height when chrysanthemum buds began to open and the dogwoods hung with berries. To the west of the Ts'ui-wei-kung, there was a mountain peak, and from the pavilion at the top a two-hundred-*li* stretch of the Ch'in River[1] could be seen laid out below like the palm of one's hand.

This was Shao-yu's favorite place, and one day he and his wives and concubines climbed there together, wearing chrysanthemums in their hair, and they drank wine together.

The setting sun cast the mountain's shadow into the broad plain below, and it began to grow dark with shadowed clouds, changing the brilliant colors of fall. Shao-yu took his jade flute and began to play a tune, sad and plaintive, full of melancholy and yearning and tears. The women's hearts were overcome with sorrow.

The two princesses said, "You distinguished yourself when you were still young, and you have enjoyed both wealth and fame for a long time. The whole world respects you in a way that has rarely been seen in this age. Now in this wonderful season, looking at this magnificent vista, with chrysanthemum petals falling in your cup among such beautiful women, what other earthly pleasures could you desire? What do you mean by playing your flute like this, so differently from other times, bringing tears to our eyes?"

Shao-yu put down the flute and moved over to them. "Look north," he said. "In the middle of that vast plain is a single lonely peak. In the light of the setting sun you can just make out the ruins of A-fang-kung, the palace of the great Ch'in Shih-huang, among the weeds and high grass. Look west. The wind is rustling the woods where the gray mountain mist hides Mou-ling, the tomb of Emperor Han Wu-ti. In the east you can see the white wall reflecting the green hills where a red rooftop pierces the sky and the pale moon comes and goes. No one leans on the jade balustrades at Hua-ch'ing-kung where Emperor Hsüan Tsung frolicked with his ill-fated concubine Yang Kuei-fei.[2] Those three emperors were for ten millennia the heroes of our history. Where are they now?

"I was just a poor scholar, a boy from the land of Ch'u who received the Emperor's favor and rose to the highest rank. You—my wives and concubines—have lived together with me in love and harmony into our old age, and even now our love for each other only increases. How could this be unless it is the karma of our previous lives that makes it so?

"After we have died and left this place behind, these high terraces will fall and the deep lotus pools will silt up with neglect and go dry. The palace where we sing and dance today will be overgrown with weeds and obscured in the cold mist.

"Boys who come to gather wood and feed their cows will sing sad songs and say, 'This is the place where Yang the Chief Preceptor played with his wives and concubines. All of his riches and his honor and all his beautiful women, elegant as flowers, with faces like white jade—all gone forever.' The cowherds will look upon this spot just as I look upon the ruined palaces and the tombs of those three emperors. A man's life is but a fleeting moment.

"There are three ways in the world—the way of Confucius, the way of the Buddha, and the way of the Taoists. Buddhism is the highest. Confucianism exalts achievements and concerns itself with the passing down of names to posterity. Taoism is mystical, but it is unreliable, and though it has benefited many, its truths cannot be wholly known. Consider the fates of Ch'in Shi-huang, Han Wu-ti, and Hsüan Tsung.

"Since my retirement, I have dreamed every night that I am bowing before the Buddha. It is clearly my karma. I must bid my home farewell and do as Chang Liang, who followed Red Pine, the immortal master, to the abode of the blessed ones.[3] I must go beyond the Southern Sea in search of the Bodhisattva of Mercy.[4] I must climb to the top of Wu-tai-shan to meet the bodhisattva Manjushri.[5] I must cast off the cares of this earthly life and attain the way that has neither birth nor death. But this means I must say good-bye to all of you with whom I have spent so many happy years. That is why you heard the mournful air of my sadness in my flute."

The women were all deeply moved. "If you feel this way in the midst of your prosperity, it must be the work of Heaven that inspires you," they said. "We eight sisters are of one mind, and we will remove to our inner quarters to prostrate ourselves before the Buddha day and night while we await your return. Surely you will meet a great teacher and good friends on your journey to help you attain the Way, and then you can return and we will be the first for you to teach."

This made Shao-yu very happy, and he said, "Since all nine of us are of the same mind, there is nothing to worry about. I will set out tomorrow, so let us all imbibe together tonight until we are drunk."

"Each of us will say good-bye by offering you a cup of wine," they said.

But just as they were about to begin pouring, they heard the sudden sound of a staff striking the stone pavement below. They were startled and wondered who would have come up so far, when they saw an old monk. His eyebrows were long and white, his eyes as clear as waves on the sea, and his bearing mysterious.

He came up to the dais and bowed politely to Shao-yu. "An old monk would like to see you," he said.

Shao-yu, already realizing this was no ordinary monk, quickly rose and returned the bow. "Where do you come from?" he asked.

The old monk smiled. "Do you not remember me?" he said. "I heard long ago that people of high rank have short memories. It seems to be true."

Shao-yu took a closer look at the old monk. His face was familiar, but Shao-yu couldn't seem to remember who it was. And then, suddenly, glancing back at Ling-po, he remembered. "When I defeated the Tibetans I dreamed that I went to a banquet held on my behalf by the Dragon King of Tung-t'ing Lake," he said. "On the way back, on Heng-shan, I saw an old monk chanting sutras with his disciples. Are you the monk I saw in that dream?"

The old monk clapped his hands together, laughing. "That's right!" he said. "But while you remember our brief meeting in your dream, you do not recall the ten years we lived together! And they say you are so smart!"

Shao-yu was puzzled. "Before I was fifteen, I never left my mother," he said. "At sixteen I passed the state examination and since then I have served the state. I traveled east as an envoy to Yen, and west to fight the Tibetans. Otherwise, I never left the capital. How could I possibly have lived for ten years with you?"

The old monk laughed. "So you have yet to awaken from your spring dream."

"And how would you wake me up?" Shao-yu asked.

"It wouldn't be hard," said the old monk. He raised his staff and tapped the stone railing a few times. Suddenly, a mist rose from every direction in the gorge and nothing could be seen.

Shao-yu felt as if he were in a drunken dream, and after a while he cried out, "Why do you resort to magic and not show the truth?"

Before he had even finished speaking, the mists vanished. Shao-yu looked right and left, but the old monk and the eight women were gone. And in a moment the terrace and the pavilions also vanished, and he found himself seated on a prayer mat in a small monk's cell. The flame had died in the incense burner and the light of the setting moon shone through the window.

He looked down and saw the *mala* of 108 beads hanging from his wrist. His hair was stubbly and rough. Clearly, this was the body of a young monk, not the distinguished old chief preceptor. It took him a while to realize he was Hsing-chen, at the monastery on Lotus Peak.

"I was scolded by my master and sent to Hell, and then I was reincarnated into the world of man as the son of the Yangs. I took first place in the national examination and became vice chancellor of the Imperial Academy. Then I served with honor as a general, retired, and enjoyed my life with two princesses and six concubines. But it was all only a dream.

"My master knew of my wrongful thoughts and made me dream this dream to learn that worldly riches, honor, and desire are nothing."

He quickly splashed some water on his face and went out to the main hall of the temple. The other disciples were already gathered there, and the master called out to him, in a loud voice, "Hsing-chen, Hsing-chen! Did you enjoy your worldly pleasures?"

Hsing-chen suddenly opened his eyes and saw his master, Liu-kuan, standing before him, looking wrathful. Hsing-chen bowed low, striking his head on the ground, and cried out, "I have been impure! No one else can be blamed for my bad behavior and the sins I have committed. Cast into the world of dust, I should have endured an endless cycle of pain and suffering, but, Master, you have awakened my mind in a dream of one night. I could never repay your kindness even in ten million *kalpa*s."[6]

"You went seeking your desires, and now you have returned, for they have faded," said Master Liu-kuan. "What have I to do with it? You say the dream and the world are two separate things, and that is because you have yet to awaken from the dream. Chuang Chou once dreamed he was a butterfly, and upon waking he could not tell if he was the butterfly dreaming he was Chuang Chou.[7] Hsing-chen, Shao-yu—which is real and which is a dream?"

"I cannot tell if the dream was not reality or if this reality is not a dream," said Hsing-chen. "Please teach me the Way so I may understand."

"I shall teach you the Great Way—of *The Diamond Sutra*,[8] but you must wait a moment, for new followers are coming," said Liu-kuan. But before he had even finished speaking, the gatekeeper came to say that the eight fairies who were the ladies-in-waiting of the Taoist immortal Lady Wei had arrived.

When Liu-kuan let them in, they came and bowed, their hands folded before them. "Though we attend to Lady Wei, we have no learning, and we have lusted after the world of mortals, unable to control our sinful desires," they said. "No one has awakened us. But since you accepted us with your mercy and compassion yesterday, we have said good-bye to Lady Wei and her court. Now we are back and ask if you will forgive our sins and enlighten us with your teaching."

"Your intention is good," said Master Liu-kuan. "But you cannot realize it without persistence and great effort. The dharma[9] is deep and profound, and each of you must find your own way. Consider carefully before you dedicate yourselves."

The eight fairies left. They washed off their face powder and rouge, and they each cut off their own hair. Then they returned and said, "We have already changed our outward appearance. We swear we will dedicate ourselves to your teaching."

"Very well," said Liu-kuan. "I am touched to see that all eight of you are of one mind." Then he went up to the teacher's seat and the light of the Buddha's brow shone into the world and flowers fell from the heavens like rain as he began to teach from *The Diamond Sutra*.

> All things conditioned
> are like dreams, illusions, bubbles, shadows—
> like dewdrops, like a flash of lightning,
> and thus shall we perceive them.

When he had finished his teaching, Hsing-chen and the eight new nuns awakened, in a flash, to the unborn and undying truth of the dharma. Seeing that Hsing-chen's faith was lofty and pure, Liu-kuan called together all of his disciples and said, "I came to bring the teachings of the Buddha to China. Now that I have found another who can deliver the dharma, I shall return to the place from which I came." And giving his *mala*, his rice bowl, his water gourd, his ringed staff,[10] and the text of *The Diamond Sutra* to Hsing-chen, he departed toward the western sky.

From that time forward, Hsing-chen taught well and oversaw the monastery at Lotus Peak, where immortals and dragons, men and spirits, all revered him as they had Master Liu-kuan. The eight nuns served Hsing-chen as their master until, by and by, all of them became bodhisattvas and the nine entered, together, into Paradise.

APPENDIX A:

Names of the Eight Women

(in order of appearance):

	CHINESE	ROMANIZATION (WADE-GILES) AS USED IN THE TEXT	MEANING
I	秦彩鳳	Ch'in Ts'ai-feng	Rainbow Phoenix
2	桂蟾月	Kuei Ch'an-yüeh	Moonlight
3	狄驚鴻	Ti Ching-hung	Shy Wild Goose
4	鄭瓊貝	Cheng Ch'iung-pei becomes Princess Ying-yang	Jasper Shell Blossom
5	賈春雲	Chia Ch'un-yün	Spring Cloud
6	李簫和	Li Hsiao-ho known as Princess Lan-yang	Panpipe Harmony Orchid
7	瀋鳥烟	Shen Niao-yen	Cloud of Starlings
8	白凌波	Po Ling-po	Whitecap

APPENDIX B:

Reading *Kuunmong* in
Chinese and Korean

While I have attempted to give as full a sense of this novel as translation allows, some nuances of *Kuunmong*'s linguistic sophistication are simply impossible to convey in English. As a postscript to the translation, I wish to offer an example of the brilliant linguistic complexity of *Kuunmong*, in its convergence of Chinese and Korean, in order to give a sense of the depth of its wordplay and to show how its language relates to its central themes on many levels.

One of the most subtle and interesting examples of the complex wordplay in the novel is the reference to Shao-yu's birthday in the last chapter. Kim writes that it was "around the twentieth day of the eighth month," which is quite curious when he could simply give a precise date—it is fiction, after all. (Gale and Rutt have rendered the date as the "sixteenth day of the eighth moon" whereas Kim Byong-Cook, in his translation of *Kuunmong* into modern Korean, has kept the actual date reference.) But with this apparently casual term, which is in keeping with approximate date references in Chinese, Kim Man-jung gives a very direct and yet elegantly subtle insight into the novel's underlying Buddhist themes. The date given in the text, 念間 (Chinese: *nianjian*; Korean: *yeomgan* 염간), can be rendered as the time "before and after the twentieth" or "sometime around the twentieth." "Twenty" (similar to the English "score") is one of the primary meanings of 念 and "interval" or "period" is one of the primary meanings of 間.

A closer reading of those two Chinese characters reveals that Kim is not being needlessly vague or imprecise about the date of Shao-yu's birth. In keeping with the multilayered word-play of the best Tang poetry, which often shows awareness of underlying pictographic elements in the etymologies of specific graphs, these two Chinese characters point to the very heart of *Kuunmong*'s theme and structure.

If we look at the semipictographic, archaic small seal script version of 念, we can see a male child being born under a roof. While the upper part of the character shows the roof, the lower part is actually the archaic pictographic version of "heart," depicting its chambers, but it also looks like a penis and scrotum:

The second character, 間, looks like an infant coming out from between the mother's legs:

In sequence, the two small seal script characters look like a cartoon depicting Hsing-chen's incarnation as Shao-yu: a male child born in a shack, which is, indeed, what happens in the novel.

Typically in fiction, a character's name can serve as an associative shorthand revealing his or her traits, as in *Jane Eyre*.[1] *Kuunmong* incorporates that technique for its main characters as well, but here Kim has used the date as a similar summarizing symbol, and we can unpack from it many other layers of meaning.

念 can also be read as "longing" or "to miss" or "to show compassion or affection for" and the bottom part of 間 is a pictogram for the moon, suggesting moonlight coming through a pair of doors. This represents Shao-yu's feelings for Ch'an-yüeh (蟾月), whose name has two characters associated with the moon. And "anxious" or "worry," which are other readings of 念, suggest his anxiety brought on by his longing and concern for her.

Another reading of 念, particularly in a Buddhist context, is "thought" or "memory," and another reading of 間 is "instant" or "moment." Shao-yu's birth, in this sense, is like a fleeting thought. Indeed, his entire dream incarnation happens in a mere moment on the prayer mat, and this ephemeral illusion is the quality of all conditioned phenomena, as indicated in the verse of *The Diamond Sutra* quoted at the end of the novel.

In Buddhism, it is understood that time is an illusion created by human consciousness, and that makes Kim's use of those two Chinese characters especially interesting. Their pronunciation in Korean, *yeomgan*, is oddly similar to the word *yeongam* (영감,令監), which means "lord," "husband," and "old man"—all three of which apply to Hsing-chen in his dream incarnation as Shao-yu. In this associative reading, Shao-yu's birth already has his old age inscribed within it. The first syllable, *yeong*, can also be read as "soul," "mountain pass," or "zero," which are also relevant to Shao-yu and the plot of the novel, especially when one considers that the second syllable, *gam*, can be read phonetically as "material used in making," "feeling," or "impression." Not only is Shao-yu's birth implicitly associated with old age, it is also imbued with the makings of emptiness (zero), pointing once again at the interwoven depth of *Kuunmong*'s Buddhist themes.

So the story that Kim Man-jung wrote *Kuunmong* in one all-night session is obviously a bit of mythmaking parallel to the story of Lao Tzu composing the *Tao Te Ching* in one night. It is clear that Kim thought deeply about all aspects of *Kuunmong*, from the allegorical plot to the underlying moral message to the interlocking meanings of individual words written in Chinese characters with their auditory and pictographic values. To his readers, most of whom would have memorized the same Chinese classics he had memorized, Kim's novel would have been profoundly resonant, echoing layer upon layer, each revealing an integrated and coherent intention. It is no wonder that many scholars call it the "crown jewel" of Korean literature.

Notes

Certain terms, names, and places may be spelled differently in the notes than in the text. While I employed the more archaic Wade-Giles Romanization in the text, I have used the standard Pinyin romanizations in the notes, except where other romanizations have become established as the familiar form. For a fuller explanation, please refer to A Note on the Translation.

INTRODUCTION

1. *Kuunmong* predates Daniel Defoe's *Robinson Crusoe* (c. 1719)—often considered the first English-language novel—by some thirty years.

2. See Daniel Bouchez's 2006 essay "On *Kuunmong*'s Title" (*Kuunmong-ui jemog-e daehayoe*), in which he gives an excellent overview of this issue and cites the relevant passage.

3. Kim Man-jung's father, Kim Ikgyeom (1614–1636), committed suicide by blowing himself up with gunpowder rather than surrender to Manchu invaders.

4. The indigenous tradition of shamanism was repressed by the Confucian state and by the institution of Buddhism during the Joseon era (and continues to be repressed today, especially by Korean Christians, who have become a major political force). Although there are elements of shamanism in *Kuunmong*, they can be seen as tied to the Taoist folk beliefs of Tang China, in which the story is set.

5. This is in keeping with what I found in the process of translation: the linguistic jokes meant to be humorous when read visually in Chinese with knowledge of the auditory Korean are in keeping with Korean, and not Chinese, authorship. At the same time, these forms of wordplay also support the theory of *Kuunmong*'s initial composition in *hanja* and not hangul. The poetry composed by the characters in the story, which is based on Tang dynasty models and alludes directly to well-known Tang poetry,

is highly unlikely to have been written in hangul. There are also formal letters and edicts composed by the characters that would not make sense written in hangul, not only because the story is set in China, but because official documents were written in Chinese even in Korea.

6. I have provided the generally accepted authorship and dating here. See Minsoo Kang's discussion of the issue of authorship and dating of the text in his new translation of *The Story of Hong Gildong* (New York: Penguin Classics, 2016), pp. x–xiv.

7. To give a sense of the royal conflict during this period, Sukjong was eventually remorseful about deposing Queen Inhyeon. When the Southern faction tried again to purge the Western faction, Sukjong had one of his about-faces and purged the Southerners instead, reinstating Queen Inhyeon. It is said that the consort Jang then murdered her by using black magic. When Sukjong found out, he had Jang, her companions, and a number of relatives executed in 1701.(But before she died, Jang so seriously injured her own son that he became sterile and had to relinquish his role as Sukjong's successor to another son.)

8. In fact, she may have aspired to be the Joseon parallel to the Tang dynasty empress consort Wu Zetian (武則天, 624–705), one of the most powerful women in Chinese history, with three sons who later became emperors. But Jang would have been associated more with the scandalous beauty Zhao Feiyan (趙飛燕, c. 32–1 BCE), of the Han dynasty, for her behavior and her humble class background.

9. See William H. Nienhauser, ed., *Tang Dynasty Tales: A Guided Reader* (Singapore: World Scientific, 2010).

10. The themes of reality/illusion (*maya*) and interpenetration (*tongdal*) are fairly explicit in the plot of *Kuunmong*, but the issue of essense-function (*che-yong*) is more implicit and layered into the language. Hsing-chen's name refers to the Buddhist *original nature*, which is his *essence*. In Buddhism, one's original nature is in keeping with Buddha nature (the unconditioned state), and it is what gives all sentient beings the potential for enlightenment. On the other hand, Hsing-chen's dream counterpart, Shao-yu (whose name can be glossed to mean "Small Visitor" or "Brief Resider"), is his *function*, representing a parallel to the world as perceived in the conditioned state. At the end of the novel, the illusion (conditioned) returns to reality (the original nature) and permits Hsing-chen to become enlightened. Thus the structure of the novel is a kind of micro-

cosmic analogy to what happens in the greater world of reality (though, ironically, the illusory world in the novel occupies most of its narrative).

11. Since Kim was writing *Kuunmong* in the second half of the seventeenth century, Korea was still resonating with the aftermath of the Hideyoshi invasions, which ended in 1598 and were opposed partially by the *uisa*, "righteous monks," who participated in the war. The leader of the *uisa* was Seosan Hyujeong (1520–1604), a Korean Seon (Zen) master whose writings were very much influenced by Weonhyo and Jinul and also Gihwa (1376–1433), who had defended Buddhism against Confucian oppression.

12. The grid shape of this diagram, like the # symbol, is also reminiscent of 井, the ancient Chinese pictogram representing the well, a reference to the *I Ching*'s hexagram 48, which happens to be about the enduring underlying structures that govern proper society and relationships.

13. *Dukkha* (Sanskrit: दुःख) literally translates as "bad space" and refers to the fact that a wheel will not spin properly when its axle hole is off center. The Chinese character for *dukkha* is 苦 (Korean pronunciation: *go*), which translates as "suffering." The Korean reading of the Chinese character can also be "bitter."

14. There is quite a lot of neuroscientific research being done in relation to Buddhist meditation at institutions like the University of Michigan, the University of California, Davis, and the University of Wisconsin. Even the Dalai Lama has taken to calling Buddhism "the science of mind." In popular literature, see Robert Wright's *Why Buddhism Is True: The Science and Philosophy of Meditation and Enlightenment* (New York: Simon and Schuster, 2017) and Rick Hanson's *Buddha's Brain: The Practical Neuroscience of Happiness, Love, and Wisdom* (Oakland, CA: New Harbinger Publications, 2009). For a description of the neuroscience that explains the phenomenology of Buddhism, see B. Alan Wallace's *Contemplative Science: Where Buddhism and Neuroscience Converge* (New York: Columbia University Press, 2007) and Tor Nørretranders's *The User Illusion: Cutting Consciousness Down to Size* (New York: Penguin Books, 1997).

15. Like those works, *Kuunmong* participates in an old tradition, found throughout the world and through time—from prehistoric Australia to Renaissance Italy—of stories about the intersection of reality and dream. For example, the Dreamtime of

the Aboriginal people is a reality that precedes and follows the one we live in, simultaneously paralleling it, and its stories offer insight into our mundane lives in this reality even while they provide a concrete historical record of the past. In European literature, works like the strange *Hypnerotomachia Poliphili* (*The Dream of Poliphilus*, 1499) by Francesco Colonna, in the tradition of romance despite its proto-surrealist use of dream narrative, also act like parables or fables whose lessons we may apply to our current lives. *Kuunmong* performs similar functions in its interweaving of mythology and folktales with a narrative that dramatizes the illusion of time and the interpenetration of reality and dream (for its main character) and the interpenetration of reality and the imaginary world of a novel (for its reader).

A NOTE ON THE TRANSLATION

1. The 1974 edition was the first part of *Virtuous Women: Three Classic Korean Novels (A Nine Cloud Dream, Queen Inhyŭn, Chun-hyang)*. https://archive.org/details/KLTI14_201701.
2. See *A Korean Classic: The Nine Cloud Dream*, Korean Folklore and Classics, Vol. 5 (Seoul: Ewha Women's University, n.d. [1973]).
3. To this distinguished company, I should add Kevin O'Rourke and Brother Anthony of Taizé, who are still translating Korean literature today and have been instrumental in educating and mentoring new generations of translators.

ACKNOWLEDGMENTS

1. Byong-Cook Kim's *Kim Man Jung's The Cloud Dream of the Nine: A Modern Korean Translation with a Critical Essay* (Seoul: Seoul National University Press, 2007). Kim's book is based on the four-volume edition of *Kuunmong*, a manuscript version in Middle Korean, held in the Kyujanggak Institute for Korean Studies at Seoul National University.

CHAPTER 1.
The Reincarnation of Hsing-chen

1. From southernmost to northernmost, these mountains extend from current Shanghai Province all the way toward Beijing.

They are collectively known as Wuyue (五嶽), usually translated as the "Five Great Mountains," which are associated with the Heavenly Emperor and have been the destination of pilgrimages since ancient times. Their positions correspond to the five directions of Chinese cosmology (north, south, east, west, and center). Imperial China considered itself to be the center of the world, with the seat of the emperor corresponding to the mirroring of Heaven on Earth.

2. Yu the Great 大禹 (c. 2200–2100 BCE) is a semimythic figure who introduced flood control in prehistoric China. There are actually no records documenting him until at least a thousand years later, and so he is generally regarded, with Yao and Shun, as one of the semimythic great "Sage Kings" of antiquity.

3. 秦始皇, Qin Shi Huang in Pinyin—his name means "the First Emperor of Qin," and he was the first great historical emperor of a unified China. His reign was actually quite short, from 220 to 210 BCE, but his influence on all of Chinese history was profound.During his reign he standardized units of measure and the writing system. He also began building what was eventually to become the Great Wall.

4. A mortal could become immortal by practicing the esoteric arts of Taoist alchemy, a diverse tradition that usually incorporated breathing exercises, meditation, special diets, and the use of medicinal and sometimes hallucinogenic plants.

5. The Tang dynasty, which lasted from 618 to 907, is generally considered the golden age of Chinese culture when it comes to literature and the arts. In the Korean literature of Kim Man-jung's era, the Tang dynasty setting was a historical fantasy backdrop, but it was also the political ideal emulated by the Korean kings. Thematically, this setting for *Kuunmong* may have additional significance because the Tang dynasty was founded by the Li (李) family. Li also happened to be the surname of the Yi dynasty (the dynastic family of Joseon Korea). Further, Tang was also briefly interrupted when Empress Wu seized control and declared a second Zhou dynasty, which lasted only fifteen years (690–705). Empress Wu (Wu Zetian) was a concubine who became "empress consort" after she married the son of her dead husband, Emperor Taizong. There is a cautionary message to King Sukjong of Joseon, a Yi (李) who elevated his own concubine, Jang, to the position of "queen consort." During Empress Wu's reign, China also invaded the Korean peninsula and caused chaos among the Korean kingdoms.

6. One of the central scriptures (sutras) of Buddhism, said to "cut through illusion like a diamond." In Sanskrit, the title is *Vajracchedikā Prajñāpāramitā Sūtra*, which is loosely translated as "The Diamond Sutra of the Perfection of Wisdom." Some of the central ideas in the sutra include nonattachment and nonabiding (which means avoiding attachment to mental constructs in one's daily life). In Chinese, it is 金剛般若波羅蜜多經, condensed to 金剛般, *Geumgang gyeong* 금강경 in Korean. This sutra is chanted regularly at nearly all Korean Seon (Zen) temples to this day.

7. Liuguan 六觀(육관)—a reference to the six sense organs or faculties mentioned in *The Diamond Sutra*. These correspond to the five senses and their sense objects (eye/vision, ear/sound, nose/smell, tongue/taste, body/touch) and the sixth, which in Buddhism is the mind and its corresponding mind objects (thoughts, emotions, etc.). *The Diamond Sutra* also lists the "six requirements" for those who would read or teach it (belief, hearing, time, host, place, and audience). Master Liu-kuan has both of these and also exhibits the "six perfections" of Mahayana Buddhism (generosity, moral virtue, patience, diligence, contemplation, and wisdom).

8. Xingzhen 性眞 (성진)—translates as "Original True Nature," but the first character can also be read as "sex" or "gender." Allegorically, this makes Hsing-chen represent the potential for carnal desire. He is a kind of raw material for returning to original innocence, but also for working out the urges of sex and gender.

9. A reference to the canonical literature of Chinese Buddhism. In the context of *Kuunmong* this would be the *Tripitaka*, or the "Three Baskets," which refers to the *vinaya* (texts regarding the rules and regulations of the monastic life), the *sutras* (texts of the Buddha's sermons and teachings), and the *abhidharma* (secondary discourses on the sutras). The *Tripitaka Koreana*, the oldest and most complete text of the *Tripitaka* in Chinese, was carved onto some eighty thousand woodblocks during the thirteenth century during the Mongol invasions of Korea. It was an act of devotion performed by the Goryeo kings, in hopes that it would help Korea expel the Mongols.

10. There are four Dragon Kings (龍王) in Chinese folk culture, each associated with one of the four cardinal points, the four major bodies of water (each a sea named for a cardinal point), and the four seasons (east/blue/spring, south/red/summer, west/

white/fall, and north/black/winter). The Dragon Kings are parallel to the figure of Poseidon in Western mythology, and they
are ruled only by the Jade Emperor of Heaven; they are deities
associated with water, every significant body of water being associated with a resident dragon or serpent (even today in Korean folklore). The Dragon King in *Kuunmong* is the one who
lives in Lake Dongting (meaning "Grotto Court"), which is
said to have giant caverns with passages leading to every part of
China.

11. In Chinese folk culture, eight fairies are associated with the
"Eight Immortals"—humans who have achieved immortality
through esoteric Taoist practices. They are folk heroes, and only
one of them is female. Here, the literal translation would be
"eight immortal women" (八仙女). 仙女 itself is usually translated as "fairy," and in Korean folk culture, they are associated
with the supernatural women who live in the court of the Jade
Emperor in the Heavenly Kingdom. The Chinese character for
"fairy" (仙) is made up of "mountain" (山) and "person" (人).

12. Also known as *The Classic of Rites* (*Liji*, 禮記), one of the *Five
Classics* of the Confucian canon. *The Book of Rites* is a collection of texts regarding the proper performance of rituals, rules
for administration, and instructions for proper etiquette. It also
includes the teachings of Confucius and biographical details.

13. The twenty-eighth and last of the Indian patriarchs of Buddhism. He is the one who brought Chan (Zen) Buddhism from
India to China. The fairies are implicitly comparing him to
Master Liu-kuan, who also came from the west to bring Buddhism to China.

14. Similar to the rosary used by Catholics, the *mala* is used by
Buddhists for keeping count of prayers or mantras. One type of
traditional *mala* (favored by Tibetan Buddhists) has 108 beads.

15. Buddhism has two major branches, known as Mahayana (the
"Great Vehicle") and Theravada (the "School of the Elders";
also known, sometimes pejoratively, as Hinayana, the "Lesser
Vehicle"). Theravada Buddhism is the more conservative and
older branch, and the goal of a practitioner is to become an
arhat, achieving enlightenment for the self. In Theravada Buddhism, there is only one Buddha, who is the historic Buddha
Siddhartha Gautama. In Mahayana Buddhism, the Buddha is
one of many Buddhas who stretch both backward and forward
in time. The goal of Mahayana is to become a bodhisattva, a
being who reaches the verge of enlightenment but then remains

in the world to help all other sentient beings achieve enlightenment first before entering Nirvana. East Asian Buddhism is primarily Mahayana while South and Southeast Asian Buddhism is primarily Theravada. Tibetan Buddhism, a special path that claims enlightenment can be reached in this single lifetime, is called Vajrayana (the "Adamantine Vehicle") and is a subbranch of Mahayana.

16. In Mahayana Buddhism, Gautama Buddha is only the fourth of a thousand Buddhas who will appear in this world to teach the dharma and compassion.

17. It was a common practice in both Tang China and Joseon Korea for families to dedicate one of their sons to the temple. In many cases, boys were "given" to a temple by poor parents who could not afford to raise them.

18. These are the figures who fetch the souls of the dead and bring them to the Buddhist Underworld.

19. King Yama (閻魔大王, "Great King Yama," usually called *Yeomra* in Korean), though based on the Hindu deity, is somewhat different. He is the ruler of the Underworld and the judge of those brought there after the end of their incarnation on Earth. In Buddhist mythology, he oversees the Ten Kings of Hell.

20. Shakyamuni means "Sage of the Shakyas," and is a reference to the historic Buddha, Siddhartha Gautama of the Shakya clan. In some versions of the story, Ananda (who is the Buddha's cousin) only enters the house of prostitution during his begging rounds and the Buddha later uses Ananda's near lapse of chastity as a moral lesson.

21. His full name is Bodhisattva King Ksitigarbha of the Great Vow (大願地藏菩薩, *Jijang Bosal* in Korean). Ksitigarbha vowed to teach all beings in the six worlds during the time between the Shakyamuni Buddha (the historic Buddha) and the Maitreya (the next Buddha in this world). His vow included the promise not to enter Nirvana until all the hells are emptied, which is why he is also known as the Bodhisattva of the Hell Beings.

22. In Buddhism, one is continuously born and reborn in the cycle of samsara because of karma. One is born with the karma one has accrued in a previous lifetime due to misdeeds, and one must strive to get rid of that burden. When one's karma is finally eliminated, one achieves enlightenment and attains nirvana, which is to leave the cycle of samsara. Although there is technically no good karma, in popular Buddhism, the idea of

working off one's karma operates much like the Western concept of changing one's fate.

23. Huainan (淮南) means "Lands South of the Huai River," placing it not far from contemporary Shanghai. During the Tang
dynasty, it was a state (also known as Wu), but Huainan is currently the name of an industrial city in Anhui Province.

24. A Chinese *li* is a traditional unit of measure that has varied
somewhat through history. It is approximately a third of a mile,
or around five hundred meters.

25. In Chinese, this is *junzi* (君子), or literally "lord's son," somewhat parallel to the Western notion of a gentleman. In Confucianism, the *junzi* is humble, loyal, disciplined, humane, and
lives in poverty. He is second only to the ideal of the sage. The
opposite of the *junzi* is the *xiaoren* (小人), the "small" or
"petty" person.

26. In Taoist mythology this is the paradisical mountain on the
mysterious island on which the Eight Immortals are said to live.
The first great emperor of China, Qin Shi Huang, is said to have
sent out several expeditions to find this island and accidentally
discovered the Korean peninsula in the process.

CHAPTER 2.
The Young Scholar

1. 潘岳 (247–300), a famous Jin dynasty poet known for his good
looks, also known as Pan An (which is still a Chinese label for a
man who is especially handsome).

2. A reference to Sun Tzu's *The Art of War* (sixth century BCE),
which in chapter 10 (on terrain) mentions the six types of tacti-
cal ground positions. The three practicalities are distance, dan-
gers, and obstacles. Sun Bin and Wu Qi were both famous
military strategists, and Sun Bin, according to some sources, is
said to be a descendant of Sun Tzu.

3. Known as Xi'an today, Chang'an (長安) was the ancient capital
of ten Chinese dynasties before the capital was moved to Beijing. The famous Terra-Cotta Army of Qin Shi Huang, the first
great emperor, is buried nearby in his mausoleum. During the
time *Kuumong* takes place, Chang'an was a walled city, and its
walls still stand today. The area is surrounded by pyramids,
and the center of the rectangular city was considered the center
of the Chinese universe.

4. Chu (楚) was the name of a Zhou dynasty state (1030–223 BCE). It covered a large area, including the setting of *Kuunmong*, and Shao-yu is alluding to it to suggest how special this particular willow grove happens to be.

5. This means she is of marriageable age and not a child any longer.

6. An allusion to one of the most popular romance tales in China. Cho Wen-chün was a widow who eloped with Szu-ma Hsiang-ju (d. 117 BCE), seduced by his zither playing. She was cast out by her father and ended up running a wine shop, her new husband entertaining guests with his musical ability. (His reputation as a poet eventually got him appointed to a high office because the emperor Han Wudi was so impressed by his abilities.)

7. Polygamy was an accepted practice both in Tang China and in Joseon Korea, but powerful men usually had multiple concubines and only one official wife. The Chinese emperors often had scores or even hundreds of concubines, reserving their official succession to the sons borne by their official wife or wives.

8. Wang Wei (699–759) and Li Po (Li Bai, also Li Taibai, 701–762) were two of the greatest poets of the Tang dynasty. Wang Wei was also an accomplished artist and intellectual, a Buddhist who retired, after being involved in great political turmoil during the An-shi rebellion, to live in semiseclusion. Li Po, on the other hand, was a flamboyant Taoist legendary for his drunken excesses, an accomplished swordsman, and an excellent calligrapher. Li Po was banished by the emperor for his outspoken excesses, and two of the best poems by Tu Fu (Dufu), another great Tang poet and dear friend of Li Po, are both called "Dreaming of Li Po." Li Po is probably the best known of the Tang poets in the West because of Ezra Pound's translations of his poems (attributed to the Japanese rendition of his name, Ri-haku) in *Cathay*, published in 1915.

9. Most likely a reference to Qiu Shiliang (仇士良), who died in 843. He was a eunuch who became very powerful during the reign of Emperor Xianzong of Tang after helping him with his bid to power. This is a curious allusion, because there was also a general named Cho Shiliang during the Tang dynasty who was a Buddhist and was known for being friendly to foreign monks.

10. The civil service examination system (*keju* 科舉, *gwageo* in Korean) began in imperial China and was used until 1905. During the Tang dynasty, this exam was theoretically open to all men, regardless of social background (except slaves and those of the lowest classes), and was based on knowledge of the classics. A

high score on the exam would win the candidate a government position and could change the fortunes of his entire extended family for subsequent generations. Korea, which modeled its *gwageo* system on the Tang system, administered the exams until they were abolished after social reforms in 1894.

11. I have used the Japanese term *go* here because that is how the game is generally known in the West. The Korean term is *baduk* and the Chinese is *weiqi* (圍棋), which means "encirclement chess." Go is played with black and white stones on a board with a grid of nineteen by nineteen lines, and its rules are very simple but the potential play configurations exceed the number of atoms in the observable universe. During the Tang dynasty, go was one of the requisite "cultivated arts" a gentleman scholar was expected to know (the other three being calligraphy, painting, and music). The image of two Taoist immortals playing go on a mountain is a common theme in traditional Chinese painting.

12. Here the reference is to Taoist immortals, who are either residents of the Heavenly Kingdom or are humans who have achieved their immortality by practicing Taoist alchemy. Taoist immortals have a status similar to the devas of Hindu culture.

13. The Koreans translate this instrument as a *geomungo*, which is based on the Chinese *qin*. It is in the same family of instruments as the zither, an instrument Confucian scholars were expected to master.

14. Peng Zu (彭祖, also Penzi) is often called the Taoist Methuselah for having lived a long life spanning two dynasties—777 or 800 years, depending on which account one reads. The term *yoga* (referring to any practice used to achieve "union" with the divine) is generally applied to Taoist practices today, though they might more accurately be called *qigong* (practices for cultivating the life force of *qi*).

15. A "cash" is a traditional Chinese coin (方孔錢) that has a square hole in the center. The coins were carried on strings for convenience.

CHAPTER 3.
Meeting Ch'an-yüeh at Lo-yang

1. The Luo River (洛河) is a tributary of the Yellow River. The city of Loyang (Luoyang), one of the "four great ancient capitals" of China, is located where the Luo joins the Yellow River.

2. The pipa is one of the most popular Chinese musical instruments, often called the Chinese lute for its similarity to the Western string instrument.

3. A love story recorded by the great historian Szu-ma Ch'ien (Sima Qian, b. 145 BCE). Szu-ma Hsiang-ju was a marvelous and unconventional poet who seduced a young widow, Cho Wen-chün, and ran off with her, defying social convention. This is alluded to again later, after Shao-yu meets Cheng Ch'iung-pei.

4. The expression *jing di zhi wa* (井底之蛙, "frog at the bottom of the well") comes from a famous Taoist fable in the *Zhuangzi*. The story, told by Kung-sun Lung to Prince Mou of Wei, is about a frog who is happy and brags of his existence in the limited world he can perceive at the bottom of a well. When a turtle from the eastern sea describes the vast ocean to him, the frog is abashed and crestfallen, realizing the smallness of his world.

5. Han Wudi, Emperor Wu of Han (漢武帝), considered one of the greatest emperors in Chinese history, ruled from 141 to 87 BCE.

6. Wei was a short-lived dynasty that lasted from 220 to 266.

CHAPTER 4.
A Mysterious Priestess

1. Han Yu (韓愈, 768–824) was an important literary and intellectual figure during the Tang dynasty. He was known as the greatest prose stylist of his time, and he was a critic of both Taoism and Buddhism.

2. Chinese music is based on the ancient pentatonic scale. The five tones, which correspond to the Taoist elements, are: *gong* 宮 (Earth), *shang* 商 (Metal), *jue* 角 (Wood/Air), *zi* 徵 (Fire), and *yu* 羽 (Water), which also correspond, respectively, to the five emotions: anxiety, grief, anger, excitement, and fear.

3. Although she is Minister Cheng's wife and the birth mother of Lady Cheng, she would have kept her own surname.

4. Also known as a litter. Small sedan chairs were typically carried by two or four men and open, unlike a palanquin, which was generally closed.

5. "The Rainbow-Feathered Robe" was the tune that originally accompanied the dance of a famous consort, Yang Guifei, as she performed for Xuanzong (Emperor Minghuang), who ruled from 713 to 756.

6. Ji Kang (嵇康, 223–262) was a Taoist philosopher and alchemist. Though he tried to avoid court intrigues, he was sentenced

to death by Sima Zhao (King of Cao Wei) for defending a friend
who had been framed. Three thousand scholars signed a petition to release Ji Kang, but to no avail.

7. Bo Ya (伯牙) was a famous musician and poet known for his *qin*
playing during the Spring and Autumn Period (770–476 BCE).

8. Shun (舜), also known as Emperor Shun, is one of the three legendary Sage Kings of China, the other two being Yao (堯) and Yu (禹).
Shun is said to have lived sometime between 2294 and 2184 BCE.

CHAPTER 5.
Tryst with a Fairy and a Ghost

1. Princess Taiping (太平公主, d. 713), whose name means "Princess of Peace," was a daughter of the infamous Empress Wu
Zeitan, whose reign interrupted the Tang dynasty for fifteen
years with her second Zhou dynasty.

2. This is a double-edged statement, since it can mean that Shao-
yu was so competent that he discharged his duties swiftly and
efficiently or that officials at court didn't really have much to
do. Here, given Kim's wit, it is likely to mean both.

3. 十三; Gale simply renders his name as "Thirteen," whereas Rutt
uses "Shih-san." It is a lucky number in Chinese for its homophonic value (similar in sound to "definitely alive"), but, given the
pervasive Taoist and Buddhist symbology in *Kuunmong*, this
name is most likely an ironic reference to the thirteen *dhutanga*s,
or ascetic practices. The Buddha himself prescribed only ten
*dhutanga*s for his monks, but his rival cousin, Devadatta, pro-
posed a stricter set of thirteen to show he was even holier. Here,
Thirteen's behavior is hardly ascetic. (The thirteen *dhutanga*s are
still practiced by some monks of the Thai Forest tradition.)

4. 王維 (699–759); one of the most celebrated Tang dynasty poets.
He was a Buddhist in his later years and also known for his
fabulous landscape paintings. See note 8, chapter 2.

5. "Peach Blossom Spring Story" (桃花源記), or "The Peach Blossom Land," was a fable by Tao Yuanming, written in 421,
about a Shangri-la–esque land where people lived oblivious to
the outside world (see also note 11, chapter 5).

6. Wulingyuan (武陵源) is a scenic area in Hunan, China, famous
for its surreal sandstone formations often depicted in classical
Chinese art and used as the setting of myths and supernatural
romances. The Wulingyuan Scenic Area is a Natural World
Heritage site.

7. Zigefeng (紫閣峰), literally "Purple Pavilion Peak"; probably a reference to the eighth stanza of Tu Fu's famous poem "Reflections in Autumn," or "Autumn Meditations": "From Kunwu, the Yusu River comes winding 'round, / The dark shade of Purple Pavilion Peak sinks into Meipi Lake."

8. See note 24, chapter 1.

9. Every six thousand years, according to Chinese mythology, the Jade Emperor and his wife, Xi Wangmu, held a fabulous banquet called the Feast of Peaches, in which they served the Heavenly Peaches to the deities to keep them immortal. The trees in the peach orchard bloomed only once every millennium, and it took another three thousand years for the peaches of immortality to ripen. In Wu Cheng'en's sixteenth-century novel *Journey to the West* (西遊記)—a story which would have been familiar to Kim Man-jung and which shares motifs in common with *Kuunmong*—one of the Monkey King's great crimes is to gluttonously eat up all the peaches reserved for the banquet.

10. This is an allusion to the Chinese legend of Wu Kang, a lazy and impatient young man who wants to be immortal. First he studies herbal medicine with a Taoist master, but gives up after only three days. Then he fails at learning the military arts. He is too impatient to study books. Wu Kang finally angers his master and is banished to the Moon Palace, the abode of the moon goddess. He is told that the only way to come back to Earth is to chop down the cassia tree that grows there. Wu Kang tries to chop it down, but the tree is magical—it heals itself after each blow of the ax—and so Wu Kang is still on the moon, chopping away. It is said that when the moon is full, one can see the shadows of Wu Kang and the magical cassia tree, and when the moon is big in the fall, cassia buds will fall from it and perfume the clouds.

11. Liu Chen and Yuan Zhao were cousins whose story, with several variants, is similar to that of Washington Irving's Rip Van Winkle. In some versions they are out to fetch water or find medicine when they happen upon two fairies playing chess. In others, they happen upon a whole banquet of immortals. Relevant to this section of *Kuunmong* is the central theme of the legend: the two men, upon their return after what they think is only fifteen days (during which they had taken fairies as wives), discover that seven generations have passed and no one recognizes them. In despair, they attempt to return to the fairies in the Wu Ling Peach Paradise, but they can no longer find the en-

trance. In some variants of the story, they kill themselves in despair and the Jade Emperor takes pity on them, appointing Liu Chen the deity of good fortune and Yuan Zhao the deity of ill fortune. *Liu Chen and Yuan Zhao Entering the Tiantai Mountains* is a famous series of ink drawings with accompanying text done by Zhao Cangyun during the Yuan dynasty (1271–1368).

12. Mount Tiantai (天台山); a mountain ("Heavenly Terrace") as well as a mountain range in eastern China considered sacred by both Taoists and Buddhists. Buddhism began to flourish there in the late sixth century. The mountains became a major center for international pilgrims, and there were as many as seventy-two major temples there at one time, some of which are still standing even after the destruction of temples during the Cultural Revolution. In the seventeenth and eighteenth centuries, the temples in the region were a center for Buddhist scholars. The Korean Cheontae and Japanese Tendai sects are named for the Buddhism (the syncretic "Lotus School") that originated in the Tiantai Mountains. Most relevant to Kuunmong is the fact that the great monk Zhiyi, who played a major part in establishing the religious culture of the Sui dynasty (581–618), settled in the Tiantai Mountains in 576. This parallels the opening of the novel, which describes how the great monk Liu-kuan established his temple on Lotus Peak in the Heng-shan range. Most relevant to this chapter (and thematically resonant with the novel as a whole) is the Tiantai doctrine, which follows the logic of Nagarjuna (who is often known as "the Second Buddha" for his wisdom) and asserts: (1) all phenomena are empty and without essential reality; (2) all phenomena have a provisional reality; and (3) all phenomena are without essential reality and are provisionally real at the same time. These three assertions are thematically central to the Buddhist reading of *Kuunmong*.

13. A reference to the abode of the Chinese moon goddess, Chang'e, whose abode includes a cinnamon tree and a rabbit.

14. Also called Lake of Gems or Green Jade Lake, the home of Xi Wangmu (西王母), "Queen Mother of the West," the goddess who ruled over a paradise in the Kunlun Mountains. She was an especially popular figure in Tang dynasty poetry. Note the parallel to Lady Wei of the Southern Peak mentioned at the opening of the story. See note 10, chapter 5.

15. Wang An-shi (王安石, 1021–1086); a poet, writer, and statesman of the Sung dynasty.

16. Meng Chang (孟昶, 919–965); last emperor of the Later Shu (934–965), one of the Ten Kingdoms located in the present-day Sichuan area.

17. Zhang Lihua (張麗華, d. 589) was an imperial consort renowned for her beauty. She was the favorite concubine of Chen Shubao, last emperor of the Chen dynasty.

18. Gale's and Rutt's translations include the poems, which are not in the edition I used as my primary source. They are dramatically extraneous.

19. In Chinese folk religion and in Buddhism as well as Taoism, those who die with unresolved issues, or die tragically, roam the Earth as *egui* (餓鬼), hungry ghosts. Hungry ghosts are not the same as the spirits of the normally deceased ancestors and they must be appeased by different means. Some hungry ghosts, who are attached to the world by unresolved desire, behave much like the figure of the succubus in Western culture.

20. *Taiji* (太極); literally, "the supreme ultimate." This is not the martial art but a reference to what is commonly represented by the yin/yang symbol in Taoist cosmology, the dynamic interplay of yin and yang qualities that gives rise to the phenomenal world.

21. Li Chunfeng (李淳風) and Yuan Tian-gang (袁天罡) together were like the Nostradamus of seventh-century Tang China. Li Chunfeng was a genius in mathematics, astronomy, and history. He wrote books on astrology and numerological prognostication, as well as descriptions of Taoist practices. Yuan Tian-gang, for his part, was the inventor of a practice called "Bone Weight Astrology." He is said to have read the physiognomy of the young Wu Zetian (武則天), who became the empress consort Wu, making predictions about her future while missing the fact that she was a girl. Yuan and Li are credited with the *Tui bei tu* (推背圖, literally "Back Massage Drawings"), a famous book of enigmatic prophecies about China's future. Some say it predicts World War III between China and the United States. This allusion refers to the previous episode in *Kuunmong* in which Yang disguised himself as a nun in order to get a look at his future wife's face.

22. The Four Seas, each associated with a cardinal direction, were considered the boundaries of China. See also note 10, chapter 1.

23. It is generally believed in Korea and China (even today) that excessive sex produces dark circles under a man's eyes because of

the loss of vital fluid. This is in keeping with the Taoist practice of preserving and recirculating the seminal fluid to enhance the cultivation of *qi*, the life force.

24. Rutt leaves this out for some reason. Gale translates: "Yang Won of Cho married a fairy and lived with her, and Nyoo Chon had a child with a ghost."

25. Once again, Rutt and Gale include poems here that are not in the edition I used as my primary source (see note 18, chapter 5). These were probably additions by someone other than Kim Man-jung during a later transcription or printing.

26. Probably an ironic reference to the statesman-poet of the early Warring States Period (475–221 BCE) who wrote "Unpopularity," which turns out to be the opposite of Shao-yu's future. Herbert A. Giles's 1883 translation of the poem, in *Gems of Chinese Literature: Verse*, concludes with the lines: "Behold the philosopher, full of nervous thought, / with a fame that never grows dim, / Dwelling complacently alone,—say, / what can the vulgar herd know of him?"

27. This is a reference to the Han dynasty tale of Emperor Wu and Lady Li, which is often cited as the origin of Chinese shadow theater. Wu was distraught at the death of his favorite concubine. A Taoist sorcerer named Shao-weng summoned her spirit within a screen of curtains, but only under the condition that the emperor observe from a distance and not come close for a direct look. The poem Wu composed afterward begins with the lines, "Is it she? / Or is it not?"

28. 春雲; Gale renders her name as "Cloudlet," but it is more literally "Spring Cloud."

29. Jia (賈). The Chinese character here is the one for a surname for which there are some interesting homophonic readings consistent with the plot of the novel: 假, fake, borrow; 佳, beautiful. When considered pictographically, the layered homophonic associations comprise a joke, especially since Jia (家), another surname homophone, is a character made from the radicals of "house" over "pig" and is typically read as representing a prosperous home. In Chinese and Korean folklore, it is often the homely woman who is the most virtuous.

30. Or Mengzi (372–289 BCE). Mencius is often called "the Second Sage" after Confucius, and his interpretations and commentaries of Confucius constitute the orthodox version of Confucianism. Mencius himself also wrote about human nature, education, and politics.

31. Clouds and rain are references to sexual intercourse in classical Chinese literature, dating back to the Yin and Zhou dynasties, when sexual intercourse was part of the ritual for producing rain. In Taoist terms, this is one of the illustrations of the profound connection between humans and nature, but it had also become a prominent theme in pornographic writing and art by the Tang period.

32. Gale adds, in what seems like an explication: "You are not a fairy, and you are not a spirit; but she who made you a fairy, and again she who made you a spirit, surely possesses the law by which we turn to fairies and spirits, and will she say that I am but a common man of earth and not want to keep company with me? And will she call this park where I live the dusty world of men, and not wish to see me? If she can change you into a fairy or into a spirit, can't I do just the same and change you, too?"

33. 姮娥, the Chinese goddess of the moon, also known as Chang-o or Chang'e (嫦娥). See also note 13, Chapter 15.

34. This is one of the significant moments when Kim alludes to the "reality" portion of the novel from inside the "dream" portion by recalling the fairy servants of Lady Wei. The entire structure of *Kuunmong* is actually like a fractal woven together with large- and small-scale examples of this type of interpenetration, and this trope—consistent with the Hwaeom (華嚴) school of Buddhism (centrally important, particularly during the Joseon period)—is another piece of evidence that the text is of Korean origin.

35. This is actually an erotically charged detail, since the "Spring Cloud" is rising to give formal thanks to Shao-yu. It refers directly back to all the lurid double entendres regarding the clouds and rain (see note 31, chapter 5).

CHAPTER 6.
The Boy at the Roadside

1. There were several major conflicts between Tibet and China during the Tang dynasty. The Tibetans actually captured the Tang capital of Chang'an in 763 during the An-shi rebellion, which had destabilized the empire. "Tibetan" was also a term that often referred to any of the "barbarian" tribes to the west, and Tang popular literature (stories like "The Tibetan Slave") often features Tibetan characters who are fearsome and large.

2. The Queen Dowager of Nanyue, a kingdom northwest of China, wanted to make her kingdom part of the Han dynasty empire during the reign of Han Wudi in 113 BCE. At the time, she was married to Zhao Yingqi, who had served in Han Wudi's court in Chang'an while he was a prince. Zhao and his queen had disagreements.

3. This sort of lavish reward is not unusual for Tang China, but it is probably exaggerated for dramatic effect. Gale's translation says "five thousand rolls of silk and fifty horses," probably because that seemed more reasonable!

4. Now known as Henan (河南)—a province in north-central China.

5. *Qilin* in Pinyin. This is typically translated as "giraffe," but it is a mythic chimera. In Chinese folklore, it was an auspicious omen heralding the arrival of a great sage or a ruler, which is appropriate here. The Chinese phoenix is also a chimera and represents the union of male and female, suggesting here that Shao-yu will soon join again with Ch'an-yüeh.

6. A talent is approximately seventy-five pounds in weight.

7. Han-tan is now Handan (邯鄲), a city in the southwest of Hebei Province in China.

8. This is an allusion to the story about King Zhuang, who saved a young man's reputation when one of his consorts broke the man's hat string for accosting her in the dark during a banquet when the lamps had gone out. By having all the men break their hat strings before the lamps were relit, he made it impossible to determine who the offending party had been. The young man became a loyal servant of the king and repaid the debt by fighting for him. See D. C. Lau, ed., *A Concordance of the Shou Yuan* (Hong Kong: Commercial Press, 1992), p. 42.

CHAPTER 7.
The Imperial Son-in-Law

1. The literal reading of her name is "Startled Wild Goose," but the meaning is likely to be "Shy Wild Goose."

2. This is a curious allusion, since it seems to refer to Li Jing (李靖, 571–649), also known as Duke Jingwu of Wei, the famous general who was a military adviser to the Tang emperor Taizong. When Li Jing was old, he was too ill to lead the Chinese invasion force against Goguryeo Korea in 644 and Taizong's army was defeated.

3. A title not quite as high as a duke.

4. The classic devoted to history, usually translated as *The Classic of History* (also known as the *Shangshu*), is one of the ancient *Five Classics* of China. A decent scholar would have memorized it.

5. Prince Jin of Zhou, called "the Immortal Prince," was the son of King Ling. The famous empress Wu, a staunch supporter of Buddhism, memorialized the tomb of Prince Jin in 699 shortly before she took a Taoist elixir to extend her life. That elixir was concocted by Zhang Changzong, whom she believed to be a reincarnation of Prince Jin. She was pleased with the elixir, and in banquets held at court she would have Zhang dress up as Prince Jin and play the flute, riding on a wooden crane. (See *Jinhua Chen, Philosopher, Practitioner, Politician: The Many Lives of Fazang (643–712)* (Boston: Brill, 2007), p. 208. Kim thus combines the associations of Taoist immortality, Buddhism, reincarnation, and romance here all at once.

6. Gale glosses her name as "Orchid" and uses that throughout.

7. Tang China had contact with ancient Byzantine Syria. In 635, during the reign of Emperor Taizong, a Nestorian Christian monk named Alopen arrived in Chang'an, the capital, on a mission. This historical event is documented on the Nestorian Stele, which was erected in 781. For the Tang Chinese, anything associated with Syria would have an exotic and mythic quality to it.

8. According to Chinese legend, Xiao Shi, the Divine Immortal, could make his flute sound like the call of a phoenix. When he married Nongyu, they flew off together, Xiao Shi riding a dragon and Nongyu riding a phoenix. See Shiamin Kwa and Wilt L. Idema, trans., *Mulan: Five Versions of a Classic Chinese Legend, with Related Texts* (Cambridge: Hackett, 2010), p. 29.

9. This is a funny bit of wordplay because the Chinese character for "panpipe," 簫 *xiao*, can also be read to mean "miserable" or "dreary." The second part of the name, 和 *he*, can also be read as "composition." So her name is potentially its exact opposite: panpipe harmony vs. miserable composition.

10. A reference to Penglai, the Island of the Immortals (蓬萊仙境), equivalent to the Land of Faerie in Western tradition. See also note 26, chapter 1.

11. Eunuchs were present in the Chinese court as far back as the Han dynasty (206 BCE–220 CE), according to historical records. They served emperors and kings, often closely, and because they were castrated (and thus could not have children or

possibly impregnate a court woman like the queen or a princess), they were considered less of a potential threat to the ruler. In Chinese literature eunuchs are often depicted as conniving villains and cunning, self-interested advisers. Korean eunuchs, called *naesi* (內侍), are documented in *The History of Goryeo*. During King Sukjong's rule, there was an entire department of eunuchs, and it lasted through the Joseon era until the Gabo reform in 1894.

12. Their names mean "Vermilion Girl" and "Jade Dew."

13. The Tang emperor Xuanzong (唐玄宗) reigned from 713 to 756 (forty-three years), the longest reign of any of the Tang emperors. It's curious that he comes up here, since he was the son of a royal consort and he lived through the brief reign of Empress Dowager Wu Zeitan (a consort who took over the throne). This is yet another cautionary allusion to King Sukjong's reign (Xuanzong was also a Li, which would be a Yi, like Sukjong, in Korean).

14. This is a layered allusion. The Han dynasty figure Dongfang Shou (東方朔, 160–93 BCE) was Emperor Wu's court jester, known as a buffoon. But he was also later known, in mythology, as a *zhexian* (謫仙), a "banished immortal." The numerous references to the poet Li Po are also to someone banished, and allude to Kim's own banishment by King Sukjong.

15. Emperor Kuang-wu of the Later Han dynasty tried to convince Sung Hung to divorce his wife and marry a royal princess. Sung Hung declined. See David Tod Roy, trans., *The Plum in the Golden Vase; or, Chin P'ing Mei, Volume Four: The Climax* (Princeton, NJ: Princeton University Press, 2011), p. 775 fn. #23.

CHAPTER 8.
Strategy and Tactics

1. Wang Xianzhi (王獻之, 344–388) was one of China's most famous calligraphers. This is a charged allusion, since Wang was famous for being able to improvise from his mistakes and still make beautiful art.

2. The game in question isn't quite clear. Rutt also translates this as "backgammon," a game that was known in China in the tenth century as *shuanglu* (双陆).

3. From *The Book of Songs*, one of the *Five Classics* of Chinese literature. This is part of a girl's lament. In Gale's translation, he changes the allusion to make it more comprehensible to

Christians: "Is it God, or Mother Earth, or devils, or men who have done it?" See the James Legge translation of Shu Li in *The Odes of Wang* (https://ctext.org/book-of-poetry/odes-of-wang).

4. She alludes to the three relationships that govern the life of a proper Confucian woman just above: she must obey her father until she marries, then obey her husband after marriage. She must then obey her son, if she has one, upon his reaching majority.

5. The life of a woman was considered hard, so one hoped to be reborn a man in the next incarnation.

6. This is another parallelism between Shao-yu and Kim Manjung. After being allowed back from his first exile, Kim returned to court in 1679 and served on the Board of Rites, a position that involved monitoring and maintaining the proper protocol for Confucian ceremonies.

7. A reference to the Confucian philosopher Mencius (372–289 BCE), who said that the relationship between husband and wife was the greatest of human roles.

8. Emperor Taizong (598–649) was the second emperor of Tang, often considered the greatest of the dynasty. This is a very clever allusion in the text (and an apt coincidence in the plot, since the proximate theme has been marriage and its effect on the welfare of the state). The Tibetan invasion of Tang was precipitated by Songtsän Gampo's displeasure at not being allowed to marry a Tang princess: Emperor Taizong had rejected the Tibetan ruler's proposal. (The invasion involved only 200,000 soldiers.)

9. See note 2, chapter 2.

10. A reference to the treatise on strategy and tactics written in the eleventh century BCE by Jiang Tai Gong (姜子牙, Jiang Ziya), also known as the Duke of Zhou.

11. The eight trigrams, each made of a set of solid and broken lines, look very much like unit symbols on a battle map. This allusion is also directly related to the previous one, since Jiang Ziya's conversations on strategy with King Wen are what is documented in *The Six Secret Teachings*. King Wen is credited with creating the most ancient configuration of the trigrams into the sixty-four hexagrams used in divination with the *I Ching* (*Yijing*), or *The Book of Changes*.

12. Mount Jishi (積石), meaning "Piled [or Long-Standing or Accumulated] Rocks," is actually part of a range (currently known as the Amne Machin) that constitutes the southern part of the Kunlun range separating China from Tibet.

13. A cruel and clever antipersonnel weapon made of sharp metal spikes in a tetrahedral arrangement designed to have one point upward regardless of how they are scattered. They look similar to jacks used in the children's game and are especially useful for disabling soldiers and horses. In modern times they have been used against vehicles to puncture tires.

14. A reference to Muné Tsenpo, who ruled Tibet for only a year or two at the very end of the eighth century. Not much is known about him, but it is said that he was sympathetic to Buddhism, which had just become the formal religion under the previous ruler, King Trisong Detsen (755–797).

15. The literal meanings of the first two names are "Sea Moon" (Chen Hai-yüeh) and "Rainbow" (Chin Ts'ai-hung). Rutt glosses Shen Niao-yen as "Mistwreath," but the three characters in her name create a complex set of associations, literally "pouring bird smoke." Since Niao-yen is the mysterious assassin who appeared from the air, this set of associations most likely refers to the way a flock of starlings can appear to swirl like liquid smoke. Her name should thus more accurately be conveyed as "Cloud of Starlings."

CHAPTER 9
Among the Dragon Folk

1. Her name refers to a white-topped wave, i.e., a "whitecap."

2. The Jade Emperor, or the August Emperor of Jade (玉皇大帝), is the highest deity in the Chinese pantheon and rules the Heavenly Kingdom in much the same way Zeus abides over Olympus. But unlike Zeus, the Jade Emperor is also the ruler of all the heavens, the Earth, and the Underworld. He is also said to be the creator of the universe, and he administers the Heavenly Kingdom with a bureaucratic structure essentially similar to the Chinese royal court.

3. Yue Lao, or Yuè Xià Lǎorén, is the "old man under the moon" who serves as the god of marriage in Chinese mythology. He binds those who are destined to marry by using red silk cords on their feet. In Gale's translation he changes this allusion to the "Grandmother of the Moon," probably to make it more in keeping with Western notions of female deities like Hera, associated with marriage.

4. Technically, these creatures would be fish, but in Chinese folklore it would be understood that they could take on the form of

men. In representations, they often have human bodies but the heads of various fish.

5. As with the Dragon King's army of sea creatures, it is understood that the Dragon King himself can change form, though in his case he may take on any number of different forms.

6. An allusion to the great Chinese novel *Journey to the West* (西遊記, 1592), by Wu Cheng'en, in which the judge Wei Cheng beheads the dragon in a dream. *Journey to the West*, in its opening episode, also features the theme of becoming depressed after reaching the epitome of worldly success. When that happens to the Monkey King, his advisers tell him he has found religion.

CHAPTER 10.
Strange Dreams

1. Hengshan is one of the mountains mentioned at the beginning of the story. Bashan, interestingly, alludes to "Written on a Rainy Night: A Letter North (to My Wife)," a poem by the Tang poet Li Shangyin (813–858, famous for his "no title" poems) in which he writes, "You ask when I shall return; / Alas, I do not know. / On Mt. Bashan the night rain / floods the autumn pools." Li Shangyin did not achieve the fame he could have because of factional disputes at court. This allusion is yet another subtle reference to Kim's own exile and his own involvement in a factional purge by King Sukjong.

2. An allusion to a cliché in Tang poetry. A famous painting by Wu Bin called *A Thousand Peaks and Myriad Ravines* (1617) touches on the same convention. It can be viewed at the Indianapolis Museum of Art.

3. This is an interesting conflation of names on the Emperor's part. He seems to be combining two figures: Yang Feng and Guo Si, who are both historical figures from the Han dynasty. Yang Feng (楊奉, d. 197) was originally the leader of bandits, and he became a general when he joined Guo Si. When Guo Si (郭汜, d. 197) turned on Emperor Xian, it was Yang Feng who protected him by calling on his bandit comrades. This is decidedly a strange allusion, since here the Emperor apparently conflates a bandit-turned-loyal-subject with a general who is a traitor. It seems that he might be sarcastic in his praise for Shaoyu. However, in an allegorical reading, this conflation makes perfect sense, since King Sukjong was known for his fickle be-

havior and for flip-flopping in his loyalty to one faction, then another, in the Joseon royal court.

4. *Retainer* is a general term for a servant (usually of a royal family), but not of the menial kind. A high-level retainer would live in the inner court and have access to members of the royal family.

5. A prefect would hold a rank below that of a magistrate or a regional governor.

6. Ban Zhao (班昭, c. 45–116) is the first known female historian in China. When her older brother Ban Gu died in 92 CE, she finished his history of the Western Han dynasty. Later, she wrote *Lessons for Women*, a text prescribing appropriate feminine behavior. But Kim may be making a sly allusion to the fact that Ban Zhao was also known for instructing the royal family on exotic Taoist sexual techniques.

7. Meng Guang (孟光) lived during the Later Han dynasty (25–220), during the time of Emperor Ming (who ruled from 58 to 75). She was said to be homely and dark complected, wore a twig for a hairpin and skirt of coarse cloth, and was strong enough to lift a millstone. She is considered the paragon of wifely virtue by Confucian standards for her devotion and moral integrity.

8. The ancient Chinese valued jade above gold and silver, and it is often found in royal tombs. Jade was called the "stone of Heaven" and held a special place in cosmology because, like humans, it connected Heaven and Earth. It is a stone associated with healing, preventing decay, and protecting against evil. It is also considered modest but powerful, and special among stones because it is naturally warm and not cold to the touch. Confucius himself said that jade had eleven virtues.

9. In the *Spring and Autumn Annals*, it is said that Wu Yun (伍員, d. 484) of the Wu kingdom (722–481 BCE), during the Spring and Autumn Period (770–476 BCE) had a special, valuable sword that had the seven stars in it.

CHAPTER II.
The Taking of Ch'iung-pei

1. What follows is a brief summary of what transpired previously, as if Kim were catching the reader (and himself) up on the plot. To avoid redundancy, I have omitted it from the text and provide it here:

The Empress Dowager had not liked Ch'iung-pei at first, but the princess, disguised as a commoner, had found a place near the Cheng house and sent the embroideries as a ruse to meet Ch'iung-pei. She had become friendly with Ch'iung-pei and come to admire her virtue and wisdom and by doing so became intimate with her. She came to understand why Yang Shao-yu would never want to give up Ch'iung-pei, and she had gone as far as to promise to live together with her like sisters and share the same husband. She had written constantly to the Empress Dowager about all of this, but eventually changed her mind.

2. See note 8, chapter 2, on Li Po. Cao Zhi (曹植, 192–232) was also an accomplished poet and heavy drinker like Li Po, but he was a prince.

CHAPTER 12.
Shao-yu's Regret

1. After Lan-yang moves to the palace, her mother cannot expect ever to see her again unless she is specifically invited to come for a visit. (Lan-yang herself would not have the authority to make such an invitation. She could only make a request to the Emperor or to the Empress Dowager.) As part of the royal family, Lan-yang would be sealed away from the outside world, so the Empress Dowager is being unexpectedly generous to Madame Ts'ui in this scene.

2. *Shijing* (詩經), also known as *The Classic of Poetry*, is the oldest collection of Chinese poetry and contains works dating as far back as the eleventh century BCE. It is one of the *Five Classics* and would have been memorized by a literary person in the Tang era.

3. Cao Cao (曹操, 155–220) was a warlord and eventually imperial chancellor during the Eastern Han dynasty. He is known as both a merciless tyrant and a benevolent ruler, depending on the source, but all agree that he was an accomplished poet.

4. The Kunlun range between the Gobi Desert and Tibet.

5. In Chinese folklore, Fu Fei is said to have drowned in the Luo River and then become a goddess, paralleling Shao-yu's idea that Ch'iung-pei has died and become a fairy in the Heavenly Kingdom.

CHAPTER 13.
Two Princesses, Two Wives

1. See note 5, chapter 6.

2. This is a loaded allusion, since in the traditional story the girl

was his own wife, whom he hadn't seen in twenty years. She refuses him and preserves her honor, which he was testing, but she commits suicide because she believes her husband has lost his own honor in trying to seduce a stranger. Shi Jinbao (1279–1368) adapted this story into a play, *Qui Hu Tries to Seduce His Own Wife*, but in that drama the wife does not kill herself (and Qui Hu recognizes her to some degree in the mulberry field).

3. Rutt continues with an allusion here: "This is like Szu-ma Hsiang-ju playing the lute in the outer court to seduce Cho Wen chün, or the daughter of Chia stealing incense for her paramour in the days of Chin."

4. An ancient independent state (蜀) that was conquered by Qin in 316 BCE. It is now Sichuan Province. Since the story is set during the Tang period, it is as if the priestess has gone back in time.

CHAPTER 14.
The Contest of Beauties

1. In traditional Chinese culture, each cardinal direction is also associated with a color, a mythical beast, and a season: east/Blue Dragon/spring, south/Red Bird/summer, west/White Tiger/autumn, and north/Black Turtle/winter.

2. Named for her village, the Woman of Wu Yen was said to be extremely ugly. According to Chinese folklore, even her picture was so ugly it was unbearable to look at. And yet, despite this, she was able to marry a prince because her mental qualities outshone her homeliness.

3. See note 7, chapter 14.

4. Yang Youji (養由基, 597–558 BCE) was a fabled archer of the Spring and Autumn Period who never missed his target. He once even shot down a deity no one else could slay, and so this is a grand compliment on the prince's part.

5. See note 12, chapter 15, on the Shanglin Preserve. The Chinese emperors had many preserves or parks set aside for their use as hunting preserves or recreational parks.

6. Rutt adds a small transition here to fill in the continuity: "Soon there were piles of game—furred and feathered—in front of the tent. The girls killed many rabbits and pheasants, which they presented to the Prince and Shao-yu for generous rewards in pieces of gold. Everyone lounged now, enjoying the music and the singing."

7. Dufu (杜甫, 712–770). Along with his dear friend Li Po, he is considered one of the greatest Tang poets. See also note 8, chapter 2.

8. Wives of semimythic Emperor Shun who were famous for their lute playing.

CHAPTER 15.
The Wine Punishment

1. Rutt continues with another allusion regarding diplomacy: "Prince P'ing-yǔan went to the kingdom of Ch'u as a peace envoy, and although he had nineteen people in his suite the one who brought peace for the kingdom of Chao was Mao Sui alone."

2. The *Chunqiu* (春秋), attributed to Confucius, is one of the *Five Classics* of Chinese literature. The Spring and Autumn Period was from 770 to 476 BCE, which covers approximately the first half of the Eastern Zhou dynasty.

3. Cui Hao (崔顥, 704?–754) was a contemporary of Li Po. Although he was an accomplished poet, his work is almost always overshadowed by that of Li Po and Wang Wei. See also note 8, chapter 2.

4. Although this plays out like a joke, Prince Yüeh is also serious here, and his suggestion refers to a form of execution or torture similar to the wine torture used at the time of Tiberius in Rome. In contemporary China, there is still the common practice (a kind of drinking etiquette game) in which someone who is late to a drinking engagement has to "catch up" by drinking the equivalent number of drinks the others have had, but all at once. In context, this is also a rather poignant scene, since (although Kim could not have known it) King Sukjong would eventually execute his favorite concubine, Jang, by having her drink poisoned wine. Sukjong was avenging his wife's death, which he believed was caused by Jang's use of evil shamanic magic.

5. The romantic story dramatizing the forbidden love of the Herder Boy (or the Cowherd) and the Weaver Girl is one of the most popular folktales in East Asia. It is documented in *The Classic of Poetry*, which is over 2,500 years old. The tale is a cosmological allegory, the boy representing the star Altair and the girl representing Vega. The two are banished to opposite banks of the Silver River (the Milky Way), because they are of different social classes, but once a year on the seventh day of the seventh month, a huge flock of magpies creates a bridge that al-

lows them to meet each other for a single day. In East Asia, this story has the resonance of *Romeo and Juliet*, though it is not as tragic.

6. Note the parallel to what Hsing-chen says to Master Liu-kuan early in the novel about being whipped on the calves as punishment. See page 9.

7. Meaning that one has a pure heart.

8. Like many of the allusions in the text, this is sexually charged. The sparrow is phallic and the clam is a euphemism for vagina. The clam can "fly" in sexual union with the sparrow, since it does have figurative wings in the form of its upper and lower shells, and it propels itself by flapping them and squirting water.

9. The daughter of the elephant hunter King Matang, as mentioned in the *Divyavadana*, a third-century collection of stories about the Buddha's previous lives. In Hinduism, Matangi is a tantric goddess equated with the Buddha. She also happens to be a goddess who governs speech, music, and art. The Shakyamuni Buddha is the Buddha of this age (the historical Buddha), called "Shakyamuni" to mean "the sage of the Shakyas." The Buddha's surname is Gautama, his given name Siddhartha, and his clan name Shakya.

10. See note 4, chapter 16.

11. See note 9, chapter 1.

12. The Shanglin Preserve or Shanglin Park was a famous preserve from the time of Han Wudi (who ruled from 141 to 87 BCE) and maintained afterward by other emperors. Wudi himself was even criticized for spending too much of his time in the preserve and indulging in its pleasures to the degree that it caused moral corruption (suggesting that there was a great deal of debauchery going on there).

13. Suggesting that his daughters are like the "goddess" of the moon. People believed that clouds moving across the moon were the fairy goddess Chang'e (or Chang-o) (嫦娥), who is often said to have fled from an abusive husband who ruled harshly over his kingdom. Note the indirect allusion to the clouds here, which is amplified when one considers that in some versions of the story Chang'e's husband was the archer Hou Yi, who was ordered by the Jade Emperor to shoot down nine of his ten sons who had transformed into suns in the sky.

14. He would have been an administrator who oversaw the logistical operations of the capital under the emperor.

15. The sons' names, in sequence, have the following meanings:

"Great Honor," "High Honor," "Younger Honor," "Late Honor," "Fifth Honor," and "Final Honor." The daughters' names mean "Tinted Rose" and "Eternal Joy."

16. See note 8, chapter 4.

17. This is a very complicated allusion, since it appears to be protesting the Emperor's surfeit of favor on the one hand, but also alludes to both Taoist and Buddhist ideas on the other.

In Taoism, a vessel is useful for its emptiness, as described in chapter 11 of the *Tao Te Ching*:

> Thirty spokes share a central hub;
> It is the hole that makes the wheel useful.
> Mix water and clay into a vessel;
> Its emptiness is what makes it useful.
> Cut doors and windows for a room;
> Their emptiness is what makes them useful.
> Therefore consider: advantage comes from having things
> And usefulness from having nothing.

In Buddhism, "the empty cup" and "empty your cup" are old Chinese Zen phrases that refer to a famous conversation between the young scholar-monk Deshan Xuanjian (782–865) and Master Longtan Chongxin (760–840). The master filled Deshan's cup until it overflowed, and when the young monk protested, the master told him that he could not teach him until he had emptied his cup.

At this point, Shao-yu is in a transition point interwoven of Confucian, Taoist, and Buddhist allusions, primed for his old master to appear from the "reality" of the novel.

The second allusion is much more self-explanatory.

18. Once again, as on page 122 (see note 3, chapter 10), the Emperor is erroneous in his allusion. The one the legendary emperor Yao asked to be his successor was actually the hermit Xu You (許由). After refusing, Xu You was so upset he washed out his ears in the river to clean his head of the request. Qao Fu was another hermit, a friend of Xu You, who is said to have avoided that river because Xu You had polluted it with what he had washed out of his ears! In the allegorical reading of *Kuunmong*, this slip-up on the Emperor's part is another indication that King Sukjong, paralleled with the Emperor, was fickle and needed good advising.

19. See note 13, chapter 7.

20. A preceptor is a teacher who also gives practical instruction, especially in medicine.

21. A fief was a parcel of land given by a ruler to his subject in lieu of a salary. The land included the peasants who worked and lived on it, and it was expected that the ruler would then receive taxes based on the productivity of that land. An additional five thousand households makes Shao-yu fabulously wealthy since he would be receiving a significant percentage of the productivity of those households.

CHAPTER 16.
Returning to the Source

1. Like the Luo, this is another tributary of the Yellow River known for its scenic beauty.

2. Yang Guifei (楊貴妃), one of the "four great beauties" of Chinese history. She was the favorite consort of Emperor Xuanzong of Tang toward the end of his reign. Xuanzong had stolen her away from his own son by having her become a Taoist nun for an interim before making her his concubine. Because Yang was implicated in the An Lushan (An-shi) rebellion of 755, as a consequence Xuanzong ordered her execution. She was strangled to death by his attendant Gao Lishi. This is an especially poignant allusion—almost prophetic—in relation to King Sukjong and the fate of his own favorite consort, Jang, whom he put to death by making her drink poison wine. Kim Man-jung did not live to see it happen because he had died in exile a few years prior.

3. Emperor Wu of the Liang dynasty (502–587) in China, who was a devoted Buddhist and actually became a monk several times, only to be "brought back" into his royal life by donations to the temple. Wu's reign was a golden age of Buddhism in China, and he is often regarded as "the Bodhisattva Emperor," although the great monk Bodhidharma put him in his place for being prideful in his promotion of Buddhism. Wu popularized repentance and the ritual of bowing as a way toward liberation. Red Pine (赤松) is the name of a legendary Taoist immortal. Bill Porter, one of the most highly regarded contemporary translators of Taoist and Buddhist texts, writes under the name Red Pine.

4. This is a reference to the bodhisattva Guanyin (觀音, also written Kwan Yin), who is derived from Avalokitesvara, whose name

means "the Lord Who Looks Down Upon Sound." The Chinese characters literally mean "perceives sound," with the implication that Guanyin abides on high, listening for the sounds of suffering in order to provide compassionate assistance. Avalokitesvara is a male figure (and the Dalai Lama, for example, is said to be his earthly incarnation), but in East Asia (China, Korea, Japan) the figure is female. Some scholars theorize that the Western figure of the Madonna converged with the figure of Avalokitesvara to produce Guanyin, who, like Mary, is often associated with the sea. Guanyin is often erroneously called the "goddess" of mercy.

5. In Korean, Manjushri is called *Munsubosal* (文殊菩薩). His name is usually interpreted to mean "the Bodhisattva of Gentle Glory," but the first two characters in his name can also be read to mean "literary distinction," which makes it a metafictional allusion. Manjushri is the bodhisattva typically associated with wisdom and is the oldest and most important one in the literature of the Mahayana tradition.

6. Sanskrit term for an aeon in Buddhist cosmology. This is generally the amount of time that passes between the creation of a world and its destruction and re-creation.

7. "The Butterfly Dream" of the Taoist master Zhuang Zhou ("Master Zhuang," 莊子) is the best known of the stories in the *Zhuangzi*, the book named after him. It is the subject of many paintings and commentaries.

8. See note 6, chapter 1.

9. The term can be used to refer to teachings of the Buddha, cosmic law, or phenomena. Here it is used in combination, particularly since we are at the end of a story that thematically addresses the interaction of the three definitions.

10. These would be the typical possessions of a wandering monk. See note 14, chapter 1.

APPENDIX B:
Reading *Kuunmong* in Chinese and Korean

1. Charlotte Brontë's *Jane Eyre* is probably one of the best examples of this technique in nineteenth-century British fiction. Jane's last name, Eyre, and its approximate homophones are a practical road map of the novel's plot. Eyre: *err* (Jane makes a grave error when she initially agrees to marry Rochester); *ire* (she is of Irish background and quick to anger); *air* (she is asso-

ciated with that element, fairies, and imagination); *eerie* (she has a strange imagination and spooks Rochester's horse when they first meet); *eyrie* (she is associated with a bird and ultimately provides a "nest" for Rochester, whose name begins with *roc*, the name of a giant bird). Meanwhile, in real life, we have amusing examples like Usain Bolt, the fastest sprinter alive.

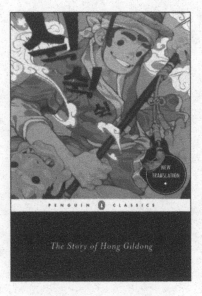